Dressed to Kiss

Dressed To Kiss

Madeline Hunter

Caroline Linden

Megan Frampton

Myretta Robens

ISBN-10:   1-5346994-7-3

ISBN-13: 978-1-5346994-7-2

DRESSED TO KISS

The Duke's Dressmaker © 2016 Madeline Hunter

The Colors of Love © 2016 Myretta Robens

No Accounting for Love © 2016 Megan Frampton

Prologue and *A Fashionable Affair* © 2016 P. F. Belsley

Cover design © Carrie Divine/Seductive Designs

Photo copyright: © Artmim (Oleg Fedotov)/Depositphotos • Photo copyright: © Novelstock • Photo copyright: © tungphoto (Mongkol Chakritthakool)/Depositphotos • Photo copyright: © v.ryabinina (Victoria Ryabinina)/Depositphotos • Photo copyright: © santiss(Александр Будиловский)/Depositphotos • Photo copyright: © svaga(Irina Smirnova)/Depositphotos

Printed in the USA

CONTENTS

PROLOGUE

London
January 1820

Felicity Dawkins had fashion in her blood.

She had been born above her modiste mother's shop, Madame Follette's, and raised among the bolts of silk and lace, picking buttons off the floor and fetching thread for the seamstresses as soon as she could toddle along and name her colors. By the time she was six, she had her own tiny pincushion to tie to her wrist and a small pair of scissors, so she could learn to make little dresses for her doll from scraps of cloth. When she reached ten, she was responsible for mending her own clothing and that of her younger brother Henry, and when she turned thirteen, she began making their clothes as well. Their father had died soon after Henry was born, and both children were expected to help in the shop, from necessity as well as to keep them out of trouble.

Her mother, Sophie-Louise, made her an apprentice at fifteen, and taught her not only how to cut and stitch a gown that fit properly, but also how to coordinate colors and embellishments for a harmonious and tasteful finished ensemble. At eighteen she became a seamstress and began taking on clients of her own, learning how to steer every client gently but surely toward a style, color, and fit that would flatter her, regardless of what the client came in wanting.

And Felicity loved it. The neat little shop in Vine Street was her world, filled with gorgeous fabrics and opportunities to create something beautiful each and every day. It was difficult work, to be sure; bending over a dress for hours at a time made her back ache and her eyes burn, as the candles burned low. But it was all worth it when the customer returned and put on the gown for the first time. Felicity lived for the moment her client's eyes would widen in delight as she saw herself in the mirror, and turn from side to side, exclaiming at the line of the skirt and the fit of the bodice.

Unfortunately, at some point those moments started becoming more infrequent. She wasn't sure when; the end of the war, perhaps, when Paris and its styles were accessible again, rendering London's dressmakers a shade less vital. Or perhaps it was the changing shape of women's gowns, away from light and elegant frocks toward gowns of heavier fabrics with more elaborate decoration. Madame Follette's excelled at the Classical silhouette, crafted of fabrics so fine they were almost sheer. Thick silks didn't drape the same way, and Sophie-Louise clucked her tongue at the puffs and ruching that seemed to sprout like mushrooms on bodices and hemlines.

"No gown needs six rows of ruffles and a tall lace collar," she vehemently declared, tossing aside the magazines filled with fashion plates of beruffled skirts and lace collars that hid the wearer's ears. "It looks ridiculous. I won't have it!"

Felicity might have agreed with her mother on some of these points of fashion, but she did not hold with Sophie-Louise's disregard for the financial impact of this decision. Women who had patronized Madame Follette's for years stopped placing their usual orders after Sophie-Louise scoffed at the trimmings they wanted. Even worse, younger women, new brides and heiresses making their debuts and country ladies finally able to come to London for a Season, did not choose Madame Follette's. To her dismay, Felicity began to see the difference between the gowns from her shop and those from rival shops. While Follette's still excelled all others in the quality of work and fit, now their gowns began to look . . . plain. Simple. Old-fashioned, even.

This sparked deep alarm in Felicity's breast. Follette's was everything to her, not merely her home and employment, but her heart and soul. She tried to persuade her mother to adapt to the changing styles, but Sophie-Louise was having none of it. "Not as long as I am at Follette's," she vowed.

But eventually facts must be faced: Follette's income had fallen to dangerous levels. Henry, who kept the shop's books, confided to her that they would have to ask for credit from the silk warehouses as well as from the lace makers—and there was no good prospect that they would be able to pay everyone back once they lost their top dressmaker, who decamped to another modiste's shop after a fierce argument with Sophie-Louise about embellishing sleeves with puffs at a customer's request.

Henry didn't say it aloud, but Felicity could read the books well enough. They were in debt, and their income was declining. If things went on this way much longer, they would be in danger of losing Follette's, and Felicity refused to contemplate that. She told her brother they must convince their mother of the danger she was courting. After her children, Sophie-Louise loved nothing more than her shop, and Felicity prayed they could overcome her stubborn refusal to change.

To her relief, Henry agreed with her. "I've been worried about this for a little while," he admitted, and agreed to come to dinner that night for the delicate conversation.

"Mama, we are worried about Follette's," Felicity began after the meal. "We have lost five customers this year"—she held up the letters they had sent in response to her queries about orders for the upcoming Season—"and gained only one."

"Faugh." Sophie-Louise made a face. "Witless fools chasing after styles that make them look ridiculous."

At this point, Felicity would make any outrageous gown a client wanted, provided it was paid for in ready coin. "That may be, but we need customers. It's well and good for you to frown on the current mode, but that is what people want now."

Sophie-Louise waved her hands irritably. "I won't have my name associated with it. We will get by with our current customers until this madness for fringe passes. Fringe! Puffs! Rubbish. It cannot last more than a year or two, and then everyone will come back."

Felicity and Henry exchanged a glance. "We aren't getting by that well, Mama," said Henry.

Immediately their mother's face softened. In her eyes Henry could do no wrong, which was why Felicity needed him to do this with her. Sophie-Louise would overrule and ignore her daughter's arguments, but she listened to her son.

"Don't worry, Henri," she told him soothingly. "I know what I am doing. Almost thirty years I have been a dressmaker. The styles will change."

3

"And that is why we must change with them," Felicity pointed out. "Please, Mama. I am worried, even if you are not."

Her mother frowned at her. "Worried? Do not be silly, Felicity. I built this shop from nothing—my designs and styles created the reputation of Follette's, and I will not allow it to be transformed into a pale imitation of Madame de Louvier's." She sniffed at the mention of a rival modiste. "*She* is not even French! And has no taste or restraint at all. I do not understand why she is still in business."

Felicity understood. Madame de Louvier embraced the style of the moment; whatever her customers wanted, she gave them. Her designs were not inspired or clever, and were often copied straight from the fashion plates of *La Belle Assemblée* without regard for the individual charms of the woman ordering the gown, but she delivered gowns in the latest styles. And for that, customers were leaving Follette's and going to her.

She turned a stern look upon her brother. He didn't like to get in the middle of arguments between the two of them, but this time he had no choice. Henry nodded. "Mama, we are surviving on credit."

"Everyone lives on credit from time to time. We have accounts at all the suppliers for this reason. When the commissions come in, we will be fine."

"No, Mama, we won't." Henry didn't blink as she looked at him in surprise. "We have been using credit for a while now. The commissions are not coming in at the rate we need. We are in danger of losing Follette's." He glanced at his sister. "Felicity is right. We need to change."

Sophie-Louise subsided, her expression troubled for the first time. Felicity tried not to feel annoyed that it took Henry's word to persuade their mother that she was right. "I don't like it."

"These are our options," Henry went on. "We could sell this building and take cheaper premises elsewhere—"

"No!"

A faint grin touched his face, and Felicity bit back her own smile. Neither of them wanted to sell Follette's, either. "Very well. We could retrench—cut back on our stock, dismiss Mrs. Cartwright and perhaps Sally."

Privately Felicity wanted this option to be aired and then rejected, for the most part. Mrs. Cartwright had to go, no matter what. She had been at Follette's for many years and was a competent seamstress, but she had no imagination for design. Imagination was what Follette's lacked. Felicity needed another seamstress like Selina Fontaine, whom Sophie-Louise had hired only a few years previously, a young woman with a fresh modern vision of fashion. Sally, the fifteen-year-old apprentice, was a harder decision. If they dismissed Sally, Felicity had a sinking feeling she herself would end up sweeping the floors and stoking the fires. They could reduce the fabrics they kept in stock, but that would hurt their productivity, as they would have to visit the warehouses more frequently and pay higher prices for each order.

But the one thing they could not do was move to cheaper premises. While Vine Street had grown a little shabby, it was still very near Piccadilly and Jermyn Street, and only a few minutes' walk from Bond Street. If they relocated, it would have to be farther away from, not closer to, those fashionable shopping areas, where rents far outstripped what they could afford. Moving would announce to all the world that they were no longer a leading source of fashionable garments, but just an ordinary dressmaker. They would have to lower prices, which would compromise the quality they could offer, and then they really would be ordinary. Felicity would stoke the fires and sew every dress herself before she agreed on this path to ruin.

Sophie-Louise puffed up angrily, as hoped. "Dismiss Mrs. Cartwright! She has been with me since you were a child, Henri! How can you suggest such a thing?"

"Because we do not have the income to keep her," he bluntly replied.

"And Sally sends part of her earnings home to help her family," Sophie-Louise raged on, her accent growing stronger with each word, as it did when she was upset. "How can you be so heartless?"

"They would both lose their positions if we go out of business, Mama." Henry's sharp retort got his mother's attention. She fell back, blinking. Henry was rarely sharp with her, and indeed, his tone was considerably milder when he went on. "There is another option, but it will require some sacrifice from you, Mama . . . Are you willing to consider it?"

"For Follette's? *Oui*, I would consider anything to save it," declared his mother. "But we will not move premises!"

Henry cast a fleeting glance at Felicity, who nodded once. She all but held her breath as her brother explained. The idea was both their

5

work, but Felicity knew it would be better received coming from Henry.

"You must step down, Mama."

Sophie-Louise's mouth dropped open in shock.

"Not forever, but for a few months—perhaps a year or two. Allow Felicity to run the shop," Henry plowed on. "She wants to bring Follette's back to prominence, but you and she are getting in each other's way."

"It is my shop!" cried Sophie-Louise. "Mine!"

"And it's failing," said Henry gently. "Felicity isn't trying to take it from you, nor am I. But Mama—we've lost so many customers. We are not gaining new ones. We must do something dramatic or we will slowly sink into impossible debt and end up losing everything."

"But why must *I* go?" his mother wailed. "I am the heart of Follette's!"

"For your own sake." Henry reached forward to take her clenched hand. "Follette's must change, Mama, and I know it will pain you to see it happen. Take a holiday to the seashore. You've spent your life working, you've earned a reprieve."

Sophie-Louise looked at Felicity with reproach. "You want to banish me from my own life's passion."

"No, Mama, not at all. Henry is right: You deserve a holiday."

"A year-long holiday," her mother said sourly.

Felicity ducked her head. "It will take awhile to turn things around."

Sophie-Louise looked between the two of them. "You are both against me. How can I win?" She sighed. "Very well, I will go. But I will be keeping an eye on each of you," she added as the siblings exchanged a glance of intense relief.

"Of course, Mama." Henry got to his feet and kissed her cheek. "No one expected otherwise."

Felicity walked him down the stairs, through Follette's main salon. They were fortunate to have a street-level shop, unlike many modistes. She and her mother shared the rooms above the shop, but Henry had taken his own lodgings years ago. "Thank you," she told her brother. "I wish she would listen to me and not require your persuasion."

He buttoned his coat and grinned. "Follette's is my concern, too. You shouldn't have to do it all."

6

"No, I—I want to do it all." She took a deep breath. "I have ideas, Henry. I can save Follette's, I know it. We only need an opportunity to prove ourselves again, refreshed and revitalized, and we'll be one of the top modistes in London."

"We have to make our opportunities," he pointed out. "Time is of the essence."

She sighed. "I know. But we'll find something." *Somehow,* she silently added.

"That's why I supported your plan to take over. I know you can do it; haven't I seen your determination up close every day of my life?" He put on his hat and gave her a grin in farewell. "I've got Mama out of your way, so step to it."

She laughed. Henry opened the door, letting in a blast of cold wind, and strode out into the January night. Felicity closed the door with a shiver and shot the bolt.

Her gaze traveled over the dark and silent shop. *I will save this,* she thought fiercely. Follette's was hers. Henry kept a keen eye on the books and was proud of Follette's, but he didn't love it the way she did. He had no interest in fashion, and he didn't want to run the shop.

And now that Mama had agreed, Felicity's mind raced. She had to dismiss Mrs. Cartwright and hire someone who could bring more flair to their work. She had to scrutinize the latest styles for elements that could be adapted and polished into Follette's own unique signature elements. She needed to refurbish, as economically as possible, the premises to reflect their new modernity. And most of all, she needed a significant event that would showcase her work and put Follette's name on the lips of every woman in London. Perhaps the Russian czar would visit again and spawn a frenzy of balls. Perhaps a handful of heiresses would make their debuts.

Ten days later, old King George died. The church bells tolled, the state funeral plans were in all the papers, and Felicity wrote one word on a piece of paper and pinned it to her wall for inspiration:

Coronation.

The
Duke's
Dressmaker

Madeline
HUNTER

CHAPTER ONE

A bright reflection blinded Selina Fontaine while she placed some fashion plates back in the window of Madame Follette's dressmaking shop. Shading her eyes with her hand, she looked to see what sent that beam of light in her direction.

A large coach had stopped in front of the shop. Its door, ten feet from the window, bore a gold and red escutcheon. The afternoon sun's rays set that heraldic carving ablaze and the glare ricocheted off the glass in the coach's carriage lamps.

She did not wait to see if the coach had passengers. She strode through Follette's street-front shop, to the door that led to the dressmaking chambers behind it. Once there she entered a fitting room where her patron, Lady Giles Woodville, waited.

"I am sure these will be perfect," Lady Giles said, sweeping her hand over the fashion plates she had chosen for her new wardrobe that were spread out on the table in front of her. "The dress for the coronation is very fine, and unobjectionable. Lady Clarice was kind to recommend you."

Selina quickly stacked the plates. "If you come in the next few days, I will take measurements and we can discuss materials."

"I thought we would do that now."

"I believe your coach has arrived already. The hour is later than we thought." It had taken this pretty child three hours to choose the plates. Selina had fought her every step of the way to make sure she did not pick the flamboyant designs that appealed to her. She might address her patroness as Lady Giles, but in her mind she dealt with a

11

schoolgirl named Edeline, much as Lady Giles's governess had, not so long ago.

Lady Giles, young, fair, pretty, and spoiled, wavered between amusement and annoyance that a dressmaker dared interfere with her fun. She chose amusement. "The carriage can wait, Mrs. Fontaine. Bring me the materials you recommend for the dinner dress and the court dress."

"It is not the same carriage that brought you. That was why I thought—"

"It can still wait." Lady Giles looked less amused.

Selina went behind a curtain to the alcove where they kept samples of fabrics and trims from the best shops. Many patrons preferred to visit the drapers and warehouses themselves, but some appreciated this convenience.

She chose quickly. All the while she tried to calm herself. Just because the state coach had come for sweet Edeline did not mean anything. It had probably been out and about in town for other purposes, and simply stopped by to collect some pretty baggage before going home.

Not for the first time she doubted the wisdom of accepting this commission, however. She had done so against all of her better judgment. She had only agreed to it because the shop needed both the work and the prestige. The owner, Sophie-Louise, had given her sanctuary and employment when she badly needed it. Loyalty dictated she take any work that would help Sophie-Louise's daughter Felicity in her current quest to enhance the shop's finances.

Nor did she have a good reason for not accepting. None she could share with Felicity, at least.

She dug through some samples of trims and plucked out several that could embellish the fabric. Muffled voices came to her, as if a hum of quiet chatter had erupted among the women looking to buy ribbons and lace in the street-front shop. Hopefully that meant another potential patron had sought them out, the sort of woman of the haute ton who would cause others to nudge and whisper.

Steps sounded in the chamber behind her curtain, the one where Lady Giles waited.

Not delicate steps. Boot steps. A man had entered.

"Oh, I did not expect you to come here," Lady Giles exclaimed.

"I was on my way back from Whitehall and directed the coach here to bring you home."

Selina's hand froze, deep in a box of colored silk cords.

"I am not really done yet," Lady Giles said.

"I assume not, if you left me waiting."

Selina's pulsed raced. Desperation wanted to give way to panic. She had only heard that voice once before, but she would never forget its terse, superior, arrogant tone. She definitely should have found a way to reject this commission.

She peeked through the curtain, hoping she was wrong.

She was not.

The Most High, Noble and Potent Prince, His Grace Randall, Duke of Barrowmore, the man who had ruined her life and her dreams in one short day, the man she would not mind strangling with the length of silken cord that she held, stood ten feet away.

"**A**re these the fashions you chose?" Rand reached for a stack of plates on the table where Edeline sat in her chair.

"Thus far. I hope you like them. Mrs. Fontaine advised me on each one, and I accepted her judgment as you told me to, even though I find most of them far too plain."

He sat across from her, and flipped through the plates. It was a hell of thing that he was doing this, instead of his sister Charlotte, or better yet, his brother Giles. Only the former was in the country pampering her husband who had managed to slice himself while practicing with a sword, and the latter had taken himself to hell knew where to escape his debts. So, in addition to his considerably more important duties, he found himself acting as arbiter of the wardrobe of his brother's young wife.

Edeline was lovely, sweet, gentle, and usually demure. Who would have guessed that she had no taste? Certainly not he, until he chanced upon her displaying a new dress to a friend the day after she received it. The modiste who made that dress should be executed.

The rest of the new wardrobe looked just as bad. Embellishments too distracting, necklines too low, colors too bright—It turned out sweet Edeline had never been let loose at a dressmaker's before. Any refinement in her clothing up until now had been the result of her mother's careful decisions. Unfortunately,

13

this spring Edeline had demanded sartorial independence and her mother had given it, since her attention now centered on the next daughter to be married off.

The entire enterprise had been a very expensive disaster. The bills would start arriving soon, not that Giles was in town to pay them. Not that Giles could *afford* to pay them, no matter where he was. Giles was another irritation and distraction that Rand did not appreciate.

Regarding Edeline's wardrobe, apparently a firm hand was needed. Fate had decreed it would have to be his.

"That is the coronation dress," Edeline said, pointing to a plate he uncovered.

"Not in this color, I hope."

"I have not decided yet. Mrs. Fontaine has gone to get some material—Where is she? Mrs. Fontaine?"

A movement stirred the air behind him. A human presence warmed his shoulder.

Edeline looked over his head. "Ah, there you are, Mrs. Fontaine. Are those the fabrics you recommend? Put them here, so the duke can see them."

A hand reached around and set a stack of cloth on the table in front of him. He looked at it, then at the plate, then back again. "So this would be for the dress proper, and this for the overdress?"

"Yes," a woman's voice said.

A very small part of him stood at attention. It had been a nice voice, deep and smooth. Mature and sensual. Its timbre momentarily distracted him.

The hand placed another stack in front of him. She had nice hands too. Elegant, with thin, long fingers. Young. "These are for the carriage ensemble, and these"—yet another stack appeared—"for the dinner dress."

"There are more plates here," he said.

"Materials of this quality can overwhelm the senses. I prefer to ask my patrons to choose a few at a time."

That made sense. Already the colors and textures created confusion. So did that voice. It kept sending rivulets of curiosity into the stream of his consciousness.

Some men possessed an expertise in fashion. He did not. He could only claim to know when a woman's garments did not reflect

14

her status and enhance her beauty. Nothing shown to him thus far fell into that category. It appeared Mrs. Fontaine knew what she was about.

Thank God he would not have to make time for this in the future.

"Are you happy with Mrs. Fontaine's choices?" His tone dared Edeline to object. He had warned her that if she purchased anything else at all inappropriate he would send her to the country for the duration of the Season and the summer.

"They are perfect."

"Then let us go." He stood and offered his hand.

Edeline accompanied him to the door. "I will come tomorrow to be measured, Mrs. Fontaine."

"Very good. I will see you then."

That voice nudged at Rand again. Something about it . . .

He turned to see the woman, in order to issue the command that would place the whole of this wardrobe into her capable hands.

One glance at her dark hair and blue eyes and her distracting, well-endowed bodice had his mind racing, searching for a thought that kept slipping away.

Suddenly an old memory flashed, and brought clarity with its light. He peered hard at the dressmaker. Hell yes, it was she. He was certain of it.

Mrs. Fontaine was really Selina Duval, the seductress who had almost got Giles to the altar four years ago.

She watched recognition slash through him like a bolt from on high. One moment he appeared aloof and barely attentive. The next moment his hot gaze scorched her from head to toe.

Selina stood her ground. She raised her chin. She looked right back at him. She pretended to have no awareness of his transformation, or of what had caused it.

The duke's change in demeanor amused Lady Giles. "I hope you are not going to threaten Mrs. Fontaine with being drawn and quartered if I end up with something you do not like."

His expression smoothed. "I never threaten women. Mrs. Fontaine knows what is expected."

Lady Giles slid her arm through his. "Then, until tomorrow, Mrs. Fontaine."

She guided her escort through the doorway. The duke looked back, over his shoulder. One raised eyebrow over one dark eye communicated that he was not finished with a certain dressmaker.

Selina pulled out the chair the duke had used, and sank into it. She gazed around the little workroom where she had found sanctuary the last few years. She had built an independent life here by exploiting her one skill and talent. She did not relish the prospect of trying to start over in another town.

"Did the consultation with Lady Giles go well?"

Felicity had stuck her head through the doorway. Since Sophie-Louise moved to the country last year, Felicity really managed Madame Follette's now. Of middling height, and with blond hair and blue eyes, Felicity was a lovely young woman. Selina also considered her a friend. Not only the long hours together in the shop had bound her to Felicity. Four years ago, when she sought employment, it had been Felicity who convinced Sophie-Louise to take her on.

"It went well, but perhaps not well enough."

Felicity came over and flipped through Selina's plates. "Did the duke approve of these?"

"I think so, but—We may not have this commission after all. He did not say so outright, but I have the feeling he was not impressed."

Felicity's face drew long with disappointment. "I so hope you are wrong. We could use this commission badly."

"I know. I am sorry. I hope I am wrong, too."

"We will know soon enough. I overheard Lady Giles speak of tomorrow. If she comes, then it is secured."

Selina doubted that, but she hoped the duke would allow bygones to be bygones. Between the current Season and the coronation in a few months, modistes all over London had more business than they could handle. A few had even tried to steal some of Felicity's seamstresses.

That meant this year represented a rare opportunity for the shop to resolve the financial precariousness that haunted it. Enough notable designs on ladies of high visibility, like Lady Giles, and Madame Follette's shop would join the list of dress designers the best and wealthiest women patronized all the time. A truly dazzling dress might even get mentioned in the ladies' journals and gossip sheets.

Upon learning one of Selina's patrons, Lady Clarice, had recommended them to Lady Giles for an extensive wardrobe, everyone employed at the shop had held their collective breath, praying. When Lady Giles wrote to request an appointment with Selina, the whole world took on brighter, happier hues. When Selina read in the gossip sheets that Lord Giles Woodville, younger brother of the Duke of Barrowmore, had departed from town, that had allayed her misgivings enough to believe she could do this without ever crossing his path.

Now her path had crossed the duke's instead. Rather than be the salvation of the business, she might damage it. The anonymity that she had found here would probably be destroyed, too. The shop might have its name in those gossip sheets, but in all the wrong ways.

Felicity gave Selina's hand a firm squeeze. "Don't look so glum. If the duke did not like your designs, he has no taste. If Lady Giles does not continue with us, we will manage as we always have, and make good of the other opportunities that are coming our way."

How like Felicity to set aside her own worries in order to soothe Selina's. She wished she could confide about why the duke would surely have second thoughts. To do so would be selfish, however. None of that was Felicity's problem. It would be cruel to give her more to lose sleep over.

If the worst happened, she would find a way to protect Felicity and the shop, even if it meant disappearing again.

CHAPTER TWO

Rand finished his letter to Lord Liverpool. The prime minister had given him an unofficial mission to try and persuade Her Royal Highness, the Princess of Wales, to leave the realm before her husband's coronation. A handsome settlement of fifty thousand pounds a year was the carrot. Humiliation at being denied a place at the coronation was the stick.

Unfortunately, his meeting with the princess and her advisors today had failed to elicit even a thorough hearing of the rationale he had prepared. It had also ended any friendship he shared with Caroline. He was now just one more lord lined up against her, in her view.

His letter completed, and, he hoped, his involvement in the whole sorry business finished too, he left his chambers in Manard House. Sounds drifted down the stairwell, of Edeline laughing with a friend who had called.

That sound brought his thoughts soundly back to that damned wardrobe. And to his brother's absence from town. And to Mrs. Fontaine.

Another unfortunate business left to him to try and fix. Not one to shirk his duty, or to avoid the unpleasant aspects of it, he called for his horse.

Selina left the shop at six o'clock. Felicity accompanied her and the other employees to the door, in order to lock it behind them.

Felicity lived above the shop, as had her mother Sophie-Louise before retreating to the country.

Bidding the others good-bye, Selina began her walk east to Panton Street, where she lived in a modest three-room apartment in a building full of similar homes for women of decent breeding but minimal income.

After bending over tables and crouching next to skirts all day, she enjoyed a good walk in the evening. She liked observing the activity of the city, unless a demonstration unsettled its normal patterns. If rain did not threaten like it did today, she might even go far out of her way to stroll along Birdcage Walk so she could study the ensembles worn by ladies taking turns there.

Today the overcast skies discouraged that. So did her state of mind. She had not forgotten the episode with Lady Giles during the last few hours, but at least work had put that at the back of her mind. Now, with each step, she paced out the details of the duke's surprise arrival, and its ramifications.

None of it helped her humor. Her emotions kept swinging between anger and indignation and fear and desperation.

Suddenly another emotion joined those. Fear.

Someone was following her.

The clip-clop of horse hooves paced in time with her feet. The presence behind her diminished all others on the street.

She quickened her steps until she almost ran. She turned onto her home's lane. The horse behind her did not. Telling herself that the day's events had made her too nervous to be rational, she walked up the steps to her building, then upstairs to her apartment. She let herself in with her key, and turned to close the door behind her.

The duke stood there, right outside the doorway. She started with surprise at how his tall, stern, dark presence simply materialized, as if conjured up by her thoughts.

"I would have a word with you, Mrs. Fontaine."

"Not today, thank you." She closed the door on him.

One strong hand pressed against it, forcing it to remain ajar. "I must insist. It is a great inconvenience for me to make time for this, and I am sure you do not want our conversation to take place in that shop. Or do you?"

She wished she had the strength to push that door closed right in his arrogant, condescending nose. Since she did not, and since she definitely did not want this conversation to take place in the shop, she released the door and stepped back.

He strode into her home and closed the door behind him. He angled his head this way and that, taking in the few chambers that gave off from the tiny reception hall in which they stood. She could imagine his thoughts as he noticed the well-used furniture bought secondhand, and the simple drapes. The one extravagance, an Indian carpet in the sitting room, had arrived from her mother unexpectedly after she wrote to Mama and told her where she was living, and how.

He headed toward that carpet. "In here, I think."

So much for any pretense that he was a visitor she had received. She followed him.

She sat in the middle of her patterned sofa. Her position covered the place where one seam had begun to fray. She did not want him taking too much satisfaction in her reduced circumstances, or, worse, pitying her.

He stood in all his majestic dukeness. He set down his hat and riding crop on the one table. Face chiseled and severe, he gazed out the long window, then at the fireplace, and finally right at her.

"There is or was a Mr. Fontaine?" he asked.

"If I am Mrs. Fontaine, there must have been."

"There is no *must* to it. Many women become Mrs. This or That out of convenience, or to ease the consciences of their protectors."

"Since I live like this, I think it is safe to say I have no protector."

He glanced down at the Indian carpet, drawing conclusions regarding the past, perhaps. "Are you currently married? Do not bother lying. I can find out."

He probably could. Dukes could do all kinds of things most men could not. Money allowed that. Their titles opened doors. He even possessed a power over his family members, like Edeline. Like Giles. Still, she was tempted to force him to go through the effort.

"Mr. Fontaine passed away soon after I married him. That was soon after I had no choice except to leave Kent after your brother threw me over and broke our engagement."

"There was no engagement."

"There were assumptions. Expectations. His pursuit of me was public and involved my family and county friends. When that ended—"

"If you permitted more familiarity than was wise, it was understandable that people made assumptions. With Giles's reputation, you should have known better than to form a liaison with him. He has never been discreet regarding his mistresses."

Liaison? Mistresses? "How dare you intrude on my home to insult me. You do not even know me. Other than that one introduction, in which you made your scorn for me very clear, we have not even had a conversation before this one."

"We had no need for one before this. I did not need to know you to see what he was up to, because I understand my brother very well."

"We were in love. I am sure that is something you can never understand."

"Giles in love is a melody he has played long and well down through the years. He is the romantic lead in every play he has ever seen. I do believe you thought him in love with you. You just did not comprehend what a shallow kind of love Giles knows."

"He told me that you interfered. He explained that when he—" She could not finish, so close was she to tears. She hated being reminded of that humiliation. Oh, the words Giles spoke had been loving and sweet to the very end, but the result had been devastating. And the gossip—All because of her foolish belief in one man's promises.

"Mrs. Fontaine, you had to know that Giles would never marry a woman of your birth and fortune. If ever he married, it would be a girl like Edeline, whose family connections and wealth were suitable to his station as my heir presumptive."

"No doubt you explained all of that when you told him to break with me."

He gave her a serious, contemplative look. Then he availed himself of the one upholstered chairs in the sitting room. She hoped he did not expect her to offer refreshments.

"Regarding my brother's wife and her wardrobe, I did not like learning the dressmaker is a woman with whom my brother had a liaison. It was an unpleasant surprise."

There it was again. Liaison. He assumed—well, what everyone assumed. She did not care what he thought. "Having you walk into the shop today was also an unpleasant surprise. It appears both our days were ruined."

"Hence my insistence on this conversation. Why ruin more days?"

"How very sensible. I wonder what role you have in all those plays where your brother is the romantic lead. Stern father? Villain?"

He almost smiled, as if he found that last role appealing.

"You had to have known who Lady Giles was, since she bears his full name. You cannot claim ignorance that she was Giles's young wife."

"It is a very large commission. Had I a choice, I might have spared my pride and refused it. We in trade live by a different set of rules than your sort do, and pride is not what governs our decisions, however."

"Perhaps you anticipated seeing him as the work progressed. I think you expected him to walk into that shop someday, not me, and perhaps play the romantic swain again. I am here to tell you that I will not have it. Giles has proven himself eternally indiscreet, but I will not have him taking up with a dressmaker so soon after his wedding."

"You are wrong in every way. I was aware he had left town. I only agreed to see her and do the wardrobe because I trusted I would *not* come into any contact with him, nor he with me."

Skepticism etched his face while he regarded her a long time.

She looked right back. She hoped she appeared proud, composed, and strong even though inside she was nervous, and silently crying for mercy. She did not want to run away from her current life the way she had abandoned her old one.

"Those fashion plates—Were they yours?"

She examined the unexpected question from every angle, but could see no danger in answering. "They are. However, I assure you that while the dresses are distinctive, they are not outré. They fit with the current fashions nicely, only not predictably."

His gaze meandered down her body, slowly. She grew self-conscious. His eyes narrowed ever so slightly and his mouth firmed. He appeared hard, but not angry, and, if she were honest with herself, not unappealing.

She had seen him thus once before, on the day Giles introduced her to him. Barrowmore had arrived in Kent unexpectedly, and found them together in the garden. Giles had been kissing her, and her bonnet was off and her hair disheveled. Barrowmore had missed none of that, she was sure.

He subjected her to the same intense gaze that day. Then, after the briefest of acknowledgments, he had turned to Giles and proclaimed they would meet privately in one hour in the house's library. Giles then escorted her home, and with every step the suspicion grew in her heart that the duke had found her lacking, and the summer idyll was over.

Now, she suffered the same scathing examination. Only she was no longer a girl desperate for his acceptance. Today that gaze contained layers not perceived the first time.

If she did not know better, she would say the duke was entertaining improper thoughts about her right now. In a day of insults, that should be the worst one. Except, if she set aside who he was and what he had done to her life, she had to admit that such inclinations transformed him. Rare would be the woman who did not react as she did. She fought the stirring his close attention evoked.

"Do you wear your own designs?"

She gazed down on the deep blue wool covering her body from neck to feet. Cut and fitted like a pelisse, with a row of closely-spaced buttons down to her hips, it kept her warm in the shop and on her walks home in the cool evenings. Most significantly, the good quality fabric felt magnificent to her hand and on her body.

"I do. Obviously I design differently for myself than for a lady like Lady Giles. Much more simply. However, it is important for dressmakers to look like they know about lines and proportions and fit even when it comes to their own work clothes."

"Like a horse." He smiled as soon as he said it, a small chagrined turning up of his lips. "That is how horses are judged. Lines, proportions . . ."

She barely heard. That smile made him a different man. Warm. Charming. It gave those handsome angles and ridges something to do besides chisel the air. She had never seen a smile transform a face like that. If she did not hate him, she might be bedazzled. As it was, for the first time she could believe he and Giles were brothers.

"Much like a horse. Except my dresses have no teeth and do not bite."

"In a manner of speaking, that is not true." He glanced askance at her bodice. Then he gathered his ducal presence around him, much as a man might wrap his cloak more securely. "I will not have Edeline hurt by talk about Giles and his paramours. That will come soon enough, hopefully when she is older and more worldly. You are not to say one word to her about that time."

"Are you saying we will continue with the wardrobe?" She wanted to gush with gratitude that he only demanded this, and had not informed her that Edeline would henceforth not be visiting the shop.

"Against my better judgment, I will allow it. The notion of spending another minute on gowns and frippery disheartens me enough that—Do the wardrobe, but never even allude to your liaison with my brother."

"I would never tell her about that, although there was not a liaison as such. I fully understand your condition, however, and will honor it."

He looked skeptical still. "Should my brother return to London, you are not to see him. I will endeavor to keep him from accompanying his wife to that shop. I can't imagine he ever would. I want your word, however, that you will avoid such a meeting even if it means you run out the back door."

"I will tell everyone there to be alert and give me warning, unlike what they did today with you."

He stood. "See that you do. Should you disappoint me, should I learn that you scheme to renew your relationship with my brother, I will make sure no decent woman ever enters that shop again. Do we have a right understanding?"

She had almost begun to barely like him. Now he threatened her future, and that of everyone in the shop.

"No, we do not. If you have reason to take some revenge, take it on me alone. At least inform me of your intentions, so I can leave Madame Follette's, and perhaps spare the others there."

He thought about that, then nodded. "Fair enough. I will take my leave now. As for the wardrobe, send the bills to me directly. If you send them to Giles, it will be years before you see a shilling."

CHAPTER THREE

"In my letter to Liverpool, I blamed myself, but also the princess's advisors." Rand sat in White's, drinking whisky with Havenstock. He had sought out the sanctuary of this gentlemen's club after his disconcerting meeting with Mrs. Fontaine. He and Havenstock not only had much in common, but what they shared was shared with very few others. Of the same age, they were both dukes. The many ways that set them apart from other men had created a bond long ago.

Havenstock could always be found at the club at this hour. The alternative was to be at home, with his sisters. He had been graced with four of them, all of whom seemed determined to remain unmarried. Havenstock often waxed eloquent about the peaceful life he would have once he ushered them into marital bliss, and kept on the lookout for likely men on whom to foist them.

Rand had only been spared because they were the oldest of friends. And because five years ago, when Havenstock broached the notion of a match with his oldest sister Clarice, he had firmly declined.

"Having survived the infamous 'trial' last year, the princess probably believes her popularity will win this contest with her husband in the end," Havenstock said. "Since none of them, not the princess and not the advisors, have ever seen the new king's temper on the subject, they have no idea how far-fetched their assumption is."

"That is the truth of it," Rand said. "It gives me an idea. I will write to Liverpool again and suggest that those advisors be given an audience with the king. Perhaps when he glares and bellows at them, they will understand the situation in its fullest."

Havenstock eyed the glass in Rand's hand. "Is that the result of your consternation with the matter? You rarely drink whisky at this hour."

"That was only one annoying meeting. My day was full of them."

"Do tell."

"Easy for you to make light of my plight."

"I meant it. Do tell. I love hearing about others' miserable days."

Rand stretched out his legs and took a good swig of whisky. "Two bailiffs found the family solicitor and issued dire warnings about my brother's debts. I was called forthwith, and had to threaten warnings of my own. Fortunately, they saw the sense of my reasoning."

"Meaning you paid them off."

"Damn it, yes. Only in part, but—" But what? It was an old story. Giles ran up debts, and Rand paid them. It had only gotten this bad once before. He had tried to draw a line then, only to have his brother outflank him in a most clever way.

Giles was good at being a charming scoundrel, he had to give him that.

"That alone justifies imbibing," Havenstock said. "What else put that frown on your face today?"

They now broached a topic Rand did not choose to discuss. He still did not even know what he thought of it. However, that visit with Mrs. Fontaine had left him badly out of sorts.

He forced himself to think of her by that assumed name lest he accidentally address her by her given name at the wrong moment.

"I saw to that business with Edeline's wardrobe. I have a hell of a life, don't I? Talking to royalty in the morning, and fussing with a girl's clothing in the afternoon." He sipped. "There is something unmanly about that latter duty. I wish I had sisters like you do who could manage all of that."

"You do have a sister."

"Lot of good she does me, up there in Scotland. How the hell does a Scot wound himself with a sword? I thought they were born brandishing them like experts. Thank Clarice for me regarding her recommendation of that dressmaker. It appears that will work out, and I am finally done with this."

Havenstock's eyes gleamed with humor. "Did you go there yourself, to make sure all was in order?"

"Briefly."

"Then you must have met this Mrs. Fontaine whom my sister likes so much."

"Briefly."

"What did you think of her?"

Rand shrugged, perhaps too emphatically. "She is a dressmaker and she seems capable. She is much what is expected."

"I assure you, she is not what is expected. If she were fifty, tending toward stoutness, and dripped French throughout her speech, that is to be expected. Not that woman." He leaned over. "Do not pretend you did not notice she is lovely, still young, has a fine form, and carries herself with the airs of a gentlewoman."

She had those airs because she was born to them. As for lovely, hell yes, she was lovely. And well formed. Good lines and proportions. If she were a filly, she would fetch a king's ransom.

Which was exactly what he had paid for her.

She did not know about that. He had realized it as soon as he entered that apartment. Giles had never told her about that part.

Of course he hadn't.

Rand had not gone to her home to collect on that ridiculous trade, which was not the same as not thinking about it once there. That bargain had been nothing more than an excuse to make Giles give up something valuable in return for once more being bailed out of debt. The goal had been a moral lesson.

The details had been Giles's idea, too, not Rand's. *I have nothing you would want that you cannot buy yourself. Except Selina. I saw how you looked at her. Pay them all off, and she is yours.*

No, he had not gone to collect, but he assumed she knew. That he had not collected lent him a principled position and the upper hand. However, since she remained ignorant of Giles's trade, that left him with nothing except—well, damned little.

"I saw her once. I brought the carriage to get Clarice and Mrs. Fontaine walked her out," Havenstock said. "She wore this dark scarlet dress, as simple as could be. Not an inch of skin showed, it buttoned clear up to her chin, yet I defy any man to see her and not start picturing what is under that fabric. Surely you know what I mean, even if you only saw her briefly."

"I have no idea at all what you mean." Only he did.

Mrs. Fontaine—Selina Duval—had been favored by nature. Her dress followed excellent lines and proportions, especially on the top. The dress had been dark blue today, not scarlet, in a hue much like her eyes, and its simplicity alone seemed to beg for speculation on just why it fit quite the way it did. Which naturally led to the picturing Havenstock now referred to. High, full breasts atop a soft, lithe body . . .

"You should get married yourself, rather than try to marry off your sisters, if you dream about a dressmaker, Havenstock."

"I thought she would make a fine mistress. She is beautiful, refined, and luscious. I considered it seriously."

Sorry, boy, she is taken. Bought and paid for.

Where the hell had that thought come from?

"But you did not make the offer?"

"Clarice suspected, and gave me hell. Her threats grew vicious. I was shocked."

Rand wasn't. Clarice had excellent taste, and an artistic eye that made her a celebrated lady of fashion. It was why Rand had taken her recommendation of this time-worn, past-its-better-days shop so seriously.

She was, however, sure to make some man's life miserable. Strong-willed did not begin to describe her.

"Just as well," he said. "Such a mistress is bound to be very expensive. After all, she knows all about luxuries, and how to get the most out of a man."

"True. Still—" Havenstock sighed.

"If it helps at all, I have reason to think the woman does not seek any protector, and would be insulted by such an overture."

"You do? What makes you think so?"

Rand stood. "Just a feeling. I am going to the card room. Care to join me?"

CHAPTER FOUR

Selina entered the shop at nine o'clock. No patrons would come this early, but there were always things to do. Today she wanted to review the plates for Edeline's wardrobe and make some notes on recommended fabrics, should the lady arrive for her measurements and want to make a few more choices.

Felicity pulled her aside as soon as the door closed. With a hiss and a gesture, she urged Selina into the shop's little office.

"She is here. Lady Giles," Felicity reported. "They arrived fifteen minutes ago."

"They?"

"Barrowmore is with her. Try to find out how much he is up for. We don't want Lady Giles choosing the most expensive of everything, only to have the duke balking at the bills."

How odd that the duke had come with Edeline. Perhaps he had rethought everything and had decided to withdraw the patronage. Selina could think of no other reason for his presence.

She walked to the back chamber, took a deep breath, and entered. The duke sat there paging through fashion plates. Not the ones Edeline had chosen. He perused others Selina had drawn and colored over the last year. He had helped himself to a big stack from a shelf.

Edeline sat across from him at the table, looking bored and tired. She kept wiping her eyes, as if sleep threatened to seal them shut.

"My apologies," Selina said after she curtsied. "I did not expect you this early, Your Grace. Lady Giles."

"He made me come." A big, noisy yawn accompanied the accusation. "He has important things to do, he says. He can't be arranging his whole day around my wardrobe, he says. He doesn't care when it is fashionable to shop, he says. *I said* he did not have to come at all, and I could have slept in."

The duke did not even look up from his perusal of those plates. "You have an artist's hand, Mrs. Fontaine. Did you have lessons?"

"There are no such lessons to take, although like most young women I was taught the basics of drawing and watercolor painting. I copied French plates and learned on my own. I am honored, however, if you think them well done."

"Very well done." He looked up. "What must Lady Giles decide today?"

"Perhaps, before she leaves, the carriage ensemble and—"

"Ooo, I want sable trim on it." Lady Giles, suddenly awake, clapped her hands.

"The ensemble is intended for summer, my lady. Fur is not advised in summer."

"It is only trim."

"Why don't we discuss it after you are measured? Excuse me for a minute only."

Selina slipped out and found Delyth, one of the seamstresses. "You come do the measurements, and I will take the opportunity to talk to His Grace about the account."

Together they returned to the chamber. "Miss Owen will take your measurements. Your Grace, perhaps you would join me in the reception salon."

"Of course." No sooner had he left than Delyth began unfastening Lady Giles's dress.

Selina led the duke to a small chamber used as a reception salon for the dressmaking patrons. Behind the storefront shop like the fitting and consultation rooms, it provided privacy for the ladies who would not want to mingle with the less elevated visitors who might arrive to buy muslin.

The duke sat when she did. The furniture was very feminine and small-boned. He overwhelmed his chair. Selina watched him deal with the discomfort of his perch.

"It is well you came today," she said. "It gives me an opportunity to learn your intentions regarding this commission."

"I would think my intentions were clear."

"I refer to the cost."

He flushed a bit. Talking about money with a woman embarrassed him. How charming.

"Of course. If I do not set an amount, she will know no restraint."

"I will endeavor to guide her to sensible choices that will not ruin you. I will try to come in under whatever you set. I do not expect you to believe that, since it does not benefit me, but I promise you that is how it will be."

"And if it is not enough?"

"There may need to be other meetings, if she insists on something that goes over the amount you now dictate."

He thought about that. "I dare not leave her to her whims, Mrs. Fontaine. Not because of the cost, nor of my need to rely on your honesty. The truth is, I think you will have an easier time of it if she insists on an extravagance you do not like, and she knows you must get my approval. If it means I must sometimes come here and talk to you about it, I will do it."

"Oh, you will not talk about the bills with me. We leave that to Miss Dawkins, who manages the shop. She will convey to me any decisions you make, however."

"Miss Dawkins? I see." He did not appear to like having Felicity involved. "How long will it take to measure her?"

"A half an hour, at least."

He pulled out his pocket watch. "Twenty more minutes. I think I will take a turn outside. Will you join me?"

"My work—" She gestured broadly at the whole shop. "My other patrons—"

"You implied we came too early, so you should have no others for hours." He stood and offered his hand to help her rise. "Walk with me. I want to ask you something."

They left the shop and strolled east down the street, away from the dust and construction that had become a daily trial while Regent Street was constructed. They strolled past other shops with other windows. Some did have the kind of patrons who arrived early. One coffee shop had filled with tradesmen prior to their opening their own businesses. The pages from the day's newspapers covered the windows, and a little crowd had gathered to read them.

"The day is fair, is it not?" he asked.

"Most fair. Was that the question you had?"

"No. I want to know how Selina Duval became Mrs. Fontaine. I am curious to know what you are doing here."

She stiffened. Her mouth formed a firm line. "I think you know the answer."

"I am not sure I do."

She kept her gaze straight ahead. "As I told you when you broke into my home—"

"Come now, I did not break into—"

"*When you broke into my home,* the gossip after Giles left was unbearable. All that attention he had showered on me. All those gifts. If not to win my hand, then for what? The answer did not flatter me. I thought to brave it out, but my mother was humiliated, and my father felt it sorely. Mama ceased leaving the house. Papa came close to calling a man out. So I left. I married the first man who asked, just to get away. When he passed I came to London and applied at that dress shop." She glared at him. "Is that enough? Because it is more than I think you deserve."

He guessed it was mostly true, but not entirely. He still did not believe there had been a Mr. Fontaine for a few months. He could not explain why he felt sure about that. Perhaps it was the little catch in her voice whenever she referred to it. Not a choke of sentiment, it sounded like a hesitation prior to forcing out a lie.

He paced on, weighing the choice in front of him. She had fond memories of Giles. She believed they had shared a great but thwarted love, done in by the villainous brother. Giles had left her with that dramatic story. Only much of it was simply not true.

Would she hate him all the more if he told her all of it? Undoubtedly.

"You do not know our village," she said. "That manor house up on the hill has been there for centuries, owned by the dukes of Barrowmore, but never used by them. Still, we were proud to be in its shadow. It made us better than other common villages. When your brother chose to live there that summer, how excited everyone was. That he included the local gentlemen and their families in his society was even better. I do not know what inspired him to visit, but for all of us, and especially me, it became a magical summer."

Giles's inspiration had been to find an obscure property where he could lie low and avoid his creditors. Just like now he was at some other such dot in the family holdings, for the same purpose.

He would berate Giles most severely for how carelessly he had used this poor woman. Ruined her, for all intents and purposes. Not that Giles would care. That summer had ended with clear and open credit for him, hadn't it?

She did not need to know the truth. It would serve no purpose. Let her remember a magical summer at least.

"We should be getting back," he said.

They retraced their footsteps to the shop door. He decided he wanted her to know one part of the story was not true.

"Mrs. Fontaine, I feel obligated to correct one memory of that time that my brother left with you. I did not order him to throw you over."

"Are you saying he lied to me?"

"Giles chose to avoid responsibility. Shall we leave it at that?"

Her brow knit. "It was long ago. I confess I have forgotten his exact words. Perhaps I misunderstood."

"More likely you believed what he said. He can be very persuasive, so the blame is not with you at all."

"If I now believe you instead, I must accept that I was a fool. A very stupid one."

"Not a fool. A woman in love, being spared more pain than necessary." He did not want her feeling a fool, or stupid, or anything like that.

She opened the door, still frowning.

Abruptly she turned and faced him. "Perhaps all that gossip and all those assumptions were not idle talk, but can be traced back to him."

"I would like to believe he did not do that."

"It is a good thing you made me promise never to see him. Because if ever I do, I cannot guarantee I would not make him pay for this."

He imagined her pointing a pistol at Giles. She would never do that, nor would he want her to, but the expression of abject contrition that Giles wore in the fantasy amused him to a disgraceful degree.

"I much prefer you angry to sad, Mrs. Fontaine. It suits you better."

She gave him a peculiar look, then turned back to the shop. "Tell the coachman that Lady Giles will be finished here in two hours."

"Certainly. Oh, and I have one more thing to say before we part. What would you say to carte blanche? If you promise not to ruin me, I will consider it."

She froze with her hand on the door's latch. After a good ten count, she turned to him with wide-eyed surprise. Only then did he realize that he had not prefaced his offer with reference to Edeline and her wardrobe. Mrs. Fontaine thought he had just propositioned her.

He was about to rush in with an explanation, but the way she regarded him caused him to pause. She did not appear insulted or angry. Rather she looked to be weighing her answer.

He waited, curious to see which way it would go, while fantasies of plucking open those buttons snaked into his head.

Enlightenment dawned in her eyes. She flushed deeply. "You were referring to Edeline's wardrobe, of course."

"If that is what you prefer."

She fumbled with the latch and muttered a little curse when the door stuck. "Of course it is." The door opened, and Mrs. Fontaine rushed inside.

Selina pressed her back against the door for support and closed her eyes. She was an idiot. A total fool. Of course the duke referred to Edeline's wardrobe.

If she could be excused for misunderstanding, which she could not, it was only because respectable patrons did not use that phrase. It was employed by the courtesans of London when their protectors had promised no restraint on what was spent on clothing and other luxuries. Not many women received carte blanche, but the shop had served a few who did.

Felicity came out of the office, navigated past some women at the counter, and sidled close to Selina. "Do you have an amount?"

Selina doubted she could manage little Edeline if there truly were carte blanche. Better to have the duke approving expenditures that got too high. "Three hundred. After that we need to consult with His Grace."

Three hundred was a handsome sum for a wardrobe, even one with unseasonal sable trim, which Selina was determined Edeline would not get.

"Well done, Selina. Should we need to consult, as you say, I will let you take care of that. He seems to like you."

"What makes you say that?" Selina snapped.

Felicity backed up, laughing. "An account of three hundred makes me say it."

Selina went to the fitting room, to finish her meeting with Lady Giles. Perhaps the duke did like her. She had misunderstood his comment about carte blanche, to her eternal humiliation, but he had not been nearly so condescending today, and he truly seemed to trust her judgment with Edeline.

It was more than that, however. When she misunderstood, while she misunderstood, he had not corrected her. He had seen it, she knew he had, and he had not offered further explanation.

It might have begun as a mistake, but a duke had indeed propositioned her today.

CHAPTER FIVE

A week later Selina sent a letter to Lady Giles, informing her that the coronation dress and the evening dress were ready for a fitting. A response came the same day. The lady had taken ill with a cold. Would Mrs. Fontaine be so good as to bring the dresses to her and do the fitting at Manard House?

Royalty conducted wardrobe business in their homes. A few very important ladies did as well. Most women, however, even those married to sons of dukes, went to the dressmakers rather than have the dressmakers come to them.

There were reasons for that. One was social. Visiting dressmakers and other shops gave ladies an excuse to be out and about in town. To see and be seen. Other reasons were very practical, as Selina noted while she prepared to fulfill this request. The dresses had to be wrapped carefully. A large box of embellishments must be taken as well, along with the pins, threads, and other sewing equipment. She hired a hackney cab, loaded all of this into it, and gave the driver the address.

Manard House proved as grand as one would expect of a duke's London home. At the corner of Stanhope Street and Park Lane, its restrained, buff façade rose five levels. A walled garden surrounded it, like a little park. If Lady Giles lived here, it meant her husband had not provided her with her own house, but instead chose to live with his older brother. Just as well, if he was going to leave town for long periods of time.

The hackney driver brought her to a rear gate where a servant took command of her packages and allowed her into the garden. The servant then escorted her into the house through a side door, where a footman took over. Eventually, she found herself and her baggage in a chamber on the third level of the house. There a thin, severe, dark-haired lady's maid took her in hand and brought her to a dressing room where Edeline waited.

Her hair down and her body ensconced in an undressing gown frothy with lace, Edeline greeted Selina with a firm blow on her nose. "Ah, there you are, Mrs. Fontaine. I knew you would not let me down. We must make progress on these dresses, but I could not go out with this red nose. I look a fright."

Selina unwrapped the coronation dress and laid it over a chair. Edeline jumped up and came to admire it. "It is lovely. So much was done in one week."

"Our seamstresses devoted themselves to it for many long hours."

Edeline turned to the maid. "Isn't it lovely, Françoise?"

Françoise gave a noncommittal nod. She came over, turned back the fabric, and assessed the stitching of a seam. Another nod, and she retreated.

"If you put it on, I will do the fitting," Selina said. She then drew the maid aside. "Is there a pillow I might kneel on?"

"The pillows are all silk," Françoise said with disdain. "They are not for use on the floor by seamstresses."

Selina fitted the dress without a pillow. She stayed on her knees while she used pins to indicate where embellishments would go. Then she rested on her heels while Edeline changed into the evening dress. Another hour of fitting and finally she was done.

She put away her equipment and wrapped the dresses again. "When you are feeling better, you can come to the shop for the others. They are almost ready."

Edeline pouted. "I much prefer doing it here. You can bring the others like you did these, I am sure."

"Of course she can," Françoise said, in a tone that managed to indulge her mistress and scorn Selina at the same time.

Selina forced a smile. "I will write to you when we are ready."

The maid called for a footman to carry the dresses and box of equipment. Selina followed him down the staircase. He did not use the servants' stairs, but took her by way of the closer main set. At the bottom, a butler's scowl awaited them.

"What is this, Timothy?"

"The lady's dressmaker, sir."

"There are two sets of stairs in this house, Timothy. See that you remember who uses which ones in the future."

Red-faced, Timothy quickened his steps. They were almost out of the large reception hall when a figure appeared at a door at one end.

"Mrs. Fontaine?"

It was the duke. Timothy froze.

"Your Grace." Selina curtsied. She gestured to poor, young Timothy. "I confess my interest in the house made me insist we come down this way. Your footman was too polite to refuse."

"I should hope so." He gave the footman a nod of approval. Then he gestured to the burden the young man carried. "What is that?"

Selina explained Lady Giles's need for a fitting despite her cold. "It is not normally done, because it takes me away for too long and I cannot see other patrons. However, I am sure Your Grace will not mind the small additional fee I will have to charge if this continues."

He gestured to the footman. "Take all of that to—wherever it is supposed to go." He turned to Selina. "I will show you the public rooms, since you are curious."

"I really should return to the shop."

"If Edeline's spoiled whims are going to force you here, you may as well enjoy yourself a little, too. We will start with the dining room."

There was nothing to do but follow him out of the massive reception hall, into the huge dining room at one end.

"My sister chose the decorations. She has good taste. Not like yours, but respectable enough," he said.

She had expected a room filled with golds and reds, ostentatious in its luxury. Instead the chamber appeared almost spare, with pale gray walls and the lightest yellow drapes. The subtle background gave the massive table and huge Persian carpet all the attention, but kept everything in balance so the eyes were not overwhelmed.

"More than respectable taste, and also unusual."

"She is nothing if not unusual. She married a Scottish earl. He talks a lot, and I can barely understand him. I just nod to whatever he tells me. It has worked thus far. Look here. This is my favorite part. In the summer we open these doors, and all but dine al fresco." He threw open two large sets of French windows at the end of the room. The ones on the left gave out to the end of a terrace, but the others opened onto a section of garden that had been planted right up to the threshold.

Fragrant early spring blooms perfumed the air. She closed her eyes and inhaled deeply. "It reminds me of home."

This view of Selina, her eyes closed and her expression one of sensual pleasure, intoxicated him. He imagined a similar expression when pleasures other than those of garden scents moved her.

Do not do it, his better half said. *She is not for you and has endured enough from the men of your family.*

Do not be a fool, his most masculine side responded. *She is a mature woman. She is smart and worldly and capable of making her own decisions.*

"Let us walk out there, unless it makes you sad," he suggested.

"Not sad so much. Only nostalgic."

If he had his way she would not even be nostalgic. There was too much melancholy in nostalgia. This woman had been wronged. He could not shake the feeling that he was partly responsible.

He had spent hours the last week, deciding if he were. He had not forced Giles to give up Selina. He had only demanded Giles give up *something* valuable. It could have been his horse. Hell, it could have been his favorite coat. Nor had he jumped to conclusions regarding that relationship. Giles had described it as a love affair, and even offered some lascivious details. Selina would not have been the first daughter of solid gentry stock to become a lover to a man like Giles.

Still, he could have been more skeptical. He had not been for the simple reason that Selina did not matter. His thoughts had been on his brother, not his brother's woman. She had struck him at their introduction as lovely, sensual and desirable, and more refined than Giles's usual tumbles. He had even reacted enough for Giles to notice. But who she was, what she was—those had been minor details in a contentious three days of confrontation over money.

He did not think he made excuses for himself. Other than finding a way to keep Giles from deploying his smiles and charms on women, and short of imprisonment there was no such possibility, the sins here were mostly his brother's. He had sworn to himself ten years ago that he could not and would not take responsibility for

Giles's excesses and sins, yet here he was once more thinking he should do so, and allow them to govern his own inclinations where Selina was concerned.

Perhaps that was because that history led him to conclusions he wanted to explore. He could not escape the reality that, in taking the moral high ground regarding that bargain with Giles, he had deprived Selina of the kind of support and security that a duke's mistress enjoyed for life. So now she labored for hours every day, making other women's dresses.

He laughed at himself. Ah, the power of desire to shade one's thinking. *By tomorrow I will have convinced myself it was a sin* not *to proposition her.*

They paced into the garden together. It appeared her thoughts were on many things, least of all the man by her side. He, on the other hand, noticed little else besides her, and saw nuances previously missed. The very tops of her cheeks possessed a faint natural blush all the time. The sun showed her chestnut hair to have dozens of colors in it. Her dress, less fitted than the blue one, had a square neckline that revealed silken ivory skin and a most attractive meeting of the neck and chest, with little valleys above her collarbone that begged for kisses.

"I admired the blue dress, though this one has its own attraction," he said.

"This is for serious work, like fitting. I move a lot, so the sleeves must be loose. And today I knelt on hard floors, so it is best if simple fabric is used."

He pictured her on her knees, pinning and bothering with Edeline's dress. "Surely a pillow at least——"

"The maid said they were all silk. I will bring my own next time."

"You will not. You already carry too much here. Next time you will use any pillow you choose, and no one will say a word. Trust me on this."

She bent to examine a group of jonquils. "By the duke's command? How generously you wield your power."

He felt foolish then, for announcing that like an arrogant ass, as if a woman like this would be impressed with such a thing.

"Mrs. Fontaine, I would like to make amends for my brother's ignoble treatment of you."

Her attention turned to him. "That is kind of you. However, you would not be making amends, but giving a gift. I have some pride left and could not accept."

"You might listen to my suggestion first. I hope you are not too prideful for that."

She stopped walking. A shrubbery with tiny flowers framed her. Give her a basket and a bonnet and she would make a fine painting.

"I think you should go back to your family, and your village. I will go, too, and explain to everyone how my brother behaved badly and took advantage of your youth and trust. In one afternoon we will rehabilitate your reputation and undo the worst of the damage."

"I am charmed that you think this would work."

Charmed? An odd word. A less than flattering one. "Of course it would work."

"Do you really believe that you can tell people to ignore all that they heard and all that they saw and their own rational conclusions, and it will be so? More likely they will grow suspicious of your interest in the matter."

"It is a hell of a thing to learn everyone does not just believe dukes. My father never warned me about that."

She laughed. A lovely sound. It reminded him of delicate chimes. Two birds in the garden began chirping as if they liked the sound, too.

"If he had not married Edeline, I would make him marry you," he said, removing any lightness from his voice. "That is the only compensation that would be fair."

Her gaze warmed. "Could you have done that? Is that one duke's command that would really work?"

"Yes."

"I would not have liked that, even if done with the best of intentions. Did you command he marry Edeline instead?"

"Giles found little Edeline all on his own. Her father's wealth made her very appealing, as did her young age." He glanced back at the house, a good distance away. The garden was large, and they had walked deeply into it. "He does not know what he has in her. No one does. Right now she is silly and vain. He should hope she remains so, and never matures in her mind."

"I expect they will work it out over the years, as most couples do."

What an optimistic thing to say. The truth was that many couples did not work it out.

Their path ended in a little grove of apple trees. Pale pink flowers decorated the newly leafed branches. Some of those petals had fallen to the ground.

"Do you like the theater?" The question just came out, without choice or decision. Only he was picturing her in one of the gowns she made for other women, sitting in a box, looking even more beautiful.

"A friend and I attend sometimes. We tell ourselves we do so to study the dresses worn by ladies of the ton."

"You can see those dresses better if you sit where the women who wear them do. Come with me as my guest and you will."

"Are you inviting my friend and me to join you in your box?"

He took her hand and held it between his. "I am inviting you alone. Edeline can be your chaperone."

So there it was. Unexpectedly. Without making a decision, he actually had.

She looked at her hand, then at him. He sensed that she weighed what danger he presented. Possibly a good deal of it. If she were young or dim, if she did not understand the risks, and had not learned the hard way the protection that discretion gave, he would not do this. Nor would he want her.

"Yes," she said. "I will attend the theater with you."

Then, lest their hands not make his interest clear enough, he kissed her.

The Duke of Barrowmore, a man she hated a mere fortnight ago, was kissing her. She could not imagine why.

Not that she worried over the question. She did not think about much at all while that mouth pressed hers and forced a new intimacy between them. He continued holding her hand, but his other palm lay upon her face, guiding her to receive and accept.

The kiss answered a question she had debated for a week. Had this man accidentally insinuated himself into her life, because of his duty to Edeline, or had that wardrobe been a mere excuse? The latter explanation seemed so far-fetched that she barely gave it consideration. He was a duke, and their history was not a happy one.

Yet, whenever he turned up, he was very much there. His presence filled her world then, and her mind. His energy stirred her physically and emotionally. Each meeting became another little invasion, much like the first.

The kiss did not last long, but longer than she expected. She felt his restraint, and also the current beneath it that spoke of greater passion. She had no illusion that His Grace was courting her. This was different. He had begun a pursuit, and anticipated a specific conclusion.

She knew all of that while she allowed it. Her soul just knew. She set the problems aside for now and enjoyed the kiss. It had been a very long time since a man had done this, and then not quite so well.

Nor was she the same person. She was not a girl anymore, all aflutter about a lord's attention. She was a mature woman, who knew full well what this duke was up to. A woman who could appreciate the sensual power that created arrows of pleasure in her with a mere glance, and much more provocative ones with this simple joining of lips. One who was flattered he had revealed some of what existed beneath his arrogance and hauteur.

She stopped it and stepped away. He held her hand until he could no longer, then let it go. She turned and hurried back through the garden, to the gate where she had entered. A footman waited there to escort her to the waiting hackney coach.

CHAPTER SIX

Felicity bade her turn. Selina took a half step around on the little dais. Felicity pulled another pin from the cushion tied on her arm and plied it into the hem of the cream silk evening dress.

"You will put them all to shame tonight," Felicity murmured.

Upon hearing that Selina would accompany the duke and their new client to the theater, Felicity had given orders about the dress. This one had been started three months ago for a lady who had abandoned them when a more popular dressmaker found an unexpected spot in her schedule. Now the dress that had caused so much heartache and cost would pay for itself many times over.

Selina thought the dress far too rich for a dressmaker to wear. She agreed to it against her better judgment. She had not yet decided what to do about the duke, and that kiss.

Her thoughts returned to that misunderstanding about carte blanche. Ambiguity had led to ambiguity, until her initial reaction had become close to real. *If that is what you prefer.* A door had accidentally opened that day, and he had now walked through it.

She would like to believe that she knew her mind on the matter, that of course she would never become a man's mistress. Had she not avoided such arrangements for years? Only this was different. It should not be, but it was. In the eyes of the world it was, and in her head.

His title made it different. His stature in the world. Like kings and princes, dukes had mistresses all the time. They always had. Highborn mistresses, often. Not mere daughters of gentlemen, but daughters of fellow noblemen. No scandal really befell such women.

44

Some became celebrated, and most continued through life with no one even blinking at their histories.

Unlike being the mistress of some middling gentleman, or even of Giles, such an arrangement would not ruin her. Rather the opposite.

So if she was correct, and a pursuit now unfolded, she would face a decision soon. However, she had not made it yet. As a result, she did not want to look like a kept woman in that box tonight, and she worried that in this luxurious dress she might.

Felicity glanced up at her, then scowled. "Not one more word from you. You are a dressmaker. If you can't turn yourself out in a fine dress, who can? You look magnificent, and everyone will be talking about this dress, and they will learn who you are and they will come here for dresses just as lovely."

Everyone will learn who you are. That was another thing that she feared. She never drew attention to herself. There might even be people in that theater who knew her family, and remembered Selina Duval.

"Take it off now. It will be ready by seven o'clock. Go home and bathe and prepare. We will bring this to you."

With Felicity's help, she slid out of the dress.

She walked home, and asked the one maid in the building to prepare a bath for her in the chamber in the basement reserved for that. She went to her apartment, undressed, and slipped down the stairs in her serviceable undressing gown.

The maid washed her hair, and she sat by a low fire to dry it.

"I can dress your hair if you like," the girl said. "I've done it before, and have a hand for it I am told."

Selina struck a bargain with the girl, and an hour later they were in her bedchamber. The girl worked her thick brown locks into something fashionable.

A sound at the door heralded the arrival of the dress. Felicity had brought it herself, along with some pins and sewing materials should they be needed. The bath girl insisted on staying for that, too.

By nine o'clock all was done. Selina stood in the center of her sitting room in the heavily embellished cream silk dress. Felicity had brought a lightweight cape in a blue wool so deeply hued it almost appeared black.

"I brought one of my mother's necklaces," she said, poking into her reticule.

"No," Selina said. "Let the dress speak for itself, and for our shop. We should not distract anyone's eyes with jewelry."

Fit, lines, proportions, and texture. Those were the essence of quality dresses. The shop had outdone itself with this one. She might be a dressmaker, but she felt like a queen. In anything else she might experience awkwardness tonight.

"A fine coach has arrived," the maid announced, from her spot at the window. She turned wide eyes on Selina. "It has one of those fancy carvings on the side, the kind that lords have."

They all waited in silence, barely breathing. Then a firm knock sounded. The maid opened the door to a footman dressed in the duke's livery. "His Grace the Duke of Barrowmore requests the attendance of Mrs. Fontaine."

Someone draped the cloak on her shoulders. She picked up the cream satin reticule Felicity had made, and accepted the footman's escort down to the coach.

Mrs. Fontaine entered his coach like a princess. Her gown made faint, pretty noises while she settled herself next to Edeline. His sister-in-law scrutinized the figure beside her, then smiled.

Edeline had resisted this visit to the theater with Mrs. Fontaine in tow. She made it very clear, in her pouting and in her words, that she thought their guest unworthy to sit in his box. Rand suspected she also worried that Mrs. Fontaine, with her access to every luxury available to dressmakers, would outshine her. The simple cape must have reassured her.

She did not see what he saw. Edeline would never appreciate the poise Mrs. Fontaine displayed. Nor could she see the slice of dress that flashed when they rode past a street lamp. Ivory colored, its lower skirt showed tiers of fine lace in the palest blue, dripping with pearlized beads.

"You are feeling better?" Mrs. Fontaine asked Edeline.

"Not completely. I had to use a good deal of powder on my nose, so it would not look terrible." Her accusatory tone was for Rand's sake, he was sure.

"It was generous of you to accompany us, so I could enjoy this rare privilege."

Edeline accepted that gratitude as her due, but added a little sniff that managed to both make her a martyr and also make a comment on the entire enterprise. Then she noticed Mrs. Fontaine's reticule, a long pale pouch with silk cords. She took it in her hands, and stroked the dangling strands of pearls attached to its top.

"I have not seen any like this," she said. "I must have one. Only red, I think, with white strands."

"If you like, we can make one for you. As for the color, we can talk about that."

Edeline narrowed her eyes. "It must be red."

"Then red it shall be." Mrs. Fontaine cocked her head. "Do you have an ensemble it will complement?"

Edeline pursed her lips. "I did. Well, I still do, but—" She glared at Rand. "Someone decided I should not wear it."

Indeed she should not. The red dress in question had been part of the first wardrobe commissioned for the Season. The dress, as scarlet as could be, suffered not only from its color, but in every way. Edeline had appeared a doll decked out in a harlot's evening gown. The least elegant courtesans at the theater tonight would look better.

"Giles likes red," Edeline muttered, still admiring the reticule.

The carriage stopped in front of the theater. The footman handed out the ladies. Rand followed and offered an arm to each.

Once inside, he could admire Mrs. Fontaine's gown. The fabric fell like weighted liquid, flowing down, its movements anchored by, but not inhibited by, the extensive but discreet embellishments. The form hinted at by her serviceable dresses was now revealed more fully. When she stood still the skirt maintained the same silhouette as all the others in the salon, but when she walked, the flow of the fabric gently glossed the shape of her legs.

She noticed him noticing. "My employer insisted I wear this, to show the world our shop's abilities."

"As it happens, the dress also shows the world your beauty."

She flushed, but also smiled in a manner to suggest she found his flattery more kindness than truth. "I am counting on Lady Giles's friends asking about the gown more than about me."

He doubted that would happen.

"Mrs. Fontaine!"

A throaty voice exclaimed the name while its owner descended on them. Lady Clarice, Havenstock's oldest sister, bore down, all smiles and curiosity.

Rand forced a welcoming smile. He imagined the questions and grins from Havenstock the next time they met.

"What have we here?" Clarice cooed. "How good of you to give your sister-in-law a night out, Barrowmore."

"He insisted I come," Edeline said. "Or rather, he insisted he come with me, as my escort."

Clarice glanced at Edeline "I am sure he did, what with Giles out of town. Do you expect his return soon?"

Edeline flushed. "Excuse me. I am going to chat with my friend Margaret. I see she just came in."

Clarice stepped back to assess Mrs. Fontaine. Her gaze devoured the dress. "Lovely. Unbearably so. Why are you wearing that, and not me?"

"It was an abandoned commission. We assumed you would be insulted by a castoff."

"Of course I would be. I hate to admit I may not have done it the same justice either. Your coloring is better for it."

Rand coughed lightly, hoping to be spared twenty minutes of wardrobe discussion.

Clarice eyed him. Not kindly. "Will you excuse us for a moment, Mrs. Fontaine? I have something I need to tell Barrowmore."

Mrs. Fontaine stepped aside. She took a position alone near the wall. Poised and elegant, she appeared not to see the glances sent her way.

"Feeling democratic these days, Barrowmore?" Clarice asked.

"I have no idea what you mean."

"I mean her." She angled her dark head toward Mrs. Fontaine.

"I fail to understand why you would make such a comment about her. She is a gentleman's daughter, after all. Nor is this her first visit to the theater."

"You appear to have learned her history. How interesting."

"One has only to meet her to know her quality. She has been as helpful with Edeline's wardrobe as you promised, by the way. Thank you for the reference."

"Do not try to change the subject. Why is she here? I hope you are not planning to lure my best dressmaker away from her current situation and into another one."

"How suspicious you are. This little theater outing is merely to show my gratitude for all the grief she has spared me. She has Edeline well in hand. I daresay when all is done I will save hundreds, as she disabuses the dear girl from the more extravagant sartorial monstrosities of which Edeline dreams."

Clarice regarded him carefully. "I am relieved you have no designs on her. My brother entertained such notions, briefly. I convinced him it would not be wise to pursue her."

"Did you warn him off so your gowns would not suffer from her absence in that shop? That is rather selfish."

"I discouraged him because she is not made of the stuff to live that life and be the better for it."

"To play devil's advocate in your brother's name, one wonders how she could be the worse for it. She may be surrounded by silks and lace in that shop, but in the end they grace other ladies' bodies. Furthermore, it is hard work that takes a toll on a woman's health and eyes."

Clarice glanced back at Mrs. Fontaine. "Look at her. One does not need to be told that all the baubles in London would never salve her shame if she became any man's mistress."

"Your brother would not have been the typical protector. Women of the best blood have been mistresses of dukes."

Her eyes narrowed, dangerously. "You have been working it all out in your head, haven't you? How your interests would not debase her? I warn you, Barrowmore—"

"Warn away, dear lady. I am not your brother, and you cannot henpeck *me*."

She turned on her heel, and strode to Mrs. Fontaine. Rand could not perceive what the deuce she said. He was able to see Mrs. Fontaine's face, however. She smiled serenely while Clarice spoke.

He extracted Edeline from her group of girls, then collected Mrs. Fontaine. Together they all took seats in his box.

Edeline perused the program. "Giles always takes me to the theater when the shows are fun and not so serious. I much prefer comedies."

"Then let us hope he returns forthwith, so you can laugh with him once again," Rand said.

You do know that his intentions are not honorable, don't you?

That was what Lady Clarice had said in the salon outside the boxes. Then, lest Selina not understand, she had outlined exactly how the seduction would unfold, and how the duke would lure her into perdition.

Selina had suffered it because Lady Clarice's intentions had been most honorable. She had spoken as a friend, too, not a patron. Lady Clarice was truly concerned.

There had been little to say in response. Certainly the truth would not do. *Thank you for your interest in my welfare. I must confess that I suspected as much, and am half way to thinking I might as well agree.*

They could both be misunderstanding, of course. If not for that kiss in the garden, all of this might be explained away.

In the box Edeline sat between them. Anyone looking over would assume Selina was Edeline's guest, not the duke's. Edeline chatted to each of them in turn whenever her attention wandered from the drama on stage, which was frequently. To Selina she pointed out dresses in other boxes that she either admired or abhorred. Selina nodded each time, but their tastes proved to be totally opposite on the dresses in question.

A few friends of the duke visited the box during the first intermission. The men smiled kindly and the women examined her dress. The duke suggested they retreat to the salon during the second intermission, to get some air. Edeline almost groaned with relief, and upon entering the large chamber went looking for her friends.

"It is kind of you to keep watch over her," Selina said.

Barrowmore turned his head to do just that, and find Edeline in the crowd. "She only turned seventeen a week before the wedding. With Giles gone, and my sister in Scotland, I had no choice. It is too easy for young women to get into trouble in London if no one is protecting them."

"Surely there is an aunt who would take up the charge."

"Several. I was tempted. However, much as I find my new sister a trial at times, I could not do it to her. Should you meet these aunts, you will understand what I mean."

"I expect they are like the matrons here who are glaring at me when they deign to look this way at all."

"Much like them. Notice how they deign fairly often. Watch that one there, in the blue. She can't resist looking. She screws up her face in its haughtiest disapproval, but she looks. That head keeps turning our way."

Just then the head turned once more as the matron in blue snuck another peek. Barrowmore caught her eye, smiled, and made a short bow. Red-faced, the matron quickly curtsied and looked away.

"That was naughty of you," Selina said, trying not to laugh.

"If Lady Trumball wants to see your dress better, she should come over and pretend conversation so she could have a good look."

"She was not interested in my dress. You know it, too. She was dying of curiosity about you, and why you have allowed a nameless nobody to stand by your side this evening. To come over would mean an introduction to someone she finds suspiciously inappropriate."

He gazed down at her. "You still do not understand, do you?"

"Understand what?"

"No woman who attracts a duke's favor is a nameless nobody. By definition she is a woman of interest. Tomorrow, when ladies write for appointments at the shop, it will not only be because of the dress they saw you wear tonight."

"Then I will not mind the pointed glances sent my way, if it will help us at the shop." What else could she say? Not one word of his explanation had insinuated anything. Even the use of "favor" only made reference to his allowing her into his circle of attention. And yet— She felt herself blushing, because it had sounded like a declaration of his interest, not Lady Trumball's. Mostly that was due to the way he looked at her as he spoke those careful words. His eyes had implied much more. At least she reacted that way.

His gaze still demanded all of her attention. He looked into her eyes so she could not escape. A little daze claimed her, and as she accepted his escort back to the box, it refused to lift. She barely noticed when the actors resumed the drama.

"Isn't he boring?" Edeline whispered during the final act. "Barrowmore, I mean. How dreadful this must be for you. Of course one cannot refuse a duke his invitation, but if he does this again and you want to say you are ill, I will confirm that indeed you are."

"I am enjoying myself. I am not bored."

"Only because I am here. Imagine if you were stuck alone with him. That is what I face in that house." She sighed dramatically. "I will be so happy when Giles returns."

Selina could not stop herself. "Do you anticipate his return soon?"

"Do not tell the duke, but I do. He wrote to me. Do not tell the duke that either. He expects to return in a fortnight or so."

"That sounds less than definite."

"Perhaps he meant three weeks. Maybe four. You must meet him when he comes back. He is ever so much fun."

Selina admitted to herself that, on the face of it, Giles *was* more fun than Barrowmore. Giles took nothing seriously. Life had been a string of jokes for him. Whoever dined with him laughed all evening. He made himself the center of attention with his wit.

The problem was that in never being serious, he said things that could be misunderstood. A passing flattery might be taken as true admiration. A poetic expression of emotion might be heard as a declaration of love. Musing speculations could be considered promises and future plans.

Oh, yes, Giles had been ever so much fun.

She looked past Edeline, at the duke. Not so glib with his wit, but also not so frivolous with his words. She doubted he would leave his new bride in the care of a brother and disappear for weeks on end. He would not leave debts all over a small town, so the people who laughed with him paid dearly for the entertainment. He would not court a woman publicly and let the world think he intended marriage when he did not. If he pursued a woman at all, he would make his intentions clear enough when it mattered.

Barrowmore looked over and caught her watching him. She should look away, but she did not. Warmth entered his gaze. Again he drew her into a silent moment of intimacy. A thrill spiraled through her.

He stretched his arm behind Edeline's chair, and reached to lift the edge of the blue wrap. Ever so carefully he raised it so it covered Selina's shoulders, to offer protection against the box's chill. It was a thoughtful gesture, quite caring, but his fingertips glossed over her back and arm in the process. The thrill turned into a whirlwind.

She turned her attention to the stage, maintaining her poise with effort.

Edeline was right. Barrowmore was not much like Giles. Giles had been a boy still, in his essence. Barrowmore was a man.

Rand really wished Edeline would disappear. At the least he wanted to foist her onto someone for the ride back to the house. He did not want to pretend to be the magnanimous duke when he and Selina entered that carriage. He wanted to grab her and—

With great effort, he pushed his urges out of his mind. There was no way to get rid of Edeline. This meant he would have to bring Mrs. Fontaine home first, and not have a single moment alone with her.

The short ride proved torturous. He sat across from the ladies, and it seemed to him his desire filled the compartment. It poured off him, an emotion he could not contain in his person. Every time Mrs. Fontaine looked over at him another wave began until he had inundated them both.

Edeline remained an island in that storm. She chatted away about some gossip one of her friends had shared. He nodded, grateful that she was too young to understand what was happening between her two companions. An older woman would have sensed it at once.

Mrs. Fontaine did, he was sure. She tried not to look at him, but kept doing so anyway. Little clues spoke of her nervousness. The way she grasped that reticule. The manner in which she kept pulling that wrap closer. The quiet, distracted tone of her voice when she responded to some comment from Edeline. She might be surprised and she might be frightened, but she was not unaware. Nor, he was almost certain, was she unmoved.

He insisted on being the one to hand her down from the carriage. He also escorted her to her building's door. He wanted to kiss her so badly that he thought he would explode from it. Kiss her and caress her and take her up to that sad apartment and make her promise to let him take care of her.

Instead they had an awkward parting with the glow of a gas lamp nearby making any privacy impossible.

"Thank you, Your Grace. It was a wonderful treat for me, and I appreciate your generosity in inviting me."

It was the kind of thing that everyone said to a duke, damn it. He did not know what the hell he expected instead, but her polite appreciation annoyed him.

"I did not intend it as a treat for you. I did not intend it as generosity. I did it as a pleasure for *me*. And you were the one who was generous, in agreeing to share your company."

She appeared taken aback.

He took one step forward, no more. Already he had dallied at this door enough to have Edeline wondering why, if she bothered to notice at all. "It was not a duke who invited you, but a man. Does that man find any favor with you?"

Her mouth fell open a bit. She visibly flustered. Then a stillness came to her. She looked right at his eyes. "Yes, I think he does."

He touched her hand, barely, the one near the door and out of sight.

She entered the building, and he returned to the carriage. He climbed in, and took his place across from Edeline. He cursed. Then he laughed.

All that discretion had been unnecessary. Edeline had fallen asleep.

CHAPTER SEVEN

There are certain times in a woman's life when she has to make important choices, the kind that will affect her life forever.

Selina knew she faced such a moment soon when a letter arrived from the duke the next day. She received it before she left her home for the shop. In it he invited her to join him on his yacht the upcoming Sunday. They would venture up the Thames. No mention was made of Edeline.

She pondered her decision on the way to the shop. Once there, a debate churned in her head while she kept most of her mind on business. The question was a simple one on the face of it. Should she encourage the duke? Did she want what he might be offering her?

As he had predicted, a few letters arrived in the morning post from new potential clients. Did one of the dressmakers have time for a consultation in the next day or two? By noon enough had come that Felicity pulled Selina into the office to discuss them.

"We will not be able to accommodate all of them," she said. "We should choose which ones we prefer."

"Not all of them will result in commissions. A good many may not," Selina said. "Some of those ladies want to consult about *me*, I fear, and have no intention of commissioning dresses. They want some information to feed to the gossip snake. The duke warned me of this."

"That complicates our responses. How do we find the ones truly interested in our craft so we do not waste time?"

"Perhaps Lady Clarice would agree to guide you. If you wrote and asked her to visit tomorrow for that purpose, she may say yes."

"Excellent idea. I will write to her at once. I am sure she knows all these names, and the characters attached to them." Felicity rose to leave.

"You did not appear surprised to learn that gossip might be abroad about me now," Selina said. "Did you expect it, despite your reassurances?"

"Curiosity is not really gossip, and curiosity was our entire goal."

"We hoped for curiosity about the shop, not me."

"You were the one in the dress. As for anything beyond that, I am sure you and the duke did nothing to invite speculation." Felicity shuffled the letters and looked nonchalant. "Did you?"

"I am sure we did not, but I fear dukes always invite speculation when they give any woman any attention."

"It will pass. He will not tolerate unfounded gossip. When you are not seen in his company again, it will— Are you blushing?" Felicity peered closely. "You are. Is there something about this that I do not know?"

Selina hung her head and nodded.

"What? Tell me now, I insist."

"He has shown some interest of a . . . romantic nature," Selina murmured.

"Did I hear correctly? Stop mumbling into your chest. Did you say he has shown romantic inclinations toward you?"

Selina nodded. "He kissed me in his garden."

"No."

"He wants to see me again. I received an invitation this morning."

"What are you going to do?"

"I do not know what to do. There is no way this pursuit is honorable." Selina stood and paced. "I will have to decline, of course."

"Are you sure that you are thinking clearly on this? He is a duke, not some clerk. Whatever his interests, this is no ordinary pursuit."

Selina almost stomped her foot. "I do not know what to do. I am out of my depths."

"I wish my mother were here. I cannot advise you as well as she could. However, it seems to me that there is one question you must ask yourself. Do you find him attractive?"

"Who would not? His attractiveness is visible to the world."

"I did not mean that, and you know it. Does your heart flip when you see him? Do you lose track of time when you look in his eyes? Did that kiss bedazzle you? Do you want him to kiss and hold you again? All of the honor and all of the benefits of his title and position will be meaningless if you feel no attraction of that kind. There are women who would suffer much to obtain a duke's generosity, but I doubt you are one of them."

Yes, her heart flipped and his gaze disarmed her. His kiss and his slightest touch did much more. She suffered not at all when Barrowmore made his interest known.

"It is not the physical part that makes me pause," she said.

"I expect not. Those born in the middle always worry about society's opinion the most. Oh, do not look surprised. My mother guessed at once that you were a gentlewoman by birth, but of the middling sort. No presentation at court for you, I think. Well born, but not well enough to ignore the rules the way the best in society do."

Felicity did not speak with scorn, of either Selina's birth or the more flexible morals of the best. She simply described what she saw through eyes inherited from her French mother, and she saw very clearly, it appeared.

"I think you should enjoy this duke's attention while you can, for as long as you can," Felicity said. "You make no promises by seeing him again. You make no decision either. If the day comes when he requires one of you, then you can make your choice."

"You are as always very sensible," Selina said, smiling. "You are correct. Why worry about a choice that I may not have to make."

Felicity came over and embraced her, then gave her cheek a little kiss. She turned to leave. "Oh, you will have to make a choice. I am sure of that. Just not right away."

A carriage called for her Sunday morning. A bright, warm sun bathed her as she entered it. The carriage brought her to the dock where Barrowmore's yacht was moored.

The yacht's sails remained down. Oars showed through holes in the hull. As she neared she saw a canopy on the deck, and beneath it a little sitting room complete with a divan, and a table with two chairs. It appeared to be just the sort of floating vessel one would expect a duke to own.

The duke appeared from below deck and saw her. He came down the little gangway to greet her and handed her on board. "We are in luck. The day is fair. No damp, no clouds, no rain, no cold."

"Luck? I assumed you commanded the weather to cooperate," she teased.

"Alas, even I cannot arrange that."

"What good it is to be a duke, then?" She paced around the little domestic vignette. All around them the crew prepared the yacht. The duke gave a nod and men began to cast off. How foolish she had been to worry they would be alone. A little navy would serve as chaperone. "This is charming."

"I thought you would prefer to travel in comfort, and not perched on a wooden bench or chair. A picnic luncheon awaits when the time comes."

"Food, too? One wonders why you bother with that big mansion behind that wall. Do you always deck out the deck thus?"

"Rarely. I will show you the quarters below, so you can see how usually this boat is less than luxurious in the things that truly matter."

She looked above her at the furled sails. "We will not sail?"

"If the wind permits it."

"Please tell me that there are no galley slaves at the oars."

"Of course there are. I promise that they are fed at least once a day." He walked to the place from where he had emerged when she arrived. "Come, I will give you a tour."

He held out his hand. In order to walk down the steep, narrow stairs she needed that support. The warmth of his hand encompassed hers. The connection unnerved her, and sent a tremor through her body.

He did not release her hand once below. She could think of no way to force that without pretending more insult than she experienced. She liked the sensation of his hand on hers. She found the hold firm but gentle, demanding but kind.

He showed her a little kitchen where a cook worked at their luncheon, and a necessary that, she suspected, was the true purpose of this tour. That was thoughtful of him. They then moved between two walls of cabinets into the depths of the yacht, toward the bow.

The skinny passageway stopped at a chamber with a bed, desk, and more cabinets.

There was no navy here. No chaperones.

"It all appears more luxurious than you believe." She tried to sound as casual as if they toured the British Museum and viewed some exotic artifact. "I do not think most captains have beds this large, covered in so many silk-dressed pillows."

"This is not the captain's."

Of course not. This was the duke's.

He still held her hand, and now he coaxed her toward him. Holding her still, like he thought she might bolt, he plucked at the ties to her bonnet. "This brim will become another sail, once we set out. The breeze will ruin it."

The slow unwinding of the ribbons unsettled her. It seemed almost scandalous for a man to remove even this small item of her ensemble, especially while in this cabin. Her mouth dried from her rapid, shallow breaths.

He lifted the bonnet away and set it on the desk. "I thought you might not agree to this outing."

"We dressmakers must take advantage of any entertainment that comes our way."

He ignored her arch tone. "I thought you might be afraid."

"Should I be?"

His lips hovered over hers. "Yes, I suppose so."

He kissed her. She did not mind. She did not resist. The sensation of that kiss warmed all of her. *Did his kiss bedazzle you?* Oh, yes. That too. The kiss, the power of his body and energy, both excited and comforted. It felt good and right even though of course it was neither.

He pulled her into an embrace, but not another kiss. She rested her head against his coats, feeling the muscles in his chest while his arms surrounded her.

"Is it your intention to ravish me down here?" She tried to sound sophisticated, but failed miserably.

"I did not think to ever ravish you. Certainly not here." His lips pressed her crown. "I will confess that I plotted a way to kiss you discreetly, however."

"I thank you for that."

He laughed. "For what? The discretion or the kiss?"

She knew what a middling sort of gentlewoman would reply. Instead she answered honestly. "For both."

The oars took them away from the dock. Once they were headed upriver, enough of a breeze rose for one sail to be used. The captain tacked back and forth, managing to move forward at a slow pace.

Barrowmore settled on the divan and coaxed her to sit there, too. They watched the shores inch by. "Fate has smiled on me, giving me this day with you. If it had rained today, and been lovely tomorrow, I would have been most vexed."

"You could have still enjoyed the fine weather tomorrow."

"Not at all. Tomorrow, I am being fitted for my coronation robes. I expect it will take most of the afternoon. I have put it off longer than I should have, so it must be done."

"Will you wear a special costume and have a special role to play?"

"I have been spared the worst, if you refer to the lucky few who will act in the ritual." He smiled slowly. "The king is dressing them all as courtiers from King Henry Tudor's time. I was not sorry to be deprived of the honor, if the king's special favor means wearing hose and a codpiece."

She angled back to take him in. "I think you would have looked splendid dressed thus. Such a pity the world will be denied the sight of you."

"I do have nice legs, if I may say so myself. How embarrassing for the men who do not. I have heard they are joining in a petition to the king to be allowed to wear high boots, so any weak calves do not go on display."

"The king is certainly making this coronation elaborate, if he is putting his retainers in costume."

"More elaborate than Napoleon's. Much more than his own father's. Normally I would not criticize, but with the humor abroad in the country, this may not be the time to spend with such abandon, and in such a public way."

He turned serious with that observation. The duke in him took over, the man whose birth had given him a say in the workings of the realm, and a voice even kings listened to. It was easy to forget, while they joked, that the robe he would wear symbolized a responsibility that he surely felt.

"Perhaps the king wants to emphasize that the crown still matters, and will continue to in the future. What with all the unrest, this display will emphasize that."

"Perhaps. I think, however, he mostly wants a big show, bigger than any remembered by anyone." He looked over at her. "He is not a young man in age, but there is still something of the boy in him."

"If you will not be a Tudor, what robes will you wear?"

"They are traditional, reserved for coronations. Ede and Ravenscroft makes them for our family. They pulled the ones that were worn the last time out of storage. They were well cared for, but it was so long ago that they were used. The duke then was much shorter than I, and I thought the fur smelled, so we started anew." He gestured to his body. "The robe encases me in red silk velvet and sports an ermine short cape. It is the same with all the peers. The only difference is in our coronets, and the number of spots on the ermine. You reminded Edeline that fur is inappropriate for summer, but tradition knows no season."

"It will be impressive, all of you lined up like that." She could picture it. She could picture *him*. She would join the crowds outside to catch a glimpse of some of it, she decided.

"It could also be unbearably hot in mid July. That will be a day when I pray for many clouds, and an unseasonably cool breeze."

"You may even wish you were in those hose. They would be cooler than wool trousers under velvet and fur."

"Maybe I will wear hose anyway. Then, once we are in place, I can part the robes and allow some cool air in." He pantomimed flipping the edge of a robe back and forth like a fan.

She laughed at the severely dignified expression he maintained while he did it. His eyes dared anyone to notice or comment on his sartorial irregularities.

A footman brought them wine then. It was very good wine, perhaps the best she had ever tasted.

When she was a girl, her family went on picnics, carrying a large basket of cold food and simple drink out to the countryside where they found a fine prospect upon which to gaze. The duke's picnic was nothing like that. It was not even a picnic in truth.

That cook had prepared pheasant in one sauce and beef in another, with well-seasoned legumes and an interesting but peculiar dish of rice and currants. They sat at the little table. All through the meal their conversation alternated between comments on the passing sights and talk about her shop and his family.

"She eloped," he said of his sister. "I have no idea why. I could hardly object to an earl."

"Perhaps it had nothing to do with you. She may have just decided to get it over with."

"I hope she welcomed the union more enthusiastically than that."

"I meant that having found the man she wanted, she may have decided to do the deed with no further ado or fuss."

"I think you have something there. Charlotte is not—" He drank some wine.

"Not?"

"I stopped because it sounds disloyal, but I think you will understand that is not intended. I was going to say not entirely normal. Not interested much in the things most women enjoy. She was a hoyden as a girl, and never came to London for a Season after her first. I had concluded she did not want to marry at all, but then, to my shock, I received the letter in February informing me that she had."

"Did she ever come back?"

"Soon after. They both came, to ask my blessing and to apologize for their hasty nuptials. I think that was her earl's idea. They stayed a fortnight, then went back to the highlands where I expect they ride out daily to count sheep with his plaid flowing from their saddles."

She sipped her wine, watching him. He spoke freely with her, more than she ever expected he would. "I think you miss her."

He looked right at her. "I think I do, too. Now, tell me about your life and your friends, and whether you still hear from your family."

She had not expected him to ask her about any of that. He had just revealed more than she expected. She could hardly now snap her own shell shut.

She chose to get the hardest part over first. "I hear from my mother on occasion. She will write a long letter when she finds the time and privacy, and fill me in on my family and the village." She did not add that sometimes Mama sent a little money too, possibly out of guilt. Mama had not liked it when she left, but she had not said the words that might have stopped it either. She had not declared to the world that no gossip was going to drive away her daughter. Amid Mama's river of tears at their parting, there had been a thick current of relief.

"I have asked her and my father to come to London for the coronation. We can watch the processions, and partake of the festivities in the streets and squares. I do not think they will come, however."

"If they do you must let me know. I will make sure they do not have to watch from the crowds."

She wondered what Mama would think if a duke, and this particular duke at that, bestowed such a gift on her daughter. Suspicious did not begin to describe the way Mama would see it. But—would she mind so much? She had not issued warnings about Giles. Only afterward had the dangers been itemized.

"Who are in your circle of friends?" he asked while he nodded to the footman who offered more wine.

"I am not a Londoner, so I do not have any circles as such."

"Even so, you must have friends." He flashed a charming smile. "Besides me, that is."

"I suppose my best friend is Felicity, who manages the shop now, although I do not think she sees me the same way. I am beholden to her, and that affects a friendship. She is not much older in age, so we have much in common and spend a lot of time together."

"How are you beholden?"

"When I came to London, I had a few shillings and a valise and nothing else except some fashion plates I had drawn. I went looking for work at a dressmaker. I found Madame Follette's easily, because the shop's entrance is on the street, not up some stairs. I had no references, and not much of a history to give them. All I had were those plates and some garments I had created and sewn for myself. Felicity's mother was not inclined to take me on, but Felicity convinced her to do so."

"It is understandable that you are loyal to her. It is all the clearer why you took Edeline's commissions."

They now skirted close to the subject of Giles, and her history with him. Barrowmore had avoided that all day. When he spoke of his family, he had mentioned the harpy of a great-aunt and an uncle of whom he was fond. He had spoken of his sister. Giles, however, had been skipped.

"I think loyalty is a good thing, when well placed. Don't you?" she said.

"Of course. I also think it is a rare thing. People are quick to rationalize it away when it suits them, and often it requires some sacrifice that becomes seen as too high a price."

"As a duke, you would know more about it than I do."

"You speak of my obligations to crown and country. Those loyalties are not so different from what is expected from any citizen. Personal loyalties, person to person, are where the real moral quandaries develop."

Their meal finished, they returned to the divan. As if on cue, the yacht made a long lazy curve to head back the way it had come. Selina watched the water and river banks glide around her in a broad arc. Her gaze came to rest on the man sitting by her side.

He was looking at her, not the views. Their gazes met in a stark connection. His eyes reflected the day's good humor, but also looked into hers so totally that he held her spellbound. It seemed a long time that they remained like that. Then he reached out and drew her toward him. He met her halfway with a kiss.

She gave herself over to the wonderful sensations that kiss evoked. Excitement and peace and pleasure all combined to create a special joy. She became free and young and so very alive. And beautiful. More beautiful than she had felt in years.

The kiss never really ended. It went on and on, first careful and luring, then harder and claiming, then invasive and deliciously shocking. She ceased caring about where they were. Thrills took over her body and a mounting desire obscured her thoughts.

He lifted her bodily and set her closer, right next to him, so their hips pressed. He did not let go of her, but wrapped her into an embrace that allowed that kiss to move to her neck and ear, to her shoulder and chest.

She accepted more enthusiastically than she ought. She rested her arms around his shoulders. She relished every evidence of the changes in her body, and the hunger they both reflected and incited. His rising passion did not frighten her, but she recognized it well enough in his kisses and firm caresses, in the tension she felt in his body and the way he forced control. She was too enthralled to worry about what it might mean or where it might lead.

Then, his caress moved to her breast and suddenly she had no choice but to think about it. Not that she contemplated her danger with any clarity. The pleasure of that caress argued forcefully that she should cast all cautions aside, give herself over to the abandon that beckoned, and assess the situation another day.

Lack of resistance hardly dissuaded him. Nor did the happy gasps that snuck out when, despite her garments, he rubbed just the right spots. The most tempting pleasures spiraled down her core and teased her femininity.

He stopped kissing her. He rested his forehead against hers, his face as close as possible, his breaths deep and ragged. His hand remained on her body, its palm on her midriff and its fingers slowly circling and sweeping her breast.

He lost whatever inner battle he fought. Abruptly he stood and pulled her up, into his arms. He took her hand and led her to the stairs. "Come with me."

She stumbled after him. Some sense found a place in her head as he handed her down below. More gelled by the time he closed the door of the cabin and embraced her again. The way he caressed her, the way their mutual desire displayed itself in hot kisses and groping holds, did nothing to help her find the words to voice the things she should say.

Only when his hand settled between her breasts and began unbuttoning her dress did her misgivings arise with force. She looked down at those fine masculine fingers opening her dress. "I thought you said you did not intend to ravish me."

"I don't." He spoke in her ear before devastating it with his tongue. "Not here, I said. Not yet."

Not yet.

A slow smile formed against her cheek. "You are completely safe. I promise I only want to feel you and see you."

Perhaps, if she were not close to ecstasy already, or if she had made her choices earlier, before pleasure swayed her, or if being undressed were not so unbearably exciting, she would have doubted his promise the way a small part of her consciousness told her to now. The truth, she knew in her heart, was that she did not want to deny him because it meant denying herself. This felt too good to stop. He had her in his spell, and she loved being there.

His fingers paused, as if he waited for her to make a choice. She looked up and met his gaze. She could only look back, helpless.

He embraced her hard, close, lifting her to a kiss that spared her not at all. Then they were on the bed entwined and fevered.

He released her and shrugged off his coat. Then he turned his attention again to those buttons.

She could barely breathe. Her dress slowly parted. Desire and anticipation made her heady. Her vision blurred. He got the dress down her arms more easily than she thought he would. The shoulders of her petticoat followed. He gently kissed the swells of her breasts above her short stays.

"You are a beautiful woman. I want to see all of your beauty, but will settle for this." He pulled the lacing that tied her stays.

With each pull of the lacing her stays loosened more. She closed her eyes to hold in what it did to her.

The stays fell aside. For a moment nothing happened. She snuck a look and the sight of him devastated her further. Dark hair mussed, expression firm, and eyes like crystals, he looked at her body, then at her face. A tremor much like fear shimmied down her body, only it affected her in ways fear never did.

He carefully lowered the shoulder straps of her chemise, and unveiled her body to her waist. His eyes narrowed and his fingertips glossed around the sides of her breasts. "Beautiful. Perfect."

Her breasts firmed and ached under his caresses. Soft hair feathered her face when his head bowed. Soft kisses praised her body and lured her toward madness. His mouth moved to the tips and began a gentle assault with his lips and teeth that drove her passion higher until she reeled from the pleasure.

She became a madwoman, insane with need, her body alive and waiting and screaming with impatience for more. She clutched his shoulders and her mind begged him to forget his promise and be a scoundrel because she would die soon if left like this.

Did he hear her thoughts? Did she utter them aloud? He claimed her in a devouring, dominating kiss that spoke of a decision to finish this the way nature intended. She kissed back, urging, triumphant, arching her body into his. Her vulva pulsed with cravings she did not think possible to know.

Surely he would raise her skirt, or remove it. Certainly the unknown that beckoned in such a maddening and physical way would be revealed.

Instead he broke the kiss, abruptly. His hand ceased taunting her, and instead slid below her in a full caress. Eyes closed, breathing hard, he rested his forehead against hers.

She almost screamed at him. For an insane moment, she could not contain her profound frustration. As if he knew, he gave her the softest kiss of reassurance. "Not now," he said, soothing her. "Not here."

She had existed in an unearthly place where her consciousness filled with only the two of them, and physical pleasures and yearnings. As he found himself and her own madness receded, the real world came into view. A cabin on a yacht, with men below and above. *Not now. Certainly not here.*

He rolled onto his back, bringing her closer so that she lined his side and his arm still embraced her. She settled her face and fingertips against the exquisite brocade of his waistcoat, and did nothing to disturb the quiet peace that descended.

What they had done, what she had allowed, could not be ignored. Even now she remained half-undressed, a state that with each moment seemed more scandalous. It was one thing to be thus in the heat of passion, and another to remain so afterward. The way her nakedness remained on view, the way he held her with that possessive arm, implied he now had a right to this much of her at least.

She could not work up much concern about that. Not now. Not here.

The truth was that she felt protected, not used, flattered, not insulted. She savored the closeness, the warmth, the strength making her small and vulnerable. Fear could not stand against the intimacy that drenched her.

She embraced the emotions and held them close, and almost wept because, for the first time in years, she did not feel all alone.

Bright light suddenly poured in the small window. Rand stirred out of the drowsy relaxation he enjoyed. Tucked beside him, her face on his chest, Selina had not moved at all. She did not sleep either. He could see her lashes raised. He wondered what she looked at.

That window perhaps. The sun had lowered enough to shine right in. Dusk could be only an hour away. The sway of the yacht indicated slow movements. The captain was deliberately taking his time, so His Grace could dally to his heart's content.

Even so, they would need to dock soon.

He kissed Selina's crown, then disentangled himself. He rose from the bed, and reached for his coat. "I will let you—" He turned and looked at her lying there, her lovely breasts still naked and her garments in disarray. "Do you need help dressing?"

She sat up, giving him another view of her body. "I do for myself every day. It is why my garments were so easy to remove."

He smiled and gave a little bow. "I will wait outside."

She turned to stretch and reach for her stays. He watched long enough to admire the sinuous line her arm and side made while she moved, then he stepped outside and closed the door.

Once there, thoughts that had been drifting through his mind coalesced. Mere musings would no longer do.

He could not remember that he had ever had a woman like that, in bed and in abandon, passionately engaged and almost begging for more, and retreated. Yet he had today.

He was not entirely sure why. Perhaps because he suspected that if he had gone further, if he had taken her, Selina would avoid ever being in his presence again.

He was not a boy. He was over thirty years old, and he knew how these things went. He had had mistresses, and he had experienced affairs of the heart. The latter were with women either unattainable or inappropriate. The former were with women who had known men before him, and knew yet more after, and for the most part his fascination with them had been a matter of desire and nothing more.

Selina did not fit neatly in either category. Whatever had happened four years before, and despite her claim of marriage, he did not think there had been other men besides that. Certainly she did not live as if a series of protectors had called with expensive gifts in hand.

If she had eschewed that life, who was he to lure her to it now?

As for the other, she certainly was inappropriate. Even Selina Duval, daughter of a gentry family of no great fortune, would have been a poor match for a duke. Selina Fontaine, woman of uncertain history and dressmaker, definitely would be.

He shook his head, and laughed at himself. He wanted her. He had soundly cursed himself even as he took the noble path today. He had wanted to kiss every inch of her, and have her every way imaginable. He still did.

However, he also liked her company. She amused him with her quiet humor and impressed him with her poise. That came from within, which was rare. It derived from her own confidence in knowing herself, not from the approval of anyone else.

He supposed, now that he considered it, that had been another reason for his retreat. He had not wanted this day, and the enjoyment it had given him, to be seen by her as merely a prelude to seduction.

The door opened, and she emerged, tidy as ever. She carried her bonnet, which he had removed hours ago. She looked lovely in the shadows of the passageway. Luminous and, it seemed to him, happy enough.

He gave her a kiss, then offered his hand and led her up to the deck.

London surrounded them. The yacht had been moving in circles. The oars dipped the water. The sail was down. Behind them, the sun hung low and orange in the sky, preparing to set.

"It is late," she said, leaning against the railing, watching the town. "I did not realize how pleasure could make time fly, or stop— or whatever happened." She glanced his way with a naughty smile.

That smile heartened him to a ridiculous extent. He did not want her worrying or regretting or any of those things women were taught to feel after such an encounter.

He slid his arm around her and together they watched the yacht make its final turn. "We have been gone so long, I should have fed you supper, too."

"I am not hungry. I do not think I will be either, for several hours. It has been a lovely day."

"I am relieved you think so."

She raised an eyebrow. "There is no telling what I will think tomorrow, of course."

"The same thing, I hope."

"I hope so, too. I am counting on it."

The yacht slid into its place on the dock. The carriage waited, to take Selina home.

"Selina, I need to say that—"

She placed her fingertips on his lips. "Do not speak. Not now. Not here. Perhaps not ever."

She gathered her skirt. He handed her over to the footman who waited to escort her to the carriage. At the bottom of the gangway, she turned and waved. After the carriage door closed, she put her face to the window, and blew a kiss in his direction.

CHAPTER EIGHT

Selina woke to a dreary morning full of fog and rain. She went to her door to retrieve the bucket of water the serving girl provided each day at dawn. Set inside it, the stem submerged, was one white rosebud.

She knew who had sent it. Or, perhaps, even delivered it himself. The gesture touched her.

It had to have come very recently, if it found the water ready. She ran to her window, to see if a carriage just now rolled away.

She set the rose on her washstand while she used the water. A hothouse flower, to be sure, but lovely and fresh. The duke must have sent a servant to the flower market before daybreak to buy it. Perhaps he had arranged it all yesterday evening. She doubted he had risen himself to tend to such matters.

She did not try to swallow the delight that rose gave her. She had returned home yesterday in a sensual daze, floating in a world that refused to feel real. Upon retiring, she assumed the morning would bring different thoughts and reactions to her time on the yacht. Only, as soon as she opened her eyes, she knew that while a good night's sleep had set her firmly in her world again, it had not brought regrets.

Dressed and ready, she walked to the shop. Already it was busy inside. Since she had no patrons calling today, she joined Alice and Sally, their two apprentice seamstresses, in the workroom upstairs, and helped with the dress on which they sewed.

An hour later Felicity opened the door and asked her to come out.

"This came for you." Felicity handed over a letter from Lady Giles.

Selina opened it. "She requests that the fitting scheduled for tomorrow be done today, and at her apartment in Manard House."

"She is a spoiled one. You have to decline, although I hate to annoy a patron of her caliber. However, we have too much to do today, and cannot spare you for the whole afternoon."

"Perhaps if I write back and say I can only do this very late in the afternoon, she will be appeased and I will not desert you for hours. I can start over at four o'clock. I am sure that any social events she has planned tonight will not start until much later."

"If you do not mind extending your day that long, that is a solution. I do not like to think of you leaving here and serving that child until night falls, however. You'll make yourself sick if that becomes a habit."

"I will gently explain to her that I cannot change plans at her whim, and that she really needs to visit us for future fittings."

Felicity made an indelicate noise in her throat, and gave a look that said she doubted much success for that plan.

To make up for the few hours she would still be gone from the shop, Selina bent over her needles all day, and shortened the midday walk she usually took to refresh herself. At half past three she began collecting the dresses and materials she would need when she called on Lady Giles.

"I'll take you, but we will have to go round a ways," the hackney driver said when he learned she aimed for Mayfair. "There's bad doings at the west end of the Piccadilly. People collecting and shouting. It could get worse as the workday ends."

Demonstrations had become part of life in London. Not only radicals and the reform-minded raised their voices and fists in public. Sometimes those opposed to change did as well. Usually none of this inconvenienced her, aside from creating an undercurrent of instability in her world.

"Round a ways" meant it took almost an hour to arrive at Manard House. This time a footman waited outside the garden portal. He waved her driver on, telling him to use the main door.

"Must be something wrong back here," the driver called back to her. "Well, if they insist I bring a servant to the main door, I'll do it."

Lady Giles had alerted the household to this visit. Footmen waited to carry up the dresses and boxes. One of them escorted Selina, offering his arm on the stairs.

"His Grace made it very clear that I was to tell you to use any pillows you chose," he said as he knocked on the door to Lady Giles's apartment.

Barrowmore knew she was coming. That must explain the different welcome she received this time. It also explained the different reception she had from Edeline's maid Françoise. The dour-faced woman immediately placed a circle of pillows on the floor.

Edeline did not look happy with the alterations in her dressmaker's treatment. She said not a word about it, but throughout the three hours of fittings she did not smile or chat. She at times stared at Selina with lights of disdain in her eyes. Selina wondered if somehow Edeline had learned about the yacht.

"You can go." Edeline's curt dismissal came as soon as Françoise helped her out of the last dress.

Edeline retreated to another chamber. Selina packed her materials. Françoise packed as well. She pulled items out of drawers and wardrobes and placed them in a portmanteau. She laid a ball gown on the divan.

"Is the lady taking a journey?" Selina asked.

"She attends a ball tonight, but will stay with her friend afterward." Françoise spoke while she examined the gown's embellishments for loose threads or damage. She caught herself, and glared over at Selina. Her expression reflected her opinion of a dressmaker asking about things not of her concern.

Footmen waited outside. They took her boxes and the dresses and Selina began her long path home. She judged it to be well past eight o'clock. Her body ached from her day's work. Even silk pillows did not keep her knees from rebelling. She would arrive home in the dark, to chambers well chilled. She did not think she would have time for a decent meal before going to bed.

As she and her footmen descended to the reception hall, a little buzz of conversation drifted up to them. She looked down to see the butler conferring with a groom. The butler spoke to another servant, then marched across the hall and disappeared.

When she reached the entry, that servant pulled one of her footmen aside and whispered something. The young man returned to her. "There seems to be some trouble in town. It is spilling west a bit. It will not affect Mayfair, but travel east of here may be difficult."

"I am sure a hackney driver can find a way around."

"I was told to ask you to wait here, while we decide what to do." He set down his boxes. The other footman draped the covered dresses over a chair. Selina sat on a bench.

A door opened, and the butler emerged. The duke came with him.

"Mrs. Fontaine. It is unfortunate that you were asked to come today," Barrowmore said. "The town is unsettled, and with evening the crowds are getting thicker and spreading. For your safety, it is best if you do not try to go home."

"I appreciate Your Grace's concern for me, but I am sure that I will be safe enough."

"Safe enough is not satisfactory. Only very safe is. If you insist on trying this, I will have to take you in my coach. I cannot turn my responsibility for you over to a hackney driver more concerned with his equipage than with your life."

She pictured his coach navigating streets teaming with unhappy people. She doubted they were in the mood to bow to a duke tonight.

Barrowmore stepped closer. Or else the servants moved back. He and she were essentially alone when he spoke again. "I must insist that you stay here, as our guest. The housekeeper will see to your comfort."

Her dealings with this man had been a series of choices. She suspected she now faced the biggest one. She should insist they call for that hackney coach.

Seeing him brought back vivid memories of the day before, of soft hair on her face and warm kisses on her breast. Of a soul-drenching intimacy that now made this austere, proud man very familiar to her. Too familiar. She risked getting in too deeply.

"It would not be wise for me to remain here," she said.

"Don't you trust me?"

"No."

"What a smart woman you are. I promise, however, that there is no nefarious plot afoot. I did not arrange for thousands of citizens to block the streets so I could keep you here."

She had to laugh, but it entered her mind that if a duke did want to make such arrangements, he probably could. "You may not have plotted it, but the result is still dangerous."

"Not so dangerous. After yesterday, you know that I can be a citadel of restraint when I choose."

She felt her face warming, because she had not shown any restraint, and they both knew it. Who was she to act like he planned an assault on her pure virtue, when all he had done was ensure she remained safe?

"I am grateful for the offer. I am sure the housekeeper will take good care of me."

"I will leave you to her, then. Will you come down after she settles you, and join me for dinner?"

"Are you not taking Lady Giles to the ball?"

"Not this one, I am relieved to say. She will be with her unmarried friends tonight, and safe enough."

She should plead exhaustion and ask that a dinner be sent up to her. Definitely. Absolutely.

"I will be honored to dine with you."

The housekeeper appeared out of nowhere. The footmen picked up their burdens. They all went back up the steps. Selina looked back over her shoulder. Barrowmore stood there, gazing up at her, watching.

"**B**arrowmore."

The feminine voice calling for his attention sounded young and petulant. He looked up from where he contemplated a low fire and weighed the wisdom of seducing Mrs. Fontaine tonight. Actually, he weighed nothing. He plotted how to do it.

"I would speak with you," Edeline said.

He stood and faced her. She had dressed for the ball, and floated through the library toward him in a haze of luxury. Head back and nose high, she regarded him more imperiously than her age or circumstances warranted.

"Speak your mind," he said.

"I do not care for the manner in which you are treating Mrs. Fontaine."

"Perhaps you should be clear in your objections," he said, carefully.

"Sending orders that she is to have use of my silk pillows, for example. I did not care for that at all."

"I see."

"Now I am told she is to stay here as a guest. That will not do."

He was not in the mood to be scolded by this slip of a girl, especially about what he did in his own home. "Having her caught in a riot because of your demands on her would *do* even less."

"It will be misunderstood if she stays here."

"You should not worry about that. I am doing what any gentleman would do under the circumstances. No one will assume that—"

"But they will. They already do. The whole world already assumes."

Edeline's world consisted of about three hundred people. Still . . .

"I cannot imagine why." He had been very discreet. None of the servants on that yacht would speak a word, no matter what they had surmised. Nor would any of those in this house.

"She was at the theater with us. That was enough to do it. Now she will stay in this house, like a guest. Everyone thinks I have befriended her, Barrowmore. *Everyone.*"

Ah. Of course. He should have known Edeline would only be noticing if the talk was about *her*.

"As if I would permit such familiarity from an inferior," Edeline continued. "It is humiliating to have such gossip spread about me, and you are the one who caused it. Now you add fuel to the fire."

A ridge of anger rose in him at the way she spoke of Selina. "Mrs. Fontaine is a gentleman's daughter. Perhaps your friends do not know that. You should explain it, if anything more is said."

"She may have been born as one, but now she is a seamstress. *My* seamstress. She should no more be strolling my gardens or chatting with a duke than should any other servant." She pouted. Her unhappiness turned her voice to a whine.

He had never liked pouting. He detested grown women whining. Both raised the devil in him. Selina never pouted.

"They are *my* gardens, as it happens, and I will decide with whom I chat. Here is the solution. Should anyone say anything, explain that she is not your friend, but mine."

"*Yours?* As if anyone will believe *that.*" With a huff, she turned and strode toward the door. "If she continues in her presumptuous behavior, I will have to end my patronage."

The hell you will. He caught himself before he flung that after her, but the retort erupted in him with an icy fury. How dare this inconsequential spoiled child look down on Selina? Edeline should pray that after living her entire life she possessed one quarter of Selina's refinement.

A footman entered the library. He carried what looked like a fat letter. He retreated after handing it over.

Rand opened it, but knew what it contained. He had not expected this until tomorrow. It was just as well he had it in hand tonight, because it appeared fate was conspiring. Whether for him or against him, he did not know.

"**I** think you have heard these stories before." Barrowmore made the observation toward the end of the dinner. He had entertained her with tales of the foibles of the ton thus far this Season, and had not shrunk from sharing the gossip that initiated the more dramatic episodes.

"Our ladies have a way of chattering on while we fit them," she said. "We hear much we should not. However, none of your stories have been told by them. All they speak of is the coronation."

"You mean Princess Caroline."

She nodded. "Everyone has opinions about that."

"They are sympathetic, I assume."

"Not all of them. But I do not think it matters to them what they believe should happen. They are too busy speculating on what *might* happen."

The topic subdued the duke. "It is a tangle, and neither will end up the better for it. It has been a miserable union from the start. Not surprising, since he was forced to marry her for diplomatic reasons. Yet, that is the lot of princes. Of most of us. If anyone should have known how it would be, it was a crown prince."

"Did you not support his attempt at divorce?"

"No. Oh, her behavior was indiscreet, even scandalous, but so was his. I did support their continued separation, and still do. He will not crown her as his queen. He will not have her present when he is crowned."

"Surely he will not bar the doors of the cathedral."

"I think he will. Literally."

"No wonder our ladies are breathless with anticipation."

"It will be the best theater of the year," he said sardonically. "No woman deserves such humiliation, no matter what she has done."

Selina drank the last of her wine. The meal finished and the table cleared, it was time to retreat to her chamber. She had enjoyed herself, though. Sitting together here, at one end of the long dining table, she could ignore that another night fifty others might be present too. Listening to Barrowmore tell stories—and he told them very well—had increased their informality.

She liked this man. She not only found him handsome and magnetic, but also friendly and very human when he shed his ducal aura. The public Barrowmore might make her tremble, but the private one made her smile.

No, that was not true. The private one made her tremble, too, but not out of awe for his station. She had spent the last two hours trembling when he looked at her. She did so right now.

"I thank you for the invitation to dine with you." She made to stand. "With your leave, I will retire now."

"Not yet." He stood, too. "Come with me. I have something to show you."

He led her to the central stairs, then up to the library. Two stories high, it showed a balcony all around above, accessed by stairs at one end of the chamber. Beautiful woods and sumptuous fabrics managed to tame the grandeur of the huge space.

He sat her on a divan, then retrieved something from a writing table. "This is for you. I arranged it several days ago. I want you to have it."

She took the thick, folded vellum packet. "What is it?"

He sat beside her. "I have been trying to come up with the right word for what it is. My difficulty in doing so is why I want you to have it now."

"Now as in not before and not later?"

"Not before because I had not thought of it before. Not later because perhaps later all the likely words to explain it would take on meanings I do not intend." He took her hand in his. "It is not compensation, you see. It is not a bribe either. Nor is it a gift. I suppose it is justice."

"Justice. Goodness." She unfolded the vellum into a large document sheet, full of words and seals. She squinted at the florid writing and pieced it out. It took longer for her to comprehend the implications. They rendered her almost speechless.

"You are giving me that manor house near my village?"

"It is not entailed, and it is almost never used. If you ever go back, you can live there. If you never do, you can still benefit from the rents and income. It is not a large property, but it is livable."

"I cannot accept this."

"It is done. It is yours. That is what all those seals and signatures mean."

"I can never live there. It does not change why I left."

"It probably changes more than you think. However, sell it if you don't want it. A better plan is to send this document to your father and ask him to have it managed for you. He owns property, and will know what to do."

She stared at the document. Not a gift or a bribe. "Justice, you called it. For what?"

He took the vellum and began folding it back into its rectangular packet. "For my family's carelessness when you were younger. For how you had to leave your home. For the hours you spend on your knees fitting dresses." He set the vellum aside. "And, if I am honest, for my showing insufficient strength in resisting my desire for you."

"I thought you displayed impressive strength yesterday."

"I am not referring to yesterday, Selina."

She could never claim she did not receive fair warning. Not that she needed it put into words. The air crackled with restless passion. He spoke as if the deed were already done, however. As if they both knew how it would be.

"I am not looking for a protector," she said. "Even with carte blanche." She had to smile when she said that, as she remembered the little misunderstanding that had started them down this path.

"I admit I would like to take care of you, and see to your security. However, if you do not want that, I will accept whatever you permit.

You will have to allow me to give you a few gifts, however. Lovers do that."

Lovers. It was not the same as being a courtesan, or even a mistress. What it had in common with those roles was the normal lack of permanence for a liaison with a duke. She had allowed herself no illusions or dreams about that. He would marry some day, maybe soon, and when he did whatever they shared would end.

She desired him as much as he did her. Just sitting here speaking of this had her excited and aroused. Her body ached to experience again the glories of yesterday.

He cupped her head with his hand and eased her toward him. He kissed her. "You are not arguing," he murmured. "You are not refusing me. You must do so now if you intend to at all."

She embraced him and kissed him back, and made her final choice.

CHAPTER NINE

She fit in his arms, perfectly. Her passion rose along with his. Having decided to give herself, she did not hold back.

Rand barely contained the urge to possess immediately. His hunger for Selina had distracted him for days, and owned his mind the last few hours. With her kisses of acceptance he experienced not only a primitive joy of victory, but also a masculine gratitude.

Their kisses turned consuming and their caresses possessive. A thought entered his fevered brain, that he should take her above, to a bed. His impatience did not want the delay, but he rose to his feet with her still in his arms and guided her toward the door. Pushing it open a fraction, he pulled away from her lips.

"Leave," he commanded through the slit. Footsteps shuffled away on carpet and marble.

"The servants?" Her question came as little more than an exhale.

"They are gone. Come with me."

He did not let her go, but drew her up the stairs, kissing her, holding her. She floated along, her body bound to his closely by his arm, her head angling to accept kisses scorching her neck.

He needed no commands in his apartment. As soon as he opened the door, another within closed. He stopped and embraced her properly so her form aligned with his and he could feel her totally, his hands smoothing over her curves. He had to part an inch so he could reach the buttons of her dress, but it was hell to relinquish the full connection.

"I favor these dresses you wear," he said while he worked the buttons. "So convenient. It is a wonder they are not more popular."

She reached down to release a few buttons herself. "Women who lack maids also favor the convenience. That is one reason ladies of the ton will not wear them. I must tell the shop to explain their usefulness to lovers, however. We may get dozens of commissions."

He made quick work with the dress and started on the short stays. Once he released her body, he ceased thinking about much at all.

Warmth. Velvety skin. He had to release her to shed his coats and pull off his boots. Then he fell on the bed with her, mad with hunger. He pulled down her chemise and lost himself in the erotic swells of her breasts, kissing and licking until her cries rang in his ears. He resented a delay while he finished undressing, hating any pause to the pleasure lest its perfection be ruined.

Finally he was atop her, his cock prodding her thigh, her head thrown back and her lips parted in her delirium. Gritting his teeth for control, he aroused her breasts until her delight pealed over and around them. He rose enough to put his hand to her mound and her cries turned anguished with need.

He wanted her badly. Ferociously. More intensely than he could remember ever wanting a woman. Each of her cries cut one more thread of his control. Eventually her abandon pushed him beyond the point of any sense at all.

He entered her harder than he intended. Harder than he should have, his mind acknowledged at once. Driving pleasure immediately buried that instant of rationality. His passion built furiously. Her cries continued, now affirming and begging while she opened to his thrusts.

It seemed forever that he took her, but also not long enough. Completion promised ecstasy, but he wanted his possession of her to be total and eternal. Finally he succumbed. His release crashed through him. It broke apart his mind and saturated his body in profound sensation.

No sooner had the blast of pleasure exploded, however, than enough self-awareness returned for him to remember the beginning rather the end.

The soft body he held in his arms belonged to Selina Duval, not Mrs. Fontaine, and up until a short while ago, she had been a virgin.

He rose up on his forearms and looked in her eyes. "You should have told me."

Selina knew what he meant. She doubted virginity could be hidden in such a situation, but she had hoped she might pull it off. "I said there had been no liaison with Giles. You just did not believe me."

"He told me there had been."

She could not imagine why Giles had lied about it. Perhaps he had told others that, too.

"I cannot blame you for believing him."

"However, I can blame him for lying. There was no need to. It was ignoble."

"Are you angry now? At me, I mean."

He kissed her. "Of course not. I am of two minds about it, though. I am relieved you were never his. But I am aware I wanted you to be experienced, because it would permit this. Then again, I am stupidly pleased to be the first."

"That is three minds, I think."

"So it is. Was there ever a Mr. Fontaine? Or did you have a white marriage?"

"He is a fiction. Being a widow explained much."

The look in his eyes said he had known that part. But Mr. Fontaine had also permitted this, hadn't he? She suspected that the mind behind that handsome face now reviewed the rules of chivalry, and how he had broken some.

"I am not a child," she said. "You asked me to be your lover, and I agreed. I think it was a splendid decision on my part." She adjusted her body enough to remind him they were still joined. "I do not regret it. Do you?"

"Me?" He laughed quietly, then withdrew and rolled to her side. "Ask me tomorrow, when I am not so damned pleased with myself." He kissed her shoulder. "Still—"

"Don't. Please, just do not. I had hoped you would not know. I do not want your guilt or apologies for something that gave me such joy."

"As you wish." A bit of the stern duke entered his tone. She suspected he really meant *it will be discussed another day.*

"I shall kill your brother if I ever see him again, for lying about me," she said after settling alongside him and resting her head on his chest.

"I will take care of him for you, in my way."

"I expect you can cut off his allowance or something."

"He does not need an allowance from me. He has his own income, in the thousands, from the portion left him by our mother. Unfortunately, he has a weakness besides lovely country girls about whom he lies to feed his own conceit. He gambles, and loses big, so he is often in serious debt."

"Is that why he is not in town now?"

"Now and in the past. I suppose I will pay off his creditors again. It is an old story between us."

She angled her head so she could see something of his face. "He is a trial for you, isn't he?"

He did not respond at once. "He is, but I think I envy him," he finally said. "Not for him were the chants about duty his whole life, or the close watch of a father on an heir. He grew up free in comparison to me. I was two people from the day I was born. Randall, and the Duke of Barrowmore. I accept the duties, and do not deny that I enjoy the power, but sacrificing the first in order to be the latter became natural and expected. Giles only had to be Giles, in all that was good and bad about that one person."

She gave him a little poke. "I forgot to ask which is my lover, Randall or the duke. How careless of me."

"They cannot be separated, Selina, even if I wished it."

She allowed herself to begin drifting to sleep. She knew all about the duke part, and what it would mean to her someday. She would make sure he never felt obliged to explain it.

CHAPTER TEN

Being a duke's lover proved more complicated than being a duke's mistress, Selina soon learned. She still went to the shop every day, where she worked hard. Only instead of walking home, she walked to an agreed-upon spot where a carriage waited to take her to him.

With the days lengthening, they twice joined at the end of the fashionable hour and rode in the park before going to Manard House. Another day the carriage made its way to the British Museum, kept open at the duke's request, just for him and his guest.

Once she did not need the carriage, because she brought Edeline four garments from her new wardrobe. Selina left the dresses in Edeline's apartment before descending the stairs to the library, where the duke awaited her.

Edeline's new coldness did not thaw with that visit. If anything, the young girl went out of her way to speak with disdain. Selina wondered if Edeline knew of the affair. They were not being secretive and most likely the word was out that Barrowmore had a new friend.

She doubted the news made more than a ripple in the gossip stream, however. She was not a notable friend, after all. Not an important lady or some old lord's wife. She was not even a celebrated courtesan. No one would remain interested in a duke's dalliance with a dressmaker.

Her own world learned the rumors. She could see it in their eyes. Curiosity sparked there, not scorn. He was a duke, after all. Thus did great power offer protection.

Selina counted the hours each day while she worked and sewed and fitted her ladies. She anticipated being back in his arms, and encompassed by the intimacy they shared. She relished their conversations before, and their jokes and easy talk after. She held her lover close to her body, and, she admitted, increasingly closer to her heart.

Ten days after that first night in Manard House, she received another one of Edeline's notes. *Bring the rose dinner dress,* it read. *I must have it by eight o'clock tonight.*

"She is too proud to be borne," Felicity said when Selina showed her the note. "I'll have a messenger bring the dress to her. We are too busy to have you at her beck and call."

"It is not finished. The hem still needs correction."

Felicity sighed. "This is not a ploy to excuse your going there, is it? I have heard the rumors about you and the duke. You do not need such intrigues for my sake."

"Nor do I, for my sake. She has done this on her own, not at anyone's bidding. I will take it late in the afternoon, and fit the hem, and have it sewn by eight o'clock."

Felicity flushed. "That is not fair to you. I apologize for what I said. Go this afternoon, and be done with it in good time."

Selina set off with the dress in a hackney at two o'clock. She hoped she would be finished by five. Barrowmore expected her to join him at the theater tonight, and she wanted to return home to dress and primp.

Edeline waited in her dressing room. No pillows lined the floor.

"I need to correct the hem," Selina explained.

"Then do so, and be quick about it."

Edeline put on the dress.

"It would help if you stood on that bench," Selina suggested.

"No. I might fall."

Selina doubted that. It was a very large, thick and sturdy bench. She went to her knees and bent low to work on the hem.

"You must stop taking advantage of us," Edeline said from on high.

Selina kept at her work.

"You must stop insinuating yourself into our lives. Barrowmore is too kind to say it, so it is left to me."

"The duke is able to speak for himself, Lady Giles. Perhaps you should let him."

"There is talk. About him and you. It is said—It is too embarrassing to have his name linked to yours. Surely you can see how bad that is. How comical, and demeaning for a man of his station."

"I think he cares less about it than you do. He does not strike me as a man who allows people to take advantage, or to insinuate themselves into his circles. Now, please turn."

"*You* will move, not *me*." Scornful and ugly, Edeline's sharp reply slapped down her presumptuous servant.

Selina scooted over on her knees so she could work on another part of the hem.

Thus it went for the next hour. Finally Edeline removed the dress and left the chamber. Selina sat near the window and sewed the hem.

Her chore completed, she rose to leave. No footman waited. She let herself out of the apartment and made her way down the main stairs, spitefully hoping Edeline saw her use of them. With each step, Edeline's own presumptions ate away at her composure.

No patron had ever spoken to her in that tone before. No one had ever demeaned her in such a direct way. The worst they saw at Madame Follette's were a few ladies who treated them like clever, talented pets. The intimacy of a dressmaker's shop created a feminine camaraderie among the women there, no matter what their roles. The womanliness of the activity, the disrobing and sartorial advice, the whispered gossip and confidences—all of that muted the differences in stations, at least somewhat.

Now Edeline had pushed Selina's nose into the ground, and all but stepped on her head. It was a wonder she had not required that her ring be kissed. If the goal had been to humble a certain dressmaker, the plan had succeeded far better than Selina would have thought possible.

Exhausted and sore, her inner strength crumbled. She was in tears by the time she rounded the final landing and began her way down to the reception hall. Through the wet blur blinding her, she saw a dark figure coming up toward her.

"Selina." The duke approached more quickly. "What is it?" He embraced her right there on the stairs. "Tell me, darling."

She shook her head, and tried to extricate herself from his arms. "It is nothing. I am fine."

He kept his arm around her and sped her up to the library. Once there he dabbed at her tears with his handkerchief. "What are you even doing here?" His tone changed with the last words, as if he knew the answer before the question was out. "Did she call for you?"

Selina took the handkerchief and nodded.

"I told her three days ago she was not to do that again. Ever."

She had never heard the duke angry before. Or seen him thus. He turned on his heel and headed toward the door.

She hurried after him and caught his arm. "Do not scold her. Please. She is young and confused and—"

"And unkind and thoughtless. I will not have her inflict her failings on you. If she reduced you of all women to tears, she must have been very cruel."

"I am fine now. See?" She forced a bright smile. "All happy again."

His anger left him. He pulled her into his arms. "Not so happy, I think. And probably tired, if she had you working for hours at her command. I will bring you home. We will attend the theater another night."

She nestled in his embrace and allowed herself to go limp against him. "Just being held by you makes me forget all of it. Your mere presence renews me. A kiss would make everything perfect."

He kissed her. In an instant she forgot about Edeline's insults and the hard floor beneath her knees. She forgot about everything, even who they were and where they embraced.

Within that sweet passion, she heard nothing except their shared breaths and her own sighs. Until, suddenly, a door closed hard, snapping her alert to their surroundings.

The next sound sent her reeling.

"I'll be damned," a male voice said. "Selina Duval. Hell, it took you long enough, Rand."

CHAPTER ELEVEN

Rand instinctively tucked Selina closer to his body. He turned his head toward the familiar voice.

"Giles. Your return is unexpected."

His brother grinned and walked forward. "I could not miss the entire Season. Besides, my bride needs me."

Selina gently removed herself from their embrace. She faced Giles with remarkable poise. Rand watched her expression assume the blandest of smiles. "It is good to see you again. I was about to depart. I will do so now, so this family reunion can continue."

Rand escorted her to the door. He told the footman to fetch a hackney at once for Mrs. Fontaine, and to ensure her safe return to her home.

"What did he mean when he said it had taken you long enough?" she asked before following the footman down.

Damnation. "I will explain that later. I will see you soon."

She looked at the door impassively, as if she saw through its panels. "It was as if I gazed upon a stranger. How odd."

Then she walked away.

Giles might indeed have been a stranger, from the way Selina had looked at him and spoken. Rand took satisfaction in that, but it did little to calm the rising rancor he felt for the man in question.

He returned to the library. Near the windows, Giles busied himself with the decanters.

"Have you surprised Edeline yet? She will be overjoyed," Rand said.

"I will go up soon. I thought to fortify myself with some brandy first." He turned with glass in hand, raising it.

Good old Giles. As always he wore a bright expression. Lights of humor sparkled in his green eyes. Rand noticed that the debt that had sent him into hiding had not prevented him from having his hair expertly cropped, or stopped him from buying what looked to be a new and expensive waistcoat.

Rand helped himself to brandy, too. "Where have you been?"

"Here and there. Living off my expectations."

Off more credit, he meant. A new town meant new merchants. Ignorant ones. The only people who could count on payment from Giles were the men he gambled with. Giles paid his gentlemen's debts first, and let the tailors and coachmen wait forever.

"It is good you are back. Your wife grows weary of my supervision, and I find the role increasingly tedious." He drank some of the brandy. "You might have asked me to do it. Not just assumed."

"It is hard to disappear if you announce you are leaving." Giles threw back his drink and set the glass down. "Selina is looking lovely. Luscious. Maturity favors her." His smile welcomed confidences of the sort Giles himself never hesitated sharing. The sort that involved lies about some women, it turned out. Ruinous lies. Unnecessary ones.

Rand put his glass down, too. "Yes. Well, about that—" He swung his fist, and landed it hard on Giles's grinning face.

CHAPTER TWELVE

Selina had hoped never to see Giles again. She had even promised Barrowmore to avoid him. She hated that she had come face-to-face with him yesterday, unexpectedly. Even worse to have been in a chamber with both brothers at the same time.

Barrowmore had said he would see her soon. Not too soon, she hoped. She wanted some time to sort through her feelings, which had turned chaotic. She had embarked on an affair with him confident in her choices. Now, suddenly, she felt no confidence at all.

At the shop, she listened to Felicity's explanation of the patrons they expected this day. She took unusual satisfaction in using her skills as the hours unfolded. Focusing on stitches and fabrics and trims kept her mind off the unease that had settled in her since leaving Manard House yesterday.

While she walked home that evening, bootsteps fell into place beside her. She did not have to look to know who it was. He had not really become a total stranger.

"Please, go away."

"Is that any way to greet an old beau?"

She marched on. "How did you find me?"

"Edeline. It took me hours to realize all her chattering about her new dressmaker referred to *you*." He tipped his head toward her. "You turned out lovely, Selina. The girl was pretty. The woman is impressive."

"You have a most beautiful wife. You should be with her today, not out on the town."

"She is beautiful, true. In a rather ordinary way. I had forgotten while I was gone how much she bores me, however. You were a much better conversationalist."

Selina stopped walking and faced him. She noted an ugly discoloration on his cheek, all blue and pink. "What do you want? Not to reminisce about a very sorry episode in my past life, I think."

Giles flashed his most charming smile. "I want your help. My brother is showing some temper." He instinctively touched that bruise on his face. "I need him to be friendlier to me. You can work your wiles and bring him around, I am sure. There are things he and I need to talk about."

"Financial things? I would be a fool to interfere. Nor would it do any good." She walked on.

Again those boots fell in alongside her steps. "You would be amazed how much good it would do. And the way I see it, you owe it to me. You only met him because of me, after all. I stood aside for him, so he could have you."

She halted midstep and pivoted to him. *"Excuse me?"*

Giles feigned chagrin. "Didn't he tell you? I was in dun territory that summer, and he came to scold the way he always does, and I could tell he wanted you. So when he demanded I give up something I treasured in return for his help, well—" He shrugged. "It broke my heart, of course, but you landed well. Look at you. Play your hand right, and you will live in luxury forever."

She could not move. She could barely breathe. *Hell, it took you long enough, Rand.*

Her voice came out strangled with emotion. "Go away, please. Do not walk beside me. Do not speak to me. Not now. Not ever." She strode on blindly, praying that Giles did not follow her again.

She was almost home when she came to her senses enough to know she did not want to go there. Barrowmore might visit. He might even be waiting for her. She could not bear to see him. His explanation would only give her more pain. Worse, her heart would want to believe anything he said, if it meant this horrible ache went away.

She turned at a crossroad and made her way back to the shop. She slipped in before Felicity locked the door, and took refuge in the workroom upstairs. She bent her head over one of Edeline's dresses, sewing its final embellishments with tiny, perfect stitches.

All the while her mind skipped through memories, of things said and assumed, of intimacies shared. She had been a fool to believe she could have a love affair with the duke, or any man, and not eventually know disappointment and heartache. She was not the kind of woman who knew how to hold back part of her heart. She admitted her emotions had become much more entangled than was wise.

She gazed at the bright flame of the candle by which she worked. In a few hours the wick would be spent and the light would go out. She wished love could end so neatly. The flame inside her would never go out while she remained here. It would probably grow until it consumed her, and make her a ridiculous figure—a woman in love with a man who had bought her from his own brother.

Hours later, halfway through the night, she finished the dress. While she wrapped it, soft footsteps outside the chamber alerted her that she had company. Felicity appeared, candle in one hand and a poker in the other, in an undressing gown and shawl, with a big cap covering her crown.

"I thought I heard something down here. I feared a housebreaker. I did not expect to find you, Selina." She set the poker against the wall. "It is three o'clock. What in the world are you doing here?"

"I wanted to finish this dress. I knew I would not sleep, so I might as well work."

Felicity examined her with curiosity. "I think you have been crying."

"I do not think so. Perhaps."

"You do not remember?"

"My thoughts were on other things. I—I think that I need to leave London for a while. I am wracked with guilt, because I know how the shop can ill afford to lose one of us now, but—" She bit her lip, and turned her attention to fussing with the dress's wrapping.

Felicity sat in a chair and beckoned Selina to sit as well. "All is not well between you and the duke, I gather."

Selina shook her head. "I have been worse than a schoolgirl, in the lies I told myself. I called it a love affair. Not for me the expensive gifts and support that made a woman a whore. Only . . ." She swallowed hard, then forced herself to go on. "I learned today that at its core, this has been a most commercial liaison."

"If you are shocked and aggrieved to learn this, perhaps you are also wrong. Wouldn't your heart know the truth?"

"Right now my heart knows nothing with security. Nor will it if I see him. My heart, you see, has been lost, and wants to believe anything that allows it to continue loving a man I never should have encouraged." Her throat burned worse with each word. Tears stung her eyes. Felicity reached to embrace her, and she broke down and cried on Felicity's shoulder.

The release brought some calm. Felicity patted her back the way a mother might. "If you must leave, then do so. We will manage. Please say you'll return, however. Our little family here will be the poorer without you."

"I promise I will return. In a month at the outside. I should know my own mind by then, I hope. Nor would I ever leave you short of help when the coronation draws near. I know how important it is. I would not leave at all if I believed I would have the strength to see him. Please believe that."

"I know you would not. Now, come above and sleep. I won't have you on the streets at this hour. In the morning you can make your plans."

Four days after his brother's return, Rand mounted the steps of Manard House, aiming for his brother's chambers. At his command, word had come down as soon as Giles was dressed.

He found Giles in his dressing room. It was much like Edeline's. The two of them had taken ownership of a vast apartment up here. Giles sprawled on a divan, reading his mail. He lay comfortably on the cushions, with his boots propped on a stack of silk pillows. They were much like the ones in Edeline's chambers. The ones too good for Mrs. Fontaine to use.

"Rand. You are up and about early."

"I wanted to be sure to see you this morning."

Giles grinned up at him. "Well, here I am. Have you rethought that idea I proposed yesterday?"

The idea had been for Rand to purchase a property that was part of Giles's inheritance from their mother. Giles must be very desperate if he was willing to trade regular income for one, quick influx of money.

"I have not. You will regret that as soon as it is done, and blame me forever. I have come to speak with you about Selina."

"Ah. How is that going?"

Rand wanted to thrash him then and there. "She has thrown me over, I think."

"You think? Rude of her not to tell a duke when she tires of him."

"She has not been at her home, nor at her place of employment, so I have not seen her. She seems to have disappeared. Do you know to where?"

Giles swung his boots off the divan and sat. He made much of pondering the problem. "I cannot even imagine where."

"Do you know why?"

His tone must have communicated how his anger strained against its leash, because Giles looked very serious all of a sudden.

"None at all," Giles muttered.

"Have you seen her since the day you walked into the library and found her in my arms? Think carefully before you answer, Giles. Should I ever learn that you lied to me today, I will leave you to the bailiffs for good."

Giles sighed and frowned. He stood and paced. Finally he turned. "I did see her, the next day. I just stumbled upon her walking on the street and—"

"One more lie and you are dead to me."

Giles gritted his teeth. "I learned she now worked at that shop, and I arranged to stumble upon her. Are you happy now?"

"For what purpose?"

Giles peered at him, confused. Then his expression cleared. "Oh. *Ohhh.* No, no. It was not what you think. I did not—I would not be so stupid as to try and revive my friendship with her, what with you and she— It was not that. I swear it."

The relief that broke was so profound it stunned him. "Then what was it instead?"

"I, uh—I wanted her to intercede with you on my behalf. You were very angry that day, and have been cold and distant since, so I have hesitated even talking to you about my situation."

"She refused you?"

"She did." A nasty glint entered Giles's eyes. "Damned high-handed she was. Dismissive. As if she were lady of the manor and not only some little—" He caught himself. "She would have never dared aim so high if not for me. She should be grateful, but instead—"

Rand found himself beyond anger. He could imagine that conversation Giles had with Selina on the street. He knew what Giles had said, to explain just how grateful she should be.

"You are my brother, Giles. I love you as such. I will be settling your last round of debts, but that is all. After this you are on your own. Have no doubt in your head that I am serious. Also, it is time to establish your own household. Your wife will appreciate that, and I require it."

Giles's expression fell. "You cannot be serious. You know I don't have enough for that."

"If you do not squander your income, you have more than enough. Many peers have smaller incomes. If you are unwilling to change, then join your wife's parents in their home. There should be a few rooms for you there. Shall we say you will be gone in a fortnight?"

Giles sank back onto the divan. "Her family? Her mother—her father— Rand, you are condemning me to hell."

"Hardly hell, Giles. Purgatory, perhaps."

He left the dressing room, and put Giles out of his mind at once. Selina had left town. Of course she had. He could think of only one place where she might have gone.

CHAPTER THIRTEEN

She could see her family home from up here, in the distance outside the village proper that stretched out at the bottom of her hill. She enjoyed standing at this window, looking down at the village's main lane. The people appeared like tiny dolls, and the buildings like miniature abodes and shops.

Her parents knew she was here, but no one else down there did. The few servants who served as caretakers of the estate had been informed of the change in ownership before she even arrived. They were already paid through the middle of the year and sworn to secrecy about the new owner.

She would have to decide soon what to do with the property. It was not intended as compensation, he had said. Nor a bribe, since he hardly needed one. Justice, he had called it. She still did not know if she accepted that explanation, after what Giles had told her. She still considered having her father find a solicitor who would sign the house and land back to Barrowmore, just as he had signed it over to her.

All of that could be discussed on Thursday, when her parents came here for dinner. Many, many things would be decided at that meal. For now, however, she gave herself permission to put it off.

She turned away from the window and took a seat on the bench that hugged a stone wall in the bedchamber she used. The entire building still showed elements of the old medieval structure at its core, even if later additions and changes made living here less Spartan. The stone walls, the beams in some chambers, the narrow windows—all spoke to the time long ago when this had been the manor house of some feudal lord whose fief included the surrounding miles.

She closed her eyes, and pressed her back to the cool stones. She had spent a lot of time on this bench the last four days. Sitting quietly, and thinking, and examining her heart. The peace of the country and the silence of the stones soothed her.

Sounds distracted her this time, however. Distant ones. Somewhere a little chaos had begun, and with each instant it grew louder. Finally she could not ignore it. She got to her feet and returned to the window.

The noise came from below, in the village. It rolled toward her, a dull buzzing on the breeze. Tiny people emerged from their miniature homes and shops to form groups. Others leaned out the windows.

The reason came into view. A grand coach rolled slowly down the lane. A magnificent one, with brass and gilt that caught the sunlight and created blinding reflections. More gilt picked out the relief of an escutcheon on the door. Four footmen rode outside, all in livery complete with wigs, pumps, and braided tricornered hats. Four immense black horses pulled the equipage.

The coachman moved very slowly, no doubt wanting to be sure those horses hurt no one. Finally he reached the end of the lane, and turned onto the drive that rose up the hill to the big house. She squinted to look in the coach's window, but all she could see was a handsome male hand resting on the sill.

It was enough to set her heart flipping like a schoolgirl's.

The door to her chamber opened. The housekeeper who tended the house with her husband burst in. "A boy just ran up from the village. His Grace's coach was seen. The duke is coming! We are not prepared for him. We are not ready." Hands flying in frantic gestures, she ran out.

Selina bent to her looking glass and tried to pinch some color into her cheeks. *I am not ready for this either. Not at all.*

"**T**hank you for receiving me," Rand said.

"You knew I would. Doesn't everyone?"

Selina sat in a chair, farther away from his than he would like. She had donned her poise like a heavy cloak. He might be paying a morning call on a chance acquaintance, not visiting his lover.

That probably was because, to her mind, she no longer *was* his lover.

He had tried to accept that. For a hellish two days he had taken refuge in anger, indignation, then guilt and regrets. Finally, unable to conquer his sense of loss, he had called for the coach.

"Do you like the house?"

"Very much." She looked around. "Although the word house sounds too diminutive for an abode of such size and history. I already knew this chamber of course, and the drawing room and dining room. I have enjoyed discovering all the rest."

"So you could come back, after all."

She speared him with a sharp glance. "I came here quietly, not down the main lane as you did. No one knows I am here except my parents and the servants, all of whom are being discreet. I came to this house instead of my parents' to spare them a revival of all that talk, although now of course the talk is well founded, isn't it?"

"It appears you regret that. If so, I am sorry I lured you into my arms."

Her tight expression broke. So did her rigid posture. "Do not be sorry. You did very little luring. I am not sitting in this house constructing lies about any of it."

"Then I should not either. Giles told you things, I think. Things that hurt you."

She began to respond, but closed her lips. She nodded.

"He did not lie. I wish I could say he did, Selina. But he did not. When I came here that summer, I found him living here like a lord, with a beautiful young woman on his arm. I confess that I assumed the worst of Giles where you were concerned. He let me. He encouraged it. Perhaps if he had not I would have been more circumspect in how I reacted when he introduced you. I would not have been so obviously entranced."

"I only saw an aloof man looking at me briefly with disdain and annoyance."

"Giles saw much more."

"So he sold me to you." Petulance entered her gaze. "Did you require that? If so, you did wait a very long time, as he said."

"I only required he give up something that mattered to him. I never—and I swear this is the truth, I swear it as a gentleman—said he had to give you up, or that he had to give *me* whatever he chose to relinquish. That, I am sorry to say, was all Giles's idea. He probably thought it gave him some advantage to cast it that way."

It was damnable to sit here, twenty feet away, while he explained this. He got up and went over to her, and knelt on one knee beside her chair so he could look her directly in the eyes if she allowed it. "If you want to blame me for letting his notion of a bargain stand, do so. I never expected to see you again. I had no intention of taking his place, so whatever clever trade he thought he concocted did not matter."

She had been staring at her hands on her lap, but now she did look right into his eyes. "And yet, eventually, you did take his place. You more than took his place."

He covered her hands with his. "That was a thing apart. A different time. The result of a happy accident."

"Not totally a thing apart, I think."

No, not totally. But in all the ways that mattered.

She looked at their hands, bound together. She managed to give his a little squeeze. "You came a long way to explain all of this."

"It was important that you know the truth. All of it. And important that you also know this truth: I do not want to lose you. I have been miserable these last days. Worthless, and dangerously out of sorts. You broke my heart when you left town without so much as a note to me. I thought . . ." He kissed her hands. "I thought we had truly become lovers, Selina. That we shared more than desire and a passing infatuation. If I was wrong, say so, and I will not try to win you back."

She removed one of her hands and placed it on his face. She gazed at him with an expression he would remember forever.

"You were not wrong. Not at all. If you had been wrong, I would never have had to leave. I would have thrown you over properly, the way those sophisticated ladies do." She leaned forward and kissed him. "I made the worst mistake, you see. I fell in love with my lover. How could I hope to recover from that if I stayed in the same city as he?"

He stood and pulled her up into his arms. "I hope you never recover from it. I never shall, I know. I want us together, Selina. I want you by my side and in my home and bound to me forever. Will you marry me so we have each other in a right and proper way?"

"Marry?" She looked confused. "Surely you must do better on that duty."

"I am a duke, darling. Not a prince. I get to marry whomever I want."

"And you want me? Are you very sure? My only fortune of note is this house now. I have been laboring as a seamstress and am known as one. I am not at all suitable."

"You are supposed to say yes, not try to talk me out of it."

She laughed. "I suppose so."

"I am very sure, Selina. This is no whim, or hurt pride talking. Nor is it my conscience forcing me to do the right thing by you. I truly want you as my duchess. I will forever be grateful if you agree."

She stretched up to kiss him. "Then I will say yes, although I fear you have gone a little mad."

"Totally mad."

They kissed long and hard while the spring breeze spun sweet scents around them. "We will do it soon," he said. "I will get a special license and we will—"

"No. Not soon." She pressed against his chest, as if to physically stop his thoughts. "I must help Felicity until the coronation. I owe it to her, and I promised. Let us keep our engagement a secret, too, so people do not gossip for months about how you proposed to a shop girl."

He did not want to keep it a secret. He wanted to tell everyone he knew. "You feel obligated to do this? To remain in that shop?"

"Only until summer. Can you stand being discreet that long?"

"If it is important to you, I can stand anything. So we tell no one that we are engaged?"

"Perhaps we should tell my parents, so my father does not call you out once he realizes that you have been having your way with me."

"It may keep your mother from crowning me with an iron pan, too."

"You are safe from her no matter what we tell them. On learning this house was now mine, she pointedly did not ask how I came by it. Mothers are practical that way if the seducer is a duke."

He took her face in his hands and kissed her like the precious, lovely woman she was. "I hope that discretion and secrecy does not require abstinence. If you prefer that, of course I will—"

She turned her head and kissed his palm. "Do not speak such impossible nonsense, Rand. In fact, do not speak at all for a long while."

He lifted her in his arms and turned to the bed. "I promise to put my mouth to better purpose, but only after I say this. I am in love with you, Selina. Hopelessly, wonderfully in love, and I won't let anything keep us apart." He kissed her. "Not here or anywhere. Not now, or at any time. We will be lovers forever."

"Lovers forever," she murmured with a smile. "Yes, before we are duke and duchess or husband and wife, let us remember we are lovers, Rand. Let us vow we will never let that change."

"I swear it, darling."

She urged his head down and gave him a sweet, emotional kiss full of their promise of love forever after.

ABOUT THE AUTHOR

Madeline Hunter is a two-time RITA award winner and seven-time finalist, and has twenty-six nationally bestselling historical romances in print. A member of RWA's Honor Roll, her books have been on the bestseller lists of the *New York Times*, *USA Today*, and *Publisher's Weekly*. More than six million copies of her books are in print and her novels have been translated into thirteen languages. She has a PhD in art history, which she teaches at the university level. You can contact Madeline through her website or her Facebook page: MadelineHunter.com and facebook.com/MadelineHunter.

~ALSO BY MADELINE HUNTER~

THE WICKED DUKE
TALL, DARK, AND WICKED
HIS WICKED REPUTATION
THE ACCIDENTAL DUCHESS
THE COUNTERFEIT MISTRESS
THE CONQUEST OF LADY CASSANDRA
THE SURRENDER OF MISS FAIRBOURNE
DANGEROUS IN DIAMONDS
SINFUL IN SATIN
PROVOCATIVE IN PEARLS
RAVISHING IN RED
THE SINS OF LORD EASTERBOOK
SECRETS OF SURRENDER
LESSONS OF DESIRES
THE RULES OF SEDUCTION
LADY OF SIN
LORD OF SIN
THE ROMANTIC
THE SINNER
THE CHARMER
THE SAINT

The Colors of Love

Myretta
ROBENS

CHAPTER ONE

"**I**'m leaving now," Delyth said to the nearly empty shop. Only Selina, the other dressmaker, and Alice, an apprentice seamstress, remained in the workroom. "I'll just be taking this with me," she added in a lower tone. As no one was paying any attention anyway, Delyth slid the copy of the *Town Gazette* into her bag and left the shop, stopping only to wish Selina a good night.

She knew she should have left the *Gazette* for Felicity, who probably hadn't had a chance to read it, but she wanted to show it to Anthea and she was also unsure of whether she really did want Felicity to see it. Delyth was beyond excited to be mentioned in such a prestigious column as "Aglaea's Cabinet," but she was not so foolish as to ignore the fact that the description was not wholly laudatory.

The distinction niggled. She adored design. She'd been highly successful in the theater, but she'd come to London (against her father's wishes, she must admit) to make elegant dresses for the elite. Nothing pleased her so much as handling sumptuous fabrics, draping flattering silhouettes, setting perfect stitches. Except maybe color. She feared that, perhaps, the theater had exacerbated that particular obsession. And in the back of her mind lurked the question, "What would Felicity think about the column?" Since taking over her mother's shop, Felicity Dawkins had been working diligently to increase its consequence, not to mention its income. Lately she had seemed even more desperate to restore the shop to its former glory and make it immediately successful. It worried Delyth.

The thought of returning to her lodgings and discussing her concerns with the good friend with whom she shared the flat cheered Delyth immensely. She was probably at the theater right now, but when she returned, Anthea would definitely have an opinion. She always did.

Delyth may have left the theater for the more genteel world of dressmaking, but her heart remained with the friends she had left behind, and her home was still with Anthea Drinkwater, her closest friend in London and the driving force behind the Thalia Theatre.

Night had fallen by the time Delyth reached her lodgings. She found Anthea sitting at her writing table before the window.

"Are you well?" she asked before she had even shed her shawl and bonnet.

"Quite." Anthea looked up from the pages she was reading. "Why do you ask?"

"You're home," Delyth pointed out as she placed her bonnet on the hook by the door and dropped the *Gazette* next to Anthea's pile of papers.

"I had noticed that," Anthea said. "It's Tuesday, you know, and I thought I'd rather work at home. Do you mind?"

"Not in the slightest." Delyth dropped a kiss on the top of Anthea's head and passed her the *Gazette*. "My gown is mentioned in 'Aglaea's Cabinet' and I couldn't wait to show it to you."

"You stole the *Gazette* from your employer?" Anthea opened the paper and went searching for the fashion column.

"I borrowed it from my employer," Delyth said, grabbing the paper back from her friend and folding it to the appropriate page before returning it to her.

"There." She pointed.

Almack's glittered in its inimitable dingy way on Wednesday last. At least, let me say that the attendees glittered, although some were more glittery than others. Although we had sufficient representation of the handsome young ladies in their first Season, clad almost exclusively in white (with the occasional interruption of pastels bordering on white), attention must be given to Lady M, whom one might be forgiven for supposing had somehow missed the entrance to Astley's and ended up at Almack's. Lady M not only glittered, she shone, she flashed, she radiated. One might say she flared. If you ventured close enough to Lady M to see beyond the dazzling array of colors with which she was adorned, you might notice that, eye-searing choices aside, the gown itself was of elegant and impeccable construction. One might hope that the creator of this extravaganza will be more judicious in the fabric choices for her next effort.

—Aglaea's Cabinet

As Anthea read, Delyth hovered over her shoulder reading along with her. Without removing her eyes from the paper, Anthea waved her hand. "Stop that." But Delyth was too excited. She backed off a bit and danced on her toes as she waited for her friend to finish.

When Anthea was done reading, she folded the paper and handed it back to Delyth. "Bringing this home was a wise decision."

"Should I show this to Felicity or will she think it's a bad thing?"

Anthea shook her head. "Are you demented?"

Delyth grinned. "Might be," she said. "Why do you ask?"

"You cannot show this to Miss Dawkins. If she hasn't seen it on her own, you might get to keep your position at Madame Follette's."

Delyth cocked an eyebrow at her friend. "Nonsense. Look at this." She opened the paper and waved it in front of her friend's face. "She says the gown was of 'elegant and impeccable construction' and the colors were 'dazzling.'"

Anthea looked as though she was trying not to roll her eyes. "Not," she said, "in a good way." She hesitated a moment and then gave her friend a puzzled look. "What, precisely did this dress look like?"

Delyth grinned again. "It was elegant and of impeccable construction and the colors were dazzling."

"Let's talk about the colors," Anthea said, "as they seem to be the real issue here. What colors did you use?"

"Oh, they were wonderful: a deep crimson with a violet over-skirt, yellow piping, and just a hint of the palest green lace."

Anthea closed her eyes. "Truly? You had a customer who wore that?"

"Of course. Lady Marjoribanks loved it. In fact, she chose most of the fabric." Delyth frowned. "You're really upset about this, aren't you?"

"And so should you be," Anthea said. "The colors . . ." Her voice trailed off.

"The colors would look wonderful from the back of the house," Delyth said.

"Quite likely, but your customer was not on stage. She was in an assembly room."

"Whatever you may say," Delyth said, still unable to suppress her smile, "my gown was mentioned in 'Aglaea's Cabinet.'"

Anthea gave a long-suffering sigh. "But not in a good way."

Anthea went back to work and Delyth returned to dithering. Although she tried to convince herself that she didn't care what Felicity thought of the article, she really did. Leaving Whitchurch against her father's wishes had made it imperative that she earn her own living, which she had done quite handsomely, thanks to Anthea and the Thalia, thank you very much. But she knew that costume design was not quite as respectable as where she was now and she could not—would not—return to her father as less than a success in proper society. If she returned at all, that is. Displeasing Felicity might assure that she never had another opportunity to step out of the back room. But she did love color so and Lady Marjoribanks was quite happy with her gown.

Not for the first time, Delyth wondered if Felicity Dawkins regretted her decision to bring an untried costume designer out of the theater and into her establishment. Granted, Felicity had praised her ability with a needle and seemed to enjoy her unorthodox use of color. Not that Felicity wasn't a perfectly lovely person and really quite delightful to work for. It's just that Felicity currently seemed so distracted. Felicity had approved Lady Marjoribanks's gown before it left the shop, but what if she hadn't really paid attention to it? What if she were surprised and upset by the bad notice? Delyth had loved that gown to distraction (and so had Lady M). She could barely conceive that it might be the agent of her downfall.

"This seems unnecessarily rude."

Simon, who was busy at his desk in the library of the house he shared with his sister, looked up. "What's that, dearest?"

"This." Louisa Merrithew waved her copy of Friday's *Town Gazette.* "The paragraph about Lady M."

"That wasn't rude," Simon said. "You were there. She did look like an escapee from Astley's."

Louisa winced. "She looked a bit . . . flamboyant. But if you looked closely—looked past the colors—the gown was an elegant and original design, as you may have said. Whoever made it is new in town and quite promising."

"Promising what?" Simon put down his pen. "The only thing that dress promised was a headache. I cannot credit that a reputable dressmaker would have let her go out in public dressed like that. What was she thinking?"

"She has a wonderful hand with draping and construction," Louisa said. "You have to find her and help her."

Simon pushed away from the desk and moved to sit opposite his sister. "I should find her and denounce her. That travesty was not an accident. I should find her and run her out of London. Surely you are jesting."

"Surely I am not," Louisa said. "I think we should call on Lady Marjoribanks."

Simon stood and stirred the fire. "We don't know her very well," he said, turning to face his sister.

"She was a friend of Mama's. She would appreciate our calling and we could perhaps give her a little push while we are there." Louisa hesitated and then added, "By 'we' I, of course, mean you." She fluttered her lashes and grinned at her brother.

"Louisa . . ." Simon's voice held a warning.

"Good," Louisa said, getting up and going to the desk. "I'll send her a note right away."

As it turned out, Lady Marjoribanks was, indeed, happy to see the late Viscountess Fulbeck's children and even happier to discuss clothing, one of her most passionate interests. Simon thought that obsession would be a bit more acceptable if the woman could tell one color from another. She obviously couldn't. The one subdued element in the room turned out to be Lady M's gray cat masquerading as a cushion.

After Simon apologized for sitting on the ill-tempered beast, he devoted himself to an inventory of the rest of the room. He squinted slightly as he took it all in, barely lending an ear as Lady M and Louisa chatted merrily about who was wearing what and which mantua-maker was coming into fashion. Normally, he would have been more than interested in such a discussion. Everything was fodder for "Aglaea's Cabinet." But examining the vibrant pink figured draperies against the shocking green damask on the wall made him think that anything Lady Marjoribanks had to say about fashion must be taken with a rather large grain of salt.

It was obvious to Simon that Lady M's most recent dressmaker had taken advantage of the fact that the peeress could not distinguish colors and had made the lady a laughingstock. He could only assume that this had been done with malice and he was currently finding it hard to forgive whoever that person was.

"Don't you agree, Simon?"

Simon looked up from his reverie, blinking against the sunlight glinting off the competing colors in the room.

Louisa, as usual, recognized his predicament. "Don't you agree that we should try her new dressmaker? She said she'd be happy to give us her direction."

Well then, that's taken care of, Simon thought. *Thank goodness for Louisa.* He turned to their hostess. "I would love to meet this person. And I'm sure Louisa would not mind if I added to her wardrobe."

Delyth returned to Vine Street the next morning with the *Gazette* tucked under her arm. Regardless of Anthea's pessimistic view of Felicity's potential response to "Aglaea's Cabinet," Delyth didn't feel that it was quite right to hide it from her. Especially since this copy was actually Felicity's. She stuck her head in the workroom and said good morning to Selina, but saw no sign of Felicity. Leaving her shawl at her worktable and taking the *Gazette* with her, Delyth went back through the front of the shop and knocked on the door to the small office where Felicity and her brother conducted the business.

"Come in." Well, that wasn't Felicity's voice, but Delyth cracked open the door and peered in.

"Excuse me, Mr. Dawkins. I'm looking for your sister."

Henry Dawkins looked up from the ledger he was working on and removed his glasses. "Not here," he said, placing the glasses on the desk. "She should be back after noon. May I help you, Miss Owen?"

Delyth stepped just inside the office door and hesitated. Should she speak to Mr. Dawkins? He was a huge and frightening-looking presence in the shop, but he always seemed kind when he spoke to any of his sister's workers. Yes, she decided, why not?

"Well . . ." she began, taking the *Gazette* from behind her back and holding it in both hands. "It's just that, well, the *Town Gazette*— that is, Miss Felicity's *Town Gazette* arrived in the shop yesterday."

Henry Dawkins put his glasses back on and peered at Delyth as if trying to read her mind. "And?" he prompted.

"And . . . well . . . I borrowed it and took it home before she saw it."

"Ah." He nodded. "That's not a problem. I see you've brought it back."

Delyth fidgeted with the paper, folding it into squares of diminishing size. "That's not the problem," she said and began unfolding the paper. When it was once again its normal size, she handed it to Mr. Dawkins and pointed to "Aglaea's Cabinet." "Here," she said. "See what it says."

Henry Dawkins removed his glasses again, polished them, and put them back on before taking up the paper.

"Hmmm. I see where you might be uneasy, Miss Owen." He put the paper to one side and looked up at Delyth.

She repressed an urge to take several steps back. "What should I do? I love my job here. I don't want Miss Felicity to send me away. I love designing clothes. I can't help it if I love color. Lady Marjoribanks adored her dress. How can that be a bad thing? I don't want to go back to the theater."

"Miss Owen!" Mr. Dawkins said. "Take a breath."

"Oh." Realizing that she had been on verge of having a fit of hysterics in front of this man she didn't know very well, Delyth deflated. "Oh, forgive me," she said. "It's only that . . ."

"Yes, I know," he said. "It's only that you don't want to lose your job."

"Yes," Delyth said. "That."

"Miss Owen, you must calm yourself. This is one opinion of one gown by one person. My sister is not so unreasonable as to fire a talented employee over something so singular."

"But Aglaea, whoever she is, is very influential."

"Possibly so," Dawkins said, pulling his ledger closer to him. "But you must trust Felicity to do the right thing."

"Thank you, sir." Delyth bobbed a curtsy and backed out of the office, wondering what right thing Felicity would do. It was too late now. Mr. Dawkins had the paper and all Delyth could do was go back to work and hope for the best.

CHAPTER TWO

Delyth threw herself into her work. Bent over her stitching, she still managed to expend a great deal of energy trying to convince herself that Felicity would not sack her for Lady M's gown and the awful mention in the *Town Gazette*. In fact, she was still trying to understand why Aglaea, whoever she might be, didn't like the gown. It was colorful and gorgeous. The color, she realized, was the problem. But Lady Marjoribanks had not demurred and Felicity let it leave the shop. She had seen it, hadn't she? Of course, she must have. She saw everything.

Felicity was absent from the shop today, as she had been since the *Gazette* came out. The shop owner had seemed distracted the last time she was in Vine Street and Delyth could only hope that she wasn't the cause. She shook her head and pushed a stray strand of hair out of her eyes. She hadn't been this nervous since she boarded the coach for London without her father's permission or, for that matter, knowledge. She hoped whatever happened didn't lead to a return trip.

One of Felicity's apprentices stuck her head into the workroom. "Miss," she said so softly that she had to clear her throat and say it again before Delyth looked up.

Delyth looked around. She was the only person in the room at the moment, so she must be the person Sally was talking to. "Yes?"

"Um, there's some people to see Miss Felicity, and no one's here right now."

"Not even Mr. Dawkins?" she asked.

"No, Miss. No one."

115

Deciding not to take umbrage over being designated no one for the second time, Delyth nodded. "Would you like me to talk to them?"

"Oh yes, please, Miss. If you wouldn't mind."

"Not at all." Delyth put her sewing aside and, smoothing her hair off her face, made for the front of the shop.

Standing by the window, examining a display gown were two of the most extraordinarily beautiful people she had ever seen. The young woman had unfashionably auburn hair, but that did not detract from her handsomeness. To Delyth, she was elegance and grace personified, her face was a classic oval and her brilliant green eyes were set in skin of purest cream. She could not have been more lovely. And she could not have been dressed more fashionably. What was she doing in Vine Street when she so obviously patronized Bond Street with the rest of the ton?

But, for all that, Delyth's gaze kept returning to the gentleman beside her. He was, perhaps, not as classically handsome as the lady, but—*oh my*—he took her breath away. Tall, lean, dark blond hair, eyes like tempered steel. He wore a solemn expression on a face that looked like it habitually smiled. The fact that he was looking particularly displeased at the moment did nothing to dim his attraction in Delyth's eyes. She had a sudden urge to do whatever it took to make him happy. Several ideas about how to do that very thing sprang, unbidden, to her mind and she blushed.

This was the first time she had greeted customers (if that's what they were) without someone else from the shop at her side and she was a bit hesitant.

She straightened her shoulders, stepped forward, and curtsied. "May I be of assistance?"

Both turned toward her. The young lady smiled, but the gentleman maintained his severe expression. That couldn't be good. Delyth concentrated on the woman.

"How may I help you, my lady?"

"It's 'Miss,'" the lady said. "Miss Merrithew."

"Miss Merrithew." Delyth dropped another curtsy.

"We're here to see Madame Follette," the gentleman said, moving a half step in front of Miss Merrithew.

"Sir?" Delyth wondered why he wouldn't let that perfectly nice lady speak for herself.

"This is my brother," Miss Merrithew said. "Simon Merrithew."

Delyth curtsied again, aware that she probably looked like a robin, bobbing up and down in front of these people. These gentlepeople, she corrected herself.

"You must mean Miss Dawkins. Miss Felicity Dawkins. She is not in today, but perhaps I may help?"

"My sister needs a new gown." Mr. Merrithew gave Delyth a piercing look. "Lady Marjoribanks spoke very highly of a Miss Owen who made a gown for her."

Delyth blinked in surprise and felt her face heat. "Did she?" she asked. "That was very kind of her. I'm Delyth Owen."

"Hmmm," Mr. Merrithew looked less pleased than Lady M purported to be.

"What sort of gown does Miss Merrithew require?" Delyth tried not to shiver. She didn't think that someone who had had the audacity to take a coach from Pembrokeshire to London and then go to work in a theater should be quite this nervous meeting two people of fashion. She stilled hands that had been twisting the fabric of her skirt into a mass of wrinkles and waited for an answer, which seemed to take an excessive amount of time in coming.

Miss Merrithew glanced at her brother, who had obviously taken over this negotiation. "Let's start with something for assemblies," he said. "And if that is satisfactory, we will want a gown for the coronation."

Delyth gasped. "The coronation?" She was afraid that her voice came out as a squeak.

"Just so," Mr. Merrithew said, looking quite pleased with himself.

Delyth's heart began to pound. If she could procure a commission for a coronation gown, Felicity would never even think of letting her go. "Very well, Mr. Merrithew," she said, hoping that she sounded businesslike rather than breathless. "If Miss Merrithew would step into our sitting room, we can begin discussing fabric and design."

Delyth started toward the room in which the dressmakers always met with their customers, but was brought up short when Mr. Merrithew cleared his throat. She turned to find that he had not moved from his position by the window.

"Sir?" It hadn't taken long for Delyth to understand who her real client was.

"We are accustomed to having our dressmakers attend us at our home," Mr. Merrithew said, examining his cuffs rather than looking at Delyth.

Delyth could not but notice that his sister sent him a puzzled look at this pronouncement, which he ignored. "Indeed? I'd be happy to do so, but I must have Miss Dawkins's approval."

"Naturally." Mr. Merrithew nodded. "We will expect you tomorrow at one o'clock. Here is our direction." He handed a card to Delyth, took his sister's arm and walked out of shop, leaving Delyth staring down at the card, feeling as though she'd been caught up in a very fashionable whirlwind.

Simon marched his sputtering sister down the street and shoveled her into their town coach. Only once they were underway did he glance at Louisa.

"We are accustomed to having dressmakers at our home?" she asked. "When did we become so high in the instep?"

Simon shrugged.

Louisa leaned forward and peered into her brother's face. "What was that all about?"

"I merely felt it would suit us better to have Miss Owen at Portman Square."

"Really?" Louisa said. "And why is that?"

Why was that? Simon wasn't exactly sure. When he'd started out today, he'd thought it would be easier to assess Miss Owen's motives in dressing her clients more easily away from the influence of her fellow dressmakers. But now, his mind kept rehearsing his first view of the notorious Miss Owen. She was a surprise. He had pictured an older woman, bitter over her fate dressing those more fortunate than she was, determined to bring down a few doyennes before retiring into solitary misanthropy. He had not expected a woman with the face of an impish angel, a cultivated, appealingly musical voice, and a disarming manner. Simon straightened his shoulders. The fact that she was attractive did not mean that he was wrong about her character. He would not let himself be distracted from his mission.

His mission. He had not shared his plan to unmask a miscreant with Louisa, judging, probably correctly, that his kindhearted sister would not approve of his ploy. Moreover, she would probably be surprised that her brother was being so devious. It wasn't something he would normally do and he had not taken more than a moment to really examine his motives. Unfortunately, after standing in the dressmaker's front room, talking to Miss Owen, he had had a hard time remembering why he was so determined to do this. However, if he was to follow through, he supposed he would have to be frank with Louisa.

"I want to see what impels her," he said, gazing out of the carriage window so that he wouldn't have to meet Louisa's eyes.

"What drives her?" Louisa sounded surprised. "That seems quite obvious. She wants to make beautiful gowns."

"Indeed?" Simon asked, glancing at his sister. "Then why do you suppose she made that atrocity Lady M wore to Almack's?"

"Are we trying to trap her? To catch her in some sort of subterfuge?" Louisa sounded indignant. "I thought we agreed that she needed tutelage and that this would be our opportunity to help her. I'm not at all sure I want to participate in a deception. Miss Owen seemed like such a nice person."

"Do you think so?" Simon returned his gaze to the scene passing outside the carriage window, fighting the inclination to agree with his sister. Meeting Miss Owen had made Simon lean toward softening his opinion. Delyth Owen was younger than he expected and seemed artless and candid. He had a hard time assigning the splenetic plot he had imagined to a person with such a pleasing look and manner. But he wasn't quite ready to give it up. "It's hard to tell on such short acquaintance, don't you agree?"

Louisa hummed. "We'll see," she said. "But I will not lie to Miss Owen regardless of what you may wish."

Simon gave her a faint smile. "I'm sure that won't be necessary," he said.

Delyth went back to her sewing, but was too excited to accomplish very much. Every time she heard a sound on the street, she jumped up to look out the window. Selina joined her soon after the Merrithews left and it didn't take long for her to become impatient with Delyth's fidgeting. Determined to avoid annoying her fellow dressmaker as much as she could, Delyth moved her work space as close to the window as she could get and contented herself with glancing out every ten seconds. She was not accomplishing any work, but she wasn't disturbing Selina, who had ceased making exasperated tsking sounds.

Finally, a carriage pulled up in front of the shop, and Delyth rushed to the front door to greet Felicity.

Felicity smiled at Delyth and headed right for her office, pulling off her gloves and shrugging out of her pelisse as she walked through the shop. She opened the office door, hung up her things, and turned to Delyth, who had trotted after her.

"Good afternoon, Delyth," she said. "Is there a problem?"

"Oh no." Delyth bounced on the balls of her feet. "At least, I hope not," she added.

Felicity waited while Delyth gathered herself and then waved to a chair. "Please sit. You are wearing me out and I'm already tired."

Delyth sat and sprang back to her feet almost immediately. "I'm sorry. I'm sorry," she said. "I can't sit still."

"Very well." Felicity raised an eyebrow. "What must you tell me that is so important?"

Delyth took a deep breath. She hadn't considered what she would say to Felicity and she was too excited to frame a coherent sentence.

"Good idea," Felicity said. "Take another breath."

Delyth followed her advice and eventually managed to tell the story of the Merrithews' visit and the possibility of a coronation commission in a manner that the shop owner seemed to understand.

"That's excellent, Delyth," Felicity said when Delyth had finally managed to communicate the gist of her meeting. "You have a possible coronation commission, if I understand your, uh, monologue."

"Yes." Delyth nodded vigorously. "But Mr. Merrithew insists that I do the consultation and fittings and, for all I know, sewing at their home."

"Indeed?" Felicity seemed to consider that for a moment. "Well, that is not entirely unheard of. Although it's usually done for the more lofty aristocrats." She hesitated another moment. "Merrithew, did you say?"

"Yes." Delyth held her breath.

"I believe that Miss and Mr. Merrithew are the children of the late Viscountess Fulbeck," Felicity said. "She was quite the leading light in London fashion until her unfortunate carriage accident."

Delyth waited, tense from the back of her neck to the tips of her toes.

Felicity sat heavily behind her desk, pulled some papers toward her and then looked up. "Yes," she said. "You may go. In fact, you should go. And good luck to you."

As Delyth left the room, she thought she heard her employer murmur, "Good luck to us all."

CHAPTER THREE

Delyth had never been in Portman Square and was mightily impressed by the grandeur of the homes and the lovely park at its center, but she was not particularly charmed by the park's locked gate. She climbed out of the hackney that Felicity had insisted she take and turned to retrieve her swatches, illustrations, and sketching supplies. She supposed she would be doing the sewing back at the shop, but she wasn't sure. Time would tell.

Delyth glanced over her shoulder in time to see the hackney driver's despairing shrug as she climbed the steps to the front entrance. She sensed some disapproval about delivering her to the front door when they pulled into Portman Square. She had prevailed, but she could see that the driver still thought she was setting herself above her station. Perhaps she was, but she had been invited here and she intended to act like a guest until someone told her otherwise.

A rather imposing personage answered her knock and allowed her to enter without so much as a raised eyebrow. *There,* she thought, wishing the hackney driver had been there to see her entrance. *I am a guest.*

"Miss Owen to see Miss Merrithew," she said. "I'm expected," she added, thinking that might be a prudent addendum.

"Yes, Miss," the personage said. "This way, please."

And so she found herself in a sunny drawing room being greeted by an equally sunny Miss Merrithew and her more cloudy brother. A footman took her valise and stood in place. "I see you've come prepared." Louisa Merrithew stepped forward and motioned to the footman. "Please take Miss Owen's things. She won't be needing them for a while."

Delyth was puzzled until Louisa said, "Your coat . . ."

"Of course." Delyth slid out of her pelisse, pulled off her gloves and bonnet and handed everything to the footman, who bowed and departed. She stood where she was, wondering what was next.

"Let us have some refreshment and discuss how we'll proceed," Louisa said.

Miss Merrithew gestured toward a chair. Before seating herself, Delyth glanced up at the glowering brother. If he didn't like her, which it seemed he didn't, what was he doing here? He obviously didn't trust her, but didn't he trust his sister? Suppressing a sigh, Delyth sat and folded her hands in her lap.

Louisa poured and Mr. Merrithew unbent enough to sit and accept a cup of tea. He still hadn't spoken.

Delyth had been trained to allow the customer to broach the initial discussion. She supposed that the Merrithews' visit to Madame Follette's had constituted that first discussion and she was prepared to take the lead now. However, she had also been raised in a gentleman's home and knew that one did not plunge into business over tea. "You have a lovely home," she said by way of breaking the silence.

She saw Mr. Merrithew raise an eyebrow, the first movement his face had made since she entered the room. She was, however, at a loss to interpret it. She decided to let it go. Mr. Merrithew had obviously taken her into dislike for some reason she couldn't fathom. Perhaps he didn't like the Welsh. Well, it was too late to do anything about that.

When she was with the theater, Delyth had asked Anthea to help her sound more like the ladies she hoped to have as customers one day. Anthea had laughed at her and told her that most ladies would kill to have her voice and she should leave it just as it was. She did, and now Mr. Simon Merrithew was frowning at her. When she had first met him, she had been sure he didn't frown at many people. Maybe it was only the Welsh.

She put her thoughts away and smiled at Miss Merrithew, who seemed all that was amiable. Apparently, dislike of the Welsh was not a family trait. "Would you like to discuss your gown, Miss Merrithew?" she asked, throwing etiquette to the winds.

Before Miss Merrithew could answer, Mr. Merrithew placed his cup into the saucer with a decided click and leaned forward. "Perhaps you could tell us a little about yourself first, Miss Owen."

Oh drat. Delyth hated this question. Not that she was ashamed of her background. She wasn't. But she also didn't think people would want to hear that she'd run away from home to join the theater. In fact, she thought that sounded rather juvenile and she was the one who had done it. Delyth was also so terrible at lying that most of the time she didn't even attempt it. She was nervous just being here. Successful lying was not even an option.

Instead, she temporized. "I have always wanted to design gowns," she said, looking as guileless as possible. "I love the feel of fabric and the interplay of colors. I love making women look their best. I want them to feel beautiful and happy." All of this was true. None of it was to the point. She knew what Mr. Merrithew wanted, and even though she knew she would eventually give it to him, she was also determined to drag it out as much as possible. Perhaps he would consume so much tea he would have to excuse himself and leave her alone with his sister, who was so much more congenial.

Rather than interrupting, contradicting, or even commenting, as Delyth expected, Mr. Merrithew merely sat back and raised that intimidating eyebrow again. She wished his eyebrows would remain in alignment. Silence reigned for more seconds than occured in normal conversation and, eventually, Louisa Merrithew began to look uncomfortable.

"You are Welsh," Miss Merrithew observed.

Ah, here it comes, Delyth thought. "Yes. I was born in Pembrokeshire." No need to provide details if she was not asked and she hoped she wouldn't be.

"You have such a delightful voice," Miss Merrithew continued. "I would love to sound like that."

Delyth smiled.

That smile knocked Simon sideways. How could someone who was obviously withholding information, who obviously had some unknown ulterior motive, have a smile like that? Genuine, joyful, real. That was not the smile of a manipulator. He almost unbent and returned the smile. Fortunately, Louisa continued talking and he was able to step back and resume his observation.

"More tea?" Louisa lifted the pot.

Miss Owen raised a hand and shook her head. "Thank you. No." she said.

Simon could have sworn she had darted a quick glance in his direction. Was he making her nervous? Should he take advantage of that?

"Miss Owen," he said, pausing as she started and then looked up at him.

"Mr. Merrithew?" Louisa was right. Her low, musical voice was extraordinarily appealing.

Simon inhaled deeply before continuing. "I understand that Lady Marjoribanks's gown was your first design for Madame Follette."

Miss Owen hesitated. "Yes," she said finally. "Although I had been working at Madame Follette's for several months before I was given someone to dress."

"And how fortuitous that it was Lady Marjoribanks."

Miss Owen blinked. "Fortuitous?"

"That you found a client who shared your sensibilities."

"Oh," Miss Owen said. "Yes. That."

Simon waited, but she said no more.

"What would you recommend for my sister?" he asked.

Miss Owen turned back to Louisa and took a deep breath. "That would depend," she said, "on what Miss Merrithew wants."

"What do you want, Louisa?" Simon turned to his sister.

"I want some time to discuss my options with Miss Owen," she said. "Alone," she added.

Simon didn't move. He wasn't ready to cede this conversation to his sister just yet. There was information about Delyth Owen that he wanted to know and that she apparently did not want to tell him. He would show her a thing or two about stubbornness. He sent an implacable glance toward Louisa and settled back in his seat.

Louisa turned to their guest. "Apparently we're not ready to discuss my options, Miss Owen. Do have a biscuit."

"Come now, Louisa," Simon said. "You know how much I enjoy fashion. Please don't banish me just when the conversation turns interesting."

The silence that followed Simon's pronouncement was deep and prolonged. Or at least it seemed that way to Simon. He was well aware that Louisa was giving him a sidelong look and that Miss Owen was looking at him in confusion. He could hardly blame either one of them. He sounded ridiculous, but he had no idea how he would pursue his quest without this particular ploy. And were anyone to look deeply into his interests, they could hardly deny that fashion was one of his enthusiasms. Of course, who would look deeply? And how would they accomplish that? He tried to imagine someone coming up to him at Almack's and asking, "Is fashion one of your enthusiasms?" Where had this train of thought come from? Suddenly he realized that the two women were looking at him in complete bafflement. Maybe they wanted to ask him if fashion was one of his enthusiasms.

At last, Miss Owen did them all the kindness of breaking the silence. "Well," she said, placing her cup on the table and putting her hands on her knees. "Why don't we retrieve my valise and we can discuss, er, fashion."

Simon relaxed. His stratagem had worked and he was strangely grateful to Miss Owen for complying so gracefully. He doubted that Louisa would have done the same.

Louisa confirmed Simon's guess by shooting him an impatient look. She called for a footman to bring Miss Owen's bag into the drawing room, and Simon sat back to enjoy the show. It was true that he had not discovered as much of Miss Owen's background as he had hoped, but he had other sources for that sort of thing. This—this example of how she worked—was the real reason he had brought her to Portman Square.

The moment her bag was before her, Delyth Owen transformed. As she pulled out fabric swatches, her eyes lit and her color heightened. No one observing her could doubt that this was her element. Simon was by turns transfixed and confused. There seemed not a shred of subterfuge about the woman displaying silks and muslins to his sister. And yet he could not shake the idea that she had deliberately made Lady Marjoribanks a laughingstock. Could she be that good an actress? He supposed he should pursue that possibility, but every moment in Delyth Owen's company made him increasingly uncomfortable with the path he had set for himself.

After some time, during which Louisa exclaimed over the various fabrics set before her, Miss Owen suggested that perhaps it would be helpful if Louisa told her what style of gown she preferred and what she had in mind for the one Miss Owen would design. Louisa declared that she would take Miss Owen to her chambers and they would examine her wardrobe.

Simon recognized that he had likely overstayed his welcome in this discussion and excused himself to make other inquiries about the mysterious and confusing Miss Delyth Owen.

What did he know? She was from Pembrokeshire. This was probably true. Her accent certainly confirmed that she was from Wales. What about her family? She had the manners of the gentry. This was interesting in light of her rather inferior position as a seamstress and aspiring dressmaker. And this was the place to start. One thing Simon knew for a fact was that Miss Delyth Owen was employed at Madame Follette's. So that was where he would begin.

Miss Felicity Dawkins was not in the shop when he arrived. Simon removed his hat. "Is Miss Dawkins ever here?"

The girl who had greeted him colored. "Miss Felicity is a very busy woman," she said.

"So it would seem. One would think, however, that she would be busy attending to her business. Is there someone I may speak to about your seamstresses?"

"Mr. Dawkins is in the office right now," the girl said, gesturing toward a door in the back corner.

"Mr. Dawkins?" Simon had never heard of a Mr. Dawkins.

"Miss Felicity's brother. He sometimes helps with the accounts."

Simon gathered this was as much as the girl knew, but it was good enough for him. "Would you ask Mr. Dawkins if he will speak with me?"

CHAPTER FOUR

"**S**he's from the theater." Simon paced the drawing room where he and his sister had served tea to Miss Owen. "The theater!"

"Good heavens, Simon. Please calm down. You say that as if she had been in Newgate or had joined the circus."

Simon could not understand how Louisa could be so unaffected by this information. "She might as well have joined the circus. What was Madame Follette—or Miss Dawkins, or whoever hired her—thinking when she hired a costume maker from the theater?"

"Perhaps she thought she was very good at what she does," Louisa said, earning her a stern look from her brother.

"Perhaps she had a moment of insanity," Simon bit out, but then stepped back. "You're right," he conceded. "She is very good at what she does, but is it possible that Miss Owen deceived Miss Dawkins in some way?"

"In what way would that be?" Louisa asked. "Did you not just tell me that Miss Dawkins's brother gave you this information? If he knows, certainly his sister knows."

Simon shook his head. "I just feel that something is wrong, but I can't identify it."

Louisa folded her arms across her chest and glared at her brother. "That much is obvious."

"And I have not been able to learn where she was before she joined the circus—uh, theater."

"Why is this so important to you? And would you please sit down; you're making me dizzy."

Simon sat and leaned forward, resting his elbows on his knees and feeling exhausted. "I don't know," he said. "Since I took over Mother's column, I seem to have developed an obsessive concern for fashion." He looked up at his sister and shook his head. "That can't be healthy."

"No," Louisa said. "It certainly cannot. But you have encountered poor dressmaking before. I have never seen you so upset. What is this really all about?"

Simon raised his shoulders. "I don't know," he said. "I wish I did."

"Well, we need to find out." Louisa stood and went to her brother, placing a hand on his shoulder. "I can't abide having you act in this deranged manner."

"Deranged?" Simon bristled, taking a deep breath before responding. Rather than answer, he just sagged back in his seat. "Perhaps I am acting deranged. But . . ." He sat up again. "I am not giving up this quest."

"Quest, is it?" Louisa strode over to the mantel and mimed hitting her head against it. "Very well, so be it. But I shall be watching you. Where do you start?"

Simon hesitated. Where did he start? Or rather, how did he continue? They had already had Miss Owen to Portman Square and he had already made his first foray into dressmaking espionage. He supposed that one way was to follow the trail to the theater.

"I will try to locate her former employer," he said, suddenly decisive.

"You mean the theater?" Louisa asked.

When Simon nodded, she continued. "What do you hope to learn there?"

Good question. "Exactly where she's from. Why she's in London. What her background might be."

Louisa blinked. "And how will this help?"

"Damned if I know, Louisa. But it's a start."

Louisa grimaced. "You know, she was very articulate and helpful when we looked at my wardrobe."

"Was she indeed?"

Louisa turned to face her brother. "Stop it, Simon. Don't take on that bored affectation with me. I know you too well. And yes, since you ask. She was, indeed. She understands patterns, fabric, and construction of clothing. I'm sure she's an excellent dressmaker."

"I notice you didn't include color in that list," Simon said.

Louisa sighed. "Not at present."

Feeling a bit more justified than he probably should, Simon nodded. "I'll find out where she lives."

Louisa put her hands on her hips, a smile overtaking her expression. "She should live here."

"I beg your pardon?" A frisson chased up Simon's spine. What was Louisa suggesting? Having Delyth Owen under their roof could not be a good idea. And yet . . .

As he retraced his steps to Madame Follette's, the idea of Delyth Owen sleeping under his roof lingered in Simon's mind. He imagined her getting into bed only doors away from where he slept. He contemplated what sort of nightdress she might wear, as he questioned the ladies at the dressmaker's shop about where Delyth lived and the name of the theater she had worked for. By the time he gained entrance to the Thalia Theatre and asked for Miss Drinkwater, he was imagining what Miss Owen looked like when she awoke, which included wondering what she would look like if he woke her.

These were not the sort of thoughts he should be entertaining. Fantasies featuring Miss Delyth Owen were completely antithetical to his plan to expose her to society. And yet, the image of exposing Miss Owen in the privacy of a guest chamber at Merrithew House would not leave his mind. It was almost as if she had cast some sort of spell over him, the little Welsh witch.

"**T**hey what?" Delyth snapped her mouth shut the moment she realized she had been standing in Felicity's office with it hanging open.

"Miss Merrithew has decided she would like to commission several new gowns and has asked that you live in her home while you work on them. She will provide you with a workroom and assistants should you require them."

Delyth's head was still spinning. "That's very . . ." Flattering? Confusing? Exciting? She was having trouble assigning the correct word.

"That's very good for us." Felicity supplied the answer. "And for you, if you do well."

"But must I live there? I have a perfectly good home," Delyth said. "And I am more than capable of getting from there to Portman Square."

"I'm sure you are, my dear." Felicity looked down to straighten some papers on her desk. "But Miss Merrithew is a leading light in town fashion, and it's a wonderful opportunity for you." She hesitated a moment. "Don't you agree?"

Delyth supposed she did. And if Madame Follette's was happy to accede, then Delyth was as well. She nodded. "Of course. When do I begin?"

"Mr. Merrithew will send a hackney to your lodgings tomorrow morning. You should bring a variety of fabrics with you. You may select them today and we'll bundle them for you. If you require anything while you are working with Miss Merrithew, just send word."

"They what?" Anthea Drinkwater stood in the drawing room of the flat she shared with Delyth with her jaw hanging open.

Delyth, surrounded by a pile of parcels, carefully wrapped and tied up with paper and string, lifted her shoulders. "They want me to move into the Merrithews' home while I design for Miss Merrithew."

"And you're going?"

"As you see." Delyth gestured to the stack of fabric that had been sent home with her.

"I see that you have brought half the shop home with you." Anthea sounded weary. Or was it worried? Delyth wasn't sure. But she knew what she had to do.

"And I am taking these with me to Portman Square. It's Felicity's wish. And," she added, "I am Felicity's employee. So I'm going."

"I don't trust Simon Merrithew," Anthea said.

Delyth was stunned. "You don't even know Simon Merrithew."

"I do now," Anthea said. "He paid a call at the theater."

Delyth blinked, trying to bring her friend into focus. "Why?"

"He wanted to know all about you, dearest. How long you'd been at the theater, where you'd learned to design, where you came from, who your people are."

"What did you tell him?"

"Not very much," Anthea said. "I couldn't very well tell him that I didn't know how long you'd been at the theater, since I was the one who brought you in. But I did not divulge any other information about you. Not that you've been very forthcoming with me about your family."

Delyth considered this interest in her background and wondered if Anthea was right not to trust it. She probably was, but Delyth's inclination had always been to think the best. "What did you think of him?" she said.

"I just told you I don't trust him." Anthea looked puzzled by the question.

"No," Delyth said. "I mean, is he not a handsome gentleman? So tall and his manners are so correct."

Anthea frowned. "I wasn't considering him as a dance partner, Delyth. I was wondering why he wanted to know so much about you."

"You worry too much," Delyth said. "He's probably concerned about the character of someone he intends to allow into his home. Wouldn't you be?"

Anthea sighed. "I suppose I would."

"Did you notice the color of his eyes?" Delyth asked.

Anthea shook her head. "No."

"Blue," Delyth said. "A cold blue. But you just know that if you could make him smile, they would warm to something like a summer sky."

"Good Lord, Delyth." Anthea threw up her hands.

"What?"

"Go," Anthea said. "Go to Merrithew House. But, please, please don't fall in love with Simon Merrithew."

"Of course I won't do that," Delyth said. "I may admire the man without falling in love. That would be totally ridiculous. Besides, he doesn't seem to like the Welsh."

Anthea stood and took her friend's hands. "Be careful, Delyth. He's up to something and I can't think that it will bode well for you."

"Well, I really have no choice unless you want me to come back to the theater."

"Of course I want you back at the theater," Anthea said. "But I know that is not where your heart lies. Go to the Merrithews. But be careful."

"Although I think you are exaggerating, I will," Delyth said. "Now help me put these bundles into some order."

Delyth was prepared. She had packed the small trunk that she had brought with her from Wales and the portmanteau she had borrowed from Anthea and checked that her bundles of fabric were properly secured. She had reorganized her sewing kit, making sure that she had sufficient needles and thread and that her scissors were newly sharpened. Everything was prepared except for her mind.

She lay in bed and wondered what it would be like to live in such a grand house. She recognized that she had not started out her life in poverty and, were she to be completely honest with herself (which was something she liked to do), she had been extremely lucky in finding employment with the Thalia and a home with Anthea. But her living situation had never come near the luxury in which the Merrithews appeared to live. Although her father was (and probably continued to be) quite prosperous, he was also one of the most parsimonious landowners in Wales. Leaving to follow her dream had never been a hardship. She had seen that Simon Merrithew, while probably not profligate, favored a rather elegant environment. It might be fun to live under his roof for a time.

And Miss Merrithew. For some reason, Delyth kept forgetting the reason she was going to Portman Square. She was to dress Louisa Merrithew and would have nothing to do with her brother. Hadn't Anthea warned her that she should be careful? But why was he asking questions about her? What did he hope to learn? Did he have an interest in her? She finally slept, with visions of Merrithews dancing in her head.

CHAPTER FIVE

"**A**re you sure you want the front door, Miss?" The hackney driver eyed Delyth's pile of parcels and her battered trunk with some doubt.

"Yes, indeed." Delyth was rather tired of officious hackney drivers, but cheerful on the verge of giddy to be ascending the front steps.

Unfortunately, the footman who answered the door looked even more dubious than the driver. "Miss?" he asked in the most condescending tone Delyth had heard since she arrived in London. And she'd been the recipient of a fair amount of condescension.

Today, however, she was not having it. "Miss Owen to see Miss Merrithew," she said, ignoring the mound of paper-wrapped parcels currently growing at her feet.

Delyth was amazed that her nose-in-the-air delivery worked. The footman executed a short bow and opened the door wider.

"Please see to my parcels," she said, suppressing a grin and sweeping inside as grandly as she could manage in her seamstress's cloak.

"If you'll have a seat, Miss—er—ma'am." The footman had gone from condescending to confused.

Delyth loved it and did not deign to respond to the implied question. "Miss Merrithew is expecting me," she said, instead. "I trust she is at home."

"Just a moment, ma'am—Miss," the footman stammered, bowed, and hurried out.

Within moments, a woman Delyth had never seen before hurried into the entry hall and greeted her. "Miss Owen. I'm Mrs. Reynolds, the housekeeper. Miss Merrithew asked that I show you to your room." She looked at the pile of packages and back at Delyth.

"For my work," Delyth said, looking apologetic.

"Of course." Mrs. Reynolds gestured to the footman. "Take these to the smaller morning room. And you." She pointed to a second footman who had appeared behind her. "Take Miss Owen's trunk up to the blue room."

Turning back to Delyth, she added, "If you'll follow me."

Delyth forbade herself the curtsy that Mrs. Reynolds's manner seemed to solicit and just smiled at the housekeeper. "Of course." She picked up Anthea's portmanteau and followed the lady out of the room and up two sets of stairs.

The blue room was lovely. The walls were covered in a soft blue silk that was echoed in the bed curtains. The rosewood furniture was polished to a high gloss and the carpet was soft under the thin soles of her shoes. She was definitely not in the servants' quarters and felt quite gratified that she had not let the driver take her around to the back entrance. Her trunk was at the foot of the bed and a maid was busily unpacking it. Delyth was taken aback. She and Anthea shared a maid/housekeeper at their lodgings, but she had taken care of her own personal needs since she left her father's house. She decided she rather liked having a personal maid and stopped herself from remonstrating with the housekeeper. If the Merrithews wanted to treat her like a guest, who was she to disagree?

"This is . . ." Delyth hesitated over the next word. She didn't want to seem too effusive. "This is quite nice," she said, finally, smiling at the housekeeper. "Where shall I wait upon Miss Merrithew?"

"Miss Merrithew desires that you make yourself comfortable and rest from your journey," the housekeeper said.

Her journey? Delyth had taken a hackney cab from Henrietta Street to Portman Square, which couldn't be more than three miles. That could hardly be considered a journey. Even if she had walked, which she could easily have done, she would not require a rest.

"But I'm—" she started to say before Mrs. Reynolds cut her off.

"You will join Mr. and Miss Merrithew for dinner," she said. "I'll send the maid up to you in time to dress."

"Th-thank you," Delyth said. She was not feeling quite so cocky at that moment. As soon as the housekeeper left the room, she whirled around to the clothes press to see if the maid had miraculously unpacked something suitable for a dinner with aristocracy. Rather high-in-the-instep aristocracy at that. Thank goodness that she was a good enough seamstress to make her own clothes. She pulled out a lovely puce and green gown that she had recently made for herself. Although Anthea had made a choking sound when Delyth had first modeled it for her, she thought it would do quite well for dinner.

A soft knock on her door woke Delyth. She sat up, surprised to find that she had fallen asleep and even more surprised that someone had entered while she slept and lit a fire in the grate. She could get used to the luxury. Smiling to herself, she allowed the maid who had unpacked her trunk to help her dress and do her hair. She looked very well, indeed, she thought as she examined herself in the glass between the drapery-clad windows. "Where am I to go?" she asked the maid.

"**S**terling tells me that Miss Owen will join us for dinner." Simon had tracked Louisa down in the library to verify that rumor.

Louisa blinked up at him. "Yes," she said, as if that was a stupid statement.

"She's a dressmaker." Simon dropped into a chair and narrowed his eyes at his sister.

"I had noticed that," Louisa said. "It's an acknowledged fact that dressmakers need to eat."

"With us?"

"If we invite her." Louisa nodded, adding, "Which we have."

"Why would you do this, Louisa?"

"What would you have me do?" Louisa leaned forward. "Make her take a tray in her room? Tell her to eat in the kitchen? Throw scraps through the door?"

"She's a servant."

"She's a dressmaker. And at the moment, she's my dressmaker. I want her at my table."

Simon noticed Louisa's jaw firming and realized that he was not going to win the argument. "Very well. I'll be there."

"Yes you will," Louisa said, picking up the book she had been reading.

Simon left the library, wondering why his sister's decision had left him so befuddled. The idea of having dinner with Miss Owen was hardly anathema. Yes, he was probably being unreasonable. He was just not sure why. He collected his hat, gloves, and walking stick from the butler and went out to cool off with a walk in the park. It would give him time to consider his response to the little dressmaker.

Taking deep breaths as he crossed the street and opened the gate to the park, he began to feel that he had overreacted. In fact, he was ready to acknowledge that he had been overreacting to everything concerning Miss Delyth Owen since he saw Lady Marjoribanks wearing that atrocious gown. Yes, he had become an arbiter of fashion since his mother's untimely death, but good lord this was taking it to unwarranted extremes. The fact that details on Miss Owen's background had been so scanty, however, caused him to still wonder if she had some ulterior motive in dressing the lady in such hideous colors. What was her story?

And why did he care? Simon found a dry bench and sat, fondling the head of his walking stick while he considered this question. He was not in the habit of deceiving himself and was ready to admit that something about Miss Owen called to him. Appealed to him? Granted, she was not what anyone would describe as a beauty. She was short and a bit more curved than the current styles called for. Granted, her hair was dark and lustrous if not particularly stylish. But what would you expect of a woman who had to work for a living? And her skin was luminous.

Simon straightened abruptly and ran his hand over his face. Her skin was luminous? Wherever did that thought come from? It was not like him to wax poetic. Well, maybe about gowns and then only in print, but not about skin—or hair! And it certainly was not like him to moon over a woman. If he were to say "her skin is luminous" to Louisa, she would fall over laughing. Shouldn't he be doing the same? He pulled his pocket watch out of his waistcoat and examined the face. How long was it until dinner?

Although he had not exactly come to terms with his alternating fascination with and suspicion of Delyth Owen, Simon was dressed for dinner and in the drawing room with his sister, thinking about a predinner glass of something stronger than sherry, when Delyth was ushered in by the footman. Simon paused in the act of reaching for a decanter and dropped the glass he was holding. Louisa hurried across the room and rescued the—whatever he was about to pour, picked up the glass, which had fallen on the carpet and not shattered, and put her arm through Simon's, turning him to completely face their guest.

Simon bit his lip, trying to school his expression. It would not do for his reaction to show on his face. But what was the woman wearing? My God! Her gown, while not as garish as Lady M's, showed a distinct . . . He wasn't even sure what to call it.

What would he write if this were for "Aglaea's Cabinet"? A distinct lack of taste. A total misunderstanding of color. He took a deep breath and tried to unfocus his eyes. That didn't help. When he did that, all he could see was the color. When he focused, he could see that the structure of the gown was lovely and quite original and that the construction was nearly perfect and that it flattered her voluptuous little body. Delyth Owen was an excellent seamstress and, possibly, an excellent dressmaker. She just couldn't pick out colors to save her life. At that moment, Simon realized that her design for Lady Marjoribanks was not at all malicious. It was just Delyth.

Just Delyth. The two words ran through Simon's mind throughout dinner and after he had retired for the night. In that one moment Miss Owen had become Delyth and Simon found himself in a muddle. He wasn't sure he should abandon his quest just yet. He told himself that one atrociously colored gown was really not sufficient evidence to acquit Delyth Owen of whatever nefarious plot she (or possibly he) had manufactured. On the other hand, he was increasingly taken with the young seamstress. She had been gracious and refined at the dinner table. Her conversation was quick-witted and amusing. She was a good companion, and Louisa obviously enjoyed her company. He needed to think.

Instead, he slept.

CHAPTER SIX

"**N**o Miss Owen?" Simon sat down at the breakfast table with a loaded plate and nodded to the footman to fill his cup.

"Miss Owen is in the workroom we've set up for her, unpacking her fabrics."

Simon winced.

Louisa sighed. "I admit that last night's gown does not bode well for what I might find when I go for my first session. But perhaps she made it out of leftover fabric from other projects, putting together whatever was available."

"Perhaps." Simon sipped his coffee. "Perhaps not. We shall see."

"Shall we?" Louisa asked, emphasizing the second word.

"Yes." Simon put his cup back in the saucer with a decided click. "I think I will come to your first meeting."

"Totally uncalled for, Simon. And a little odd."

"Perhaps, but I need to know what she is up to. And I need to make sure you are dressed properly."

Louisa lifted her fork and poked at the eggs on her plate. "I am a grown woman and have been choosing my own clothes for some time now. And I shouldn't have to point out that Miss Owen's design and technique are excellent. I will admit that her color choices are a bit . . . unusual."

Simon shook his head. "I feel involved, somehow," he said. "I am no longer convinced that Lady M's gown was done with malice, but I feel that I should follow through with this."

"I wonder," Louisa said, "what your real reason is."

"I beg your pardon?" Simon lifted an eyebrow. "What kind of a question is that?"

"It wasn't a question," Louisa said. "It was a statement."

"Then what kind of statement is it?"

Louisa frowned at her brother. "Men!" she said. "You are all impossible."

Simon had lived among women his entire life, particularly this woman, whom he had known from an infant. And yet, they remained a mystery; their thoughts and conversation were frequently cryptic. The longer he lived with Louisa, the more he was able to decode her thoughts. But there were times when he was completely baffled. This was one of them. He wondered whether to pursue this discussion or abandon it as hopeless. In the end, he couldn't resist.

"Granted," he said at last. "I'll agree that we are impossible if you'll tell me what you mean."

Louisa inhaled deeply and gazed at her brother in contemplation. "I think," she said, "that you are no longer suspicious of Miss Owen. Or at least are less suspicious. But you won't let it go. Why is that?"

Simon felt like grinding his teeth. Cryptic. Nothing clarified. His sister was so annoying. "I'll join you in the workroom," he said.

"Very well." Louisa threw her napkin on the table and stood. "I'll be there, but don't come in until later. Miss Owen will be taking measurements and I'm sure no one wants you about for that."

Simon wandered into the library and sat at his desk. He opened his account book, but could not muster the will to deal with today's bills. He opened the newspaper and found nothing of interest. He opened a book and then another and finally dropped onto a sofa and closed his eyes.

He supposed that Louisa was right about many things. She needed no help in choosing her wardrobe. And he didn't doubt that she could easily deal with any problems that might arise with Miss Owen. But he needed, or rather, wanted to be there while Delyth worked with his sister. Louisa was right about that, too. His reasons were no clearer to himself than they were to his sister. He wasn't sure whether he wanted to expose Delyth Owen or help her. Or perhaps both. In the back of his mind, he had a niggling suspicion that he wanted whatever would put him in close proximity to Miss Delyth Owen. The idea bothered him enough that he was happy to push it as far from his thoughts as possible. If, indeed, that were possible.

Rising from the sofa, he went after his hat and gloves. Maybe some fresh air would clear his mind.

Delyth had just finished Louisa Merrithew's measurements when someone knocked on the door. Louisa was behind a makeshift screen with her maid, getting back into her clothes. Delyth was sitting with her paper and pencil, sketching some ideas for additions to Miss Merrithew's wardrobe.

"Enter," she said.

Simon Merrithew cracked open the door and stuck his head in. "Am I too early?"

Delyth jumped up from her seat. "No," she said, a little out of breath. "Not at all."

Louisa peered around the screen and said, "Just in time, Simon. Take a seat." And then disappeared again.

Simon looked pointedly at Delyth, who was confused until she realized that he was waiting for her to be seated. Without speaking, she dropped back onto the stool on which she had been sitting to take Miss Merrithew's measurements and picked up her sketching tablet. Simon sat.

Delyth bent over her work, her pencil flying. She could feel Simon Merrithew's eyes on her back and it made her anxious. But she didn't stop her work. She was here for Miss Merrithew. And Mr. Merrithew seem to have softened a bit since her arrival. Perhaps he was getting used to her. Maybe she'd ameliorated his dislike of the Welsh. She flicked her eyes in his direction. He wasn't frowning. Surely that was a good sign. She smiled to herself and continued drawing. She had not changed her mind about him being a very handsome man. He was even more handsome when he wasn't looking forbidding. A second glance confirmed that he seemed much more relaxed and the lines of good humor around his eyes made her heart beat a little faster and, she feared, brought a blush to her face. She bent lower over her tablet.

Miss Merrithew finally glided out from behind the screen, looking as elegant as ever. She dismissed her maid and took the chair next to Delyth, looking over her shoulder as she sketched.

"Oh! I like that one." Louisa pointed to the upper left corner of the sheet.

Delyth turned the drawing around so Louisa could see it more clearly. "Do you?" she asked and then pointed to another drawing. "What about this one? It's similar but there are small differences."

"Yes, I see." Louisa took the tablet out of Delyth's hands and looked closely. "Very nice. I'd like to have them both. In different colors, of course."

"Of course." Delyth jumped up and went over to the corner where the fabrics she had brought with her were draped over the back of a settee. She had brought a wide range. She knew that not everyone liked the brilliant colors that she loved. She was afraid that Lady Marjoribanks might be the exception to the general taste and thanked the fates that had brought her into Madame Follette's. She would start with what she liked, though. Miss Merrithew had chosen her after visiting Lady Marjoribanks. There must be a reason for that.

She picked a deep crimson from the array and then reached for a daffodil yellow. Out of the corner of her eye she saw Miss Merrithew jump up and, when she turned her head, she noticed that Mr. Merrithew was wincing. These were, apparently, not successful choices. She stood where she was as Louisa crossed the room to join her. So much for hoping that the Merrithews shared Lady M's sensibilities.

"Perhaps something not quite so . . . bright," Louisa said, removing the fabric from Delyth's hands. "I like both of these colors," she continued, "but perhaps not together."

Mr. Merrithew joined them at the settee, looking over the display of fabrics. "Why did you make this choice, Miss Owen?" he asked.

Delyth flushed slightly, but straightened and looked Simon Merrithew directly in the eye. "I like these colors," she said. "They are vibrant and can easily be seen from—from a distance." She had almost said "from the last row," but stopped herself. She was not ashamed of her time in the theater, but she thought that Mr. Merrithew might not want a costume designer dressing his sister. And she wasn't sure that Miss Merrithew would want that either.

"I see," Mr. Merrithew said, cocking his head as he examined the fabrics. "From a distance."

Delyth hesitated. She supposed they were bound to find out eventually anyway. And this way she could go back to her home. She was sure Anthea missed her. "I . . . I began designing in the theater," she said, keeping her voice low. She definitely wouldn't be heard from a distance.

"Ah." Simon Merrithew's blue eyes looked into her face and perhaps into her brain, as if he were probing her thoughts.

"It's true," she said. Did he doubt her?

Delyth saw Simon glance at his sister and some unspoken communication pass between them. Was this where they'd tell her to pack her valise and go home? "I'll get my things."

"No," Mr. Merrithew said, as Delyth turned and began gathering up the material on the settee.

Louisa reached out and took her hand. "Wait. Where are you going?"

"You can't want a theater costumer dressing you," Delyth said, blinking her eyes.

"No," Simon repeated. "Don't go. Let us help."

Delyth dropped her fabrics and stared at Simon in amazement. "Don't go?"

Louisa looked up at her brother and then nodded. "Stay," she said. "You do beautiful work. I want you to design my gowns. But . . ." And she looked at Simon again.

"But," he continued for his sister. "I—We would like to help you decide how to choose colors. Are you willing to do this?"

Delyth couldn't speak, but managed to nod vigorously until she regained her voice. "Yes," she said, a delighted grin supplanting her earlier distress. "Yes, please."

CHAPTER SEVEN

That smile. As Simon prepared for what he thought of as The Education of Delyth Owen, he couldn't keep the image of that incredible smile from his mind. He thought back to the first time he'd seen her smile, her genuine delight when his sister had complimented her voice. He thought, now, that moment had been his first insight into who Delyth Owen really was, the moment he knew he was wrong to suspect her of subterfuge. Her smile when she realized that she was not to be dismissed for having worked in the theater left him breathless and made him want to know so much more about her. But this time he did not want to find where she had come from. He wanted to know what she thought, what she felt and, he admitted to himself in the privacy of his own chamber, what it would feel like to hold her in his arms.

He shook his head. That was impossible. She was not someone he could court and he was not someone who would seduce her.

"Damn."

"Sir?" Simon's valet dropped his hands from the cravat he was tying and stepped back.

"My fault." Simon shook his head at the man and lifted his chin to signal that he should continue. "My mind was wandering." And it was, to places it shouldn't ever step into. He would have to discipline his unruly thoughts if he was to be any help to Delyth. Miss Owen. He should also stop thinking of her by her given name.

Miss Owen. There, that wasn't so difficult. Miss Owen was waiting for him in the front hall. He was relieved to see that her street clothes were fairly subdued. He had half expected to find her in an aubergine

144

pelisse and green bonnet. Instead, he found her in a drab gray cloak and matching bonnet. It was so unlike her that he almost missed the outrageous gown she had worn to dinner. And then she smiled at him, and everything around him had more color. How did she do that?

"Miss Owen," he said. "I see you are prepared for our adventure."

"I am." She appeared to be shifting from foot to foot in excitement. "What are we to do?"

"We are taking a walk," Simon said, offering her his arm.

Delyth looked startled, but took the proffered arm as he nodded to the footman and escorted her into the sunny afternoon.

Once they were on the street, Delyth looked up at him. "Where will we walk?" she asked.

"We are going to Bond Street." Simon turned her in the proper direction. "And we will observe and discuss what the ladies we pass are wearing."

The sky was clear and the breeze was remarkably fresh for a spring afternoon in London. Simon took a deep breath and looked around. It was a mild, spring day, and he felt particularly happy to have the adorable, if drably dressed, Delyth Owen on his arm. As they made their way down Oxford Street, Simon wondered if he would have preferred that she wore something reflecting her extravagant taste in color. An interesting question. He'd have to give it some thought.

Bond Street was alive with color. The trees were a new green and the ladies were wearing their spring fashions. There was a lot of blue this year, he noted. Also pink. Always pink. He could see some pale cloaks with brilliant scarlet linings and a few pelisses in salmon or a rich green. Not in the same garment, fortunately, or unfortunately depending upon your point of view. He looked down at Delyth—Miss Owen—trying to gauge her reaction. She looked disappointed.

"What do you think of the colors?" he asked.

Miss Owen stopped in the middle of the pavement and looked around her. "They're rather dull, aren't they?"

"Do you think so?" Simon discreetly turned her toward the lady in the salmon. "What about that? It's a vibrant color."

Miss Owen brightened. "Yes. Yes. That's a lovely color and the construction of the pelisse is very fetching . . ."

"But?" Simon sensed her hesitation.

"But." She took a deep breath. "But imagine it with some pea green piping or maybe violet gussets." She looked up at Simon, her eyes dancing. "Or both."

Simon groaned, noticing that his reaction had done nothing to diminish the dressmaker's enthusiasm. He extended his arm again. "Come along."

The walk continued in much the same vein. "Notice how the hint of carmine lining accentuates the rich gray of the cloak."

"Gray? Why do ladies wear gray? It's as if they are trying to be invisible." When Simon gave her an inquiring glance, she elaborated. "I mean ladies of fashion. I'm just a dressmaker. The cloak would be much better with the red on the outside and perhaps a jonquil lining. Then it would stand out."

"Well then." Simon spotted another smartly dressed lady coming toward them. "There's a lovely jonquil dress, nicely set off by the fawn spencer."

"Oh yes." Delyth smiled at him again. "The dress is lovely. I think that it would look better with a brighter spencer. Tangerine, perhaps, or pistachio."

Simon was suddenly hungry. "Let me buy you tea."

As Simon steered Delyth toward a tea shop he liked to patronize, she grasped his hand and tugged him toward a shop window. "Look."

He found himself looking into the window of Percival & Condell. P&C had a good reputation as a draper and the window today was awash in colored linens and silks. Delyth had not released his hand, and Simon did not feel inclined to bring that to her attention.

She stood, eyes shining, taking in all the colors. "Oh my," she whispered. "Just look at these."

At this moment, Simon's latest suspicion was confirmed. Delyth Owen loved color, loved it in all its variations, loved the richness of good fabric, loved the way colors played off one another. Any colors. Her eye did not look for harmony, it looked for joy. Her love of color was disastrous and infectious. As she stood in front of the draper's window, reveling in the sweep of color before her, she was impossible to resist.

Tea with Simon Merrithew. Delyth was floating. Walking through the streets of London today, looking at the fashionable ladies and in the shop windows, talking about clothes and fabric and color had been an afternoon outside of her experience. And then tea. During her time in London, Delyth had nearly forgotten that she had been a child of privilege, had actually presided over tea, had entertained neighbors, had planned menus with her father's cook, had wandered the fields of her home. And yet, remembering all that today as she and Mr. Merrithew were seated at the little table in the confectioner's shop he had chosen, she still could not remember a single moment as wonderful as this afternoon had been.

Tea and dishes of sweetmeats were placed before her. She licked her lips in anticipation and glanced up at Mr. Merrithew, who was watching her face with an absorbed gaze. Had she done something wrong? She gave her companion an inquiring look.

He shook his head as if coming out of a dream and smiled at her. "Try these." He edged a small plate closer to her. "They're my favorites."

They were small and brown and shiny. Delyth had never seen anything that looked quite like these. She gave Mr. Merrithew a half smile. "You're not trying to poison me, are you?"

He smiled back and popped one in his mouth.

Delyth did the same. "Oh my," she murmured, placing her fingers over her lips as if to keep the flavor in. She could describe colors in her sleep, but flavors were another story. She knew that this was wonderful, but had no idea what to say about it. "It tastes like a warm day in autumn," she said, finally.

Simon Merrithew cocked his head to one side, sliding the sweet around in his mouth and examining her face. "Yes," he said after a while. "I believe it does."

Why did his agreement make her feel warm all over? This afternoon had revealed an entirely different Simon Merrithew from the one who had glowered at her at the shop, glowered at her in his drawing room, and glowered at her over the dinner table. This was the Simon Merrithew she had guessed lay beneath all that glowering, the one whose habitual expression was one of good humor. At last, he had dropped the angry façade and had enjoyed the day with her. Maybe being Welsh was not such a problem.

"What has happened?" Delyth asked, no longer willing to wonder why he had changed.

Simon (Could she think of him as Simon? She wanted to.) looked confused. "What has happened?" he repeated with a different inflection.

"You have been so kind to me, today," Delyth said. "I thought you didn't like me."

Simon sighed. "I apologize. My pique was unreasonable and uncalled for."

"Well, yes it was," Delyth said. "I'm pleased you've realized that. But what happened?"

"Someday," Simon said. "Some other day, I'll try to explain."

It was obvious that she wasn't going to get the answer today. But it still had been a marvelous afternoon and she was not going to let her companion's reticence on this subject spoil it. "Very well," she said with a slight smile and raised her cup to her lips.

"Shall we leave?"

Delyth had finished her tea and eaten as many sweets as she could manage without making herself sick or looking like a glutton. Neither condition was desirable. She supposed that they should leave. As delightful as this interlude had been, they really did eventually have to get back to Portman Square. Back to normal life.

Taking Mr. Merrithew's arm, Delyth allowed him to lead her back into the street. Dusk was upon them and the crowds had thinned if not altogether vanished. It was a lovely, soft night and Delyth found herself leaning toward Simon Merrithew, her head close to his wool-clad shoulder, the scent of him in her nostrils. It was delicious.

As they walked back along the route they had taken from Merrithew House, Delyth felt Mr. Merrithew's arm relax and unbend. She started to release her hold on his arm and step back, when she felt his hand slide down her arm and grasp her hand, lacing their fingers together. Her whole body responded, a luscious surge beginning at her toes and working its way up, weakening her knees and creating a strange warmth in parts of her body that usually didn't warm on their own. She let her eyelids fall shut for a moment to simply enjoy the sensations Mr. Merrithew's actions were generating.

And then reality crept back in. This could not be good. As wonderful as the day had been and as delightful as she found Simon's—Mr. Merrithew's—company, she was a dressmaker. (At best. Perhaps just a really good seamstress.) She was no one Mr. Merrithew could consider as other than a . . . a . . . Well, she couldn't even formulate the words for what he might consider her as. Her face heated to the roots of her hair and she stopped dead, trying to pull her hand away.

Simon looked down at her in consternation.

"Stop," she whispered.

He shook his head and whispered back, "Trust me."

Oh Lord, she wanted to. She didn't resist when he tugged her into a narrow side street and urged her into the shallow doorway of a closed shop. She didn't resist when he loosened her bonnet ribbons and slipped it off her head. She didn't resist when his hands came up and cradled the back of her head. She didn't resist when he lowered his head and his lips brushed against hers.

She whispered against his lips, but this time the word was, "Yes." As Simon's hands slid from her head and gathered her closer, Delyth could feel her hands move to his shoulders, seemingly of their own volition. Control of her body was beyond her at this moment. She softened under his kiss, allowing him entrance to her mouth, allowing him anything he wanted. She wanted it, too. Whatever he was offering, she was taking. Whatever he wanted, she was offering. God help her, nothing, no taste, no sound, no sensation, no color, had ever made her feel as good as she felt right at this minute.

CHAPTER EIGHT

It took every ounce of his resolution for Simon to release Delyth from his embrace. She was unbearably sweet and her kiss was enthralling. He was well and truly ensorcelled by his Welsh witch. He knew he should be questioning both his actions and his reaction. He knew that he was taking advantage of a woman in an inferior position, a woman he could never marry. Simon liked to think that he was a rather broad-minded aristocrat, but, even so, he could not forget that he was the son of one viscount and the brother of another. He would not embarrass his sister by marrying a seamstress. And what was he thinking, to take a kiss in a darkened doorway and consider it a prelude to marriage? What nonsense. He just needed to step away. Mustering all of his resources, he did step away, looking down at the flushed and flustered face of Delyth Owen.

"Forgive me," he said.

Delyth looked as though she had just awakened from a deep sleep. "What?"

"Forgive me," Simon repeated. "I shouldn't have . . ." He waved his hand toward the doorway they had just left. "I shouldn't have . . . done that."

Delyth looked back over her shoulder as if to remind herself what they had done. The rosy color of her cheeks became even deeper and she took a deep breath. "Think nothing of it," she said.

Simon was momentarily dumbfounded. *Think nothing of it?* How was that possible? Surely Miss Owen was not thinking nothing of it. Simon would be mightily surprised to learn that she had ever been kissed like that before, if, indeed, she had been kissed at all. One look at her face told the whole story. That was her first passionate kiss and she had participated freely and enthusiastically. Possibly, this was a genie that could not be put back in the bottle.

Drawing a deep breath of his own, Simon stepped back onto Bond Street and offered Delyth his arm. His plan at this moment was to pretend the kiss had never happened.

Simon was able to put the plan into action all the way back to Merrithew House. He kept the conversation light and directed once again to the clothes of the people they passed. "What do you think of that redingote, Miss Owen?"

Delyth's response was subdued, listless. "It's very nice." Gone was the exuberant discussion of color of the earlier afternoon. Gone was the passion for clothes. Simon suppressed a sigh. Perhaps she was just tired. Surely a single interlude in a doorway would not break the spirit of someone as vivacious as Delyth Owen.

Louisa was waiting in the drawing room for their return. When Delyth dropped a quick curtsy and excused herself to go change, Louisa threw Simon a concerned look. "Is Miss Owen unwell?"

"No," Simon said, perhaps a bit too quickly. "That is, I don't believe so. The walk may have tired her."

Louisa raised a Merrithew eyebrow as she took a seat. "Probably," she said.

Silence reigned in the sitting room. Louisa sat quietly for a moment, then picked up some embroidery from her workbasket. Simon examined his fingers. Would Miss Owen return for dinner? The minutes ticked away and Simon began to doubt it.

What had he done? And what was he to do? The kiss had been so out of character. He was not given to cornering girls in doorways. His flirtations were always conducted with ladies of his class and were usually light and enjoyable and did not involve shepherding them into secluded alcoves and kissing their shoes off. What would he say to Louisa if his actions caused Delyth to leave?

Just as Simon was beginning to decide how he would explain Delyth Owen's departure to his sister, Miss Owen appeared in the doorway to the sitting room, resplendent in her puce and green gown. She was smiling that infectious Delyth Owen smile. She was here. Simon felt the relief of her presence flood through him. And noted that the gown no longer made him cringe.

"Miss Owen." Simon sprang from his chair and crossed to Delyth, extending his hand.

Delyth took his hand. "Mr. Merrithew." Her grin was a sly indictment of the tremor in his fingers. She looked as though she knew every thought that had passed through his mind since she left him at the door. *The witch.*

Louisa had put down her embroidery and crossed to where Simon was standing. She looked pointedly at him, making him realize that he was still holding Miss Owen's hand. He dropped it, probably too quickly, and Louisa gave him a curious smile. "Shall we dine?" she asked.

Simon extended both arms and escorted his sister and Miss Owen into dinner with not a little trepidation. Which turned out to be unfounded.

"Did you enjoy your afternoon, Miss Owen?" Louisa asked.

Eyes shining, Delyth nodded. "It was wonderful," she said. "And would you please call me Delyth?" She looked uncertain and asked, "Is that all right? For you to call me Delyth?"

"Yes." Louisa laughed. "It's fine and we would be delighted. Wouldn't we, Simon?" She turned to her brother.

"Er," Simon said. "I'm not—" He stopped abruptly when he felt the toe of Louisa's shoe meet his ankle. "Yes," he said. "Absolutely." He was in such trouble.

"And you must call us by our first names," Louisa said. "At least when we are among family."

Delyth blushed, which, of course, Simon found charming. "Thank you, Miss Merrithew."

"Louisa," Louisa said. "Now tell me about your walk."

Delyth's smile bloomed again. "It was so beautiful," she said. "And Mr. Merrithew—Simon," she amended, blushing again, "tried so hard to show me how colors should be used together." She looked down at her dress. "I'm afraid I'm hopeless."

"You are not hopeless," Simon said. "You merely have a more exuberant idea of how color should be used than the average woman."

Louisa turned a stunned look on her brother. He could have sworn he heard her whisper, "How the mighty have fallen," under her breath, but that couldn't be right.

Delyth fluffed her pillow and tried a different position. There was no doubt that this was the most comfortable bed in which she'd ever slept. There was also very little doubt that she was not going to get any sleep in it tonight. Every time she closed her eyes, the events of the afternoon and evening marched through her mind like a particularly well-staged play, one she had seen so many times that each scene was as vivid as if it was actually being performed before her eyes.

Each instant of the afternoon, from the moment she and Simon (Simon!) left Portman Square to the moment in the doorway when he kissed her repeated in her mind. In fact, every other part of the afternoon seemed to be rushing ahead at top speed so her memory could get back to that doorway. That was why she wasn't sleeping. She was back in the shallow doorway right off Bond Street being kissed by Simon Merrithew. Every time she thought of that—relived that—kiss, her toes curled and, worryingly, her nipples hardened and she felt as though she was melting somewhere in her middle.

Delyth considered whether or not she might be coming down with an illness. Consumption? Typhus? Influenza? The Black Death? An inflammation of the lung? But she was not a stupid woman and she had read some of the books Anthea tucked away in the back of her bookcase. She knew she wasn't ill. She didn't know exactly what name to give the way she felt but she knew what, or rather who, caused it.

However, identifying the cause was not helping her to sleep. Identifying the cause was only exacerbating the restlessness pervading her body (and concentrating in certain spots). She threw the covers off and slid out of bed, lit a candle, and looked around to see if this lovely room had any hidden bookcases. If she couldn't sleep, she could at least read. She wouldn't object to something like Anthea's hidden stash of illicit literature. In fact, she was in just the mood for such a thing.

There was, of course, nothing to be found, not even a treatise on agricultural practices, which, from her reading of Minerva Press novels, she had gathered was a staple of gentlemen's libraries. But perhaps that was only gentlemen with country estates. Minerva Press had also given her to believe that creeping out of bed to a gentleman's library in the middle of the night in her nightdress would lead to more of the kind of thing that had happened in the doorway. She stopped to consider that for a moment. She wouldn't entirely object to another such encounter, but she hated to be a cliché. Then it came to her. She would go down to the workroom that Louisa had set up for her and get her drawing tablet and pencils. She might as well use her time to work on some designs for Miss Merrithew. She could worry about the colors later.

Delyth picked up a shawl, slipped out of her bedroom door and crept down the hallway, careful to not make any noise. Once downstairs, she hesitated outside the library door. The room was dark and she stood for a moment considering whether she would go in. In the novels, sometimes the heroine was in the library first and then the handsome hero appeared. No. It would be better to go to the workroom.

The workroom was as dark as the library, but Delyth quickly lit a branch of candles from the single stick she had carried from her bedroom. Much of the room was in shadow, but she stood for a moment admiring it. Miss Merrithew had arranged a room that was very nearly perfect for the purpose of creating clothing. Delyth walked over to the worktable where her drawing supplies were set out and picked up the tablet. She started at the front and paged through it. Someone had written notes beside each drawing, suggesting colors and materials. Who had done this? Louisa? Simon? It must have been one of them. No one else in the house had the knowledge or interest. Delyth looked through each description, understanding, for perhaps the first time, why these colors had been suggested. Before her afternoon with Simon, she would have thought the choices were deadly dull. Now, although she might not agree with the subdued suggestions, she understood them in the context of what society ladies were wearing.

Picking up her pencil, she made some adjustments to her existing drawings and sketched out two additional dresses, taking the time to make some notes of her own as to color and fabric. It would be interesting to discuss these with Miss or Mr. Merrithew. After nearly an hour, the room had cooled considerably and Delyth had done all she wanted to with her drawings. Wrapping her shawl around her, she blew out the candles and made her way back toward her room.

This time, as she passed the library, she noticed light filtering out from under the door. She stopped and considered. The smart thing would be to continue to her room and get some sleep. She was, however, feeling neither smart nor sleepy. Gently easing the door-latch open, Delyth edged into the room. Simon was standing by the fire with his back to the door, in a contemplative posture.

"Oh!" Delyth said. "I didn't know anyone was in here."

Simon turned toward her and smiled. Or perhaps he smirked, which she knew she deserved. In a voice that was both low and amused, he said, "Indeed?"

Without shifting his gaze from her face, Simon began pacing toward the door. Delyth had sudden second thoughts and began backing up, her hands groping for the latch. Before she could find it, however, Simon was directly before her. He was still dressed in the shirt and trousers he had worn at dinner but he had discarded his jacket and waistcoat and—Delyth looked down—his shoes and stockings. *My, but the man has elegant toes.* Her own toes curled a little.

Simon stood for a moment not moving, then removed the candlestick from Delyth's grasp and placed it on a table. He put his hands on Delyth's shoulders and moved a step closer.

Delyth's arms went limp and her shawl fell to the ground. There she was, standing so close to Simon Merrithew, wearing only her night rail and—she looked down again—no shoes or stockings. Her toes were not nearly as attractive as Simon's. When she raised her head, Simon was still staring at her, his steel-blue eyes holding a warmth she had not seen before. What now?

Simon lowered his head and hesitated, his lips a bare fraction of an inch from hers.

"Yes," she thought and then, when Simon's mouth touched hers, realized she had said it aloud. At first it was a mere feather-touch of a kiss, his lips lightly moving over hers, all warmth and coaxing. He increased the pressure and she responded, winding her arms around his waist and allowing her hands to move up his back, gripping the long, lean muscles that had been so well hidden by his jackets.

Simon's hands skimmed down her arms and slid around to her buttocks, drawing her fully against him as he kneaded the sensitive flesh. Delyth was well-read. She knew what the hard ridge that was pressing against her stomach was. But she had no previous experience of it. Nor had she expected what happened to her body when Simon pulled her flush against him. Her knees turned to water and the rest of her to fire. She gasped and Simon's tongue entered her mouth, beginning a sensuous dance in which her own tongue soon became a willing partner.

As the kiss deepened, Simon's hands roamed up her back and eased the sleeves of her night dress off her shoulders, tugging it down until her breasts were exposed to his gaze. Then one hand slid upward and closed around a breast, holding it gently for a moment before he found her eager nipple. The moment he took it between his fingers, the warmth that had manifested itself between Delyth's legs when Simon had first kissed her threatened to turn into a blaze. She groaned. And when he leaned down and drew it into his mouth, she thought she might explode.

And Simon stepped back. Delyth blinked at the sudden withdrawal of the voluptuous sensation of Simon's mouth on her. She looked up at Simon's face, trying to read his thoughts, his feelings.

Simon looked as though someone had just thrown a bucket of water over him. He brushed a hand over his eyes, then pulled Delyth's night rail back over her shoulders. He bent to the floor to retrieve her shawl and wrapped it around her. Then he bent forward and placed a gentle kiss on her forehead.

Her forehead! "Simon," she said. "What . . . ?"

"No." Simon placed two fingers against her lips. "Forgive me. That was wrong. I should never . . . I don't know what I was thinking."

Delyth just stood, dumbfounded and frustrated. "I beg your pardon?"

"I have no business making love to you."

"You weren't alone in this activity," Delyth said, folding her arms across her chest to secure her shawl and hide her nipples, which seemed to be still mourning the loss of Simon's touch.

Simon sighed. "Thank you, Delyth." He touched her cheek. "It is kind of you to try to absolve me. But this can lead to no good end."

Delyth bit the inside of her cheek to prevent herself from saying something she might regret.

"I understand," she said finally. "I am aware of what I am and that my standing is far too inferior to warrant a future for us. However . . ." She tightened her shawl around her shoulders.

"However, the future I was envisioning had not progressed beyond this room. So perhaps you should calm yourself and we'll just return to our former, er, positions."

Delyth put her hand on the door-latch. "If you like, I can return to Madame Follette's tomorrow. I would appreciate it if you wouldn't mention any of this—"

Simon stopped her. "This will remain between us," he said. "And, no. Please stay. Louisa enjoys your company and is looking forward to your designs. I would also enjoy continuing to work with you. As you say, we shall return to our former positions."

He didn't look convinced, but Delyth chose to ignore that. "Thank you, Mr. Merrithew." Delyth dropped a small curtsy, even though she felt foolish doing so in her nightclothes and bare feet, and marched out the door and up the stairs.

Once in her room, she threw herself on the bed and pulled a pillow over her face. "Stupid, stupid, stupid," she said into the linen. "Now I will have to tiptoe around the Merrithews and pretend that Simon has not made me fall in love with him." Maybe she should go back to the shop. She would have to see what the next day would bring.

CHAPTER NINE

Simon returned to his bedchamber and, after getting into his nightshirt and banyan, spent half an hour pacing his floor and berating himself for his stupidity. There was no excuse for approaching Delyth as he had. Although, perhaps the way she looked in a nightdress and bare feet was sufficient provocation.

No. He was a gentleman and gentlemen did not accost women who were working for them. Cads and knaves did that. Rakes and scoundrels. Not the sons of viscounts. Well, perhaps some sons of viscounts, but not Simon Merrithew, son of the late Viscount Fulbeck, and brother of the current viscount. His brother would be in a towering rage if he learned what Simon had done.

Brandy! Yes, that would help. Simon strode to the sideboard under the window. Brandy in hand, Simon retired to the chair before the fire and gave the guttering flames a poke. He was worried about tomorrow and about the day after that. He was worried that he had hurt Delyth and he was worried that Louisa would read his mind as she so often seemed to do.

Delyth had not appeared to be hurt. She was definitely angry, which he richly deserved. He wasn't quite sure whether she was angry because he had kissed her or because he had stopped. That was an interesting question and one for which he thought it would be wise not to seek the answer. Unfortunately, he wasn't sure he was that wise. He also wasn't sure he wouldn't want to kiss her again, and more. It probably would be best if she left the house, but his heart quailed at the prospect. He had gotten used to having Delyth in his life so quickly. It was nearly impossible to believe that little more than two weeks had passed since he had thought her a petty dressmaker with an ulterior motive. He could not remember being more foolish and that included his school years when he had been quite foolish, indeed.

Simon finished off his brandy, hoping that it would be sufficient to put him to sleep. There was so much going on in his head (and other parts of his body) that he doubted even alcohol would help. He left a candle burning when he crawled into bed, thinking that he would read if sleep evaded him. The book he chose was a tome on modern agricultural practices. True, he had no estate, but he had found it in the library and he kept it by his bed for nights when he couldn't sleep.

Tonight, crop rotation wasn't working. His mind kept skittering back to discussion of ladies' dresses, and the way Delyth Owen's lips had looked when she tasted the caramel sweetmeat, and the way Delyth Owen's lips had tasted when he kissed her, and the way Delyth Owen's toes had looked peeking out from beneath her night rail, and the way Delyth Owen's breasts had looked peeking out over the top of her night rail. Simon dropped the book. And the way Delyth Owen's breast had felt between his lips when he had taken her nipple into his mouth.

"**W**here is Miss Owen?" Simon stumbled into the breakfast room after a restless night, feeling as though he would need at least five cups of coffee to clear away the fog in his head.

Louisa looked up from the morning paper. "She had to go to her shop today."

"Is she coming back?" The anxiety Simon had felt last night returned in full force.

Louisa looked puzzled. "Of course she's coming back," she said. "Why wouldn't she?"

Simon shrugged and waved his cup at the footman, who responded with a stream of steaming coffee. "Excellent."

"What?" Louisa's puzzled expression intensified.

"The coffee," Simon said. "It's excellent."

"Are you feeling well?" Louisa nodded to the footman, who refilled her cup with the excellent coffee.

"I am a little tired, since you ask." Simon took a deep draught from his cup and choked a little. "I had a little trouble sleeping last night."

"Interesting," Louisa said. "Miss Owen looked a bit tired herself when she came down earlier."

"Indeed?"

"Yes," Louisa said. "Indeed."

Simon looked into his coffee and nodded.

"Simon." Louisa drew out both syllables into a long, exasperated sound.

"Louisa?"

"What is going on between you and Miss Owen?"

Simon tried to cover his hesitation by taking his plate to the sideboard and examining the offerings.

"I'm waiting." Louisa put her cup into its saucer with a sharp click.

"I'm trying to tutor her in the use of color. Is that not what we agreed on?"

Louisa looked as though she was debating whether or not to believe him. She was annoyingly perceptive. "That is what we agreed on," she said. "But I don't think that's all you're doing."

Simon was silent, but, apparently, Louisa was not to be put off by lack of communication.

She sat up straight in her seat, her back not touching the chair, and just stared at him.

Simon had a vivid memory of his mother giving him just such a look until he succumbed and told her everything she wanted to know. He had been helpless in the face of his mother's piercing blue eyes and he was quite sure that he would be no more successful against Louisa's green ones.

"I kissed her," Simon said quietly.

"You what?" Louisa leaned forward and cupped a hand around her ear. "I don't believe I heard you clearly."

Simon looked around the room and nodded at the footman, who slipped out the door, closing it behind him. Once he was alone with his sister he raised his voice just slightly above his previous whisper. "I kissed Delyth Owen," he said. "Twice." Then he sat back in his chair, wincing and waiting for the gale of his sister's displeasure.

Louisa remained motionless and looked at Simon as if assessing his state of mind. Simon could almost swear he could see a glint of amusement in her eyes. "Did you indeed?"

What was he to make of that? "Is that all you have to say?"

"What would you have me say?" Louisa asked.

"You could remind me that I'm a gentleman and should act like one."

"I could, but I imagine you've been doing that to yourself already. All night by the look of you and the way you're inhaling the coffee."

"I have," Simon admitted, closing his eyes in distress.

"Simon!"

"Yes?" Simon opened his eyes and looked at his sister.

"What are your feelings for Delyth Owen?" she asked.

Simon opened his mouth, but could not seem to formulate the correct words. He opted for more coffee.

Delyth had received a cryptic message from Selina that morning during breakfast and, having made her excuses to Miss Merrithew, hurried off to Madame Follette's to see what Felicity's urgent meeting was about. She awoke this morning looking forward to working with Louisa Merrithew today. She was not happy about being pulled away from her plan by a problem at the shop and she was worried about what the problem might be.

Nothing looked amiss when Delyth entered the shop. She greeted Selina, Sally, and Alice and went to her usual worktable. Taking out the drawing of the dress she was working on and Miss Merrithew's measurements, she spread out some muslin and began working on her pattern. Although she was glad to be back among the people she worked with, she wondered why Selina had sent her note. She looked around, but Selina was deeply engrossed in her own work and didn't look up.

When Felicity walked in everyone looked up and put down their work. She looked as though she had something important on her mind. Within a matter of minutes, the sky had fallen. Felicity announced that the building was being torn down and that she would find another place for Madame Follette's.

Felicity was so sincere and Delyth desperately wanted to believe her, wanted to believe that she would continue to have a place with Felicity Dawkins. She glanced at Selina, but her impassive expression gave nothing away. Delyth wondered if Selina felt as uneasy as she did. "You're quite certain everything will work out well?" She knew there was no real answer, but she had to hear it.

It had been a strange and upsetting day. The weather was fine, so Delyth walked back to Portman Square to give herself time to think. Felicity had tried to be optimistic about the future of her shop, but things did not sound promising. What if she had to reduce the number of dressmakers? Surely that unfortunate notice in "Aglaea's Cabinet" would put Delyth on the top of the list to be dismissed. She had tried to put the best face on Aglaea's mention of her color choices, but, in her heart of hearts, knew that it wasn't good. Still, it hadn't really made a difference until this moment, when it might be a factor in what her future would look like. Now, she was both angry and frightened, although she tried not to acknowledge those emotions. They were not her customary responses to obstacles.

Think about something else, she told herself as she crossed Great Marlborough Street. Naturally, the first thing that came into her mind was Simon Merrithew or, rather, how delightful it was to kiss Simon Merrithew. The kiss in Bond Street had been unexpected but far from unwelcome. Ever since he had begun smiling, she had barely been able to keep her eyes off him. Since he wasn't holding her Welshness against her, he had been entertaining, almost lighthearted, interested in her and her work and—yes—adorable. As much as she enjoyed working with Louisa Merrithew, something in her craved the company of Simon.

But last night. *Oh my!* That encounter in the library had been more than a kiss. If she read her Minerva Press novels correctly, that encounter could have ended up on that velvet-covered sofa near the fire. It didn't, however, and Delyth was a bit put out with that. Oh, she knew what Simon was doing. Simon was being a gentleman. She liked that about him. She really did. But she would have liked some less gentlemanly behavior just as well. Perhaps better. Delyth gave a little sigh as she headed toward Oxford Street. It seemed as though she was not going to get the opportunity to find out. Too bad.

Delyth had been born into the gentry. She knew how gentlemen (and ladies) were supposed to act. However, she thought she might prefer the sort of thing that went on in her novels: more gazing into eyes, more touching, more kissing, more . . . Of course, she also knew about fallen women and unmarried women with babies and women who relied on men to whom they weren't, and never would be, married. She didn't think she would like to engage in that sort of thing. It was a quandary.

Contrary to her hope, Delyth had not resolved her feelings by the time she reached Merrithew House.

CHAPTER TEN

It was early afternoon when Delyth returned to Merrithew House. "Where is Miss Merrithew?" she asked the footman who had opened the door for her.

"I'm right here, Delyth." Louisa strode into the entry as if she'd been waiting for Delyth's return. "Is there a problem?"

Delyth took a deep breath. There were so many problems she didn't know where to start. No. That wasn't true. With Louisa, she should start with the dressmaking problems and not with the fact that she was in love with her brother. The brother problem was one Louisa couldn't solve and wouldn't want to hear about. "I would like to discuss our work," she said, trying to sound as she imagined Felicity would sound in a business negotiation.

"Let's go to the workroom." Louisa linked her arm through Delyth's and led her away.

The workroom was just as Delyth had left it the night before. Her tablet was on the table by the window, the fabrics had all been organized on a nearby bench. Delyth's sewing tools were tucked neatly into her bag. It didn't look at all as if the world had changed.

"Now," Louisa said. "What is wrong?"

Before Delyth could answer, the door opened and Simon stepped into the room, and she completely forgot what she was going to say. Her heart began to beat faster and she knew that color was flooding her face. She felt lucky that she didn't faint. Good heavens! Was it going to be like this from now on? She could not possibly work this way. Something had to be done.

Delyth nodded at Simon and, straightening her shoulders, turned to his sister. She was convinced that she desperately needed the coronation commission in order to keep her position, but wasn't quite sure how to go about getting it. Should she beg? Begging might work. Louisa Merrithew was a compassionate person. The next moment, Delyth realized that she didn't want a commission based on pity. Did such a thing happen in the dressmaking world? Perhaps, but not to her.

She opted for the truth. "I'd like to know if you really want me to design a gown for the coronation." Before Louisa could answer, Delyth continued, "I know that it was to be contingent on my other work for you, but . . ." She closed her eyes and spoke very quickly. "But there is not much time and I am afraid that I will lose my job if I haven't brought in any important work."

"Lose your job?" Simon stepped forward. "Has Miss Dawkins threatened you?"

"Oh, no!" Delyth shook her head. She could not bear for anyone to think badly of Felicity. "It's just—I hate to say this. You probably don't know, but I had a very bad notice about Lady Marjoribanks's gown in that 'Aglaea's Cabinet.' Miss Felicity never said anything to me, but I know she's seen it. It was about one of her customers. Of course she did. Someone who causes a public fashion scandal cannot be good for her shop. And now, if she has to cut her staff, I just know I'd be the first one to go."

Simon glanced at his sister with a look that Delyth couldn't interpret. Now that she had told the Merrithews about "Aglaea's Cabinet," she would probably be removed from the house. So much for compassion.

Hunching her shoulders, Delyth turned toward the worktable and began to pack up her things.

"Wait." Louisa hurried over to her. "What are you doing?"

"Leaving," Delyth said. "Isn't that what you want?"

Simon came and stood at her other side, so close that she could feel the heat of his body. "No," he said. "That is not what we want." He looked over at Louisa, who nodded at him. "We want you to continue with the new dresses for Louisa's wardrobe."

"And," Louisa said, "we want you to stop offering to leave and to begin working on ideas for my gown for the coronation."

The blood seemed to rush from Delyth's head. She gripped the edge of the table to keep from toppling over. She felt Simon's hand under her elbow and then, surprisingly, around her waist.

Slowly, he walked her to a chair and helped her sit. "Take deep breaths," he said, and crouched down in front of her, taking her hand and looking into her face.

Delyth did as she was bid, taking deep draughts of air into her lungs, never taking her eyes off Simon's. She wasn't sure what all this meant, but she was too light-headed to try to make it out. They were going to let her continue. She was going to make a coronation gown. She would save herself and make Felicity proud. She would not be going back to the theater.

"Are you feeling better, Delyth?" Louisa handed her a small glass of sherry.

Delyth sipped and suppressed a grimace. It was not her favorite restorative. Gently, she set her glass on the small table beside her. "Thank you, yes." She realized she still had a grasp on Simon's hand and tried to break it, but he tightened his grip and stayed where he was. What was he thinking? What would Louisa think?

She drew in one more deep breath and rose from her seat. Of necessity, Simon released her hand. "We should get to work, then," she said, brushing her hands together. She returned to the worktable and took out the pieces of the pattern she had cut at the shop. "I'll baste this together and we can proceed from there." She spoke directly to Louisa. "It shouldn't take me long. Why don't you think about what fabrics you prefer?"

"**S**hall we?" Simon gestured to the selection of fabrics piled on the bench. Delyth had immediately started pinning pieces of muslin together and seemed to be trying her best to pretend he and his sister weren't in the room.

Louisa looked as though she wanted to leave Delyth to her work, but he wasn't ready to do that. He wanted to stay in here and coax Delyth into talking about cut and color and texture. He privately acknowledged that he could happily listen to Delyth Owen rhapsodize about fashion for long periods of time. In fact, he had not yet determined what his limit was, or if there was one.

"Simon." Louisa looked and sounded perturbed by his insistence on staying. "Let the woman work and then we will consult with her about fabrics." She took his arm and started to drag him out of the room. "Come with me."

Simon looked back over his shoulder at Delyth, who was bent over her sewing with a sly smile on her face. He felt his own mouth shape into an answering smile and let Louisa lead him out of the room.

Louisa didn't stop until she reached her favorite drawing room where she pushed Simon into a chair. "Sit," she said. "Stay." And she rang for tea.

"What do you think you're doing?" Louisa asked, once the tea arrived and she'd passed Simon a cup he didn't particularly want.

"Apparently, I'm having tea," he said.

"I mean, what do you think you're doing with Miss Owen?"

"Nothing." Simon attempted an uninterested shrug and took a sip of tea. "I'm here having tea with you."

Louisa rolled her eyes. "You are the most impossible man I know."

"Quite possibly," Simon agreed.

"This morning you told me you kissed Delyth. Is that not correct?"

Simon nodded.

"And then you asked me to remind you to act like a gentleman."

"Also correct," Simon said.

"And yet, you insist on mooning around the workroom while Delyth sews a pattern. What is the meaning of that?"

"Mooning?" Simon asked, appalled at the characterization. "Mooning?"

"Yes. Mooning. Now, make up your mind, Simon. I am your sister, not your conscience. I'm not going to make you do anything. You have been an adult for quite some time now and—I thought—a gentleman. If you think you should act like one, you are perfectly capable of doing so on your own." Louisa set her cup down and stalked out, leaving Simon alone with his cooling tea and his teeming thoughts.

Simon's relationship with his sister had always been open and honest. Yet, this was the first time he could remember being the recipient of so vehement a lecture. It was a lot like having tea with his mother.

What would his mother say about his ambivalent feelings about Delyth Owen? Would he even tell her? Although he probably would not have shared even as much as he had with Louisa, he did wonder how his mother would feel about Delyth. She was lovely. Lovely and refined for someone who had worked in a theater. Wait! She was refined regardless of her background. If he didn't know she'd worked in a theater, he would have thought she was a member of the gentry. She would appear to advantage at any social occasion he could imagine taking her to. Except, probably, for the color of her gowns. But that, he now realized, was neither here nor there.

Delyth Owen was not the sort of woman a gentleman dallied with. Had he met her in a ballroom instead of a workroom, he would have courted her. He would have considered marrying her. And now that he'd met her at a dressmaker's shop, how was he to proceed? Maybe he needed more tea.

Maybe he needed something stronger than tea. Although brandy or even sherry might be the better way to work through his predicament, two o'clock in the afternoon was probably not the time to start drinking. Simon considered going after Louisa to continue their fight. That was always invigorating and sometimes fun. Today, however, it hadn't felt like fun and it had confused him more than anything. He decided to go back to the workroom and see how Delyth was doing. Yes. That would be appropriate. And he wouldn't be mooning. Indeed! What was Louisa talking about?

Delyth had finished putting the pattern together and was laying it out on a table to examine the form. She stepped back and walked around the table to consider it from another angle. Simon stood in the doorway and watched her contemplate her work until she noticed his presence and stopped.

"What color will you make it?" Simon asked.

Delyth blushed. Simon hoped that their little educational walk down Bond Street hadn't dampened her enthusiasm. He might not agree with her color choices, but he craved her own delight in them. If she began restricting her designs to pastels and whites, he thought he might feel as though he had personally drawn a veil over the sun. It would be a travesty.

Simon realized he was smiling at the turnabout in his feelings about Delyth's use of color. He hoped the change was due to some new insight he had gained and not because all he could think about when he watched her nimble fingers straightening pins was how he could manage to have those fingers upon himself. Nor because watching her sweetly rounded body leaning over the worktable made him wonder how he could uncover it and charm it into his bed.

He almost stepped out again, but, at that moment, she looked up and smiled at him. Her generous mouth turned up at the corners and her eyes twinkled. Simon was transfixed. His body flooded with heat and it was all he could do not to snatch her up and carry her away.

"I think," Delyth said, her smile widening, "that I will try tangerine and pistachio."

"If you are trying to make me hungry," Simon growled. "You have already succeeded."

CHAPTER ELEVEN

The sound of Simon's low growl went right through Delyth's body. It was impossible for her to think when he looked at her like he was right now and when he spoke in that low, seductive tone. She dropped her pincushion to the table and turned to him, ready to do whatever he had in mind. The thought that she was in a peck of trouble moved fleetingly through her mind and disappeared. She moved to him and put her hand on his chest, right over his heart, and he lifted his hand to cover it.

"Come with me," he said, still in that low tone.

"Now?" Delyth's tone was in a higher register than her usual voice. Being around Simon Merrithew seemed to make her squeak.

"Now." He closed his fingers around her hand and turned in the doorway, taking her with him.

"Where are we going?"

Simon stopped and Delyth thought he looked a bit puzzled. "We're going for a walk," he said, finally.

"I'll get my shawl."

"Not necessary," Simon said, apparently more certain of their destination than he was a minute ago.

Not letting go of her hand, he led her to the library and through the French windows to the small walled garden in back of the townhouse.

Delyth had never been here before and wondered if she were about to get a lesson in floral hues.

Simon led her to a bench off to one side of the garden, against a wall of espaliered laburnum, just beginning to bud. It was a lovely setting, but Delyth wondered what it was a setting for.

Simon indicated that she should sit on the bench which, being stone and in the shade, was just a bit cool on her nether parts. But she sat and stayed seated. Simon sat next to her, and Delyth noticed that he had not flipped up the tails of his coat. Fine. He had extra protection from the stone. They could be here forever before his nether parts became chilled.

She imagined he had some reason for bringing her out here although she could not, at the moment, imagine what it was. Still, this was Simon, the man who had kissed her on Bond Street and kissed her again in his library, the man who had just now used his seductive voice and irresistible smile to lure her out to this cool bench. She was willing to wait to see what he had in mind. She rather hoped that he had changed his mind regarding that speech about being a gentleman that he had given her in the library. She thought that might be it and, heaven knew, she was ready.

"Miss Owen," Simon said, raising her hand to his lips. "Delyth."

"Yes?" Delyth raised her face, giving Simon an inquiring look.

Simon hesitated again. Was she going to have to initiate this seduction? She was perfectly capable of doing so and would if Simon did not make his move. Delyth waited patiently as Simon lowered her hand and stroked her fingers. She knew he wanted to say something. She wanted him to say something. But his proximity heated her blood and the stone bench cooled her bottom.

Before Simon could find the words he was obviously searching for, Delyth rose from the bench and, bending over Simon, took him by his lapels, drew him up, and kissed him with the full force of her longing, kissed him as she wanted to be kissed, as she had been kissed, kissed him until he took her in his arms and kissed her back. Once his arms were around her, Delyth sighed, loosened her grip on his jacket and wound her arms around his neck, giving herself up the joy of being in his arms, of being kissed by the man she loved, refusing to think of what would happen next, what this meant for her future.

After a kiss that went on forever and didn't seem long enough, Simon took her by her shoulders and put her away from him. "Wait," he said. "Wait just a moment."

"What? Wait?" Delyth was stunned by the sudden loss of his warmth and confused by his command. "Why?"

"I brought you out here to say something, to ask you a question." Simon's voice was low and his expression serious but not angry.

Delyth was still confused. "Then why haven't you done so?"

"I . . ." Simon hesitated again.

"My God, Simon. If it's too difficult for you to say, then perhaps you should just let me go back to my work." Delyth shrugged out of his grip and turned to leave.

"No!" Simon grabbed her arm. "I want to marry you."

"What?" Delyth dropped back to the bench and looked into Simon's eyes. She no longer felt the coldness of the stone. She couldn't even feel her legs. She could feel nothing in her body except the fierce beating of her heart. "You what?"

"Marry me, Delyth Owen. Live your life with me." Simon sat back down and reached out to draw Delyth into his arms.

"Are you daft?" Delyth pushed at his chest. "I'm a dressmaker. And even worse, I used to be costume designer in the theater. You can't marry me." She was obviously going to have to be the rational person on this cold bench.

"Can you marry me?" Simon asked, refusing to let go of her.

"Well, of course I can. In marrying you, I would only be improving my position."

"Do you love me?"

"Not the point," Delyth said, and asked, "Do you love me?"

"I just asked you to marry me."

Delyth sighed. He was not going to say he loved her, and she felt as though he ought to be able to do it. She'd give him one more chance. "So you did and I just asked if you loved me."

Simon nodded.

"You seem to be having a hard time saying things this afternoon," Delyth said. With that, she extricated herself from Simon's arms and marched back to the house.

The day had gone from bad to worse. Delyth had not exactly turned down his marriage proposal, but she certainly hadn't accepted it before she stormed back to her workroom and locked herself in. She had asked for a tray in her room rather than joining the

Merrithews for dinner. She was avoiding him and Simon feared that he had, in some way, irrevocably offended her. He had thought a marriage proposal would make everything right and it had had the very opposite effect.

"What happened?" Louisa glared at Simon over the dinner table as he pushed his food around his plate.

Simon didn't pretend not to understand. "I don't know," he said.

"Men!" Louisa continued to glare. "What did you say to her?"

"I asked her to marry me."

Louisa's expression softened. "You did? That's excellent."

"Is it?" Simon wondered how excellent it could be if he felt as though he had a large object lodged in his chest.

"You love her." It wasn't a question.

Simon nodded.

"And she said . . . ?" Louisa took a sip of wine as she waited for the answer.

"And she didn't say no," Simon said.

Louisa frowned.

"But she didn't say yes," he admitted after his own swallow of wine. "And she hasn't spoken to me since. Nor allowed me entrance to the workroom."

"Yes," Louisa said. "I had noticed that. What are you going to do?"

"Sleep on it," Simon said, throwing his napkin on the table and stalking out of the room.

Simon lay in bed staring at the canopy. He supposed that coming to his room was a better option than sitting at the dinner table, not eating, with Louisa alternating between glaring and sympathy. Neither of those responses were tolerable at this moment. However, despite his parting remark to Louisa, he was not going to be able to get any sleep. It seemed possible that he was going to die of either starvation or exhaustion unless he was able to resolve the debacle left in the wake of his marriage proposal, his ridiculously inept marriage proposal. He imagined he probably deserved a long, uncomfortable death. And he imagined that both Delyth and Louisa might agree at this moment.

He turned over and pulled the covers over his head. What was he going to do? Despite his failure to tell Delyth that he loved her, he realized that he did and that he could not conceive of a future without her in it. Abruptly, Simon sat up and punched his pillow. *Damn.* He really wasn't going to sleep tonight. Throwing off the rest of his covers, he got up, lit a candle, and fumbled for his banyan. He hoped he had a book worth reading in the room. He was certainly not going down to the library tonight.

Simon found *Sense and Sensibility* beside his chair. Had he really brought that up to his room? Louisa must have left it for him. She'd talked about it enough that he was aware that it was about family, one of Louisa's favorite subjects. Why not? He picked it up and turned to the first page. There was a death in the third paragraph. Just what he needed.

He was paging ahead to see if anyone else was scheduled to die right away when he heard a knock on his door. "Enter." Yes, he was snarling, but he was in no mood to see anyone . . .

Except the person who slipped through the door and closed it behind her. Delyth, in her night rail and shawl and bare feet, almost as she had looked when they met in the library. Delyth. The one person he did want to see, although he had no idea at this moment what he was going to say to her. He dropped the book and stood, looking, he suspected, particularly stupid.

"Am I disturbing you?" Delyth asked in a low voice.

"As you see." He held his hands out.

"Oh. You're reading." She craned her neck, trying to read the title of the book.

"*Sense and Sensibility,*" Simon said to save her time. "And no. You're not disturbing me." Except in the most irrational way.

"I . . . I thought we should talk," Delyth said. "I left you rather precipitously in the garden."

Simon took her hands and led her to a chair. "Nothing I didn't deserve," he said.

"You didn't. You had just done me a great honor and I marched off in a temper. I came to apologize and . . ."

"And?" Simon asked, still holding both her hands.

"And to say yes," Delyth said, taking her hands from his and sliding them around his waist. "You don't need to tell me that you love me. I know."

Simon blinked. It seemed that his life had changed completely in the last minute. "You do?"

"Yes. I knew by the way you kissed me," Delyth said, turning him toward his bed. "Now, let us see what other ways we might tell each other."

Simon's entire body came to attention. Delyth Owen, round, smooth, delectable, delightful Delyth Owen had come to his room to take him to bed. Who was he to deny her?

The covers were a rumpled testament to his poor attempt at sleeping. He thought about straightening them, but decided to put his time to better use. He leaned down and kissed Delyth until she softened against him, and then dragged her nightdress up her body until it bunched at her shapely hips.

Delyth immediately took the hint and raised her arms, allowing him to pull the gown over her head.

Simon's first inclination was to tumble her onto the bed. His second was to inspect the treasure that had been delivered to him tonight. He stepped back and examined the woman who had said she'd marry him. "You are even more beautiful naked," he said.

Delyth blushed, and Simon could see that her entire body turned a delicate shade of pink. Her rosy nipples darkened and, as he looked at them, crinkled and stood up. Her cloud of dark hair floated about ivory shoulders, her tongue darted out to moisten her plush lips, and her blue, blue eyes dilated.

Then Simon tumbled her, lifting her into his arms and dropping her into the center of his bed, following her down as her limbs came around him and her opulent little body pressed against his. Her mouth opened in invitation, which Simon accepted. The kiss became a duel of tongues and the duel of tongues became a duel of arms and legs. Delyth bowed against him and Simon responded, entering her without hesitation. Making her his in a single moment. The moment extended into others, time moved out of ken, their bodies met in passion and in love and, when Delyth cried out her release, Simon was there with her.

CHAPTER TWELVE

Delyth rolled over and stretched, then sat up with a sudden start. Where was she? She looked around and sighed. She was in her assigned room at Merrithew House. She flopped back down on her pillows and took a moment to recall how she got here.

She had started out the evening in Simon Merrithew's room. In Simon Merrithew's bed! The soreness of her muscles (indeed the soreness of muscles she was sure she had never used before last night) and the tingling sensation elsewhere in her body were palpable reminders of how she had spent the time before she crept back to this room in the early hours of the morning. She had agreed to marry Simon. Even now, luxuriating in the afterglow of anticipating their wedding vows, she wondered what people would think when Mr. Merrithew announced his betrothal to a dressmaker. The thought put a damper on the fires still smoldering within her, but not enough of a damper to cause her to leap from her bed and take back her acceptance.

She still had a workday ahead of her. Regardless of a proposed marriage to a gentleman of the ton, Delyth was still determined to dress his sister for the coronation and to do whatever else would please both Louisa Merrithew and Felicity Dawkins. She owed them both so much. Delyth threw back the covers and pulled out the clothes she would wear today. Nothing good enough for the affianced wife of Simon Merrithew, but it would do for Miss Merrithew's dressmaker.

My word. She had slept late and no one had awakened her. There was still breakfast on the sideboard and still a footman presiding over coffee and tea, but neither Simon nor his sister was in the breakfast room. Delyth accepted the tea offered her by the footman and asked, "Is Miss or Mr. Merrithew in the house?"

The footman blinked, and Delyth realized this was the first time she had ever addressed him. She waited until she thought he might have had time to process the question and then asked it again. "Not at the moment, Miss," he replied.

Very well. That was an answer. Not one she knew what to do with. She supposed she could go to the workroom and begin another pattern. Time was drawing short and clothes must be made. She should also make sure she had sufficiently detailed sketches for the coronation gown. That should be started right away. Delyth knew she would need help to meet the deadlines she had set for herself. She could feel anxiety flooding her system.

What was she doing? She had promised to marry Simon and yet was agitated about his sister's wardrobe. Would the betrothal mean she couldn't make gowns? She didn't know how this was going to work. And she could not bear to disappoint Felicity after all she had done for her, plucking her out of the theater and giving her a chance for a respectable career. Her heart gave a hard thump. A respectable career that would result in marriage to the brother of a viscount. There was trouble somewhere on the horizon. She just knew it.

Trouble ahead or not, Delyth proceeded with her day. Spreading out her drawing materials in the workroom, she began adding details to the sketch of Louisa's coronation dress. She would need to have Louisa's decision by the end of the day if she were to complete this on time. If she were to make the coronation dress and finish the other wardrobe additions that Louisa has already chosen, she would need the help Felicity had offered. This couldn't wait. Leaving her paper and pencils where they were, she went back to her room to fetch her bonnet and shawl. She needed to talk to Felicity about using Alice or Sally or whether she should find another helper and where she could get one.

Neither Simon nor Louisa had returned by the time Delyth was ready to leave the house. She supposed she could leave a message with a footman, but decided it would be better to leave a note. She headed to the library, since that seemed to be the preferred location for both the Merrithews when they were at home. She stuck her head in, briefly recollecting what had happened in there with Simon. And briefly shivering in remembered arousal. She had to put that out of her mind if she were to get anything done today. No one was about, so Delyth walked to the desk to leave a note.

She knew where Simon kept his paper and pulled open a drawer to retrieve a clean sheet. As she reached for the pen, she noticed a half-filled piece of paper laying on the desktop. She averted her eyes. She was not here to spy on Simon, who seemed to be the one to use the desk most of the time. She would not read his correspondence. And then something caught her attention.

To Editor, *Town Gazette*. Please find "Aglaea's Cabinet" for the next edition, Simon Merrithew

The handsome Miss S, London's newest diamond, showed the rest of the ton how an incomparable should look. Her sea-foam green silk gown and silver net overdress—undoubtedly the work of Madame Cecily—was the perfect foil for Miss S's silver-blond hair and flawless skin. Her turn as a delectable sea creature did not go unnoticed by the formally-clad fisherman of Almack's.

On the other side of the beach was Lady V, looking distinctly crablike in her red satin panniers. Do au courante ladies still wear panniers, I ask you? Someone should whisper the news in Lady V's shell-like ear.

One could go on, but perhaps one shouldn't.

Delyth dropped into the chair and took up the letter with shaking hands. No. She definitely shouldn't have read this. But she had and now her world had flipped onto its head. Everything she knew, or thought she knew, and everything she felt was a fraud. She had to leave. She scrabbled around the desk until she found the paper and pen that she had come for and began to write her own letter.

Simon Merrithew was out of sorts. He had spent the day talking to his man of business, his solicitor, his vicar, his banker, two purveyors of fine textiles, and Anthea Drinkwater. He had much rather have spent the day with Delyth, planning their life together, but he had, at least, put everything in motion to see that the marriage would happen as soon as possible. When the footman who opened the door answered his first question by telling him that Miss Owen had left the house before noon and had not yet returned, Simon's mood turned even darker.

"Is Miss Merrithew in?" he asked.

"Yes, sir." The footman nodded.

"Good." Simon strode off toward the library.

Louisa wasn't in the library, but arrived almost immediately after Simon entered.

"Where have you been?" she asked, taking her usual seat near the fireplace.

"Arranging a marriage." Simon stopped in front of his sister and dropped a kiss on her forehead.

"Whose?"

"Mine." Simon sat opposite his sister. "But I can't seem to locate the bride."

"Delyth?" Louisa sprang from her chair.

"Delyth," Simon said. "Have you some objection?"

"None." Louisa clapped her hands. "I love Delyth. But I suspect that there will be objections from other quarters. The viscount will certainly not be pleased."

"I could not be less interested in what Robert thinks of my choice." Simon stood and hugged his sister. "But do you know where the future Mrs. Merrithew might be?"

"I . . . No." Louisa looked puzzled. "She did not come down to breakfast at her usual time." She stopped and gave Simon an assessing look, which he chose to ignore. "And, according to Sterling, she left right after she broke her own fast. I thought she had things to do at the shop, but now I think she might have had something else on her mind."

"Well, I wish she'd get back. This has been a wretched day without her company." It has not occurred to Simon until today, as he went from one meeting to the next, how much brighter his days had been since Delyth had joined the household. He could barely wait until the arrangement was permanent.

Louisa, who had wandered over to the desk to look through a pile of correspondence, paled. "You had better see this," she said, showing Simon a piece of paper.

Dear Miss Merrithew,
Madame Follette's has my designs and will bring you the dresses you chose
for fitting. Thank you so much for your kindness, your hospitality, and your
friendship. It has been a pleasure to spend this time with you and your
brother. I will send for my things within the next day or two.

Delyth Owen

Simon read the note twice and looked back at his sister. "What is this about? Did I propose marriage to an insane person?"

"No," Louisa said. "I'd say she was quite sane. Take a look at what was on top of your desk when she came to leave a note."

Simon moved to the desk, glanced at the top, and dropped into the chair with a thud. His knees felt incapable of holding him up. "How . . . ?" he began and realized what a stupid question that was. Of course, he was at fault. He'd left out the damned, half-finished column and with his name on it, no less. Not only was it a stupid question, its answer was that Simon Merrithew was a stupid person.

He let the letter to his editor float back to the desk and looked at his sister in despair. "Can I make this right?"

"I certainly hope so," Louisa said. "I like Delyth immensely and I think you'll be miserable if she doesn't marry you. Which," she added, "looks like a distinct possibility at this moment. Now do something."

Simon rose and paced the library for several minutes, running his hands through his hair. "I need to think," he said, and left the room.

Simon strode though the Merrithew portrait gallery on the way to his room. He glanced at his father and wondered how he would feel about giving birth to such an inept son. He thought the late viscount would probably like Delyth and might even approve of his son's unorthodox choice of wife. But he knew his father's approval was not a factor in his choice of Delyth, nor would it have been if his father were still alive. Simon loved Delyth and that was the only factor as far as he was concerned. He gave his father a small salute and moved down the gallery, coming to stand in front of a portrait of his grandfather painted in 1765, the year Simon's father had been born.

His grandfather had been painted in a long frock coat and breeches of what Simon supposed he would call violet damask. The waistcoat was a lighter purple and the white shirt was excessively ruffled. The viscount's stockings were also white, but his shoes were heeled, crimson, and displayed a rather large diamond buckle.

Simon chuckled. Delyth was obviously born in the wrong decade. She would have loved these clothes. Recognition thrilled through Simon's body. "Louisa!" he shouted.

A footman stuck his head out of a concealed door at the end of the gallery. "May I help you sir?"

"Yes." Simon took a moment to lower his voice. "Tell Miss Merrithew to meet me in the attics, immediately."

"What are you doing?" By the time Louisa entered the attic, Simon was wildly pulling clothes out of a trunk.

"I must find Grandfather's clothes. I'm sure they're here." Simon did not stop his search but opened another trunk. "Yes!" He beamed at Louisa. "Here they are."

"Are you demented?" Louisa asked. "Why are you rummaging in these trunks?"

Simon pulled out the very suit his grandfather had worn for the portrait. "Look at this," he said. "Wouldn't Delyth love this?"

Louisa blinked. "Yes. I imagine she would. But . . ."

"Do you think it will fit me?" He held up in front of himself and looked down.

"It looks as though it will."

"Good. Find me stockings and look for the satin dress shoes Grandfather would have worn with this." Simon continued his search and pulled out a heavily embroidered, lime-green waistcoat. "This one," he said.

Louisa grimaced. "Are you sure? I think there's a matching waistcoat in there somewhere."

"No," Simon said, shaking out the garment. "This is the one. Trust me."

Ultimately, everything fit but the shoes. When Louisa pulled them out of another trunk, it was immediately obvious that the Merrithew foot size had increased significantly in the last half-century. "Drat," Simon said. "They're perfect. Ah well, I suppose I'll have to wear dancing slippers."

Louisa sighed. "I suppose you will." She looked at her brother, splendidly arrayed in fabulous color and sumptuous fabric. "I think I know what you're up to," she said. "I hope it works."

Failing to find a hat appropriate to the suit, Simon elected to go bareheaded, taking only his walking stick, which he thought would work in almost any century.

"Hush," Louisa said to the footman who opened the front door for Simon. "And put your eyes back in your head."

Simon managed to ignore the astonished faces at Madame Follette's when he stopped to inquire whether Miss Owen was there. Everyone was polite, despite the fact that they obviously thought he had lost his mind, and one kindly suggested he go to Henrietta Street. This had been his plan if Delyth wasn't at the shop. He executed a graceful bow, wishing he had the appropriate headwear to doff, and continued on his errand.

Anthea Drinkwater was not pleased to see him. "I think you have probably done enough damage today," she said, opening the door only far enough to peer at him with a beady eye.

"Please," Simon said, wishing once again he had a hat to remove. "Please. I must speak to her."

"Why?" Anthea had put her foot against the door and was not about to relent.

"I need to grovel," Simon said. "A lot."

"In that case." Anthea gave a grudging shrug and swung the door open.

Simon stepped inside and followed Anthea up the stairs to her drawing room.

"Wait here," Anthea said. "I'll see if Miss Owen is in."

"Thank you, Miss Drinkwater." Simon figured it wasn't too early to begin the groveling.

After a few minutes, Delyth entered the room without Miss Drinkwater. Her eyes were red, but her face was composed. The moment she saw Simon she came to a dead stop and clapped a hand over her mouth. "What," she said, "are you supposed to be?"

"I am," Simon said, "a man in love."

Delyth snorted.

"Please," Simon said, dropping down on one knee and taking Delyth's hand. "I have no reasonable explanation, but please let me apologize. I do love you."

"Oh Simon, you fool." Delyth pulled him back to a standing position. "I know you love me. No man who hated my color choices as much as you do would propose for any reason other than love."

Delyth stood back and examined him from head to toe, which stirred interest in some of the more easily excited parts of his body. She put her hands on her hips and cocked her head. "What are you wearing?"

"Don't you like it?" Simon asked. "It's my grandfather's."

"In fact, I do like the colors," Delyth said with a slight smile. "But, Simon, the embroidery! The buttons! I think I can get Anthea to put you on the stage. Where's your hat?"

"Yes," Simon said. "I knew I needed a hat, but I couldn't find the right one. Why did you leave without talking to me?"

"You hurt me, Simon. You said things about Lady Marjoribanks's dress that might have cost me my job and then you didn't tell me you were Aglaea. What kind of a name is that anyway?"

"It's Greek," Simon said. "But never mind that. I didn't mean to hurt you. Or perhaps I did at the beginning, but when I began to know you and understand your passion for color, I was so sorry."

"Then you should have said so."

"Yes, I should have. Is it too late?"

"You foolish, colorful man." Delyth took his face in her hands and went up on her tiptoes to kiss him. "I suppose I am going to have to marry you to keep you in line—and properly dressed." She stepped back. "I do like you in violet."

EPILOGUE

Reverend Hodgson expected that St. George's had rarely, if ever, seen a wedding like the one presently assembled in his sanctuary. It wasn't a large group, but it was certainly . . . interesting. Lord Fulbeck was in a front row, along with his viscountess and his sister, Miss Louisa Merrithew. Although Lord Fulbeck was looking rather dour and his wife absolutely grim, Miss Merrithew exuded enough happiness to make up for the rest of the row. A few other members of the haute ton were scattered among rows behind them.

On the right side of the center aisle, a prosperous-looking and well-dressed gentleman, who had introduced himself to Mr. Hodgson in a broad Welsh accent as the bride's father, sat next to a lady the vicar thought he might have seen on the stage at some time. Behind them, there were several other interesting persons, all of whom looked like they might be theatrical people. He hadn't asked. Behind these was a group of less flamboyantly dressed young women and one very large man. And, rather incongruously, the Duke of Barrowmore. Other than the duke, he hadn't the vaguest idea where they were from, but they looked happy to be there.

Right now, all he must do was stand next to the groom and await the bride. The groom was well known and well liked in London society and the vicar was surprised that his wedding had collected such an odd assortment of guests. Mr. Simon Merrithew, however, did not look the least bit discomfited, nor did he evince the usual jitters Reverend Hodgson had come to associate with his grooms. He looked calm, confident, and, one might say, triumphant as he turned toward the door through which his bride would enter. In fact, he looked the ideal bridegroom if one discounted the fact that, over the traditional bridegroom attire, he was wearing a violet damask dress coat from the previous century.

When the door opened and the bride appeared, everything became clear. Miss Owen's gown was a celebration of color: violet to match her groom's jacket, with pale yellow piping and crimson gussets. Rather than a bonnet, she wore a wreath of vibrant flowers. Her prayer book was the only subdued element about her. Oh, but she glowed. She seemed lit from within, her smile wide and joyful. All else about her paled in the light of that smile.

As the bride began her solitary walk down the aisle, the groom left his place in the chancel to meet her halfway. The vicar smiled. This would be an interesting marriage.

ABOUT THE AUTHOR

Myretta Robens has been nominated for a RITA, and has won the Holt Medallion. Her most recent work is a contemporary short story in the anthology *Jane Austen Made Me Do It*. She was a founder of the Republic of Pemberley Jane Austen web site, which she continues to manage. Myretta lives near Boston with her giant Corgi and a clowder of geriatric cats. You can find her online at www.myrettarobens.com.

~ALSO BY MYRETTA ROBENS~

JANE AUSTEN MADE ME DO IT
JUST SAY YES
ONCE UPON A SOFA

No Accounting for Love

Megan
FRAMPTON

CHAPTER ONE

"**D**o you suppose it's a good time to go in? I don't want to seem as though I was waiting until he was there."

Katherine suppressed the urge to roll her eyes. "But you have been doing precisely that," she said as she glanced at the watch, given to her by Effie's mother, pinned to her dress. "For nearly two hours." She tried to keep her tone as neutral as possible. Not easy when one had been enclosed in a carriage for so long. "So you might not wish for it to seem as though you were waiting, but you do have to acknowledge that you have been."

Two hours of listening to her charge as she discussed each and every facet of Mr. Henry Dawkins, whom Katherine was beginning to wish had never been born. Not that she begrudged the man his ability to exist, she wasn't that cruel, but she did wish he wasn't the focus of Lady Euphemia Hammond's usually flighty attention.

Apparently he was not only handsome and well-spoken, but more importantly, to Effie, at least, he was one of the very few not to have fallen sway to Effie's charms which, Katherine had to admit, were many. That made him far more unusual than merely being blessed with looks and wit.

Effie was petite, nearly as short as Katherine, but without Katherine's ample figure. Her hair was a lustrous gold, shining bright as the sun, many a suitor had told her—usually adding accolades for her sky-blue eyes, porcelain skin, and perfect nose.

Katherine had to wonder at times if there was a common vernacular amongst all of Effie's admirers, since they tended to use the same words to describe her: an angel, a goddess, a delicate fairy.

Anything but a woman, which was what Katherine most definitely was. A curvaceous woman whose appearance seemed to cause a certain reaction in the opposite sex, one that made her wish she could just swath herself in fabric like one of those Egyptian mummies so that no one could see her.

But even if she could swath herself, it just wouldn't be possible. In addition to being curvaceous she was also poor, so even though she was the daughter of a viscount, she had to make her way in the world. And since she was a lady, she wasn't allowed to work in anything other than a capacity in which it would appear she was not working at all.

Even though being Euphemia's companion in her first Season felt like work most of the time.

Effie could be very sweet when she wanted to, but she was also prone to temper tantrums, sulks, and the kind of self-absorption Katherine had found in the very wealthy and the very beautiful. Both of which Effie was.

Which meant that her parents, the far more sensible Earl and Countess of Kilchester, wanted to ensure their delightful slip of a daughter did not fall in love with one or more of the available men who were searching for a fortune, not a wife. So they hired Katherine, although the conceit was that Katherine was an old family friend merely visiting for a time. That way, honor could be maintained and Effie's honor would be kept intact until the appropriate man was found who could relieve her of it. And if she suited, Katherine would be kept on to help launch the marriage journeys of Effie's younger sisters.

As for Katherine's own honor, she was grateful she hadn't had to surrender it in order to survive. She was twenty-three years old and thus far had had six dishonorable offers, with none of marriage. She was on the brink of despair when Effie's parents had contacted her with their offer, which she had gratefully accepted. All she had to do, they explained, was chaperone Effie through her first Season, since her parents recognized that their young and spirited daughter was too much for them to handle themselves. Since Effie's sisters were, according to everyone but Effie, far less determined although just as pretty, Effie's Season was Katherine's baptism by fire. She was looking forward to the far less fiery girls. *Only one Season,* she kept repeating to herself. And then she would be launched on a career that wasn't a career at all, since ladies didn't work, it was understood, but it would keep her in food, clothes, and housing, so it was nearly as good as (if far more discreet than) actual work would be.

She would see to it that Effie only received honorable offers, and help guide her to making the decision as to who would be most appropriate to lavish adoration on Effie for the rest of her days.

This Mr. Henry Dawkins was not, as Katherine well knew, at all appropriate or seemly for Effie to consider, even if he seemed disposed to adore the girl. Which he wasn't anyway. He was a mere mister, not even landed gentry; his father had been Effie's grandfather's solicitor, which is how the two had met. Mr. Dawkins's sister was a businesswoman, proudly earning her living by owning a dress shop, while Mr. Dawkins was a bookkeeper.

Mr. Dawkins, Effie had heard, was working on the books in his sister's shop, which was why Effie was here. It wasn't enough for her to have captured the interest of most of the young men in her world; she seemed to feel a need to make certain that Mr. Dawkins recognized that he had, indeed, made an enormous mistake when he rebuffed her three years ago, when Effie was fifteen and just coming into her fairylike goddessness, or something like that.

Now that she considered it, Katherine had to say that she admired the unknown Mr. Dawkins; most young men would have leapt at the chance to compromise an heiress. Even if he had been immune to her appearance. Not only had he not pressed his advantage, he had told Effie in no uncertain terms that she needed to be wary of young men in the future who might not be so circumspect when she approached them in that way. So instead of wishing Mr. Dawkins to the devil, especially after two hours of waiting outside the dress shop, perhaps she should thank the man for not taking advantage of the young girl.

"I'm going in," Effie declared in the tone that meant that there was no arguing with her. In other words, her everyday tone of voice. She rapped on the door for the footman, alighting from the carriage, and barely paused to wait for Katherine's own descent before walking to the door.

"Wait a moment," Katherine said, tugging the edges of her cloak around her. Clothing tended to get disarranged when one had awkward things like bosoms and hips to contend with.

"What is it?" Effie spun around to face Katherine, her lovely face twisted into a grumpy pout. "You cannot convince me not to go in there, it is entirely proper for me to patronize Miss Felicity Dawkins's shop, given our family connection."

Katherine finished fussing with her cloak, taking a deep breath before she replied. "I was not going to try to dissuade you"—since that task was impossible, Katherine had found—"but I didn't want you to enter on your own, since that is not proper."

Effie's expression eased, and Katherine suppressed a smile of triumph. Since becoming the young lady's companion she'd learned to suppress many things, but at least she was surviving. That alone was worth enduring a spoilt debutante who, when it came down to it, had a good heart, even if it was buried under glorious golden tresses.

"That makes sense," Effie admitted, nodding in accompaniment to her words.

"Excellent," Katherine returned, grasping the handle and swinging the door open, allowing Effie to enter, then following her into the shop.

Katherine's first impression was of vast femininity, a profusion of gorgeous fabrics everywhere, with ribbons and buttons and jaunty feathers in colors that had never actually appeared on a bird. Three dolls were arranged on the shelves, dressed impeccably. There were a handful of live women inside, all of whose clothing was far grander than Katherine's shabby cloak and less shabby, but no less dull, dress underneath. She didn't think she had ever owned a gown in any of the colors on display here, and she wished, not for the first time, that she was less poor, less curvaceous, and more able to wear whatever she liked.

"Can I help you, ladies?" A woman, speaking in a soft Welsh accent, stepped out of the cluster of females and glanced between Effie and Katherine, a pleasant smile on her face, wearing a garment in a wide variety of colors.

"I am an acquaintance of Miss Dawkins." Effie was using her simpering voice, the one she employed when she wanted something. Again, one she used all too often. "Is she here?"

Katherine and Effie both knew perfectly well that Miss Dawkins was not here, since they had seen her leave a half hour prior.

The woman shook her head, a sincerely regretful expression on her face. "No, she has gone out. An acquaintance, you say?"

Effie nodded.

"Miss Dawkins's brother is here, do you know him? Perhaps I can see if he can spare a few moments."

Effie simpered even more. "I am acquainted with him, yes. That would be wonderful, thank you."

It was hard to believe more people didn't see through Euphemia's machinations, but then again Katherine was often startled at how oblivious people could be. Maybe obliviousness was one of the better side effects of having wealth and position, or in this case, a gown that distracted your thought process—you seldom noticed individuals who had less of both. Katherine, having no wealth and only a tenuous position, was in the unfortunate circumstance of being forced to pay attention to everybody most of the time. That she found amusement in trying to discern motivation in others' actions was perhaps her own welcome side effect. Even though it was terribly lonely.

"I will go ask him," the woman replied, turning on her heel and walking quickly toward the back of the shop.

"Did you see how fast she went?" Euphemia said. "I can only imagine what the ladies here think of Mr. Dawkins," she said, her tone indicating what she thought of the other ladies' chances.

Katherine hadn't noticed a change in the woman's expression, but perhaps Mr. Dawkins had dazzled this lady as he had Effie. Katherine would have to be on her guard around him, then—she had no wish to be caught up in admiring someone who would not admire her back. She had learned, painfully learned, that the male of the species did not want her admiration. They usually wanted something else, something that had everything to do with how she looked and nothing to do with who she was.

"He'll be out here in a minute," Effie whispered, sounding less worldly than she did usually. "I can't believe he is here!" she said, nearly hopping in her excitement.

"Of course he is, you made certain he would be," Katherine whispered back.

Effie's hopping stopped as she scowled. She did not appreciate it when Katherine reminded her of her own subterfuges. But since she was usually on to another subject within a few minutes, her ire did not last long.

"Well, he will be surprised to see me," Effie said in a more subdued tone of voice as she patted her already flawlessly arranged hair.

That reminded Katherine that her hair was likely less flawless. Actually, she knew for certain it was; it was too boisterous, too unruly, and definitely too red. But since both she and Effie anticipated that Mr. Dawkins was going to be struck dumb by Effie's beauty, she wouldn't have to worry about how she looked. He would not notice her.

"Lady Euphemia?"

The voice was low and rumbly, the voice of a man, not a boy. Katherine looked to where the voice came from and felt as though her heart stuttered in her chest.

This was a man. A very large, very virile, very large—but she'd said that already, hadn't she?—very attractive man. The only thing wrong with him, as far as Katherine could see, was that his eyes were behind spectacles, which perhaps explained why he hadn't seen Effie's beauty properly.

No wonder Effie was so determined to conquer him. Katherine wanted to at least storm his gates, and she hadn't even been introduced to the gentleman in question.

He walked toward them, a puzzled expression on his face. As he moved closer, Katherine could see that his large form—had she thought he was large? He was *huge*—was testing the limits of fabric. His coat, although modest enough for the bookkeeper he apparently was, was fitted perfectly, his trousers encasing legs that were probably twice the size of hers, and she was not a small woman. In height, yes, but not in width.

She'd never had such a visceral reaction to a man before. It terrified her, albeit in a very pleasant way. Pleasantly terrified wasn't something she was familiar with feeling, however, so she concentrated on keeping her breathing steady as he approached.

"Mr. Dawkins." Effie held her hand out, and up, since he was so much taller than she. And since Effie had a few inches on Katherine, she felt as though she were standing at the foot of a tree staring up at the leaves. A tree she would very much like to climb.

"Lady Euphemia, of course it is a pleasure to see you, but—?" His eyebrows drew together above the spectacles, and then

Katherine wanted to laugh, because how could he ask Effie what she was doing there without being rude?

It appeared he realized that himself, since he shook his head. "Never mind. It is a pleasure to see you."

Katherine nudged Effie with her elbow. If she was going to stare at Mr. Dawkins, she at least wanted to give him the privilege of knowing the name of the woman who was transfixed by his massive self.

Because although he was large, it was clear that almost all of his size was muscle. Did he drag around trees that ladies stared up at or something? Perhaps he was a literal bookkeeper, in that he kept the books—all of them—and had to lug them around for people who wished to read them.

That, or he was just naturally muscular and large.

"This is my companion, Miss Katherine Grant." Katherine thrust her hand out, for once not feeling as though she was too large herself. He could probably lug her and all the volumes of Gibbon's *The History of the Decline and Fall of the Roman Empire* without even breathing that hard.

"It is a pleasure to meet you, Miss Grant." He gazed into her eyes as he spoke, and she felt her legs tremble. As in if she were not corseted up within an inch of her skin she would actually fall. His eyes were a dark, dark blue, so dark they almost appeared black, and his brow was furrowed as though he was concentrating very hard, and it felt almost as though he were concentrating on her.

My goodness. No wonder Effie was all aflutter. And no wonder that impetuous fifteen-year-old Effie had flung herself at this man, this handsome giant. Thank goodness he hadn't reciprocated. Never mind the ensuing scandal, he might have crushed her under his weight.

"The pleasure is mine, Mr. Dawkins," Katherine replied, not untruthfully.

It seemed as though he held her hand a fraction longer than was necessary, and Katherine felt the impact of that touch through her entire body. She wanted to shift, to relieve some of the pleasant discomfort—another oxymoron she'd have to pick apart at some time when she wasn't quite so befuddled—to keep his hand in hers, to find out what his muscles felt like under her fingers.

Plainly put, she wanted. And she had never wanted like this in her life. Pleasantly terrified, indeed.

CHAPTER TWO

Henry tried to keep his expression from revealing what he was feeling, mainly because if Lady Euphemia knew just how dismayed he was at seeing her here in his sister's shop, she would likely redouble her efforts to capture his interest. And he knew precisely that that was why she was here—she hadn't taken well to being rejected three years ago, when she was just coming into her beauty, and he knew her well enough to recognize the determined look in her eye as she regarded him.

If only Effie weren't so piqued, he wouldn't have been standing in this bastion of femininity feeling like he was a very large, very male intruder. Worried he was going to bump up against one or another of the ladies in the shop and cause them to faint or scream or something. This was why he preferred to stay in the back with the books. A solid desk and door between himself and the customers.

He wished his mother and his sister had found an affinity for something less . . . frilly. Like books, or the piano, or, or—well, come to think of it, there were very few things a respectable woman could make a living at. And his sister needed to make a living, since his earnings, even though he was getting more clients, were not enough to support her. Not that she'd take money from him anyway. He just wished how she had decided to make money was less filled with women scurrying about, making him acutely aware of just how large he was in comparison. Although the chances of his having found anything else to do were unlikely, since he'd grown up—and up, and up again—in the shop.

He darted a glance at Effie's companion, a woman who looked nearly as out-of-place as he did in the shop. Not that she wasn't a woman—she most definitely was—but her clothing was as dark and plain as his, and she was worrying her bottom lip with her teeth as she glanced around, her hands doing some sort of unconscious fluttery movement by her skirts.

He understood uncomfortable people; most people were uncomfortable when confronted with his size. She didn't seem to be bothered by him, more bothered by the place she found herself in, but that just meant he could try to put her at ease, as best as he could. And the bonus was that it meant he wouldn't be paying as much attention to Effie, so perhaps she would get the hint.

"Miss Grant, is this your first time in London?" He tried to keep his voice low and measured, but its timbre still caused a few of the ladies in the shop to start in surprise. He suppressed a wince. He felt comfortable among numbers as he never felt comfortable with people. Numbers didn't make him feel too large, too muscular, or too brutish. They accepted him as he was. Why couldn't the rest of the world?

But never mind that, the lady was responding. "Actually," she began in a dry tone, "I have lived here my entire life. So if you consider that I have never left, then yes, this is my first time in London."

Wonderful. He had asked her one question—*one!*—and it had been the stupidest thing in the world to have said.

"But I can understand you thinking I have just arrived." She gestured to her dress and offered an embarrassed smile.

Now he wished he could just sink into the ground. Not only had he asked an inane question, she had assumed he had asked because her clothing was not what most polished ladies in town would wear. And she wasn't wrong, but he couldn't very well acknowledge that.

Not for the first time Henry wished he had been born smaller. Or mute.

"Ah, yes. Well, then." Because that was the most intelligent response he could think of. He wished he could smack himself in the head.

"Mr. Dawkins," Lady Euphemia began, then stopped herself to giggle, putting her tiny little hand in front of her rosebud mouth. "It feels so odd to be so formal, and yet in town you are not Henry, and I am not Effie." She giggled again.

"But it would not be correct for Mr. Dawkins to address you so familiarly, Lady Euphemia," Miss Grant said with a glance toward Henry. He could have sworn she had a look of repressed irritation, and he didn't feel quite as bad for being an idiot. Because if she felt comfortable enough to share that kind of commiseration about Effie with him, maybe he hadn't insulted her irreparably.

Effie's rosebud mouth turned a bit . . . thorny, as she twisted it into a pout. An adorable pout, to be sure, but a pout nonetheless.

"Well, *Mr. Dawkins*," she said, over-enunciating as she glared at her companion, "I came by because it has been so long since I have seen your sister, and you, of course, and I was hoping I could purchase some gowns, but since she is not here, perhaps you could inform her I called, and if you would be so kind as to escort me and Miss Grant to our carriage . . . ?" And she tilted her face up to his and nearly flattened him with the brilliance of her smile. It really was blinding, and if he had ever wondered if he felt an iota of attraction to his family acquaintance, he could answer that now. Definitely not.

He shot a desperate look at Effie's companion, hoping the woman would be able to deflect some of Effie's focus.

"Effie, before we go, we should see if Miss Dawkins's shop has any blue ribbons that could go on your new hat." Miss Grant took Effie's arm and steered her away toward a table covered with, presumably, ribbons. That were blue.

She glanced behind her, a wry smile on her lips, and Henry heaved a deep sigh of relief. Perhaps Effie would get so distracted by the prospect of ribbons she'd forget all about the prospect of him.

Although if that happened, it would mean she'd realized she didn't require the attention of every single person in the room. Which would never happen.

Katherine suppressed a snort at seeing Mr. Dawkins's face. It didn't make any sense, but seeing him so discomfited only made him more attractive, although Katherine would guess Effie wouldn't feel the same way. There was something so warmly appealing about him, even beyond his admittedly good looks and impressive physique. Even his glasses made him look appealing. As though there was a shy person hiding inside the hulking giant, a man only Katherine could see.

"And we will get you a ribbon or two as well," Effie was saying, now leading the way to the table. Katherine still felt his presence behind her, his gratitude nearly palpable in the small shop.

"That is not necessary," Katherine murmured, even though she knew it was useless to argue. She already had a collection of things Effie had insisted on purchasing for her, even though she protested she didn't need anything. If Effie were to somehow decide to buy her a small cottage somewhere, that would be useful, but as of now, Katherine's bedroom was cluttered with porcelain figurines, jewelry that was not to her taste, and many, many ribbons in bright colors, all of which would clash with Katherine's drab clothing.

Not that she didn't appreciate Effie's generosity—she did, and she knew the girl was motivated by kindness. It was just that there were only so many small pottery horses a woman could own without feeling as though she was somehow expected to transform into a small horse herself, just to fit in.

Dear God, what if Effie's younger sisters also deluged her with gifts? She'd end up overcome with stitched handkerchiefs, ferns in glass cases, or perhaps just numerous portraits of themselves painted by their swains.

Please don't let them get painted by too many swains, Katherine thought.

"Oh!" Effie exclaimed, spinning around to face Mr. Dawkins. Katherine did as well, telling herself it was just to follow what Effie was saying. Not because she wanted to look at him again. "I've just had the most wonderful idea." She clapped her hands and blinked as Katherine braced herself for what was to emerge from her charge's mouth.

Mr. Dawkins, poor fellow, clamped his teeth together so tightly she saw his jaw muscles clench.

"It is for Henry—Mr. Dawkins, that is," Effie corrected with a flutter of her lashes, "to be my partner to practice my dance lessons."

"Lady Euphemia," Katherine began, while at the same time Mr. Dawkins said, "My lady," each of their respective tones exhibiting their skepticism at the plan.

"It will be perfectly respectable, and since you are such an old friend of the family, there will be nothing untoward about it. Plus Katherine will be there, so it is all aboveboard."

This was precisely the kind of trouble Katherine had been engaged to circumvent, and yet here she was, unable to think quickly enough to halt the ridiculous plan in its tracks.

"I cannot dance." Mr. Dawkins's tone was abrupt, and entirely awkward.

Oh, thank God, Katherine thought.

Only— "Excellent! So we can learn together," Effie said brightly.

"But," Mr. Dawkins began, only to have Effie wave a delicate finger in his direction.

"I am considering who will be making the gown I will wear to the king's coronation. I do wish to give the honor to your sister, but if you cannot do me this favor . . ." She let the words dangle there, but Katherine felt as though she could see the words nearly wrap around the poor man's throat.

"I agree," he said at last in a low voice.

"I knew you would," Effie enthused. "Come to my parents' house tomorrow at three o'clock. It has been so lovely seeing you," she said, taking Katherine's arm and heading for the door.

Henry stood gaping long after the door to the shop had shut behind the two ladies. How had he gotten enmeshed in Effie's schemes—again? He'd thought that once she was a lady in town that she would change, but apparently not. And he had hoped that once he was older, he would be able to withstand any female machinations thrown his way, but again, apparently not.

Dancing. If his sister were to get the dressing of the admittedly lovely Lady Euphemia, he would have to dance with her. Not to mention dance to her tune. He chuckled without humor at the thought.

Effie's companion had tried to speak up, but Effie had just rolled right over both of their objections, as he should have predicted she would.

Not for the first time, he cursed his appearance. He knew full well he attracted more than his fair share of female attention, and Lady Euphemia was not the most obvious nor the most unsuitable lady he seemed to have acquired among his list of admirers, but she was the most persistent. It had taken him an hour to persuade her that no, she was not in love with him, and no, he would not risk everything to be with her. And that had been when she was fifteen.

She was eighteen now, and her self-absorbed interest in him did not appear to have abated.

He groaned as he removed his spectacles, rubbing his palm over his face, wishing he could just be left alone to do his work and help his sister. Although that was what he'd be doing, wasn't it? Helping her? If she were known to be dressing Lady Euphemia, who was likely the reigning beauty of the ton, then customers would be flocking to her shop to have her do the same for them. Then maybe he wouldn't have to be so worried about her future, and their mother's. It was their mother's dress shop originally, but his sister had taken over after Henry had shared some hard truths about the shop's finances with their mother. She had protested vehemently, but had finally seen the sense in relinquishing the shop to Felicity. It would take a tremendous success—something like dressing the desirable Lady Euphemia—to make it so he would worry less.

Not that he found Effie at all desirable. Beautiful, yes, but not the kind of woman he could see himself with.

Her companion, on the other hand. Something about her intrigued him; perhaps it was her shockingly red hair, or pale skin, or dark brown eyes. Or, most likely, it was that she was built like a woman, not a waif or a statue. She had curves that made him want to touch her, and he wondered what she would look like if Felicity had the dressing of her as well—all those curves encased in something other than the drab cloak and dress she wore.

He didn't share his sister's knowledge and skill with clothing, but he had enough of an eye to know when something—or someone— would be remarkable if just given the right context. What would Miss Grant look like if she were given a chance to shine? He probably shouldn't be thinking too much about that, given that he was in a shop filled to the rafters with ladies, and they would notice if he— well, he just couldn't.

He felt his face get hot, the way it always did when he was embarrassed. Damn it. He hadn't actually done anything, just thought something. And his face had turned red, and other parts of him had reacted as well.

And he was obliged to see the lady in company with Effie as he was trying to dissuade the latter from her interest in him?

That scenario just felt like a romp from a Shakespeare play. If Shakespeare had written about a lovely red-haired woman whom there was no mistaking for anything but a woman.

Damn.

CHAPTER THREE

Katherine fully expected Euphemia's parents would balk at having Mr. Dawkins reenter their daughter's life, but apparently not—Effie had taken her mother aside and whispered something that made her mother brighten up and nod, and that was it.

He was to help Effie dance, even though he did not dance himself and Effie's own dance skills were already well-honed, since she'd been attending balls in the country from the age of sixteen.

It was such a clear subterfuge it seemed ridiculous.

"It's nearly three," Effie pointed out, as though she hadn't been reporting on the time since noon. "I told Hen—Mr. Dawkins three o'clock, and he is not here yet."

"It is nearly three," Katherine reminded her. "Not three right now. He should," she began, but stopped when she heard the knock on the door.

Thank goodness Mr. Dawkins was prompt. She did not want to have to listen to Euphemia report on the time every other minute.

"Lady Euphemia, your guest is here." The Kilchesters' butler did not look pleased at Mr. Dawkins's arrival. Unlike Effie, who positively beamed.

"Show him into the ballroom, Jenkins, and please make sure we are not disturbed." Euphemia gestured to Katherine to follow, then both ladies made their way to the ballroom.

Each time Katherine saw it, she felt a pang of—of loss, or wishing, or regret. The room was enormous, empty of any furniture except for a few chairs against the wall and a piano in one corner. The windows were huge as well, going from floor to ceiling, with heavy green velvet curtains covering them. Effie had ordered that the curtains be pulled back, so the light—meager though it was, given that it was London, after all—streamed through the windows, throwing a golden glow on the polished wooden floor.

It was a room devoted to pleasure, designed only to provide adequate space and a lovely surrounding for parties. For events where every lady would have a dance partner, and the drinks would be sparkling and bubbly, as would the conversation. Where someone like Katherine, even, could find a moment of pleasure herself, a relief from her everyday cares and worries.

It wouldn't ever happen, not here, not anywhere, which was likely why the room filled her with such regret. She was well past the age of such fancies, and yet she had never experienced them in the first place, so her imagination insisted on dreaming up scenarios where she would be the belle of the ball, which was laughable, not when females like Effie existed, not when Katherine herself was so old, poor, and not attractive to marriage-minded men.

"Katherine, would you mind playing the piano?" Effie gestured to the corner where the instrument stood. "Henry, that is, Mr. Dawkins," she said with one of her delightful giggles, "you just stand there, and we can begin. Oh, I do so love dancing," she said, clapping her hands together in her enthusiasm.

Katherine suspected that what she really loved was the opportunity to capture Mr. Dawkins's interest, but she dutifully made her way to the piano and sat down, flexing her fingers.

"Play that waltz that I can never remember the name of," Effie said as she smiled up at Mr. Dawkins.

Mr. Dawkins, Katherine noticed, didn't smile back as much as grimace. Perhaps it wasn't that he hadn't learned to dance so much as he just wasn't able to? In which case, Effie's toes would take a beating, since Mr. Dawkins was so much larger.

And that led to some very inappropriate thoughts. She'd wondered if she'd exaggerated his largeness and general good looks, but no, she definitely hadn't. If anything, in the nearly empty room he looked even more massive, as though he were a Greek statue come to life.

Come to life to dance with Euphemia. Katherine sighed and turned her attention to the music.

She hadn't had cause to play much, not since taking up residence at the Kilchesters' house. Before, when she was Effie's age, she had played the piano and sketched watercolors and done all those things genteel young ladies did to show their gentility.

She had yet to meet a gentleman who was passionate about a lady's ability to stitch neatly, but if such a gentleman were to exist, perhaps she could dazzle him with her talent.

And while she was dreaming, perhaps she could find a gentleman who didn't assume that her hair color and generous figure meant that she was wanton.

"Faster!" Euphemia's voice interrupted her thoughts, thank goodness, since the last thing she needed was to continue being mournful about her lot in life. She had a home, currently, her duties weren't too onerous—even if they could be aggravating—and she was able to enjoy the benefits of regarding Mr. Dawkins.

"Yes, of course," Katherine replied, taking a quick look over her shoulder.

The two were dancing, sort of, but it appeared that Effie had taken the lead, while Mr. Dawkins looked as though he were trying to tiptoe, which looked almost ridiculous, especially on someone as large as he was.

But it was only almost ridiculous, because honestly, the man was so impressive-looking he could have been playing leapfrog and still looked handsome. His face was screwed up in concentration and what looked like embarrassment. No wonder he was embarrassed, since he obviously could not dance.

"This way, Henry," Effie said in her impatient tone of voice. Katherine smothered a grin at seeing just how quickly Euphemia's need to have things go the way she wanted them to overshadowed her desire to appear . . . desirable.

"I can't," Mr. Dawkins replied, sounding equally aggrieved.

It was obvious that the two had known each other for some time. Actually, they behaved more like brother and sister than anything romantic.

Katherine shrugged, returning her attention to the music. It wasn't her place to categorize Euphemia's relationships. Although actually it was, since it was Katherine's responsibility to keep her from embarking on anything unsuitable.

But given how Mr. Dawkins seemed to regard Effie, she didn't think she had much to be concerned about.

"Here, you try dancing with him." Euphemia's pouty tone took on a much more sinister meaning when Katherine understood what she was saying.

She shook her head without even thinking about it, playing a very strident chord in the process. "I have to play for you, I know you do not enjoy playing, Lady Euphemia." Perhaps if she reminded Effie that it was Katherine's place to take the less pleasant tasks, she wouldn't make her dance with Mr. Dawkins.

Who, she could see, looked just as discomfited as she felt, which made her feel worse. Was the prospect of dancing with her so terrible? *No, you idiot, he just doesn't like to dance. He isn't thinking of you at all.*

Which also made her feel worse.

"No, you don't need to play." Euphemia came to stand beside her, her arms crossed over her chest. "You can just hum as you dance. I insist." Judging by her tone—and by the fact that the girl was the most stubborn person Katherine had ever met—she knew it was either comply now, or comply in half an hour after hearing a litany of reasons why she should comply. And since she had no idea if Mr. Dawkins had any other engagements that day, she took the path of least resistance, rising from her seat and glancing toward the gentleman in question.

"Effie." He paused and looked skyward, heaving a deep breath that made his chest and shoulders seem even broader. "Lady Euphemia, that is, this is not going to work. I cannot dance. I told you that."

"You can't give up now." Euphemia sounded resolute. And she should—probably the last time she had been told no was when he had told her no three years ago.

Maybe it was just as well Katherine wasn't a raving beauty. Imagine being so spoilt that one assumed everyone would do as she asked.

Oh, now that would be a hardship, Katherine thought to herself, a wry smile curling her lips. Poor Euphemia. Too beautiful to ever be denied.

"Fine." Mr. Dawkins glanced at Katherine, as though just realizing that she was there. His cheeks started to turn pink, and

Katherine resisted smiling even more at how adorably odd it looked on such a male specimen. Blushing, of all things. All because he did not want to dance with her. Or anyone, it seemed.

"Miss Grant, I assure you it is not that I don't wish to—" He waved his hands in the air as though the words were somewhere out there. "It is just that," he continued, only to stop and shake his head. "You will see. Lady Euphemia, you will most definitely see as well, and then you will rid yourself of this foolish notion."

Henry didn't think things could get worse, but then Effie got it into her head that he should be dancing with Miss Grant, and he could feel his face turn hot as he contemplated it—holding her, being close to her, stepping on her feet. He wanted to be doing two of the three things, but not enough to cause her any pain or embarrassment, and both things would occur if they danced. Plus they'd only just met the day before, and all he knew about her was that she seemed to have a secret, sly wit and her looks appealed to him in a way he'd never felt before.

He hadn't been lying to Effie when he said he didn't know how to dance. He'd been taught, many times, but just couldn't get the steps right. Ever. Eventually, Felicity had banned him from the exercise since she was tired of having her toes mauled.

"Well, Mr. Dawkins," Miss Grant said as she regarded him, another one of those half smiles on her lips, "I suppose we should attempt this, since Lady Euphemia will not take no for an answer. I promise I have very sturdy toes," she said as she stepped toward him, holding her arms out from her body.

Henry swallowed, bracing himself as she walked closer. He kept his eyes focused on hers, not wanting to slide his gaze down her figure because he already knew the effect she had on him.

Not that looking at her face was a hardship, either; her mouth was as lush and curved as the rest of her, and her brown eyes seemed to hold a spark of humor, a glimmer of something that promised fun, if he could just figure out how to unlock it.

He should not be figuring out any unlocking at all. Nor even thinking about it.

He held his arms out as well and she stepped into them, the skirts of her dress—another abysmal color, he couldn't help noticing—brushing his legs.

He placed his hand at her waist as she put hers on his shoulder. They clasped their other hands together and then just stood there.

"I believe here is where you are to hum, Miss Grant," Henry said at last, feeling like the stupidest clod in the world.

"That's correct, you have to hum, Katherine," Effie ordered from where she stood, about ten feet away. Henry had nearly forgotten she was still there, since he was so engrossed in not staring at certain parts of Miss Grant. He wondered if this was the first time someone had overlooked Effie's presence.

Henry was just wondering what Effie would do if he admitted to having forgotten about her when Miss Grant spoke. "Certainly. Humming is one of those skills young ladies are taught in the schoolroom. I can do that."

"Was it?" Henry asked, surprised enough that he actually spoke.

She laughed, shaking her head. "No, although we learned plenty of other fairly useless skills. Do you know I can ask for more sugar in both French and Italian?"

"Impressive," Henry replied, enjoying how her eyes lit up even more when she was speaking.

"Any time now," Effie's impatient voice cut through the moment, and Henry nearly jumped. Thank goodness he hadn't, since he likely would have landed on Miss Grant's foot, and he did not want her not to be able to dance either.

Although her foot would improve. He had no hope of his dancing ever being improved, no matter what Effie said.

He forgot about that when Miss Grant followed Effie's directive and began to hum, the same tune she'd played on the piano. He took a deep breath and began to move, wishing again that he was smaller, nimbler, and actually not in this room at all doing this thing.

But that would mean he wouldn't be holding Miss Grant's hand, which he did rather like doing.

But he couldn't talk to her now. Not only because she was humming, so she couldn't respond, but also because he was concentrating on counting the steps in his head, and if he stopped doing that, he would surely step on her somehow.

This was delicious agony, if such a thing could be said to exist. The delicious part? To be holding her hand, to possibly share a sense of humor—even though he had yet to display his, but he had shown his appreciation for hers. To be dancing in Euphemia's company, as he desperately tried not to reveal just how much more he admired Effie's companion than Effie herself, was the agony part of it.

"Oh, drat," Effie said, interrupting the humming as well as Henry's dangerously conflicted thoughts. "I forgot I promised to take a drive with my father this afternoon. I must go get ready, if you'll excuse me." She waved her hands toward them. "You can continue as you were. And Katherine," she continued, "could you walk with Henry to the shop and pick up more of those blue ribbons we selected? I think they will look lovely on Mother's second-best hat."

Miss Grant's expression changed to one of confusion, and her mouth opened as though to speak, but then her eyes narrowed and she snapped it shut again.

Henry was just grateful it appeared he would no longer have to dance.

"Of course, Lady Euphemia," Miss Grant said. "Do have a lovely time with your father."

Euphemia smirked, and Henry wondered if she was actually going to drive with her father—or perhaps had arranged to meet with some other gentleman, and was using their appointment as a cover for her subterfuge. But then why involve him? And make it seem as though she continued to be interested in him?

He could live to be a thousand years old, and yet he didn't think he would ever understand women.

Effie waved at them again and was out the door in seconds, leaving them standing together in the middle of the vast empty room, still holding hands, poised as though to dance again.

Miss Grant snatched her hands away and put them behind her back, looking down at the floor, but not so much that Henry didn't see the wash of color on her face.

It was good to know they had blushing in common as well.

"What do you—?" Miss Grant began, only to shake her head and stop speaking.

"There are so many ways I could answer that, Miss Grant." Now that he no longer had to dance, or move at all, he felt much more comfortable. And also somewhat scandalously and inappropriately delighted that he and Miss Grant were alone together.

Did Effie consider her companion so old that there was no need for chaperones? Or since she was a chaperone, she had no need of one?

Not only did Henry not understand women, he didn't understand the careful societal constraints under which they operated. But if this meant that he could be alone with someone who didn't make him feel short of breath, or entirely awkward, then he didn't care.

"I could think that perhaps you were wanting to know, 'What do you want to do now?' and I would have to answer, 'Not dance.' Or maybe it was 'What do you think of the weather today?' and I would say it is temperate, and surprisingly sunny. Or 'What do you find to be most uncomfortable—being in a room with a complete stranger alone, or being forced to dance with a complete stranger in a room while someone watches you?'"

Her expression froze, and he continued.

"That is it, isn't it?" He shook his head in mock dismay. "And here I thought you wished to know what we should do, and if the weather was conducive enough to support those efforts."

She grinned, and he smiled back, surprised that he had been able to put together a few sentences that weren't idiotic and didn't also manage to insult her. Maybe there was hope for him yet.

"I am not certain what answer is best to that last question," she said with a laugh, "just that you and I, complete strangers though we are, are in complete agreement."

He gestured to the door. "Shall we walk to my sister's shop, since it seems that that is what Lady Euphemia requires? It would take us out of the room, which would remove one of the issues."

Miss Grant nodded, and he felt his chest relax as he let go of a deep breath. Not that he was breathless at being in her company—only damn, it seemed he was.

CHAPTER FOUR

Well. As though she hadn't found him attractive before when he was just an awkward handsome man, now she found him irresistible. He was still awkward, but in such an endearing way it made her heart kind of wobbly.

As well as her legs, and other parts of her as well.

But a lady, even if she was only an impoverished lady companion to a raving beauty, did not admit to feelings in Other Parts.

Other Parts were for Other Women. Women who could be ladies, yes, but women who had hopes of finding love with the gentlemen who caused those feelings.

She had no such hopes. Mr. Dawkins was a nice man, and definitely caused those feelings—no matter how inappropriate they were—but she knew full well she was not the type of lady he would ever wish to be with. She was accustomed to men looking at her, assessing, surveying, and making her feel as though she were being scrutinized, and most often found lacking (or too much, if she were to be honest with herself).

Long before this, when there had been more funds and fewer curves, she had entertained a few thoughts of what it would be like to be a wife, a mother. But she'd pushed all those dreams aside when it became clear that there was not enough money to live on, not if she wanted to keep her curves and not starve. And she might wish she were smaller, sometimes, but not so much as to wish to waste away from not eating.

And because of her choices, she still got glances from men, men whose gazes drifted from her irrepressible hair to her even more irrepressible figure.

But he kept his eyes focused on hers, not even drifting.

She wished he would drift. Even to let her know he'd seen her, not just thought of her as a companion to his persistent and stubborn childhood friend.

It was wrong, no doubt, that she wanted from him what she had gotten from so many others, and not wanted it then.

Perhaps it just proved how perverse she was. She sighed, then realized she hadn't replied to Mr. Dawkins. Had he just been standing there, waiting for her?

"Oh, my goodness, I am so sorry, yes, let us walk to your sister's shop and collect those very important ribbons." She fluttered her hands as she spoke, but he still kept his eyes locked on hers, despite her general waving about.

Perhaps he was just very, very focused?

And why did that thought make her get all shivery in that Other Parts Feelings way?

She swallowed and nodded, mostly because of course she had to emphasize her agreement with general hand-waving and head-nodding. She should exit the room before she decided she would entertain Mr. Dawkins with her pirouettes.

Just because she could dance better than he did not mean she should be pirouetting at any time.

"Well, then, let us go, shall we?" She plastered a smile on her face, trying hard not to allow her gaze to travel over him. But it was so, so difficult, because he was just so much there, and handsome, and there was so much of him.

Even her thoughts were nonsensical.

She strode ahead of him wishing she could just burst into flames of embarrassment and be done with it.

Henry followed Miss Grant out of the room, at last relaxing his vigilance and letting himself look at all of her.

Her dress was plain, but at least it fit relatively well. Her figure was lush and appealing, to him at least, and his hand still tingled from the contact with hers. Neither of them had been wearing gloves, which would have been scandalous from someone who wasn't a mere bookkeeper and a lady's companion, but he was grateful for the lack of fabric between them.

And it seemed she was just as awkward at times as he, despite her initial ability to converse. That made him feel another type of kinship with her, something that set something off low and warm inside. And not just *there*, although *there* was certainly interested as well.

It wasn't that she was particularly beautiful, even though she was definitely pretty. It was that she looked approachable, touchable, and he suspected that he wouldn't squash her with his size, should he happen to accidentally fall on her or otherwise bash her with his body somehow.

There was something to be said for that kind of attribute in a woman. The 'not getting flattened when accidentally fallen upon' attribute.

He chuckled to himself as they walked into the main room, where the imperious butler was already waiting with his hand on the door. No doubt Euphemia had informed him they would be departing soon.

One of the footmen arrived with Miss Grant's coat, and Henry took it from the man before he could be the one to put it on her, instead holding it out for her to thrust her arms into. She smiled up at him, and he felt the smile all the way down to his toes. Which reminded him—he hadn't stepped on her toes, had he? Maybe there was hope for him yet.

Or maybe he had found the perfect partner.

Which was far too dangerous as well as a treacherous line of thought.

The idea of it clung to his brain, even as they began the twenty-minute or so walk back to his sister's shop. That she was perfect, for him, even though the thought terrified him. He couldn't find anyone, not now, not when his family needed him. Not when he was accustomed to being the enormous oaf whom ladies admired but didn't want to actually speak to. To get to know. And yet it seemed she did.

"When did you arrive in London, Mr. Dawkins?" She glanced at him from under the brim of her bonnet, and he was grateful for the opportunity to look at her again. She really was pretty. "Or have you been here forever as well, like me?" She smiled in a teasing way, but not as though she were offended by his idiocy of the day before. More as though they were sharing a mutual joke.

Oh, how he hoped they were sharing a mutual joke, and that smile wasn't just her disguise for "I cannot stand being in this gentleman's company, I have to tolerate it for now, and I cannot be rude."

Maybe that was why she was walking so quickly? That is, she wasn't walking too quickly for him—nobody could, his long legs ate up miles like a hungry child confronted with sweets—but he hadn't had to slow his stride to allow for her to keep up.

"I—well, my mother came here from France and settled in London." That didn't answer the question, did it? And here she was likely thinking he wasn't a complete idiot. "And she opened the shop, the dress shop that my sister is running now. I was born here, and we've lived in London all during that time."

There. That did answer the question.

Only now it was time for him to ask something, and he didn't know what to choose—"Are you as uncomfortable as I am?" was hardly something any lady would wish to answer. And how could she possibly answer that without making both of them more uncomfortable?

"How long have you known Lady Euphemia?" There. That seemed safe enough.

"About three months." She paused, and the hand on his sleeve tightened. "Her parents asked me to assist her in her come-out. It is my responsibility to keep her out of any inappropriate situations." She stopped walking, and turned to look up at him. "I do hope that her acquaintance with you will not cause one of those."

He didn't process her words for a few moments, too engrossed in looking at her, and when he did, he felt his entire body heat up, and knew his face was more vividly-hued than any of the fabrics in his sister's shop.

Her eyes widened, and then she, too, blushed, only the pink on her cheeks merely made her look prettier. "Oh my goodness, Mr. Dawkins, you must think me the rudest person!" She slid her fingers down his arm to clasp his hand. "I know you have no such intentions toward Lady Euphemia, it is just that she is so impetuous, and persuasive, and I wished to warn you." She shook her head, her face bearing an expression he'd seen often in his own looking glass—one with equal parts mortification and annoyance. She took a deep breath, and Henry worked hard not to glance down at where her lungs, and other parts, were. "Warn you that Lady Euphemia is likely to rope you into something that you don't wish to do—"

"Such as dancing?" he interrupted, then wished he had just kept his mouth shut. Because now her pink blush turned a fiery red, and he realized what his words could mean to her, especially if she was as awkward inside as he was.

"Not that dancing with you is something I don't wish to—" he began, then dropped her hand and flung his arms in the air. "Look, I cannot say anything without getting it wrong."

"We have that in common," she muttered.

"Yes!" he said, reclaiming her hand. "We do have that in common. It is already so different from my conversations with most ladies. And we've only just met. Imagine how many more wrong things I can say to you as we get to know one another."

Her lips curled in a tentative smile. "Does that mean you wish to get to know me?"

This he could answer without getting it wrong. "Yes."

For the first time in her life, she wished she could just kiss someone. And then wondered why it had never crossed her mind before. Because if she were kissing someone, she wouldn't have to worry about what to say—her mouth would be occupied.

But probably the reason it had never occurred to her was that she had never met a man she had wanted to kiss, not until she'd met Henry. He was so endearing, and handsome, and large. Not that it seemed he had any interest in kissing her; he was charming, in his entirely awkward way, but his eyes didn't travel anywhere but her face, and she wished that didn't bother her, even though it bothered her the other way when men did let their gazes wander.

Perhaps she was never to be satisfied, no matter what happened.

But then the thoughts of satisfaction made her think of those Other Parts, and what's more, of Other Things, Things she shouldn't know of, but did, because she wasn't completely ignorant. Even though she was in a physical sense completely ignorant. Given that she had never even thought about kissing someone, much less those Other Things.

216

But he had said yes, hadn't he? That he wished to get to know her? That was something. And it wasn't as though she wanted anything more (even though she absolutely did); she had a duty to Euphemia, and the earl and countess, and that duty did not include distracting a very large, handsome acquaintance of Effie's.

Only—what if it did? What if she could make it clear to Euphemia that her old friend was simply not interested in her— because he was interested in *her*? Far too many hers. But if she could engage Mr. Dawkins's interest, at least enough to show Euphemia that he was not going to join her cadre of admirers, she would be rescuing Mr. Dawkins from Effie's attention and ensuring her charge was not acting, or anything else, inappropriately.

She could even say that her attempt to engage Mr. Dawkins's attention was entirely altruistic.

If she weren't lying to herself.

But it could possibly be a very good thing to do, not just because of how much he seemed to intrigue her.

She took his arm again and began to walk. She liked that she could make her stride as long and as fast as she wished, and he could keep up with her. So few people could.

"In the interest of getting to know you, Mr. Dawkins, how about we ask one another some questions?" She didn't wait for him to respond, which immediately made her break her own suggestion. "I already know you don't like to dance. What do you enjoy?"

She felt him shrug, and shivered a bit at the sheer strength she felt under her fingertips.

"I suppose I am happiest when I am with my family. My sister is hardworking and dedicated to the shop, and my mother is a strong woman. How could she not be? She survived the Terror by fleeing France and built a life here. I owe her so much." His tone resonated with intensity. "But that doesn't precisely answer your question." He gave a derisive snort, only now she knew it was directed at himself. "I know it sounds odd, but I really do like working with numbers and accounts and such. There's something so gratifying about putting things into their proper place, and making everything work together. So few things in real life do."

That last part piqued her interest. "Have you often been disappointed in real life, then, Mr. Dawkins?"

Another pause. "I suppose that it is not disappointment as much as it is I find I often have a lack of hope, Miss Grant." He shook his head. "I can't explain it properly, likely because I am not entirely sure what I mean myself."

"That sounds so sad." The words just came out of her, and she hoped he wouldn't think she was being presumptuous.

Thankfully, he didn't seem to take it badly. "It's not that as much as it is just . . . not. Not hoping is different from having had hopes, only to have them dashed." She felt him shrug again, as though it didn't matter. *It does matter,* she wanted to scream, only that was more about her own feelings than his. Even so. *It does matter. For both of us.*

But she definitely couldn't tell him that.

"What about you?"

"You want to know about my disappointments?"

He paused. It seemed to be a habit of his, to mull over his words before he spoke, and yet he still managed to sound awkward and unclear at times. What would he say if he didn't think things through first? Her mind boggled.

"I do. If you want to share them, that is."

This was a deep conversation for her to have with a gentleman she'd just met. Or even with just a gentleman. Or anyone, actually.

The closest she'd come to this kind of conversation was when she was by herself, late at night, and she was exhausted. Not at all the same thing.

"I think I am disappointed that this is the first time I've ever thought about such things as disappointments," she said, trying to keep her tone neutral. "It seems as though one would have thought of such things in the course of one's life."

"Maybe it's that you haven't been disappointed that often," he replied.

She smothered a snort. "No, it's definitely not that." She thought of it all—how she'd had a few Seasons, but had no offers. Offers that were honorable, that is. How her parents didn't have enough money to provide for her, so she had to take employment, genteel though it was. How she longed to wear gowns like the ones sold in Mr. Dawkins's sister's shop, only that would require funds, someone to wear them for beside herself, and a figure that wasn't more womanly than would fit into such a gown.

But she definitely couldn't share any of that. Not even with herself.

"I suppose I am disappointed that I haven't," and she stopped herself, Henry Dawkins-style, before she said something really awkward and uncomfortable.

"Haven't been kissed?" he completed in a low voice.

CHAPTER FIVE

From the expression on her face, Henry knew that wasn't what she was planning to say—what lady would even think of saying such a thing, anyway?—but after a moment she bit her lip and nodded.

And he felt himself breathe out.

Because he hadn't been planning on saying it either, but the words had just fallen from his mouth, and he couldn't, and what's more, didn't want to, take them back.

"We cannot here in the middle of the street, of course," she said in a low tone, one designed for intimacy, for the sharing of thoughts with one other person alone. And then she froze, right as he was calculating just where they could go that would be both nearby and discreet. "Unless you didn't mean a kiss with you, but in general." She covered her face with her hands. "Oh, my goodness, please don't tell me"—she peeked out at him from between her fingers—"please don't tell me you are now horrified at my behavior, or that—"

She stopped speaking as he reached to take her fingers away from her face, rubbing his thumb over the back of her hand. She slid the other hand down his arm and grasped his wrist. "I meant with me. Only with me," he said, and as he spoke he felt a fierce burning within him, a feeling he'd never had before, one of pride and possession. He knew other men often had such feelings, the ones that made a man puff up his chest and make it clear the female in his company belonged to him. Henry had never seen the point, either of puffing up his chest—he was big enough already, thank you—or of claiming a woman as his.

But now he'd met her, and now he wanted to claim her, but it was also reciprocal; he wouldn't mind if she put her brand on him in some distinct way.

And he had just met her. He'd never felt this kind of connection with anybody before. It was the kind of connection he felt with numbers and accounts, but numbers and accounts didn't converse with him, and they definitely did not have a figure that made him want to touch them all over.

Because that would be unaccountably—so to speak—odd.

"Well," she said in a more normal tone of voice, "then it seems we are in agreement. I would very much like to be kissed by you, Mr. Dawkins." She chuckled, squeezing his wrist. "Only I suppose I should call you Henry, and you should call me Katherine, if we are to be so intimate."

Intimate. The word hung between them, nearly shimmering in its intensity, and Henry's throat thickened, the want and desire rising up as it never had before.

No wonder so many other men did anything they could to assuage their base instincts. Only his instincts didn't feel base, not to him; they felt as though they had been smelted out of some celestial material, some higher substance that he hadn't been worthy of having.

Until now.

And wasn't he becoming fanciful as he became lustful? Who knew the two would go hand in hand?

"That explains so much about poetry," he muttered, "and here I always thought Byron and Blake were being hyperbolic."

"Pardon?" she said, her brows drawing together in confusion.

He placed her arm in his and began to walk, faster now, confident she could and would keep up. "Never mind. I know where we should go."

At his words, Katherine's entire body felt as though it had been lit from within. Never mind that he hadn't seemed to notice her; she could tell by his urgency and the tone in his voice that he did want to kiss her. Perhaps more, but a lady, even if she had Other Parts, wouldn't even allow those thoughts to cross her mind.

They walked quickly and silently, her hand gripping his arm, which she found, to no surprise, to be solid with muscle.

"If you're a bookkeeper," she began, hearing how breathless she sounded, but not caring in the least, "how do you maintain your . . . ?" And she paused, because she knew well enough it wasn't polite to ask a gentleman about his body, although of course it also wasn't polite for said gentleman to be speeding his way through the streets en route to a private place for a kiss . . .

"My physique?" he completed, not sounding breathless at all. He chuckled. "I finish most days going to a club where I find pleasure in hitting a bag filled with sand. It relieves the troubles of the day and allows me to indulge in as many sweets as I wish. I have a sweet tooth," he confided, as though it was something he usually kept hidden from people.

She found all of that adorable, not to mention rather exciting. The image of him engaged in that kind of physical activity—well. "I should like to see you," she murmured, emphasizing her point by squeezing his arm.

When he spoke, after a few moments of silence, his voice was husky. "I would like you to see me as well," he said, and somehow that made her general state of . . . attentiveness to him, to his whole personage, even more enhanced.

At last they arrived at a medium-sized, rather nondescript building. Mr. Dawkins—Henry, that is—withdrew a set of keys from his waistcoat pocket and selected one, inserting it into the door.

"Where are we?" Katherine asked, nearly in a whisper even though there didn't appear to be any people within earshot.

"These are my lodgings," he replied, also in a low voice. "Unless you don't wish . . . ?" And his voice trailed off, the expression on his face revealing his uncertainty.

Adorable. And exciting.

"I do wish," Katherine said, stepping ahead of him to push the door open and walk inside.

Henry followed, his throat thickening with desire. He'd kissed a few women before, ladies who, he thought, might have wanted to discover who he was beyond his size and appearance. He'd only been disappointed, but this time—this time, he felt as though she was different, that she could empathize with his difficulty among people, and feeling out of place no matter where he went.

She turned to look at him, her expression curious. "You live here by yourself? Not with your mother and sister?"

Henry shook his head. "Felicity and I thought it best that I take my own lodgings. I am not sure you have noticed"—and then he heard himself snort, of all things, but she merely smiled in response—"I am not very good in company."

She looked at him for a few moments, that warm smile on her face warming him inside, as well. "You might not be, but you seem to be very good company. To me."

And then she took his hand, placed it at her waist, and put her own hands on his shoulders, tugging him down to her mouth.

Oh. Oh, this. Her mouth was soft, and so warm, and Henry allowed his lips to rest on hers for a few glorious seconds, his other hand coming to rest at the other side of her waist.

Both of them standing nearly still, their mouths moving, the roaring in his ears the only sound he heard.

Well, that and how the fabric of her gown rustled as she shifted, how it seemed he could hear every move she made, even though she was almost unmoving.

Her fingers reached up to tug at his hair, and he lowered his head so she didn't have to stretch so far. His glasses shifted on his face, and he withdrew for a moment to remove them, placing them on the table. And immediately returned to what they were doing.

And then, when his lips had gotten to know the shape of hers, and he was feeling as though every part of him was acutely and intensely alive, her mouth softened, and her lips opened, and he felt the point of her tongue at his mouth, and he groaned, and opened, allowing her tongue to slip inside.

It was delicious. She nibbled at his mouth, and he could feel how she was on her tiptoes, reaching for him. He tightened his hold on her waist so she could get more support from him, and he felt how she stretched more, her mouth still on his, both of her hands now in his hair.

He let her take the lead, relishing how it felt for her to lick him, to tangle her tongue with his.

How her body felt pressed against him, just—

"Oh, Pythagoras!" he said as he stepped back, hearing how loud his breathing was in the quiet room.

She looked at him, surprised, her mouth red and moist from their kiss, her own chest—no, he couldn't look there, he shouldn't look there, but he couldn't help himself, her bosom was so lush and lovely, and—

"Are you laughing?" he said at last, when it was clear that she most definitely was.

She nodded, a quite unladylike snort emitting from her. "It is just—Pythagoras?" she said, her voice rising in disbelief.

And once again, Henry felt awkward. He had almost felt normal for a few minutes there, while they kissed. But now? Now he was once again the idiotic oaf who couldn't open his mouth without embarrassing himself.

But that wasn't fair. They had spoken, and for some time, without him wishing the earth would open up and swallow him whole. He picked up his glasses and placed them back on his face. Feeling as though he had just drawn a curtain over that moment with the gesture.

She shook her head, her eyes dancing with laughter. "I have never heard such an original expression, Mr. Dawkins," she said, and then she turned a becoming shade of pink, no doubt because it was odd for her to address him so formally when her lips had been pressed against his. They had agreed to use one another's Christian names, after all. But she must have forgotten.

And then it didn't feel so awkward anymore, not with her all flushed and rosy and smiling.

"I know it is not polite to curse in company, or anywhere, really. And I have my mother's temper, she's French, you know, and—"

"And French people are more likely to have quick tempers?" She arched an eyebrow. "That is a sweeping statement."

Henry ran his index finger inside his collar, suddenly feeling it was rather snugger than before. It didn't have anything to do with his wanting to take his clothing off—and hers, also, in the spirit of égalité—did it?

"Saying that is preferable to saying my mother has a quick temper." He shrugged in imitation of his mother's Gallic gesture. "If an entire people have a certain attribute, it is less noticeable when one person has a lot of it."

She chuckled, as he'd meant her to. He hadn't thought before of how making that kind of generalization could erroneously tar someone's reputation. He liked that she was smart enough to question it, smart enough to notice the anomaly, and yet didn't present her challenge antagonistically. That took art, a skill he knew he lacked entirely.

Not that he'd ever had cause to challenge anyone before; usually, people took a look at his size and demurred to whatever he had to say. Except for his mother and sister, of course, but they knew him. Did this mean she already knew him better than most other people?

Beyond the fact of touching one another's mouths, he'd have to say she did. And he liked it.

"But why did you invoke the name of Pythagoras in the first place?" She'd drawn nearer, her hand resting on the back of one of his two dining room chairs.

What could he say that wouldn't sound insulting?

Nothing, which was why he should probably just tell her the truth.

"Would you care to sit?" Not the answer to her question, or even the truth. Perhaps more of a prelude to the truth. An appetizer to truth, perhaps.

"Thank you, yes." She glanced around the room, and he almost apologized for how sparse it was. But she wasn't here to assess his living quarters. And he thought he knew what she was here to assess, and she had not found it lacking.

If he were honest with himself, he'd have to admit to being a hypocrite at this very moment. For so long, ladies and women of all sorts had made it clear they appreciated how he looked, and he'd felt as though they didn't truly value him.

But with her, he felt as though he were truly and entirely valued, for his outside, yes, but also for his inside. Perhaps it was the same for her.

She drew the chair out and sat, gesturing across the table at the other seat. He swallowed and sat as well.

He'd never had anyone but his relatives here. It felt odd, but also oddly right.

Like her.

CHAPTER SIX

"**W**ell, I have to say I have never been in this kind of situation before."

Mr. Dawkins made some sort of embarrassed inarticulate noise and took his glasses off, even though he'd just put them back on again, glowering at the lenses. He withdrew a handkerchief from his pocket and began to wipe them furiously, as though it was their fault he was so awkward.

"Do you mean the kind of situation where you are in a gentleman's house unchaperoned, or you've just been kissed by said gentleman, or merely that you are unaccustomed to sitting in the type of chairs I have?" He put his glasses back on and regarded her, that telltale stain of pink flushing his cheeks.

She tried not to laugh. But a little delighted giggle emerged, nonetheless.

"All of those things?" She wiggled in her chair. "That is, I don't have any quibble with your chairs. But the first two things, certainly."

And then his face turned an even brighter shade, and his eyes went wide behind his spectacles. "I certainly didn't mean to ask if you made a habit of this kind of thing, it is just—" And he stopped short, likely unable to find any acceptable words.

She had to laugh then. "Of course you didn't mean to ask if I was in the habit of being with gentlemen in their homes getting kissed. I was the one who said I've never been in this kind of situation before, and you were merely exercising your right to be curious." She took a deep breath. "I like that. Your curiosity. So few people are genuinely curious about one another."

His color receded, and she thought perhaps he wouldn't spontaneously combust. At least not right at this moment.

"I find myself . . . very curious about you," he said at last. His voice was so low she could barely hear it.

But she could feel it. His words resonated throughout her body, and it was as though each word—"I" touching her mouth, "find" making its way to her chest, "myself" making her breasts feel heavy and full, "very curious about you"—well, she couldn't even say to herself where those words had gone, but she thought she had a fairly good idea.

And it wasn't to her toes.

He swallowed, and she saw how his throat worked, the strength of even those muscles evident under the cloth of his cravat.

Oh, goodness. All of that was interested in, apparently, all of her.

Which made all of her very interested in return.

She rose so suddenly her hipbone smashed into the table, and she staggered back. "I—I should be going," she said, wishing she sounded more authoritative and less breathy.

But he had taken her breath away, hadn't he?

He stood as well, as was polite, of course. "I will escort you home." This time, the tone of his voice didn't do anything but make her feel terrible. As though she'd missed a moment, which of course she had.

But if she had taken the moment—if she had continued down that line of curiosity and getting to know one another and all of that—she might do something she would irrevocably regret.

Or at least know was not something she should be doing.

And she had the suspicion that he would regret it as well, since she already knew he had a strong sense of honor—look at how he could have engaged Effie's affections to secure his future—and she didn't want him obliged in that way to her.

Never mind how wonderful it felt to be kissed by him. To walk in the street beside him, knowing that she was safe, and secure, and he was interested. In her, of all people, and although she knew he was interested in her in that way—that kiss proved it—she also felt that he was interested in her. Just her. Without thinking about what she could do for him, or to him, or any of those things.

"Do you suppose Lady Euphemia will insist on more dance practice?"

227

He sounded as though he'd just asked, "Do you suppose I will have to continue having splinters put under my nails?"

"Why do you dislike it so much?" she asked.

"Beside the fact I cannot do it?" He snorted. "That is probably it, to be honest. There are few things I have set out to do that I have not accomplished, but dancing, it seems, is one of those things. And yet when I see people dancing, and hear the music, it seems like such a lovely activity. I wish I could."

"We can practice again, if you like," she said, her words rushing out before she could even register that she'd spoken. "If you want, if you'd be more comfortable with me, since—" And then she stopped, because how she could say it?

"Because we've kissed," he said in a less splinter fingernail voice.

Apparently he could say it just fine.

"I appreciate the offer, Katherine," and the way he said her name sounded so intimate, "but I don't think there is any hope for me."

"Don't say that," she rejoined, instinctively clutching his arm more tightly. "There is hope for everyone. Yourself included, Henry."

"And what did you do today, Henry?" He busied himself with washing up his dishes from his evening meal—something simple, and warm, and filling, as usual, although he couldn't say just what he'd eaten.

And why was he delaying answering, when he was just talking to himself?

"I kissed a woman who is the most appealing lady I've ever met. And that terrifies me."

He sat down in his chair, the one he'd sat in opposite her so briefly, and removed his spectacles, laying them on the table and rubbing the spot between his eyes.

"Why does it terrify you, Henry?" He'd found, through the years, that since he lacked someone to confide in—since he definitely was not going to share any of this with his sister—he just had to rely on himself.

Which was the problem, wasn't it? He'd spent so long relying on himself, and being the one that was relied upon, that he didn't know what to do when confronted with something he wanted, and not something he needed to do.

And what, precisely, did he want? "What do you want, Henry?" he muttered in a low tone, getting up to fetch a bottle of whisky and a glass. He poured out a healthy amount and sat back down, staring at the settling liquid in the glass rather than downing it right away. He was good at that, at seeing things he wanted, that he desired, and then letting them be. That was why he had a nearly full box of candy in his cupboard, even though he'd been honest about his having a sweet tooth. He rationed them out, one every few days, in some sort of test of his will.

But he didn't know if he could pass the test of resisting her, not after tasting how sweet her mouth was, or how it felt as though he wasn't entirely and unutterably alone.

He hadn't realized until she'd come into his house that he had felt so alone. He'd been grateful, at first, not to have the chatter of his mother and sister around him constantly. But now it wasn't the absence of chatter he heard but the silence. The quiet that meant that only he was there, and only he would be in the room, and only he would speak, and be spoken to.

"Why does it terrify you?" he asked again, lifting the glass of whisky to his mouth and taking a sip.

He still couldn't answer that.

He sat for another moment, an exhalation of frustration escaping his mouth. And then he leapt up, going to his desk where he kept papers and pencils, returning to his seat and putting his materials on the table.

Another sip. "This should be as easy as accounting," he murmured. "I can list all the things that are of concern, and see what conclusion I can draw."

It sounded so simple.

"In the first column, we can list Miss Grant." He wrote her name down, then underlined it sharply. "In the next column, we have my family." He wrote "Family Obligations" in the next column. "And that is it," he said, laying the pencil down, then picking it up to underline "family," since that would make its format the same as "Miss Grant."

He was nothing if not consistent. Perhaps he was nothing without his consistency, he thought sourly. He was a large obligation-keeper, at least in terms of how he saw himself. He knew that his family would insist that he do what he wished to do, but that made him run into the essential problem: He didn't know what it was he wanted to do.

Although he knew who he wanted to do whatever he did want to do with.

He stared down at what he'd written, all four words of it, then picked the paper up and crumpled it, tossing it onto the floor and raising the glass instead.

He downed the rest of the whisky, shrugged, and poured himself some more. Perhaps logic and lists and accounting weren't what were needed now. Perhaps he just needed to feel. To figure out what it was that would make him less alone, more full of hope, and less . . . obliged.

CHAPTER SEVEN

"Oh, you're back!"

Katherine started guiltily at hearing Euphemia's voice. *Yes, I've returned, and I've been thoroughly kissed. By the man you wish to capture for yourself.*

Thankfully she did not say any of that. "Yes, I'm back, although I believe I have forgotten the ribbons." She dug through her reticule, willing the heat in her cheeks to subside. Not that Effie would notice; Katherine could be on fire, and all she'd say was that she no longer felt the chill, so could Katherine put her shawl somewhere?

"Never mind them." Effie glanced around in a theatrical manner, reminding Katherine, as though she could forget, that the girl was only eighteen. Not that Katherine had ever been that dramatic, even at Effie's age, but she supposed drama came with that much beauty. "Let's go here so we can talk." Effie dragged her by the arm into the earl's little-used library; it was dark and cozy, and Katherine was probably its most frequent visitor, since she often stole down here to read when she couldn't sleep.

"What do we need to talk about?" Did she know about the kiss? She couldn't, not unless she was a mind reader, in which case the kiss was the least of what Effie might have gleaned from Katherine's brain.

"Henry," Effie said, uttering his name in a heartfelt sigh.

"Mr. Dawkins," Katherine corrected, acutely aware that it would be more appropriate—if not at all correct—for her to call him "Henry" since she had, indeed, kissed him, and that would seem to put one on a Christian name basis.

231

"Isn't he everything I said he was?" Effie continued, clasping her hands to her chest in a gesture definitely better suited for the stage.

At least it was reassuring to know that if Effie suddenly became less of an heiress she could make her living by acting.

Hopefully Katherine was good at subterfuge as well. She wished she could confide everything to the closest person she had to a friend, at least in near proximity; all her old school friends had married and gone to the country or somewhere.

And what did that say about her? Although that would have to rank after the fact that she'd kissed a man the day after she'd met him. Probably having a vainglorious debutante as a friend was slightly less awful than that.

"He is." She turned to look at Euphemia, feeling her brows draw together. "But why did you leave, if you wished to resume your acquaintance with him?"

"Oh, that!" Euphemia said, flipping her hand in the air. "You see, I told Mother that I had hopes of pairing Mr. Dawkins off with you, which is why she agreed so readily to his coming here. She worries that you will remain unwed, even though she does wish you to take charge of the girls."

That makes two of us, Lady Kilchester, Katherine thought.

"And I know that when you get to know Mr. Dawkins as I know him, you will be able to persuade him that he is indeed a suitable man for me to marry."

Oh dear. This was precisely the kind of circuitous plot a young girl would hatch, and one that Katherine had been hired to circumvent. Only—

"Did he say he wished to marry you?"

Katherine couldn't keep the skepticism out of her voice. Because a man who was in determined pursuit of one lady yet also convincing another to kiss him—well, that man would have to be a far better actor and definitely more polished than Mr. Dawkins was.

At this point, she should just purchase tickets to Drury Lane. Apparently she was desperate to see a theatrical production.

Effie shrugged in that delightfully artless way that seemed part of being a rare beauty. Katherine knew if she attempted the same she'd look confused rather than dainty. "He hasn't yet, no, but he will. I am so much older than I was three years ago"—yes, three years older,

Katherine wanted to point out—"and he must see me as a woman now."

"And so your plan is to pretend that he might become interested in me while you engage his interest?" Effie nodded in pleased satisfaction. "And then when he has proposed marriage you will tell your parents it was you he was interested in all along?" Effie nodded again, positively beaming.

"But don't think my parents will take that to mean that you have not done your job properly," Effie said earnestly. Even though that would be exactly what it meant. "They would know that even if Mr. Dawkins was interested in you initially, he would have no choice but to fall madly in love with me." And then she sighed, as though picturing it.

Katherine closed her eyes, resisting the urge to shout. At herself, at her charge, or even, perhaps, at the adorably large Mr. Dawkins. Henry.

If she could just keep Effie from him until the girl lost interest— *oh, very altruistic of you, Katherine*, a sly voice said, *keeping him occupied yourself.* But she knew Effie well enough to know that eventually Effie would find one of her admirers to be more appealing than Mr. Dawkins.

It was just up to Katherine to keep Mr. Dawkins occupied until that time.

And if she succeeded in this, she could handle any number of feckless young ladies. As long as she didn't break her own heart.

"It is nearly three o'clock. He did understand it was to be three o'clock today, didn't he?" Effie glowered at Katherine, as though it were her responsibility to ensure Mr. Dawkins—Henry—knew where he was to be and when.

It had been four days since that day. The kissing day, which had reached such importance in Katherine's mind that she now thought of it as The Kissing Day, just as important as Christmas, Boxing Day, and the Queen's Birthday.

She didn't know what she thought of herself, much less him, for having engaged in the activity. And even if she could take it back— which she knew full well she could not, it was not as though time traveling was one of her skills, she had enough trouble with embroidery—she didn't think she would.

What if that was the only lovely kiss she ever received? She would have to honor The Kissing Day for the rest of her life, if that were so. To recall that day when a man, a very handsome, awkward, and totally adorable man, had wanted to kiss her. Her, Katherine, of the red hair and the curvaceous figure and the occasional sly wit.

It felt wonderful. To recall the moment, even as it drifted into the past, to hold the few memories of the day in her mind and know that for those moments, for that time, she was desirable, and desired, and not just for salacious purposes. Though that was certainly an element.

"Katherine?" Effie's sharp tone snapped her from her thoughts. Her charge was still regarding her, now less glowering and more quizzical. If she were to ask just where Katherine's thoughts had been—well, she was going to have to think of a believable enough lie, since Effie was a very keen observer when she wanted to be. Although she and Effie had, much to Katherine's dismay, had the same thing on their respective minds.

Effie had continued to explain her plan of getting Mr. Dawkins into her vicinity under the ruse of having him get interested in Katherine. It was awkward for Katherine the first three times Effie went through it; the remaining dozen or so iterations were downright painful. She would feel terrible about it if she didn't know that the two of them would be a terrible match, that Effie's parents would never allow it, and she was fairly certain Mr. Dawkins would never be coerced into loving someone.

Just coerced into kissing them.

"Katherine!" Effie said again, more stridently. She was not accustomed to being ignored.

Katherine straightened. "Oh, yes, I am so sorry." She glanced at the clock, which was five minutes shy of three o'clock. "You sent Mr. Dawkins the note, and he did say he understood." Katherine was hoping that Mr. Dawkins was just as prompt as he had been the first time, or she would have to speak of him and what he knew and what he understood for much longer.

Please let him be prompt. If not to see me again, at least to allow Effie to stop speaking of him.

They both heard the sharp knock on the door after a minute. She couldn't help but look at the clock again; four minutes to three. She exhaled, not realizing she'd been holding her breath in the first place. He was here. Was he regretting their actions? Had he come to regard the day as worthy of capital letters?

Had he even thought of it?

What if he were so accustomed to kissing ladies that this was just another moment in his life? And it didn't matter to him, not at all?

But she knew, from his reaction, that their kiss was not a usual circumstance for him either. Unless he was just as awkward each time he kissed a lady, and she doubted that anyone, even someone as awkward as he, wouldn't have learned at least some finesse along the way.

She exhaled again, relieved to know she had talked herself out of believing that this was a habit for him. And wondering if their kissing would occur again, in which case it might indeed become habitual.

"Mr. Dawkins is here," the butler said.

Henry stepped forward, nodding in greeting. "Good afternoon Lady Euphemia, Miss Grant." His gaze lingered on her face for a moment longer than it did on Effie's, and she felt the heat of a blush steal onto her face.

"We are so glad you are here, aren't we, Katherine?" Effie's smile was one of the blinding ones she used on her admirers, only now it was directed toward Katherine.

The girl could not be more obvious. Katherine restrained herself from wincing.

"Well, you did make it very clear," Mr. Dawkins replied wryly.

"Yes, I did, didn't I?" Apparently Effie was incapable of recognizing when someone was less than delighted by her persistence, judging from her tone. "Let us proceed to the ballroom. I am attending a party in a few days and I do not want to be shown up by any of the other ladies."

"I doubt that would happen," Mr. Dawkins said as he waited for Effie to walk past him.

Katherine followed Euphemia, a sharp pang of jealousy at his words. But it was only the truth; there was no possibility of any other lady being as beautiful or charming (when she wanted to be) as Lady Euphemia.

"She is not aware of anyone but herself, is she?" Mr. Dawkins murmured as he walked beside her. Katherine felt his fingers touch her elbow, just briefly, but long enough to warm her thoroughly inside. "It is not outward beauty that attracts, but something that shines from within," he continued, but then he turned to her, an aghast look on his face. "Not that you are not beautiful, it is just—"

She trailed her fingers on his forearm and smiled at him. "I know what you mean."

And she did. She knew just what he meant, and what he really meant to say, which was that he found her more attractive than Euphemia, incredible though that might seem. And the fact that she knew that, even more than that he thought that, made her even warmer inside, making her feel as though it might not be her permanent lot to be alone.

Not that she was counting on Mr. Dawkins to remedy her lonely situation; they had only kissed once, and she wasn't given to the same flights of fancy other young ladies were. For one thing, she couldn't afford them, either in terms of her peace of mind or in actual fact. Flights of fancy, when it came to romance, were for ladies who didn't have to worry about where they would be living or if they would have enough to eat.

It did not escape Katherine's notice, however, that it was Euphemia's own flight of fancy regarding Mr. Dawkins that had allowed Katherine to meet him.

"Just as before, Katherine, you can play while Hen—Mr. Dawkins and I dance," Effie said in her usual peremptory tone. Mr. Dawkins looked pained for a moment, and Katherine had to repress a grin at just how uncomfortable he seemed to be.

She pushed that aside, stepping to the piano, which had now seen more use in the past week than it had during the entire time she'd been here. Effie scorned doing anything that didn't involve seeing and being seen, and it was Katherine's job to accompany her. And not on the piano.

She searched her mind for what she could play; she hadn't thought that music would be one of her duties in the Kilchesters' household, so she hadn't brought her music with her. Not that there was much music to be had in the first place. Her parents' house, once they were gone, had been handed to her father's heir, a distant cousin whose youth and general foolish exuberance gave Katherine pause. It wouldn't have been appropriate for her to live with him—not that he'd offered. He'd been too delighted at the prospect of setting up house in London to worry about where his newly-discovered cousin was going to live.

She could have stayed with him, she supposed, but it would have been awkward. And not in the deliciously adorable way Mr. Dawkins was awkward, but truly awkward—in the week or so before she quit the house, her cousin had already brought home two women with suspect professions and a half dozen inebriated men from his club, a few of whom had regarded Katherine with that look that made her skin prickle unpleasantly.

Thinking of that week, however, reminded her of a song that one of the women had sung to entertain her cousin and his friends—a simple tune that she had played for practice. She placed her fingers on the keyboard and began to play, casting a few surreptitious glances at Mr. Dawkins as he and Effie danced.

He really was terrible. Perhaps he wouldn't have been so bad if it hadn't been obvious—painfully obvious—that he was absolutely uncomfortable with his size, and that he might crush a random passerby if he stumbled.

But he wouldn't crush her, would he? She was—quite literally—made of stronger stuff. And the thought of having him pressing on her, all that muscle pushing against her, was enough to make her—

"Miss Grant!" Effie's tone interrupted her thoughts just as they were taking a very dangerous turn. She jumped, banging out an unpleasant-sounding chord.

"Pardon?" Katherine turned to look at Mr. Dawkins and Effie, both of whom had stopped moving (in his case she couldn't precisely call it dancing) and were looking at her.

"Your playing. It is nearly as bad as Henry's dancing," Effie said, sniffing disdainfully to emphasize her point.

"It is definitely not as bad as all that," Henry added, a rueful grin on his face.

"I think you should practice a bit. Both of you," Effie said, gesturing to the two of them. "Katherine, you can work on your scales and Henry, you can practice the waltz. I have to go look in on my mother to see if she needs anything." She ran out of the room, leaving them alone.

237

And this was where Mr. Dawkins would know that Effie was up to something, if he really knew Euphemia. She hoped he didn't know her that well. Although if he did, that would guarantee he would never fall in love with her—not that Katherine didn't want him to fall in love with her, only—*oh, hush, Katherine. You don't want him to fall in love with her. For so many reasons.*

"Do you suppose Effie is up to something?"

Well, he might have been awkward, but he was definitely not unobservant. And he did know Effie fairly well after all.

Katherine rose from the piano stool and smoothed her skirts. She had no desire to practice her scales, of all things, just because she'd been distracted by thoughts of Mr. Dawkins. Besides which, he was still here, which meant he would only distract her further.

It was best to face the source of her distraction, never mind that facing it—facing him—was far more pleasant than playing piano. Or eating ice cream on a hot summer day. Or doing anything that wasn't speaking with him, or looking at him, or anything to do with him.

Pythagoras, I'm doing it again!

She started to giggle at the thought, and his lips curved in an answering smile.

"What is amusing you?" he asked in that low tone. The one that made her get all shivery.

She waved her hand. "Nothing, really."

"Is it really nothing?" He spoke in a tone that blended hesitancy with confidence. As though he knew the effect he had on her, but didn't want to presume he knew.

She shook her head as she stepped toward him, walking into the circle of his arms. "Not entirely," she murmured, placing her hand on his shoulder. "Not at all, in fact." She felt herself start to blush and thought she probably ought to change the subject before she blurted out everything she was thinking. "I think we should start slowly. Perhaps practice preparing to dance rather than actually do it."

One eyebrow rose up over his spectacles. "You mean to pose in a sort of pre-dancing position? Like this?" He put one hand—his large, strong hand—on her waist and took her hand with the other.

She was grateful for his relatively low occupation, since it meant he wasn't required to wear gloves, and she wasn't able to because of her piano-playing. So their hands touched, bare skin touching bare skin, and the contact made her Parts—those Parts she shouldn't even be thinking about—spark up, as though he were actually touching her there.

"Are you all right?" he asked in a concerned tone of voice. Apparently her thinking about her Parts made her face go all odd and her knees buckle.

"Fine," she said, taking a deep breath. "How does this feel?"

She meant the pre-dancing position, but she knew right away that it was ambiguous enough to possibly mean something else, something she shouldn't be saying to him.

Now who was the awkward one? She felt her cheeks flush, and hoped she was not quite as red as she felt.

"It feels marvelous," he replied, his eyes focused on hers with a meaningful gaze.

"Oh."

"**H**ow did it go? Did he speak of me?" Euphemia had popped out from wherever she'd been hiding as soon as the door closed behind him.

They'd spent another twenty minutes in the room with Mr. Dawkins perfecting his pre-dancing position, although both of them knew it was just an excuse to touch one another in a nearly acceptable way.

He'd left at a quarter to four since he had an appointment. Otherwise they might still have been in the ballroom standing together and holding hands.

Why weren't they still together in the ballroom holding hands?

"Uh—well, no, but he didn't speak at all, actually." And Katherine willed herself not to turn red again, since that was the truth, but the additional truth—if there could be truth on top of truth—was that they'd just spent the time looking at one another, moving occasionally, both of them silent except for when they laughed.

It felt marvelous, and Katherine knew he wasn't silent because he was concerned about saying something awkward, but the opposite—because they were so comfortable with one another.

How could two people be so comfortable with one another after only a few days' acquaintance?

"Oh." Effie looked disappointed, but still adorable. Her expression quickly changed, however, as did her focus. "I was going through the most recent invitations with Mother, and there is a benefit performance at the theater, I have no idea what they will be performing." Hadn't she just been thinking about going to the theater? Perhaps another of her dreams would also come true. "And then we began discussing what we would wear," Euphemia continued. "I cannot be seen in the same gown more than once." Her lips curved into a sly smile. "Which means we will go to Felicity's shop to order some items." She glanced at Katherine, one perfect eyebrow lifted in appraisal. "And you will accompany me, of course, so we will order a gown for you, I believe."

All of Katherine's other thoughts—including her memories of The Kissing Day—fell away at those words. *A gown for you.* Something that would fit her, that might suit her, that wouldn't be brown or scratchy, something she could wear that would make his eyes light up as he saw her. Not that they didn't seem to light up already; she trusted that he did find her attractive, but in a new gown—a gown designed by his sister—he might find her breathtaking.

And then he would do things that would leave her breathless. A fair trade. Something that would right the accounts. She nearly snorted at her thinking in terms of his profession, but had to stifle herself, aware that now Lady Euphemia was regarding her with a quizzical expression on her face.

"Uh—yes, that would be lovely, but I cannot afford it," Katherine replied, quashing any hopes of breathtaking or breathgiving or any kind of breathing at all.

"Pish," Effie said, waving her hand in dismissal. "It won't do to have you garbed less than perfectly." She raised her chin. "After all, you are my companion; if you do not look your best, I might not look my best."

Katherine wanted to laugh at how aghast Euphemia sounded at that prospect—unlikely though it was—but didn't, merely going over to embrace the younger woman, who seemed uncomfortable at the gesture.

It was far, far better than another miniature horse.

"You are too generous, Lady Euphemia," Katherine said, knowing that there was a kind person buried somewhere inside the narcissistic young girl.

"Yes, well, I want to look my best," Euphemia replied. "Which means you should, too."

"Oh goodness." Had she thought about being breathless with him? Because he was most definitely not here, and she wasn't certain she would ever catch her breath again.

She stood on the small platform in Follette's dressing area, directly in front of strategically placed mirrors. Lady Euphemia was seated on a chair just behind her, while Miss Felicity fussed with the hem of the gown.

"You like it." Felicity said as she shook out a piece of the crimson fabric.

"Oh goodness," Katherine said again. Would she ever be able to say anything else? But truly, the gown was outstanding. An evening gown, it had tiny puffed sleeves that hung just barely on her shoulders. It was cut daringly low—at least in Katherine's eyes—in the front, allowing the swells of her breasts to show. The fabric encased her like a thoughtful glove; not too tight, so as to make things look pinched in and unpleasant, but not so loose as to be sacklike. The gown had the high waistline currently in fashion, which often made Katherine look shapeless, since her bust and hips were so curved. But in Miss Felicity's hands, her figure was stunning. Almost too much to look at, with every curve hinted at, but not exploited.

She looked beautiful, she could admit that. If only to herself.

"You look lovely." Apparently Miss Felicity could admit it as well.

"Thanks to you," Katherine said, unable to take her eyes off her reflection.

"And it complements my gown so well," Effie said in a satisfied tone of voice. Her gown was a light pink trimmed with darker pink ribbons, and it would indeed look good next to Katherine.

Katherine was grateful that Effie was so confident, in fact, that the thought of her companion outshining her would never cross her mind. There was a lot to be said for the kind of person Effie was; she was not petty or jealous. She demanded her due attention, of course, but she didn't begrudge others getting theirs. Which was why she was so insistent that Katherine have new clothing, even though she had perfectly adequate garments for whatever event she was required to accompany Effie to.

"I'll just need to make a few minor adjustments," Miss Felicity said, crossing her arms over her chest and scrutinizing Katherine.

Katherine resisted the urge to cross her arms over her chest as well; experience had taught her that her arms were just not large enough to obscure everything, and besides, Miss Felicity would likely be annoyed that Katherine was wrinkling the fabric.

"You'll have the gown to us by Friday, though?" Euphemia asked. Her tone made it clear that she wasn't asking a question.

"Friday, yes," Felicity replied. "Are you attending the benefit? My client Lady Marjoribanks has generously offered the use of her box that evening, so my brother and I will be in attendance as well."

But now it did feel as though the gown was tight, too tight, since she couldn't seem to breathe again. And after she had regained it so well just a few moments before.

Her brother. What would Henry say—more importantly, what would he do?—when he saw her?

She must have made a sound, since Miss Felicity was looking at her with a concerned expression on her face. "Did I poke you with a pin?"

"No, no, it's"—*it's just that the thought of your brother seeing me in this gown is making me light-headed*—"it's nothing to be concerned about. Merely something catching in my throat."

Felicity frowned in confusion, since Katherine hadn't eaten anything since arriving at the shop, but thankfully Effie had a question about feathers for her hair or something, and Katherine's inability to breathe was forgotten.

CHAPTER EIGHT

"You look splendid. Stop fidgeting."

Henry tried to be still, but his sister was smoothing fabric, and fussing with his cravat, and assessing him with her dressmaker's eye. Something he usually avoided—in the first place, she did not make gentlemen's clothing, and in the second place, he wasn't actually a gentleman, so he had no need to dress like one.

But tonight he was in the guise of one, since Felicity had requested that he escort her to some sort of performance at the theater.

He did not generally like the theater. He preferred facts and figures, and the theater was basically an excuse for people to stand in front of other people lying.

"Why do I have to be there anyway?" he asked, perhaps for the hundredth time.

His sister curled her hand up into a fist and punched him. And then smoothed out the wrinkles she just put in his coat with a brisk yank. "Because you said you would go with me." He couldn't argue with that. He had. "And besides, Lady Euphemia told me Miss Grant will be there tonight," his sister added, making him start, which made her face twist up into an almost smile.

"Oh?" He tried to sound as though he didn't care.

"As though you aren't intrigued by her." Part of his sister's success was her ability to read people, to gauge the effect her gowns had on the ladies she dressed. Unfortunately, she'd gotten her first experience at reading people with him, and she hadn't stopped, so he wasn't able to fool her, not for a moment.

"I suppose I am." He might as well admit it, she wouldn't believe his denials anyway. "But she is a lady, and I am not."

She snorted. "Of course you're not."

He glowered at her. "That is not what I meant, and you know it."

She sighed, blowing a few pieces of hair up around her face. "I know, but you are from a good family, and she is a lady, but an impoverished one."

"Which just means she is not for me, Felicity." Left unspoken was his responsibility in case Felicity wasn't able to make a go of the shop. Not to mention that a visitor to the shop had just pointed out some water damage to the front room's ceiling, so there was another expense they had to account for. Felicity might argue the point, but Henry didn't even want to imagine what would happen to their mother if neither one of them could provide for her.

"Things can change, Henry," she said, but he just shook his head, knowing he couldn't entertain the idea of it. The list he'd made mocked him still; it lay on his table, the few words written on it a reminder of everything he wanted—and everything he could lose.

"You should enjoy yourself tonight is all that I am saying." Felicity gave his jacket one last pat, then nodded in satisfaction. "Thank you for going with me."

He pushed his glasses up his nose and smiled at her. "It is not as though I had a choice. But I will do whatever I can to help you," he added. Because if she did succeed in her business venture and he no longer had to worry about her, or his mother—well, then perhaps he could worry about himself. Do something for himself that wasn't making fruitless lists or imagining what it would be like if he didn't have responsibility.

"I know, Henry." His sister's tone held an honest resonance that let him know she was well aware of what thoughts were going through his head.

It wasn't very long before the hackney they were in pulled up to the street the theater was on. Felicity looked splendid herself, as usual, and Henry hoped that her appearance would bring in a few more clients. The shop was regaining its earlier prestige, but it wasn't yet certain that they were out of the financial woods. Henry knew, from his other clients, how quickly things could get upended, and he also knew that a dressmaker's reputation could be won or lost in a moment—there had been a few mentions of the shop's designs in the fashion columns, not all of them favorable, and that had caused him no small amount of distress.

But a business's reputation could be made as well, and that was why it was imperative that Felicity's designs be displayed to their best advantage. Which meant, Henry thought with a sense of doom, that he needed to play out whatever it was Euphemia was planning.

"There she is," Felicity said in a whisper, nudging him in the side. He glanced at the door to the box seats and felt as though she'd punched him in the heart.

Because yes, Effie was there, and that was the "she" Felicity had referenced, but his "she" was also there—Katherine. Looking glorious, as beautiful as he'd ever seen her, and he'd thought she was beautiful before.

She wore a brilliant gown made of scarlet satin, a bright color in a sea of pale pastels. Her hair should have clashed with the color of the gown, but it just heightened it, making her entire appearance like a symphony in red.

He nearly rolled his eyes at himself—*a symphony in red?*—but was too busy keeping his eyes in his head as he kept staring.

"Stop that," Felicity murmured. "You're staring."

Damn his observant sister.

"Miss Felicity, Mr. Dawkins." Euphemia glided toward them, looking perfectly lovely as always. He could see that, even though he had no reaction to her. Not the way he felt as though every part of him was reacting to *her*, wanting to reach out and touch all that loveliness.

He felt his cock stir inside his trousers, and he willed himself to stand down. Literally. He did not need to make even more of a spectacle of himself at a public event where his sister's livelihood was on the line.

He lowered his hands to cover that part of him, attempting to look as casual and polished as he ever had. Even though this was likely the most awkward he had felt, even including when he was dancing, and that was definitely saying something.

"Good evening, Lady Euphemia." He cleared his throat. "Miss Grant." A pause. "It is a pleasure to see you this evening."

Her eyes met his, and he lost himself in her gaze, not worrying about what he looked like, or where he was, or anything but her.

The warm expression in her brown eyes seemed meant for him, and only him, and he wanted to drown in them. To walk up to her and take her in his arms as every part of him was currently clamoring for him to do.

"Likewise, Mr. Dawkins," she replied, her voice low and husky. As though she were thinking the same thing about him.

This was—this was forbidden heaven, this moment of looking at her and wanting her so much it felt as though he would burst. Knowing he couldn't have her, not like this, not without some assurance that he could keep her. Because if he had her and then had to let her go? He might just break.

"Mr. Dawkins, you haven't told me how you like the gown your sister made for me." Effie's voice was a nearly welcome intrusion into his thoughts. This was why he was here. For Felicity, for the shop. Not for himself.

"You look splendid, Lady Euphemia. My sister did a wonderful job." He couldn't help but look at Katherine again after he'd paid Effie the compliment. He'd known Felicity was making something for her as well, but hadn't realized until now just what a genius his sister was. "And you, Miss Grant. You look lovely." His tone was raw, and he wondered if she could hear the unvarnished honesty in his voice.

"Thank you." She glanced down at herself, her eyes widening in what might have been astonishment. "I have never worn anything like this."

"I have been telling Katherine she is to wear nothing but Miss Felicity's designs from now on," Effie announced. She smiled, a genuine smile, at her companion, who started to turn that adorable shade of pink that Henry hadn't realized he admired so much. "She might be chaperoning me, but there is no reason she has to look like one of those musty chaperones." Effie's little nose wrinkled in disdain. "I told my mother that if she didn't want to see me to all of these functions this Season, I would not be saddled with some frump who didn't want to do anything." She nodded toward Katherine. "Even if she is older than I am."

Henry felt Felicity's hand on his shoulder as he opened his mouth to defend his Katherine.

Wait. His Katherine? Dear God, she was his. On his list, in his arms, in his kiss. No, that didn't work. But still. His.

He wasn't usually an aggressive man—being the size of a tree had a way of making it seem as though one was aggressive when one wasn't—but right now he wished he could just stomp through the crowd and haul her away where he could strip her bare of her lovely gown and worship her even lovelier body.

Felicity spoke before he could consider what route he would take. "Lady Euphemia, would you care to join us in our box? My client offered me its use, and it would seem empty with just the two of us," she said, gesturing toward him. "Or perhaps you could allow me to pay my respects to your mother." She turned to Henry. "You do not mind escorting Miss Grant to Lady Marjoribanks's box, do you?" She addressed Euphemia again. "That is, if it is all right with you, my lady."

"Of course," Euphemia agreed.

His sister took Euphemia's arm, tossing Henry a triumphant look back as they walked away.

Leaving them alone. Oh, Felicity was a clever woman, and was also, at this moment, the best sister ever. The only sister he'd ever had, granted, but still. The best.

Alone, and with him bursting full of thoughts about Katherine, and what she looked like, and what she was doing to him, and that he couldn't do anything about it. Not here, not ever. Not unless things changed in his life.

"Are you feeling all right, Mr. Dawkins?" She glanced at him from under her lashes, a look that did things to his insides. "You look positively murderous." She accompanied her words with a faint, knowing smile, as though she knew why his expression was so fierce.

And she did. She did know him, she'd been able to read him from the first time they'd met. As he had her.

"I'm torn," he replied, keeping his voice low. "I don't relish the idea of having another man—other men—admire you, even though you look"—and here he paused, hoping he would be able to phrase his words the right way for the first time—"you look spectacular, and you deserve all of the attention. No matter what I may feel." He shook his head and turned his gaze to the floor, where he could see her feet encased in frivolous little slippers that matched the gown.

"Thank you," she said in a voice so low he could barely hear her.

CHAPTER NINE

The way he was looking at her—well, if looks could kill, then they could probably do other things, all of which it felt as though he was doing them to her right now.

Her body tingled, all over, especially in those Parts, and she was fiercely, proudly glad she had come out this evening. She had come close to telling Effie she had a headache; the prospect of sitting in a dark theater while people fell in love and got what they wanted on stage was not an enjoyable one. And whatever notice she got was usually not notice she wanted.

He was noticing her. But what felt right was that he was giving her as much scrutiny as he had before she'd put this gown on. It was just that everything was *more,* from the color of the dress to the look in his eyes to the way she felt as he looked at her—all of her—the heat of his gaze seeming to brand her.

She shivered, and that was apparently all it took for him to take action.

"You're cold, let's go outside." And then he shook his head, a rueful grin on his lips. "Although of course it is colder outside, so you'll get colder, and I don't want that." She saw how his cravat shifted as he swallowed. "It was an idiotic thing to say, I just—"

"I want to go outside with you." She didn't wait for his reply, she just took his arm and began to lead him toward a small door that presumably led to a balcony.

He was a palpable force at her back. And if she had been cold before, which she hadn't been—her shivering was a direct result of him, and how he was looking at her—she was on fire now, her whole body feeling as though it were heating up from the inside.

From those Parts. That now she was beginning to think really weren't things she could ignore, never mind that a lady shouldn't think about such things.

She was, and she couldn't stop. What's more, she didn't want to stop.

The balcony was small, and there were others leading out from other of the large windows, but nobody stood there. Probably because the play was about to begin, and who wanted to miss a play? No one, thankfully. Except them.

"Come sit," she said, taking his hand in hers and guiding him to the small stone bench at the other end. A large, leafy tree blocked out what little moonlight there was, so they were nearly in darkness. She sat down, the coldness of the stone a shock to her backside. He did the same, the heat of his thigh next to hers a marked contrast. Her whole body, her whole self, was a study in contradiction; she was hot, she was cold, she wanted, but she didn't want to presume, she knew what she should be doing and yet here she was.

Never mind all that. She knew what she wanted most right now: to be here, with him, whether hot or cold or somewhere in between, which sounded far more intriguing in her mind than just saying "lukewarm."

She couldn't repress her grin at her ridiculous thought, and she clapped her hand over her mouth as she started to laugh. He smiled in return, sliding his hand over her back to settle at her waist on the opposite side.

Oh my. It felt so good sitting there next to him, his fingers at her waist, his whole body seeming as though it was claiming ownership. Of her.

Her breasts, tighter in that dress than they usually were, felt prickly, but in an intriguing way. As though they craved a touch.

Oh, who am I trying to fool? I wante him to touch me, on my breasts, and on my skin, and anywhere his large hands could travel.

My goodness. Now that was a thought that made her whole body react.

"You really are cold. This is a stupid idea," he said, beginning to get up. "We should go back to the play."

She clamped her hand on his thigh. "No."

He froze, his gaze looking down at where she was touching him.

"Uh . . ." he began, and his voice sounded shaky, and she had a momentary pang at having made him shaky. But that was silly. She should be proud that she had made this powerful, honest, wonderful man nearly as weak-kneed as she felt.

"I wish we could leave here and return to your house," she said, keeping her hand on his leg. "But Lady Euphemia is my responsibility, and—" And Effie would be upset if she thought that Katherine was actually interested in Mr. Dawkins, much less kissed him and wanted to do Others Parts-ish things with him. It almost upset Katherine herself, only she'd have to say she was less upset than she was intrigued.

"And what would we do there?" he asked, his voice returning to its normal low rumble. It sent another shiver spiraling through her body. "That is, I know what I would do," he continued, putting his hand on top of hers on top of his leg. *Oh my.*

"And—and what would you do?" she asked in a breathy voice. Was that her? Sounding as though she had run a long distance?

No, that wasn't it. It was as though she were running toward something, catapulting toward it, every fiber in her body yearning to grab it, to take it, to make it hers.

That was how she felt.

"I would remove your gown from your body," he said in a low voice, "but slowly, since I wouldn't want to wrinkle it. It is spectacular work, my sister truly is a genius," he said, almost in an aside. "And then, when you were just in your shoes and stockings, I would kiss your feet and work my way up until I got to your mouth."

"Oh."

She'd only been able to say "oh goodness" when she'd first seen herself in the gown; that was twice the amount of words she was apparently able to muster right now. "Oh," she said again.

"I've never felt this way before," he said, and she knew it was honestly, painfully true.

"Me either." Two words again! Perhaps she wasn't rendered entirely incoherent.

She opened her mouth to speak, but found she had nothing to say. Nothing that wasn't something she shouldn't say, at least. It wasn't as though they could leave, nor could they act on any of their desires, not without serious consequences. It would have to be enough that they sat here, on the balcony of a public theater, her hand on his leg, his words ringing in her head, his warmth so close but not.

It had to be enough.

But what if it wasn't?

"**K**atherine! Mr. Dawkins! There you are." Euphemia peeked out through the doors just as Henry was wondering how obvious it would be if he just flung Katherine over his shoulder and stalked out.

"Yes, here." He raised the hand that had been on hers in a wave. She snatched her hand away, leaving a cold ache on his leg. Well, an ache in another area as well, but he couldn't think about that. Especially since he had to stand after Effie had spotted them. He was entirely grateful for the relative darkness.

A gentleman trailed after Euphemia, and Henry squinted to make out the man's features, which were shadowed by the bright light coming from the theater hallway.

"Mr. Dawkins, I have returned your sister to Lady Marjoribanks's box. And Katherine, my mother sent me to find you so you could meet Lord Waddell." Effie turned and flashed a brilliant smile at the gentleman, who staggered a bit at the impact. "Lord Waddell was just asking what I thought of the play, and I told him, quite truthfully, that I couldn't tell him anything about it."

Neither could he or Katherine. "It is a pleasure to meet you, my lord." Katherine curtsied, and then took Henry's arm. "And this is Mr. Dawkins."

"A pleasure, my lord," Henry said, bowing to the shorter man.

Lord Waddell nodded and smiled again, as though ensuring he had been entirely pleasant before turning to look at Effie, that slightly stunned expression still on his face. "Would you like a glass of punch? I believe we have time before they ring the bell for the play to begin again."

She took his arm and flashed another smile. "That would be delightful, my lord," she replied. She nodded smugly at Henry and cast a knowing look in Katherine's direction before walking back into the ballroom on Lord Waddell's arm.

Henry heaved a gusty sigh.

"That relieved, are you?" she said in an amused murmur.

"Is it that obvious?" he asked, turning to regard her. Her face was tilted up to his like a flower opening to the sun.

God damn it, Henry, first a symphony in red and now this. He shook his head disgustedly.

"It is. But, I think, only to me. I know Effie can be quite persistent."

"And you know I don't want her, not in that way." He heard how his words emerged strangled from his throat.

"I know. I also know that I am her companion, and I should go ensure she is not doing to Lord Waddell what she attempted to do to you, much as it seems the gentleman might appreciate it. I have a duty," she said, sounding resolute, standing as she spoke.

One problem down, now that Effie seemed to have veered off her course, but now he had a much greater problem, one that he didn't know how to solve.

How could he make himself and his family happy at the same time?

"Lord Waddell is glorious, isn't he, Katherine?"

Katherine grinned into her book. This was only the tenth time Effie had said nearly the same thing.

"He is quite a good-looking gentleman," Katherine replied. *Even though he is not as tall as I like, nor quite as broad.* Oh, she couldn't lie to herself. He couldn't be as glorious as Henry simply because he wasn't Henry.

"And it is a good thing I did not encourage Mr. Dawkins," Effie continued blithely, as though she weren't lying. She *had* tried to encourage him; it was just that he was immune to her charms. "Because if he had proposed, and I had accepted, it would be quite shocking. That is, a lady of my standing, even someone in your standing, would find it quite lowering to marry a person who is not a gentleman, even if he comes from good stock."

"Oh, yes." She had thought of that, but not quite in those terms. As in, she had considered what it would be like to be married to Henry in some ways—mostly Other Parts ways—but she had not thought that people would consider it a disgrace if she were to marry someone like him. Not that it would matter to her, but it would matter if his sister's shop could suffer. And it might, knowing how judgmental and fickle Society could be. He would never allow that, which meant he wouldn't even dream of marrying her, even if she was willing.

Oh no.

But what if she were to approach him and ask him to—she could barely articulate the thought in her mind, which showed just how shocking it was.

But if she did, she would know. And then she would be able to totter off into her spinsterhood, chaperoning all of Effie's sisters and perhaps more beside, and she wouldn't regret anything.

"I promised Lord Waddell I would go driving with him in the park this afternoon. In his curricle. There is only room for two, so you are free to do whatever you like," Effie said. "Mother said it would be perfectly respectable, since we will be in the park and he is so eligible," she continued, neatly deflecting Katherine's concerns about proper chaperonage.

Which meant that if this was to happen, it would happen today. This afternoon.

Without any sort of proper chaperonage.

She hoped to God he didn't have a previous appointment. Or her entire life would not be irrevocably changed, and she would be very disappointed about that.

He heard the knock on the door as he had just returned from his last appointment. He stood abruptly, knocking the chair he'd been sitting in to the floor, where it made a loud bang.

He glowered at it for a moment before flinging the door open. And felt his mouth drop open as he saw her. Her, standing in his doorway, an odd expression on her face.

"Can I—can I come in?" she asked after a moment of them both standing there.

"Uh, yes," he said, stepping aside to let her enter and closing the door. "Is something wrong?"

She shook her head as she removed her bonnet and set it on the table. Right on top of the list that had her name on it. It had lain there for days with him unable to throw it away, as he should be doing. "No, nothing is wrong, or everything is wrong, depending on how you look at it." She turned to him and he saw a wild, nearly frantic expression in her eyes. He locked the door.

"How do you look at it?" he asked, moving closer to her.

She lifted her face to his and smiled. Not the brilliant incandescent smile that Euphemia often had, but something warmer. Something softer. Something just for him. "I came here to ask you something."

"Oh?" he said, feeling his whole body spark to life. He wouldn't be coy, not to himself, and pretend he didn't know what she was about to ask him. The question really was, what was he going to do when she did?

She took a deep breath and stepped forward so they were nearly touching. And then she did touch him, reaching her hand forward to place it on his chest. "I want you to do what you said," she said in a voice so quiet he could barely hear her. Only he heard her loud and clear, like a bell setting off alarms all throughout his body. Especially there.

Although that was an odd image, so he wouldn't think about it too much.

"Do what I said?" he repeated, his words coming out in a croak.

She smiled, as though she understood. And he knew she did. She was as uncomfortable in certain situations as he, and in this situation—which he presumed was this situation—neither one of them had any experience, so at least they were equal there.

"Do you mean about the gown and the stockings and such?" he asked in a low voice.

She nodded. "Yes. Please."

He felt his chest tighten at how determined and vulnerable she sounded, all at the same time. Swallowing, he reached his fingers forward to undo the knot of her cloak, then slid it off her shoulders and placed it over one of his chairs.

Instead of starting with her gown, however, he knelt swiftly at her feet, sliding his palm over her ankle, feeling the delicate bones under the sturdy stockings she wore. Her boot was made of soft material, the footwear of a lady. She was a lady.

He paused, thinking about that, thinking about what it might mean if—when— he were to do this thing she was asking. It wasn't as though he wanted to stop it. He wanted this more than anything, but he thought that this moment in time would change him forever.

That she would ruin him for anybody else. Even though he was about to ruin her.

"What are you doing?" She sounded hesitant, and he glanced up.

"Nothing. Just thinking."

She bit her lip and he saw the pink flush wash across her cheeks. She was so perfectly pretty, he almost couldn't stand it.

Good thing he was kneeling, then.

"Thinking we shouldn't? That is . . ."

"No." He spoke as firmly as he ever had, and that included when his sister had tried to use him as a mannequin when she first became interested in fashion. "I want this, more than I've ever wanted anything before." And it was the truth, only he was worried he would continue to want, more than he'd ever wanted before, after as well. And forever, in fact. But she was a lady, and ladies didn't marry bookkeepers, and he couldn't dare jeopardize his sister's livelihood.

First things first. He couldn't think about any of that now. She was here, she wanted him, and damn his future if he didn't want her back.

CHAPTER TEN

It felt so odd to be standing above him, to look down at him kneeling at her feet. Holding her foot and ankle as though they were precious things. His body was so large it obscured her view, so all she could see was him. His broad, strong back, where his hair curled close to his collar. She had a sudden urge to lean over him, to wrap her arms around him and press her face to his back. To breathe in the scent of him, all warm, and masculine, to bury her nose into one of the doubtless numerous muscles on his body.

But she didn't.

Instead, she stood still as he undid her boots, placed them tidily on the floor next to her, then slid his strong, large fingers up her legs, making her shiver.

His thumbs were on the inside and his palms covered her legs entirely, the bottom of her gown coming to rest on his shoulders as he kept moving inexorably up.

What was it he'd said? *"I would remove your gown from your body, and then when you were just in your shoes and stockings, I would kiss your feet and work my way up until I got to your mouth."*

"Aren't you doing this the opposite way?" she asked in a voice she barely recognized as her own.

He looked up, one eyebrow raised, his chest rising and falling rapidly. "The opposite—?"

"Yes, when you said it, you said you wanted"—and she took a deep breath herself, wondering how she dared to say such things, but knowing she would regret it forever if she didn't—"to remove my gown first, and then have me in my shoes and stockings. You've

256

already removed my shoes," she continued, nodding to where they were on the floor, "and I was wondering if you had decided to go about it a different way?"

He leaned back, resting his hands on his thighs as he continued to look at her. Her heart froze as she waited for him.

And then melted as she saw his mouth curve into a smile, a knowing, clever smile that sent shivers of want and need spiraling through her body.

"I did say that, didn't I?" He rose, graceful for such a large man, then walked around her so he was in back of her, his hands at the nape of her neck.

"You know, people in my profession have to be methodical. Concise." He undid a button and then placed his large, warm palm on her shoulder. "We also have to be very conscious about not wasting anything. Waste leads to too much expenditure, and that is exactly what bookkeepers are hired to work against. So if I should do one thing, such as this," and then his hand lowered down her front to rest on her breast, his palm cradling it in his hand, "while also doing this," he said, undoing more buttons with his other hand in what seemed to Katherine to be a shocking display of dexterity, "then I am definitely doing a good job."

"Oh, yes, you are," she replied, keenly aware of his every touch on her body, counting the buttons down as he undid them rapidly and efficiently.

"And now," he continued, his voice more ragged than before, "now we will get you out of this gown and I can see you. All of you." And the way he said it, as though he were reverent, and wanting, and passionate, made her feel a warmth throughout her body without the hint of embarrassment she'd always assumed she'd have in this situation.

Because she wasn't anything like Effie, or any other of the traditionally beautiful women she'd seen; she was shorter, and more full-figured, and her hair was an unfashionable red, and her eyes were plain brown, and yet right now she felt as though she could eclipse any of those ladies. In his eyes, at least.

He slid her gown off her shoulder with his left hand, his right still on her breast until he reached up to her neckline, drawing the gown down until it puddled at her feet. Then he did probably the most surprising thing ever; he wrapped his arms around her and picked her up, as though she weighed nothing. He turned her in his arms and cradled her body against his broad chest, looking down at her with an intensity that made her breath catch.

"And now I think I'll take you to my bed," he said in a soft voice, moving as he spoke. She wrapped her arms around his neck and reveled in the feeling of being carried, which she hadn't felt since she was small. But the wonderful thing was, compared to him she was still small. She was nearly dainty when juxtaposed against his solid, large form, and she wanted to fling her head back and laugh at the joy of it, but she could hardly explain her amusement—*I am laughing because I am a somewhat large female, and yet here you are carrying me around like I'm made of thistledown or something.* It was not something she wished to remind either of them of. So she just smiled to herself and breathed in his scent as he lowered her gently onto his bed.

He frowned as he looked down at her, and she felt a moment of panic, but knew he wasn't regretting this. Likely he was realizing that he hadn't removed her chemise, which was an oversight of efficiency.

She sat up to kneel on the bed, raising the bottom of her chemise with one hand while steadying herself with the other against his chest. "I have to say, I am not as impressed with your forethought as I was before. I am not entirely and completely naked, Mr. Dawkins. Not yet, that is." Then she pulled the chemise over her head and dropped it on the floor, resisting the urge to cover her breasts from his gaze.

And she was entirely glad she hadn't, since his eyes had narrowed, his gaze even more intense as he looked at her. With passion. With want. With need.

"You should be entirely and completely naked as well, come to think of it." She lay back down and made an imperious gesture. "Go ahead. Undress. I will watch."

His hands went immediately to the buttons on his waistcoat, which was off in less than a minute. He yanked his shirt from his trousers and pulled it over his shoulders and then that, too, was on the floor.

She wished she could ask him to slow down so she could just look, but her mouth was dry and she didn't think she'd be able to speak. His chest was more magnificent than she had even dreamed—a broad expanse of muscle and dark hair in a T-shape and then ridges lower down where his hips were. Dipping into his trousers as though they were an arrow pointing her in the right direction.

His shoes came off, then his trousers, followed by whatever he wore underneath them, and he was gloriously and completely naked, and she wondered if a woman could expire from having seen too much beauty at one time.

Because he wasn't just tall; he was large, *everywhere,* and it looked as though his muscles had muscles.

"Come here," she said, reaching up to him.

He looked shy for a moment, and she wished she could laugh at the ludicrousness of that—him, shy, when he had a body that was meant to be viewed and appraised and cherished and there was nothing for him to be awkward about, finally. Not when he was standing in all of his naked glory, each and every part sheer perfection. In her eyes, at least.

He put one knee onto the bed and hesitated, and she rolled her eyes and took his arm and yanked him so he fell on top of her.

"I don't want," he began, and she reached around him and grabbed hold of his—of course—firm arse and squeezed.

"You don't want to crush me, and you're not, Henry. You're not. It feels amazing. Stop worrying." She paused, and squeezed again. It was remarkable that two people's same body parts could feel so different. "This is where it is excellent that I am . . . sturdy," she said, after a hesitation.

"You are gorgeous," he said, no hesitation at all. He stroked down her side, lingering near her breast. "All this luscious female in my bed, and I—I just don't know what to do."

She widened her eyes in mock outrage. "You don't? Well, I certainly don't either, so what will we do? I mean"—and then she lifted her hands from his glorious self and waved them in the air over his back—"that is, I have a general idea, but have you not done this before either?"

He smiled, a shy smile reminiscent of his awkward self. "No. I have not. Although as you say, I have a general idea."

"Well, let's try it out together. Just like our dancing practice, only—"

"Only far more enjoyable."

He might not have done this before, but she couldn't tell the difference; each and every one of his caresses felt perfect, and he couldn't stop murmuring about how much he liked looking at her—"you're beautiful," interspersed with his mouth moving over her skin, "I want to do this forever," and the best of all, "I cannot believe we are here doing this together, I never thought I would find anyone—" Only then he stopped, and it made her heart hurt.

Because she never thought she'd find anyone either, and yet here they were, but it was only temporary. Could be only temporary because of their respective obligations. She couldn't jeopardize his family's livelihood, and she knew he was aware of the disparity between them; he'd made that clear in his attitude toward Euphemia's interest in him. So much that was different about them, and yet so much the same.

"Touch me." His words were ragged and wanting, and yanked her from her thoughts, thank goodness. His male part was thick and hard against her thigh, and she reached down between them and put a tentative hand on it.

He hissed, and she made to remove her hand, only he clamped his fingers around her wrist. "Do not stop," he said. "Like this," he continued, and he drew her curled fingers up and down his shaft, squeezing so tightly Katherine was concerned it would hurt him.

But apparently it was doing the opposite, since his expression was intense, and full of desire, his eyes heavy as they gazed at her, his mouth slightly open allowing his panted breaths to escape.

"I need to," he said, and she nodded, understanding precisely what it was he wanted.

"I need you to, too," she said, guiding his male part toward her own Other Part, anticipating the moment with an almost feverish intensity.

He pushed, and she felt the pain of it, only it was a delicious pain, if such a thing were possible. His entire body felt as though it were tensed, and she grabbed hold of his shoulders and pulled him closer to her, which made him push all the way inside.

"Ahhh," he said, sounding agonized. Only happily agonized.

She slid her hands back down to his firm arse and grabbed hold as he withdrew, but not entirely. And then pushed back in.

And that felt even more wonderful; she was crushed underneath him, yes, but it felt right, as though he were owning her, branding her, making it impossible for her to be anywhere but here.

As though there were anywhere else she'd want to be.

"Kiss me," she said, and he did, devouring her mouth as he rocked inside her. It felt as though his part was making things happen down there, and she broke the kiss, unable to concentrate on anything but what he was doing, and how he was moving, and his whole massive self and this moment, and—

"Ahh," she moaned, a rising intensity of feeling building inside her, a movement that felt inexorable to its finish, even though she had no idea what the finish would feel like, only—"Ahh," she said again, only this time loudly on a cry as she reached wherever it was she was supposed to go, and she was so, so grateful she'd gone. That he'd taken her there.

His movements got more rapid, his body shifting and pushing in and out of her, his eyes closed, his jaw clenched, until he thrust and stayed there, shouting out his own pleasure.

And then collapsed on top of her without saying one word about his crushing her, and she smiled to herself that he had allowed himself that pleasure, that she had brought him that pleasure, so much that for once he wasn't concerned about anything—not his size, not his awkwardness, not anything but this moment and them.

"Dear lord," he said at last, his words muffled into her shoulder.

"Yes, indeed," she said, kissing his jaw.

"That was—that was," and then he stopped talking, instead just shaking his head.

"Yes," she agreed.

CHAPTER ELEVEN

She'd been gone about an hour, and Henry still sat at his table, looking at the list he'd made before. The list didn't matter, not now; now that he'd had her, felt what it was like to be with her, to share something so powerful, so wonderful, it didn't matter. No, that wasn't right; it *did* matter, but it couldn't matter, not if he had any chance of finding happiness in his life.

He knew his sister would punch him and tell him to go on with it. That the shop would survive any scandal, if there was even to be a scandal. He just wasn't sure Katherine—and he had to think of her as Katherine now, not Miss Grant, not when he'd been inside her, and felt her climax, and kissed all the parts of her skin he could manage, not when he'd held her full, round breasts in his hands, and felt how soft and curved and delicious she was—would want to marry him. She was a lady, she was not of his world, and he would be asking her to give up so much to be with him.

Unless she became pregnant, which would be another reason entirely. Which, idiot that he was, he hadn't even thought of. Mostly because he'd been incapable of thought.

But then again, she'd already proven herself to be a daring and enterprising and wanting young lady, coming here this afternoon with a specific desire in her mind, and acting on that desire. If she didn't want him, she would tell him. She wouldn't feel obligated, just because of this.

He nodded as he stood, feeling resolute about going to ask her— because he was going to ask her, not demand that she do the right thing by marrying him. He snorted at his own ridiculousness as he clapped his hat onto his head.

He would go, and ask her, and he hoped as much as he ever had that she would be as willing to forgo what was sensible to do what was right.

"**H**enry won't be too upset, will he?" Effie said. "It wasn't as though there was an understanding or anything. He knows well enough that my parents would never allow it anyway, I am certain that is why he hasn't spoken before this."

Lady Euphemia had returned from her drive with Lord Waddell, at which point the young man had spoken to her father, with the result that Effie was now an engaged young lady. Katherine couldn't help the feeling of relief when she heard the news. It seemed there was now no impediment to her feelings for Henry—*fine, Katherine, call them what they are, you're in love with him*—but it remained to be seen if he would want what she wanted. She rather thought so, them being in such harmony of mind, it seemed. But if he kept true to his course, remained awkward about who he was and what he was allowed to do—well, then, she would cherish this afternoon as a sweet memory and try not to think of what might have been if he had been less him. Although she wouldn't change a thing about him, so that wasn't fair.

She just hoped, is all.

"Miss Grant?" The Kilchesters' butler interrupted her thinking.

"Yes?"

"Mr. Dawkins is here. I have put him in the ballroom."

"Oh!" Katherine exclaimed.

Effie frowned. "And why is he here today; we hadn't arranged dancing practice. Do go see what he wants, and if you could perhaps tell him—?" Euphemia's face shifted into her adorable expression, and Katherine smiled back. She was an entirely self-absorbed and often selfish young lady, but she did have a good heart.

"I will tell him," Katherine promised.

Henry waited in the ballroom, running his fingers over his hatband, shifting the hat in his hands. If she said no—

"Good afternoon, Mr. Dawkins." She turned and shut the door behind her, leaning on it as she looked at him.

She was so lovely, and he didn't deserve her, but for the first time in his life he was going to be selfish—wanting something he shouldn't have, asking for something he should barely suggest.

"Katherine." He strode up to her and placed his hands flat on the door over her head. She grasped his waist and smiled up at him.

"Katherine, I know I have only known you a short time, and I know I am not who you should be marrying, but I want to tell you that . . ." He paused, his mouth dry, his heart racing. "I find I cannot imagine life without you, and I want you to consent to be my wife, because I am only entirely comfortable when I am with you. Even though, as we have agreed, we are both awkward at times."

Her smile deepened, and he felt a modicum of hope.

"You wish us to get married because that makes us both comfortable?" she asked in a teasing tone of voice.

"Pythagoras, that is not—that is, I didn't mention, did I, that I happen to love you? Because I do. I love you, Katherine, and I want you to marry me."

She had tears in her eyes, but he knew, even though he couldn't quite believe it, that the tears were of joy because of how her entire face seemed to glow with happiness. "Yes, Henry. I love you, too. Yes, I will marry you."

"Oh, thank God," he said before lowering his mouth to hers for the least awkward kiss in history.

ABOUT THE AUTHOR

Megan Frampton writes historical romance under her own name and romantic women's fiction as Megan Caldwell. She likes the color black, gin, dark-haired British men, and huge earrings, not in that order. She lives in Brooklyn, New York, with her husband and son. You can visit her website at www.meganframpton.com. She tweets as @meganf and is at facebook.com/meganframptonbooks.

~ALSO BY MEGAN FRAMPTON~

WHY DO DUKES FALL IN LOVE?
ONE-EYED DUKES ARE WILD
NO GROOM AT THE INN (NOVELLA)
PUT UP YOUR DUKE
WHEN GOOD EARLS GO BAD (NOVELLA)
THE DUKE'S GUIDE TO CORRECT BEHAVIOR
HERO OF MY HEART
BARING IT ALL
WHAT NOT TO BARE
A SINGULAR LADY

A Fashionable Affair

Caroline LINDEN

CHAPTER ONE

May 1821

Vine Street was a very ordinary lane in London, no longer fashionable and never stately. The brick buildings slumped together in comfortable shabbiness, relics of a frenzy to throw up anything to support the rapidly expanding city. A mixture of shops occupied the ground floors and curtains fluttered at several narrow windows on the upper stories. Vine Street offered cheap lodging and reasonable shopping, a hidden pocket of threadbare gentility only two streets away from the thriving bustle of Piccadilly and the gleaming new boulevard being built from Carlton House toward the elegant neighborhood rising in Regent's Park.

And it was all coming down.

Evan Hewes, Earl of Carmarthen, surveyed it dispassionately as he rode the length of the street. In a year's time Vine Street would look vastly different, with wider pavements and improved drainage, modern sewers, pipes laid for gas, and buildings of clean white stone. There would still be shops with lodgings above, but they would be modern and new, crisply uniform in appearance and no longer a dark hodgepodge of Stuart brick and Tudor half-timbering. It was a new century, and Vine Street would soon be just as new.

The prospect filled him with excitement. Rebuilding always had, ever since his ancestral manor burned to the ground only a month after his father died, and Evan was faced with the monumental task of rebuilding. He soon realized it was more like a shining opportunity. The stone shell remained, but everything within the house, which dated from the time of the Plantagenets, had been wood, and thus burned to ash. Evan moved his weeping mother and younger sister into the dower house and hired a brash young architect who helped him rebuild a house that featured none of the odd corners, strangely shaped rooms, smoky chimneys, or stairs so tight and narrow the footmen couldn't go up them without stooping. Now the manor had clean gracious lines, a modern aesthetic, and every convenience.

He meant to do the same to this grubby little corner of London. It was near the fashionable shops, and once it was rebuilt, the whole area would be revitalized.

The milliner on the corner, the stationers next to it, and the teahouse at the end of the block had all recently accepted his offers to purchase their properties. He already owned almost everything else. There were some tenants who would need to go, but his solicitor had secured settlements with most of them and Evan expected the rest to follow soon. He was giving generous inducements to uproot and move elsewhere.

There was, however, one tenant who had refused all offers. He bent a grim and impatient look upon the premises of Madame Follette's, modiste. It sat near the midpoint of the street, the bow window slightly warped from the settling of the building. The door was painted a bright blue and the steps were neatly swept, but nothing could disguise the careworn feel of the place.

He dismounted in front of the shop. His solicitor had tried for several months to secure the cooperation of the owner, to no avail; when Evan finally declared he would go see her himself, Grantham expressed doubt.

"She's an older lady, a Frenchwoman," the solicitor explained when Evan expressed frustration over the delay. "Stubborn as a mule."

"Offer her more money."

"Tried it twice." Thomas Grantham leaned back in his chair. "In reply she sent a three-page letter that was mostly in French and insulted my intelligence, my manners, and my clerk's penmanship. At the conclusion she refused your generous offer, and for good measure added that she would refuse an offer five times as high."

Evan scowled. If Grantham—who was known for being smooth and persuasive—had failed, the old lady must be a regular shrew. "Did you tell her everyone else in Vine Street has accepted, and the improvements will happen regardless?"

"I did," said Grantham pleasantly. "Her reply to that was a single page of paper containing one word, writ large: *No.* I hope you have an alternate plan, or can demolish and build around her."

By some great feat of restraint he didn't curse out loud. He couldn't demolish around the dressmaker's shop without fatally compromising its structural integrity, as it shared at least one wall with its neighbor. That was part of what made Vine Street so attractive a proposition: Everything needed to come down. He could demolish the buildings on the other side of the street, but the approved plan called for *both* sides of the street to be rebuilt. Leaving one half in place would add insurmountable obstacles, in time, engineering difficulty, and expense, to say nothing of spoiling the elegant uniformity of design he envisioned. The dressmaker had to go.

So here he was, determined to oust the obstinate modiste personally through some combination of charming persuasion and subtle intimidation. He tied up his horse and went in.

A tiny bell tinkled as the door opened, and he stepped into a room that stretched the width of the building. He supposed some would call it bright, and it was for this street, but he couldn't help thinking how much nicer his new buildings would be, when the sun could reach the ground floor windows and illuminate the whole room, instead of only a small area at the front.

But otherwise it was a pleasant room. The floor was impeccably clean, the walls were soft blue, and behind the wide counter shelves held bolts of silk and lace. A selection of periodicals was spread on the counter, and three gorgeously attired fashion dolls stood on shelves near the fabric.

At his entrance a woman emerged from the curtained doorway at the rear. "Good morning, sir," she said, her voice very faintly tinged with French. "How may I help you?"

The answer that came immediately to Evan's mind was rather risqué. If he'd known seamstresses were this attractive, he would have personally escorted his mother and sister to every fitting. The woman before him was lovely, with dark gold hair and vivid blue eyes. He couldn't stop himself from taking a swift but thorough survey, from the top of her blond head to the hem of her skirt. Round hips, trim figure, splendid bosom, and a face he'd very much like to see flushed with passion.

"Sir?"

He snapped his gaze away from her very kissable mouth. *Business, then pleasure,* he told himself. Buy the building, then flirt with the seamstress. "I've come to see Madame Follette."

Her soft pink lips parted in surprise. "Have you an appointment?"

By God, she was beautiful. He leaned against the counter and grinned. "No, but I hope she'll see me all the same." He produced one of his cards and slid it across the polished wooden surface.

A thin puzzled line appeared between her brows as she reached for the card. It vanished as soon as she read it. Her eyes flew back to his, and this time they shone with a more cordial light. "My lord."

"Will Madame see me?" he asked, lowering his voice to a more intimate register.

"But of course!" She smiled, and his stomach took a drop. There was a dimple in her cheek, and he was sure that smile was coy, almost inviting, as if she felt the same attraction he did . . . "I am Madame Follette."

It was so unlike what he had expected Evan was struck speechless. "You?" he said stupidly.

Her eyes flashed, but her smile didn't waver. "Yes. What did you wish to see me about?"

Inside his head Evan cursed his solicitor. An older Frenchwoman, stubborn as a mule, eh? He'd been prepared for that sort of woman. This woman—young and attractive and dangerously appealing—threw him.

But only for a moment. He straightened his shoulders and assumed a contrite expression. "I beg your pardon. I was expecting an older woman. I'd been told Madame Follette was a Frenchwoman about my mother's age."

"Ah." Understanding softened her demeanor. "That will be my mother, who founded Madame Follette's and ran the shop until a year ago. She has taken an extended holiday to the seashore. But I would be happy to assist you. Have you come to inquire about a gown for Lady Carmarthen?"

"Er . . . No." Behind him the bell chimed again.

Madame's face brightened at once. "One moment, my lord," she murmured to him. "Lady Marjoribanks! Come in, Miss Owen has been expecting you. May I offer you a cup of tea?"

"Not this morning," said Lady Marjoribanks as she stooped to set down a ball of gray fur she was carrying. "Midas isn't well today, he didn't want to be alone. I hope you don't mind."

Evan didn't see the slightest flicker in Madame's face as a pair of malevolent yellow eyes winked open amid the gray fur and glared up at her. "Of course I don't mind. Come, I'll show you to a private room and tell Miss Owen you've arrived."

As they crossed the shop, the older woman caught sight of him. "Carmarthen! What are you doing here?"

"Delighting in our chance encounter," he said smoothly, giving her a bow. "A great pleasure to see you again, Lady Marjoribanks."

She seemed amused. "And you, my boy! I hope you've not come to haggle with Miss Dawkins. She's a wonderful girl, so clever with a needle and thread, and if you reduce her to tears, you'll have me to deal with." She shook her finger in admonishment.

"I wouldn't dream of it," Evan replied, covertly noting the way Madame—Miss Dawkins?—flushed and avoided looking his way.

"Very good. Keep an eye on Midas, would you, while I have a word with the ladies about my gown." She turned her attention to the proprietress, still at her side. "I saw the most original style the other day. Four shades of fringe! Do you think Miss Owen could create something similar?"

He couldn't make out Madame's reply as she guided her client through another doorway. With a sigh he rested his elbow on the counter and regarded the cat still crouching on the floor where Lady Marjoribanks had put him. He knew the viscountess was eccentric, but carrying her cat around with her? From the baleful look on his face, Midas didn't seem pleased to be here, and as soon as his mistress had gone he crept under a nearby chair.

Evan tried to use his moment alone to reassess his approach. It galled him that he'd made such a mistake about the owner, no matter what Grantham had said. Still, it could work to his benefit. An older woman might be reluctant to move, but surely a young woman would see the value in what he wished to do. Surely she couldn't like the way her floors slanted, or that her windows only got an hour of direct sunlight every day. Surely a young woman must want modern plumbing and gas lighting. Evan had done his research, and this was one of the oldest parts of Vine Street. There was no record of it having significant improvements in the last several decades, and he certainly didn't see signs of any now that he was here.

On the other hand, he couldn't afford to be distracted by a pretty face and a splendid bosom. Regretfully he pondered that point a moment. There must be someone else he could speak to, if only to persuade them to intercede with the actual owner.

Madame—Miss Dawkins?—emerged. "I apologize, my lord," she said as she went behind the counter again. "Have you come to inquire about a commission? We are quite busy, but I'm sure we could accommodate you." Her hand drifted toward the fashion periodicals.

"No." He paused as another woman burst out of the same doorway where Lady Marjoribanks had disappeared. With a murmured apology she took some of the periodicals and went back where she'd come from.

"That is Miss Owen, one of my head seamstresses," said Madame. "She has a dramatic eye for color and flair, and designs garments unlike anything else in London. Lady Marjoribanks is devoted to her."

"I've come about a financial matter, Madame." He paused. "Or is it Miss Dawkins?"

Slowly her hands curled into fists before she put them below the counter. "Dawkins is our family name. Follette was my mother's name before she married my late father. What sort of financial matter?"

"One I must discuss with the owner. My solicitor has been corresponding with your mother, I believe, whom he understood to be the person holding the deed to this building." He waited a moment, but she just stared at him, her eyes darkening. Too late Evan thought he ought to have heeded Grantham's advice and stayed out of it. He didn't want to make this woman hate him, but he had plans—investors—promises he had to keep. "Where might I find her?"

"Yes, my mother is the owner. But I am managing the shop now." Her chin came up. "You can speak to me, my lord."

"Perhaps I could speak to your man of business," Evan said hopefully. Surely her man of business, or her solicitor, would see reason and help argue his case.

That was the wrong thing to say. Her mouth flattened and she set back her shoulders with a little twitch. "You can speak to *me*," she repeated, a hard stress on the final word.

There was no other choice, it seemed. He nodded and tried to look rueful. "Don't mistake me—it would be my pleasure to speak to you. Are you aware of your mother's correspondence with my solicitor, Mr. Grantham?"

"No."

"That explains it." He gave an abashed grin. "I feared as much, which is what brought me here today. I've a business proposal to make, but your mother is unwilling to listen."

Her expression didn't change. "As I said, I am managing Follette's now; my mother has retired from the trade. What is your proposal?"

He doubted she was empowered to accept it, but she could help persuade her recalcitrant mother. Evan propped his elbow on the counter again and leaned toward her. Lord, she had the most magnificent eyes, and the way her face tipped up to his . . . "I couldn't help but notice your floor slopes and your windows are warped. This building must be nearly two hundred and fifty years old." He knew it was; building records showed it had been built before the Great Fire, one of the small pockets of London that survived unscathed. And from the looks of things, it hadn't changed much since.

"Yes," she allowed, "but it's home. Surely you have a home, my lord, all the more endearing for its quirks and oddities."

He didn't mention that he'd had that building completely rebuilt, in part because of its oddities. "Of course! But there are quirks, and then there are . . . failings. The drains in this street are appalling; it must flood in every heavy rain. And there's no gas, I noticed. All the shops in Piccadilly have gas lighting now."

A mixture of discomfort and longing flickered over her face. "That is true. But there are great improvements happening just a few streets away, and I expect the tide will eventually reach Vine Street."

"You are exactly right." He smiled. "Very soon, in fact. That's what I've come to discuss. I have submitted a plan to improve Vine Street just as Mr. Nash is doing in Regent Street."

"Oh!" Her eyes brightened, and a pleased smile curved her lips. "That is very welcome news! And you've come to let the tenants know? How good of you, sir."

"It will be absolutely splendid," he went on, growing enthusiastic as he always did when talking about his plans. "Modern sewers, gas to every building, wider pavements. The shops will be brighter, the rooms above supplied with water closets and pipes for pumps, to say nothing of taller ceilings and perfectly proportioned rooms."

"That sounds delightful," she said in bemusement, "but how will you change the proportions of the rooms?" Her voice trailed off as she spoke.

Evan went for the bold strike. "I would like to buy this building, Miss Dawkins. Everything in Vine Street will be torn down and built anew, exactly as I said—and you're right, it will be delightful, and a vast deal better than this." He swept one hand around the shop.

"What?"

He ignored the horror in her exclamation. "Mr. Nash himself approved the plans, and the work will be carried out with his advice. This street is very near Piccadilly, but has frankly grown too shabby to be fashionable. In two years' time, it will rival Bond Street." He paused, but she only gaped at him, her face pale. "I'm prepared to make a very handsome offer, Miss Dawkins."

"No," she said faintly.

"An offer you would never receive from anyone else," he said softly. "This is an old building. The work in Regent Street will disrupt traffic for years and cut you off from the fashionable part of town when it's complete."

"No!" Her expression grew stormy. "You cannot sweep in here and have my shop for the asking! I presume you've come because my mother has refused all your solicitor's previous inquiries"—he said nothing, and she jerked her head in a knowing nod—"and you should know that I agree with my mother. We will not sell Follette's!"

Evan sighed. As pretty as she was in a fury, he didn't have time for this. "That would be foolish."

"Foolish?" She raised one brow in disdain. "How arrogant, to presume you know anything about my shop or my concerns. Good day, sir." She swept around the counter and went to the door. The bell jangled sharply as she jerked it open, and Midas hissed from beneath the chair.

He tugged at his gloves, studying her through narrow eyes. By God, she was throwing him out. "It would be foolish to stay," he said coolly," because I have already bought every other building around you." Her eyes went wide, and he gave a small shrug. "Vine Street is coming down, Miss Dawkins. If you stay, it will come down around your ears, and when the work is complete, yours will be the lone spot of drab in the middle of a gleaming new street, devoid of all the modern trappings I just described. How much will it be worth then? If, however, you accept my offer now, you'll get good—no, *exceptional*—value for it. I could even sweeten the offer by extending you a lease in the new premises at favorable terms," he added.

She swallowed. "When do you expect this destruction to begin?"

"The last tenant will be out by the end of the month." He put on his hat. "I expect to begin tearing it down the next day."

"The end of the month," she gasped. "Why so soon?"

Evan rocked back on his heels. "So soon? I've been acquiring property for almost a year. Did your mother not mention the multiple letters my solicitor has sent her?" She blanched. "No? Because I assure you, this has been several months in the planning." He took out another card and laid it on the counter. "You may inquire with my solicitor, Thomas Grantham, if you don't believe me."

For a long moment she just stared at him, her blue eyes wide and unfocused. "Good day, my lord," she finally said.

Confounded woman. Annoyed, Evan strode past her, only to pause on the pavement beside his waiting horse. "Look around, Miss Dawkins," he warned her, waving one hand at the shop across the street. The tailor had already gone, and the windows of his shop had a blank, dead look about them. "Soon every window on this street will be dark except yours. Soon the street itself will be torn out. Your clients won't be able to drive to your door, and dust from the demolition will seep through the cracks in your windows and ruin every bolt of silk you possess. Do you really want to run your shop under those conditions?"

For answer she closed the door with a snap, and remained behind it glaring at him, arms crossed over her chest. This time Evan didn't even glance at her splendid bosom. "Think about it," he said again. "And when you reach the obvious conclusion, you have my card." Somewhat sardonically, he bowed to her, then got back on his horse and rode away.

CHAPTER TWO

Felicity glared at the hateful man until he vanished into traffic at the end of the street. As satisfying as it had been to slam the door on him, she couldn't so easily shut out his words.

She gave a despairing huff. Her first sight of him was dazzling: tall and handsome, exuding confidence and wealth. Felicity's imagination had run away from her for a moment, imagining all the commissions such a man might have come to make, and she'd got butterflies in her stomach at the prospect of outfitting his mother, his sister, his wife, his daughter, even his horse if that's what he desired. After dealing with Lady Marjoribanks, no request would make her blink.

Instead he'd come to ruin her. Sell Follette's! Move away! The very thing she'd vowed never to do. And all so he could raze it to the ground and build something new, probably with rents she could never afford. Felicity had seen the building going on in Regent Street. While it had cleared away some ramshackle old buildings and improved the general tone of the area, she couldn't help noticing that those pristine new shops had contributed to her own business's decline. Why venture to Vine Street when one could find plenty of shopping only two streets away, situated along a broad, well-lit, perfectly paved boulevard?

And Mama had known, for months, that that—that *predator* was preying on them, but not said a word. Felicity pressed the heels of her hands to her forehead, trying to calm her temper. It seemed her mother had steadfastly refused His Dazzling Lordship, which gave her a vengeful delight, but how could her mother keep such a thing secret from her and from Henry?

Her hands dropped. Had Mama kept it from Henry? "She must have," Felicity whispered. Surely her brother would have told her, even if Mama had tried to swear him to secrecy for some reason . . .

She strode through the shop and into the tiny office at the back. She grabbed a short cloak hanging on a hook and threw it over her shoulders, then tied on her bonnet. She shouldn't leave the shop, but this was an emergency. Stopping only to ask Selina Fontaine, the other head seamstress who had no clients in at the moment, to mind the salon for a while, she headed out to see her brother.

Clutching her cloak with one fist, her lips pressed into an irate line, she strode toward Henry's lodgings. Although they weren't far from Vine Street, the trip required her to cross Regent Street, forcibly driving home the truth of Lord Carmarthen's words. Construction made a mess. The shop would be filthy, even if she swept twice a day. And the familiar buildings that she'd beheld every day of her life would be gone, torn down just because they were old.

She tried not to think of the burst of delight she'd felt for that brief moment when she imagined Lord Carmarthen's vision of new sewers and gas lighting benefiting everyone already living in the street, not merely himself.

She knocked firmly on Henry's door, not certain if her brother was awake. He would be soon, she grimly vowed, and knocked again.

"That sounds like my dear sister's way of pounding on the door," said Henry as he opened that door. He was in shirtsleeves and had clearly been lingering over his breakfast. "Good morning, Fee."

Felicity pushed past him. "Henry, did Mama ever tell you someone offered to buy Follette's?"

His eyebrows went up as he shut the door. "No."

She sighed, although she wasn't sure if it was relief or dismay, and pulled off her bonnet. "A gentleman came to the shop today and claimed he's been making Mama offers to buy the shop for months. Obviously she refused him."

"And you thought I wouldn't have told you, if I'd known?"

"No," she murmured, abashed at his frown. "But I had to be sure. If Mama had sworn you to secrecy . . ."

He gave her a deeply disappointed glance, but his frown faded. Henry was extraordinarily good-natured. Sometimes Felicity thought she'd got all the temper in the family, and Henry all the forbearance. "What gentleman wants to buy a dressmaking shop?"

"The Earl of Carmarthen." Felicity held out the expensive card the earl had left on her counter. "Do you know anything about him?"

"No," said her brother slowly, appearing quite thrown. "Felicity, why on earth would an *earl* want Follette's?"

"So he can tear it down. He says he's bought every other building in Vine Street and will demolish them all around our ears. He's got plans for improvements like in Regent Street," she said, trying not to spit out the word "improvements." Those plans would improve things for the landlords and the wealthy shopkeepers looking for shiny new premises. Felicity was dreadfully afraid, though, that those plans were meant to force out her and other ordinary shopkeepers. *Clearing away the rabble,* she thought grimly.

Henry's brow furrowed again. "He's bought every other building? I noticed Mr. White's tailor shop had closed, but never imagined . . . Did you ask the neighbors if that's true?"

She shifted her weight. "No. Not yet. When do I have time to visit the neighbors and ask if anyone's offered to buy them out? Besides, we're one of the few tenants who owns our building." That was thanks to Sophie-Louise's foresight decades ago, when she'd been determined never to be poor or homeless again. Their mother had fled revolutionary France during the days of the Terror, and it had left a deep mark on her mind.

"It would be good to know," Henry pointed out. "If Mama refused him, perhaps others did as well. He may be trying to cozen you."

"Do you think he lied?" Her heart rose hopefully. How she would love to call Lord Carmarthen's bluff, and see his handsome face fall as he realized he'd been bested by a woman . . .

Henry shrugged. "He wouldn't be the first. It should be easy to verify, though. The parish must have records of the deed holders."

"Would you?" She saw his face; he was not enthusiastic about the prospect, but he would do it. She gave him an adoring smile. "You take such good care of us, Henry, and of Follette's. Mama would be proud—"

"Mama," he repeated. "What will we tell Mama, assuming this fellow's claim is true? If he tears down the whole street, it won't be good for Follette's. And to be clear, Fee, I doubt he'd say he owned everything if it weren't substantially true."

Her mood darkened again. "We can't move, not now." The king's coronation was swiftly approaching. No lady of quality planning to attend would want her gown from a modiste in Bloomsbury or Islington. Bloomsbury and Islington, though far more affordable than Piccadilly or Bond Street, smacked of middle class, not the leading edge of fashion. In the last year and a half, Felicity had fought fiercely to push Follette's back to that edge. She had hired Delyth Owen, a new seamstress with a keen, bold eye for design, and promoted Selina, and all three of them had been creating bold new interpretations of the latest styles. They had staunched the decline of their clientele and even attracted a few prominent new clients who placed expensive orders—and absolutely nothing could be allowed to interfere with delivery of those commissions, because Follette's entire future depended on them.

It was not enough for a dressmaker's shop to produce handsome clothing of good quality. To be considered a fashion leader, a modiste must produce exquisite garments of superior quality *for the right ladies*. Outfitting a merchant's family, no matter how wealthy, or a country squire's wife, no matter how beautiful, would not put a modiste's name on everyone's lips. That required patrons of some prestige, although notoriety could be just as good.

From the moment the old king died, Felicity had set her sights on the coronation of the new king. As prince, George IV had proved himself a man of lavish tastes, exceedingly fond of spectacle, and the stories printed in the papers promised that this would be his crowning moment in every sense of the word. With days, even weeks, of dazzling festivities planned in celebration, every peeress and lady of quality would want a new gown or five, gowns they would wear in front of the most rarefied society in all of Britain. Felicity was determined that at least a few of those splendid new gowns would come from Follette's. But to make that happen, she needed to avoid anything that would disrupt work at the shop.

"How much did he offer?" Henry's question broke into her thoughts.

Felicity flushed. "He didn't say. He said he'd give exceptional value and offered to grant us a lease on favorable terms after the reconstruction is complete." She grimaced, absently straightening some of the dishes on Henry's breakfast table. "Which won't be for a year or more."

"Exceptional value," repeated her brother. "I'd like to know what he thinks that is." She shot a furious glare at him. Henry put up his hands defensively. "I didn't say we should accept it. It's just hard to know what the property is worth. And . . . er . . . We might need a mortgage."

"What?" she cried. "You never mentioned that!" Sophie-Louise would be appalled. Debt was evil, in her mind. It was the threat of not being able to pay their accounts that had persuaded her to let them take over the management of Follette's, after all.

"Nigel Martin is tightening our credit," he said, naming the owner of her favorite silk warehouse. "He wants to be paid in full. I wonder now if he knew about this plan for Vine Street and foresaw trouble for us."

Felicity seethed. *Curse Mr. Martin,* she thought, *and curse Lord Carmarthen, too.* She wasn't going to sell her shop. She was going to see those gowns produced, one way or another, even if she had to mortgage the shop thrice over in order to take a single room in the middle of Mayfair . . .

And there her thoughts paused. The middle of Mayfair would not be a step down. If she had a shop there, it would show that Follette's was moving *toward* fashionable London in light of the destruction of Vine Street, not away from it.

Lord Carmarthen wanted her shop very badly. That much was clear from the way he'd come himself and tried to convince her how greatly his plans would benefit everyone in Vine Street. He also knew she wanted to stay, just as he knew she could become a large thorn in his side. For all his bluster about tearing everything down around her, Felicity knew that her shop shared a wall with the building next to it. He couldn't pull down that wall without destroying her property. But it meant he would probably accept almost any remotely reasonable terms she proposed as the cost of moving out of the shop . . .

"I have an idea," she said softly, still thinking hard.

Her brother tensed. "What?"

She gave him a sharp look. Henry was too amiable to send into battle against Lord Carmarthen. Besides, she wanted to best the earl all on her own. It still rankled that he'd asked to speak to her man of business, and only broached his true purpose when she insisted she was in charge of Follette's. "Never mind now. I'll deal with this." She went up on her toes to press a quick kiss on her brother's cheek. "Thank you, Henry."

He still looked wary. "Please promise me I won't have to rescue you from Newgate. Assaulting an earl is a capital crime."

She laughed as she put her bonnet back on. "No, no. It shall be perfectly legal and proper. I've decided the evil earl may help us yet."

CHAPTER THREE

Evan strode into his solicitor's office, still incensed by his encounter the previous day with Miss Dawkins, or Madame Follette, or whatever her real name was. "How much can I tear down in Vine Street without damaging the modiste's shop?" he demanded without preamble.

Thomas Grantham looked up over the top of his spectacles, and put down his pen. "It didn't go well, did it?"

"No." He flung his hat and gloves into the waiting arms of Grantham's clerk. "Do you still have the engineering reports at hand?" Perhaps there was a way to tear down everything except the dressmaker's shop. Evan told himself he had to be coldly logical about this, and not let a stunning pair of blue eyes shake his resolve. Miss Dawkins had had her chance, and she'd refused it. He was convinced she'd change her mind once work began and she was forced to deal with the dirt and noise and upheaval. She would be on his doorstep begging for another chance to accept his offer, which would not be quite as generous the next time.

Grantham looked at his clerk. "Fetch the reports, Watson." The man nodded and left. "How badly?" the solicitor asked, leaning back in his chair and smiling, once the clerk was gone.

Evan glared at him. Thomas Grantham was not just his solicitor but his friend, a fellow student at Cambridge who had tutored Evan to a surprisingly strong showing in mathematics. Grantham had an engineer's mind, precise and logical, but his father, an attorney, had decreed Thomas would follow in his footsteps and read law. At the time Evan had privately thought it sounded dry and dull, but in recent years he'd come to appreciate his friend's training. As his interest in improvements had grown, he'd realized how vital a good solicitor was to the job, and had promptly put the opportunity to Thomas, who accepted on the spot.

This partnership between them put the best of Grantham's skills to full use: He was able to make sense of the engineers' reports and estimates, and he knew how to guide a large renovation through the byzantine bureaucracy of Whitehall. It had been his task to buy all the property and smooth the way for the construction, while Evan dealt with the architects and tradesmen, to say nothing of using his position to get the necessary approvals.

But now Thomas was enjoying Evan's failure to acquire one dressmaker's shop a little too much. "Horribly," he muttered grudgingly, before turning the barb around. "In part because you neglected to tell me whom I'd be facing."

Grantham's brows went up. "Who? The sole owner is Sophie-Louise Dawkins, widow, although she uses her maiden name, Follette, in her business. Is she even more shrewish in person?"

"No." Evan rested his hip against the windowsill and folded his arms. "I never saw *her*, the older Frenchwoman who refused you so belligerently. Instead I made a fool of myself because her daughter is running the shop now, and the mother has left London." He cocked one brow. "That seems like something we ought to have known, don't you think?"

Grantham frowned at the pointed question. "Yes. I sent a man to visit the shop several months ago and he spoke to her. She must have left since then." He leaned forward and rang the bell. "What's the daughter like? I take it she's no more receptive than her mother was."

"Not much, although she forbore to swear at me in French."

At that Grantham grinned. "That must count as progress, Carmarthen. The mother insulted everything but my parentage."

"The daughter threw me out of the shop," he retorted.

His friend laughed. "Now I wish I'd gone! That must have been a sight."

"Even more amusing will be the contortions required to proceed without being able to touch a brick of her shop," said Evan drily. "I hope my memory is failing me, and that that shop does not, in fact, share significant structural support with the building next to it."

The amusement faded from the solicitor's face. Before he could reply, there was a knock at the door and a clerk poked his head in. "Sir—"

"Did we send someone recently to Vine Street to query tenants?" Grantham asked. "Specifically Madame Follette's, the dressmaker shop."

The clerk looked startled. "Er—I'm not certain, sir. But you've a visitor—"

"I'm engaged at the moment," said Grantham, tipping his head toward Evan.

"I believe you'll want to receive the lady, Mr. Grantham," said the clerk.

Evan exchanged a look with the solicitor. A lady? "Who is it?"

"She gave her name as Miss Felicity Dawkins, of Madame Follette's shop." There was a whiff of smugness in the clerk's voice. "Shall I send her in? It will save time, although I could go 'round to her shop if you prefer."

"I should sack you for laziness, Watson," said Grantham. "Instead I'm forced to compliment your timely interruption. Show her in." The clerk grinned for a split second, then closed the door. "Felicity. Such a joyful name for a shrew."

"I never called her a shrew." Evan straightened his posture without moving away from the windowsill. He told himself not to show any sign of interest or pleasure at her appearance. *This is business,* he told himself, and Grantham would catch any betraying sign of weakness on his part. He must keep his mind focused on how obstinately she closed that door in his face, and how she'd glared at him through the window, arms folded under those beautiful breasts . . .

The door opened again and she walked in. If Evan's first glimpse of her had stirred his interest, his second glimpse threatened to knock him senseless. Today she wore a dress of brilliant blue, as rich as the twilight sky over Carmarthen Bay, and the way the skirt swayed as she walked made Evan's mouth go dry. She had already removed her pelisse and bonnet, exposing her fresh complexion—and splendid bosom—to his fascinated gaze. Her dark blond hair was swept up into a cluster of curls that looked soft and tempting, and the smile she gave Thomas Grantham almost made Evan lose his balance.

"Good morning, Mr. Grantham," she said, the hint of French adding a purr to her words as she made a graceful curtsy. "Thank you for seeing me without an appointment."

If Grantham had blinked once, Evan hadn't noticed. "Of course," said the solicitor. He cleared his throat. "Pray, be seated, Miss Dawkins."

With a swirl of skirts she seated herself. "I understand you have been corresponding with my mother, Sophie-Louise Dawkins."

Grantham caught Evan's fulminating look and sat forward in his chair. He would know what Evan was thinking: If Miss Dawkins had come to them, she must have reconsidered her refusal of the previous day. She must have come to accept, or perhaps to bargain.

But the infuriating woman hadn't looked his way once, and Evan could only glare at Grantham impotently and try to signal that the solicitor should bring the sale to a swift and immediate agreement. The sooner this woman was out of Vine Street, the happier he would be.

"Yes, I have, for several months now," said Grantham.

Again she smiled, somewhat ruefully, as if they shared a private joke. "I understand she was not very receptive to your overtures."

One corner of Grantham's mouth tilted. "Unfortunately not." Like a good lawyer, he was letting her speak, waiting to see where she began.

"I must tell you, neither my brother nor I knew anything about it," she went on. "A little over a year ago, Mama decided to step down and turn over the shop to us. She has gone to Brighton and has little to do with Madame Follette's."

"But she does still hold the deed of the property."

A faint flush colored Miss Dawkins's cheek. Evan told himself he was watching her closely to detect signs that she was weakening, and not because he was fascinated by her skin. "She does, but she has also put great trust in my judgment. If I intercede with her on your behalf, I believe she would accept your offer."

"That would be very good of you, ma'am." Grantham paused. "What would inspire you to intercede? Lord Carmarthen came away from his visit to your shop yesterday disappointed."

The flush deepened. Now Evan knew she was avoiding looking his way to spite him. The single pearl earring that hung from her ear trembled. "I did not expect him, and he caught me off guard with his wild declaration that everything in the street was to be destroyed in a few days' time."

Evan shifted his weight and scowled. That was not how it had gone. He hadn't said anything like that.

"However, now that I've had some time to think about it, I believe we may be able to reach an equitable compromise." She smiled again.

"I'm very pleased to hear that." Again Grantham stopped, leaving the next step to her.

Miss Dawkins didn't appear rattled. "It would be a tremendous inconvenience to relocate my shop. Not only is Vine Street ideally situated for my clients and for my employees, but a move would disrupt our work unpardonably. In addition, I have an extensive stock of fabrics and other materials, and it would cost me a great deal to remove it all, to say nothing of the expense of setting up new premises."

"Yes," Grantham allowed, "but that is why Lord Carmarthen made such a generous offer."

"He has offered money," she replied rather dismissively, "which addresses only one of my concerns. The other two are equally important. If, however, they can be addressed to my satisfaction . . ." She raised her chin. "Then I would be prepared to advise my mother, very strongly, to accept your offer for Number Twelve Vine Street so that Lord Carmarthen may proceed with his improvements."

For a moment there was silence. Grantham darted a glance at Evan, who was thinking furiously. Her other concerns were the inconvenience of moving—which he didn't know how to eliminate—and the "ideal situation" of Vine Street—which was by definition confined to that location. "What would be sufficient to your satisfaction?" he asked.

Miss Dawkins hesitated, then turned her head slightly toward him. "To run my business, I require a suitable set of rooms, including space for receiving clients, fittings, a workroom, and storage of supplies. Since I also live above Number Twelve, any new premises must include respectable lodgings. I don't wish to pay higher rent than thirty pounds a year. And, most importantly, it must be located where it will be more convenient, not less, for my clients and employees. Those are the only circumstances under which I shall leave Vine Street."

Grantham looked at Evan, who nodded once. This was what he'd wanted, after all. As hoped, Miss Dawkins had recognized that she had to give way. She even had a fairly reasonable list of requirements for a new situation, which meant she should be able to relocate soon and not delay his plans. He tried not to think about the matter of her lodgings; did she live alone above Number Twelve? She'd mentioned a brother . . . He pushed that rogue thought from his mind.

"I understand, Miss Dawkins, and that is all very commendable," said the solicitor. "But how can you be sure your mother will be persuaded? She was quite firm in her refusal of Lord Carmarthen's last offer."

"She wants what is best for Follette's. If my brother and I assure her this will be to our benefit, she will accept." There was no shade of doubt in her tone. It was still a risk, but Evan thought it was one worth taking. Surely Mrs. Dawkins couldn't prevail against both her children as well as the ravages of construction.

"We can allow some time for you to locate these new premises, Miss Dawkins, but we must know with certainty whether, and when, we will acquire the property," Grantham went on. "His Lordship has contracted with a number of tradesmen who will need instruction. Can you guarantee an answer by the end of this month?"

"I?" Miss Dawkins raised her chin. "I have no time to ramble about London viewing properties, Mr. Grantham. This is a very busy time for us, with the Season in progress and the coronation approaching. I will use my influence with my mother if, or when, *you* locate new shop quarters and lodgings for me."

"I beg your pardon?" Evan lurched forward indignantly.

At last she met his gaze head-on. Lord almighty, her eyes were blue. "You came to my shop personally," she pointed out. "You offered exceptional value for it. You plan to raze the entire street to the ground, and then rip out the street itself. You yourself, my lord, pointed out that Vine Street will be utterly destroyed because you've bought everything else in it and made contracts with tradesmen already. That must have been an enormous investment. After all this, you would be deterred by finding one shop for a dressmaker?"

Evan stared in disbelief. Even Grantham seemed speechless.

Miss Dawkins was pleased to have brought them to a stand. "I know you cannot pull down everything if I stay. My shop shares a wall with Number Eleven; there is only a single course of brick dividing one side from the other, and I must tell you, it is not in pristine condition. You may own Number Eleven, but if you try to take it down, you will cause great damage to my property and I assure you my mother would file suit and pursue it forever." She tilted her head at their prolonged silence. "If you want me to leave Vine Street, you should be able and willing to find a place for me to go."

"We're not estate agents," Evan began, his shock at her bold demand wearing off.

In reply Miss Dawkins cast a pointed look toward the door. The bustle of clerks in the outer office was audible. "You have plenty of people to help you find one, sir."

His mouth thinned. She might have grasped that he was going to win the battle eventually, but she meant to make him fight for it. Unfortunately for him, he had no choice but to do it. The indignity and inconvenience would be worth avoiding the ruinous delays he'd suffer otherwise. "Very well," he bit out. "We'll find your new premises."

"Very good. Thank you, Lord Carmarthen." She beamed at him, a sunny but somehow coy expression that did terrible things to Evan's baser instincts. When had Fortune turned against him so cruelly, casting an enchanting siren as the obstacle to his ambitions? If Felicity Dawkins ever turned that smile on him for more seductive purposes, Evan had a bad feeling he would make an absolute fool of himself over her.

With some unease he forced those thoughts away. "Will you require us to find men to move your household as well?"

He'd said it drily, trying to push back against her presumption, but she merely nodded, her blue eyes wide and somber. "That would be very kind of you. Thank you, my lord; Mr. Grantham. You may send word to me when you have located a suitable property for my inspection." She curtsied again and left in a swirl of blue skirts.

The silence was deafening. "Well," said Grantham a full minute later. "I suppose that counts as success."

"Barely." Evan crossed the room and closed the door. "She wants us to do our part before she even begins hers, which may or may not succeed."

"We'll have to make sure of it, then." The solicitor reached for the bell again and rang for his clerk. "Watson," he told the man, who appeared almost instantly, "locate an estate agent immediately. We need to find premises suitable for a dressmaker's shop within the next month."

"Yes, sir. Where?"

Grantham glanced at Evan, who shrugged. "Anywhere." He listed Miss Dawkins's requirements. "And then go query everyone left in Vine Street personally to be certain each and every tenant has made arrangements to be elsewhere by next month. I want to know everything about everyone in the street, to ward off any other unpleasant surprises."

"Yes, sir."

"Tell the estate agent to send his list of properties to let to me," Evan told the clerk. "I'll take care of this myself."

Grantham looked surprised. "I'm sure it's not necessary."

"No." He flexed his hands, remembering the pleased light in Miss Dawkins's face. She did this to spite him, but they had a bargain now. On no account was he going to let her wriggle out of it. "I want that shop closed as soon as possible. If she dallies or delays for months, it will cause enormous headaches—she's right about the structural wall, isn't she?"

Grantham hesitated, then nodded once.

"I'll hold her to her word," Evan vowed. "If I have to show her every available property in London, she'll be out of Vine Street within a fortnight."

CHAPTER FOUR

For two days Felicity all but held her breath, waiting to see how the Earl of Carmarthen would react to her demands.

Every time she thought of his stunned expression, a warm bubble of satisfaction welled up in her breast. He was used to getting his own way in everything, she was sure. It galled her to no end that he was going to get his way this time, too. Mama might own Number Twelve, but Felicity had spent enough time around wealthy peers to understand that the world was organized to help them. Eventually he would find a way to pry them out, which meant her chances of getting something in return were at their best right now.

She felt rather proud of herself for coming up with this plan. Instead of being racked by dismay at the impending upheaval, she thought it entirely possible that it would be a godsend. If Lord Carmarthen could find a comparable set of rooms for the low rent she had named, even closer to the heart of fashionable London, Felicity would walk out of Vine Street without a backward glance. It had been her home all her life, but Lord Carmarthen was going to destroy it all sooner or later, and she might as well wring every possible advantage out of the situation.

But that was all supposition and hope. If Lord Carmarthen couldn't locate a suitable alternative, or simply decided it was beneath him to try, she would have little recourse or aid. Henry had checked, and it was absolutely true that Carmarthen had bought, or was in the process of buying, everything else on the street. All the tenants had been given compensation on the explicit understanding they would be gone by the end of the month. Felicity recognized that she had been dealt a losing hand months ago, before she even knew anything was at stake, and now she could only hope her opponent wanted to win graciously.

She was working on a sketch for one of her longtime clients, Lady Euphemia Hammond, when the bell jingled. Loath to stop working—Lady Euphemia was expected later in the day and Felicity wanted to have this sketch ready for her—she cast a hopeful glance at her brother's back. He sat across the office from her, working at the books. As if he could feel the weight of her gaze, his shoulders hunched slightly. He didn't want to go.

That might be her fault. Henry only came to the shop a few days a week to maintain the account books, and today she had taken up the first hour of the day with recounting her visit to Mr. Grantham's offices. By the time she finished relating every detail, her brother looked slightly dazed. Although he gamely expressed hope that her tactic would work, she could tell he thought it wouldn't. He'd been scrutinizing the books ever since, as if trying to find another way out of their dilemma. With a sigh, she put down her pencil, smoothed her skirts, and squeezed past her brother's chair.

The Earl of Carmarthen stood in the shop, his hands clasped behind his back and his head tipped up as he studied the ceiling. Felicity stopped short at the sight. Her irritation with him had obscured her memory of how attractive he was, but as the clear morning sunlight illuminated his face and figure, she was very keenly reminded of it. His dark hair was just long enough to brush the collar of his perfectly cut gray jacket, and when he turned to face her, the light behind him made his shoulders look very broad and strong.

"Miss Dawkins." He bowed.

Squashing the inexplicable butterflies in her stomach, she came to the counter. "Good morning, my lord. How may I help you today?"

One corner of his mouth curled, but his piercing blue gaze didn't falter. "Don't you want it to be the other way around—that I come to help you?"

"Which would help you in turn," she pointed out.

"Indeed." He strolled across the room and rested his hands on the counter. "Are you always so direct in your dealings with others?"

Her heart skipped, and she could feel her face growing warm. "I like to avoid misunderstandings."

"Oh?" He smiled. She'd seen his smile before, but this time she *felt* it, deep inside—which horrified her. "Very good; so do I. Will you come for a drive with me?"

Disconcerted by the warmth of his expression and the unexpected question, she froze. A drive? Why would he ask to take her driving?

"I've located a property that should meet your requirements," he added. "I presume you wish to view it before taking it."

"Oh," she said, then again as his meaning sank in. "Oh! Yes, I would, naturally." What a ninny she'd become for a minute; as if an earl would ask her to go driving for any other reason! Flustered, she turned to fetch her bonnet, and nearly ran right into her brother, coming out of the office. "I'm going out for a bit, Henry. Ask Miss Owen to mind the salon, please. She has no clients expected until later today."

Henry looked past her at the earl. As amiable as Henry was, he was also quite a big fellow and could look intimidating when he wished to. "Where are you going?"

She took a deep breath. "My lord, my brother Henry. Henry, this is Lord Carmarthen, who wishes to purchase the shop. He has found a potential new location for us, and I'm going to inspect it."

Her brother gave her a measured look. He thought she'd lost her mind, leaving the shop in the middle of the day. Either that, or he was in shock that her mad scheme might possibly be working. "Now?"

"As you see, Lord Carmarthen is here and has offered to escort me there."

Henry didn't appear convinced, but he didn't protest further. Felicity shook her head and hurried to get her things. Her fingers fumbled a little with the bonnet ribbons as she tied them. It would have been polite of Lord Carmarthen to send a note, instead of arriving out of the blue and expecting her to drop everything to go off with him. She preferred not to dwell on the fact that she *had* jumped to do so, instead of thinking of her responsibilities at Follette's. She buttoned on her spencer and went back into the main room, where Henry and the earl were standing in the middle of the salon, gazing up at the ceiling.

"I doubt it's unsafe, but it's a sign of decay," the earl was saying. He broke off as she returned. For a moment he gazed at her as if caught by surprise. Felicity tugged on her gloves. She knew she dressed well. Her appearance, she reasoned, was an advertisement for Follette's and as such she took pride in it. Her dress today was simple, but her spencer was a glorious blue and gold damask with a silk ruffle starched into a graceful arch for the collar. She'd made it over from an old polonaise jacket, bought secondhand for the fabric. It must have been a duchess's, and it made Felicity feel bold and confident—something she needed with the earl about.

"I'll keep an eye on it," Henry said. His head was still craned back as he squinted at the ceiling. "Thank you, my lord."

"Of course," murmured Carmarthen, his gaze locked on Felicity. "Shall we go, ma'am?"

He helped her into his curricle in the street. At the corner he turned into Regent Street. The southern end, near Piccadilly, was almost entirely new construction, from the gleaming curved Quadrant north to Oxford Street. Some of the houses were still being finished, and Felicity pressed a handkerchief over her mouth as a cloud of dust rose around them, kicked up by a wagon loaded with bricks. "London's barely fit to live in, with all the building going on," she muttered.

"I daresay this is a better method than having it all burn to the ground," said the earl.

"A fine argument to make to those displaced," she said wryly.

"No? A fire sweeps all away before it, without warning or recompense. Planned improvements, on the other hand, offer everyone an opportunity."

She gave him a jaundiced look. "I have the opportunity to uproot myself and my business. You have the opportunity to build expensive new shops, without having to endure any of the inconvenience yourself."

He laughed. "Anyone who thinks there is no inconvenience associated with rebuilding an entire block of buildings has obviously never done it."

"So this isn't your first time turning people out of their homes?"

The earl's easy smile stayed in place, in spite of her provocative queries. "I've never turned anyone out of his home. However, I have made fair and reasonable offers to purchase in areas that were primed for improvement."

"All at a tidy profit to yourself, of course."

"Of course," he agreed, "but not only to me. Think of the bricklayers and surveyors, Miss Dawkins, the plasterers and ironmongers who were able to pay their rent and feed their families because I employed them."

"How many of them were able to afford the houses you built?"

"Some. But all of them were paid on time, and what they did with their earnings was their choice." He slanted a curious glance at her. "Surely you can't disapprove of providing employment to so many men."

Felicity pressed her lips together. "No," she conceded. "But on that philosophy, we should keep building everywhere, all the time, so that anyone who wants to work may have a job."

"That would be ridiculous. Why build houses or shops where no one wishes to live?"

"Why tear down and rebuild houses and shops that are already occupied?"

He inhaled a deep breath, then let it out, the sound of patience being tried. "Because they are old, Miss Dawkins. Because they are unsound, and often it would cost more to repair them than to tear down and start anew, only this time with modern methods and conveniences included."

"At a tidy profit to yourself," she said again. He was not doing this out of altruism, no matter how worthy he made it sound.

"Surely the man who brings functioning sewers and drains to Vine Street must deserve a little something."

"Perhaps," she admitted, thinking of the gleaming new buildings in the Quadrant, now several streets behind them. "Although so do the people who will be displaced."

"I never said otherwise." He paused. "I couldn't help but notice that your own shop, so dear to your heart, has a leaky roof. Water has been coming down inside the walls and is responsible for the stains on your ceiling."

She darted a wary glance at him. "Yes, but it's been repaired."

"When?"

"Several months ago," she said slowly. It would have been done sooner, except that the leak had been behind a wall hanging in her mother's room, hidden from view. By the time Sophie-Louise left, the damage had reached the ground floor and thoroughly ruined the wall behind several cupboards in the workroom above. Henry had exclaimed over the bills for the repairs.

"I suggest you don't hire those workmen again," said the earl. "It's still leaking. There are fresh signs of damage in your main salon."

Now she regarded him with dismay. "I'll have someone in to look at it."

"Don't you believe me?" he asked with amusement. "Why would I possibly tell you your roof was leaking if it were not?"

"Because it's another mark against the building, a sign that you're correct in wishing to take it down—and for a lower price as well, no doubt." Felicity spoke pertly, but his words gave her real alarm. She knew Number Twelve was old. The floors all sloped, the stairs squeaked horribly, and the back chimney had a terrible draw. If Lord Carmarthen had offered to buy the building next winter, once all the commissions for the Season and the coronation festivities were completed, she would have been far more likely to accept. Now she could only say a prayer that she could stave off structural damage, and the earl's persuasions, for another few months.

Carmarthen grinned. Felicity's gaze lingered on his mouth for a moment before she resolutely looked away. "I give my word not to lower my price," he said. "Though if the leaking roof makes you more inclined to agree promptly, I shan't be disappointed."

She laughed reluctantly. "It does not. There are other reasons why I cannot accept, which I made quite plain to you and Mr. Grantham."

"So you did." He pulled up the horses and set the brake. "I trust you'll keep your side of that bargain as quickly as I've kept mine."

Felicity looked around to get her bearings; she'd been so caught up in their conversation she hadn't paid much attention to where he drove them. It was a small street, quiet and quaint, but now that she thought about it, she didn't remember turning west. "Where are we?"

"Frith Street, near Soho Square." The earl jumped down and held out his hand.

She could only look at him in dismay as her heart sank. "No . . ." Soho Square was not the right part of town. Soho was practically Bloomsbury, even farther from the fashionable customers Felicity desperately needed to attract.

"No?" Astonished annoyance flickered over his face for a moment, quickly masked. "It's an excellent property. The light is good, the rooms are quite large, and the rent is reasonable. And the roof is entirely sound." He waved one hand, indicating a wide storefront of red brick behind him.

Felicity shook her head. "I'm sorry, my lord. It's not acceptable." She ignored the hand he still held out to help her down.

Carmarthen stared at her. "I beg your pardon. It fits every particular you listed—"

"No, it doesn't," she returned quietly. Sitting in his glossy black curricle in the middle of the street made her self-conscious. It seemed passersby were watching everything. "Please take me back to Vine Street, sir."

The earl looked utterly flummoxed. He stepped closer to the carriage and put his hands on his hips. A thin frown creased his brow. "Tell me why you object to this manifestly suitable shop," he said in a low voice.

Against her will she glanced at it again. A gentleman waited on the step, conspicuously facing away from them; no doubt the estate agent with an agreement to let in his pocket. Lord Carmarthen was certainly eager to get her out of Vine Street. And it did look like a handsome shop, with tall mullioned windows that would expertly display wares . . . to the wives of the prosperous merchants who lived nearby.

She turned away. "I'm sorry, my lord," she said, softly but firmly. "It is not acceptable."

"Is that all the explanation you're going to give?" he exclaimed.

"If you drive me home, I will explain." Unlike him, she was trying to keep her voice low. Even though she couldn't possibly bring Follette's to this street, it was a clean and well-kept neighborhood, and she had no wish to offend anyone who lived here.

For a moment she thought the earl would lose his temper. His mouth flattened, his eyes flashed, and Felicity felt her own temper stirring. If he upbraided her in public—

"Very well," he said curtly. "A moment, please." He stalked away and spoke to the lingering gentleman. Then he came back and stepped into the curricle. With a snap of the whip he started the horses. "Explain what was so deficient you could not even set foot in the place."

"The shop itself looked large and pleasant," she said. "Please don't think I found it lacking, particularly the sound roof. The problem is with the location."

"In what way?"

She heard the cynicism in his voice and it poked at her temper again. "You don't understand fashion, if you need to ask."

Carmarthen frowned. "Obviously I do not. What has fashion got to do with shop premises? Is your ability to stitch silk and lace compromised by the general character of the neighborhood? I confess, I'd no idea seamstresses were so susceptible to such vanity, particularly at the paltry rent you wish to pay."

"I don't pay any rent at the moment. Even thirty pounds a year will be an increase."

"Yes," he said—through his teeth from the sound of it—"but you shall have the money from the sale of your current shop."

"Which must also be spent on preparing the new premises, moving my household, replacing any fabric damaged in the move, and many other expenses! And once it is gone, that sum will be gone forever. My mother may well wish to set something aside for her old age; her life's work and savings are invested in Follette's." She glared at him. Only a wealthy man would carelessly brush aside the issue of money.

Felicity's plans, if they came to fruition, would push her family's income back to comfortable levels, but she was keenly aware that the Dawkinses were still far from secure. Until she, her mother, and her brother had healthy sums saved and invested, with a thriving shop to support them without touching the capital, she would not stop tracking every shilling. She couldn't. If they lost Follette's, their options would be too terrible to contemplate.

The earl fell quiet. Felicity felt flushed and irritable, which made her feel awkward as well. She wished they were already back in Vine Street. Carmarthen simply didn't understand. He called her vain— and a mere seamstress—while brushing aside mention of thirty pounds, which was a very handsome bit of coin to every seamstresses Felicity knew.

"What sort of neighborhood did you hope for?"

His voice made her start. She dared a glance at him, but he was serious. He met her gaze, and she sensed he was as disappointed in the morning's outing as she was. For different reasons, no doubt, but somehow it took the edge off her irritation to know that he was honestly trying to satisfy her conditions.

"A dressmaker in Soho Square attracts a very different sort of client than a dressmaker near Bond Street," she explained. "You may wrinkle your brow and declare that it makes no difference in the sort of clothes one can sew, but examine your own habits. Do you patronize a boot maker in Whitechapel? Do you venture to Holborn for your shirts?" He said nothing, but his jaw tightened. Encouraged, Felicity went on. "I have no objection to clothing the wives of merchants and bankers. Indeed, they are often wonderful clients! But the success of a modiste may fairly be judged by the elegance and status of the ladies she clothes. To have a gown worn to Court is a triumph; to be spoken of in the ballrooms of Mayfair puts your name, and your work, in front of women whose patronage can set the style and ensure a steady stream of other clients."

"So you wish to be near Bond Street."

"Yes," she said, unable to keep the longing from her voice. Bond Street was a bounty of fashionable needs, from milliners and glovers to drapers and dressmakers, but also of bookshops, wine merchants, hairdressers, and jewelers. To be in Bond Street meant a merchant had reached the pinnacle of taste and desirability.

Unfortunately, the rents charged for shop frontage there reflected this fact. The next best thing was to be near Bond Street, and it had been solace to Felicity that Vine Street was only a short distance away, a few minutes' walk down Piccadilly. But now Mr. Nash's Quadrant and Regent Street sliced through the neighborhood, acting like a gleaming wall between the elegance of Mayfair on the west, and the slowly fading area to the east.

Carmarthen didn't speak again until they reached Vine Street. When he stopped the curricle in front of Follette's, he turned to her before getting down. "You never said you wished to be in Bond Street when you came to Mr. Grantham's office."

Felicity's lips parted. Was he trying to blame her for this? "I don't require premises *in* Bond Street," she exclaimed. "I never said that. I was quite clear, however, that I do require a situation that would be *more* convenient for my clients and employees, not less. Soho Square would be a great deal less convenient, as they would all be required to cross the great swath of chaos that is Regent Street. You can see even this short drive has been filthy." She pointedly brushed at some of the dust that had settled on her skirt. "If you were uncertain of what constituted convenience to me, you could have asked at any time."

The door of the shop opened and Henry stepped out. He must have been watching for her return. Felicity beckoned to him, and he jumped forward to help her down from the earl's elegant but high carriage. "Good day, my lord," she said, giving him a curtsy. "Thank you for driving me home." Carmarthen nodded once, but didn't say anything. Feeling unexpectedly let down, she went into the shop.

Henry followed her. "It did not go well, I take it."

Felicity hung up her bonnet and spencer. "He found a shop in Soho Square, and didn't seem to understand why it was all wrong."

Her brother cleared his throat. "Why *was* it all wrong?"

She sighed. This was why she was in charge and Henry was not. She loved her brother, and knew him to be intelligent and thoughtful, but the finer points of the fashion business weren't important to him. Henry was meticulous at keeping the books and he excelled at dealing with vendors and bankers, but he felt as Lord Carmarthen obviously did: A gown was a gown, and where the sewing took place had no impact on the final product. "Because it would mark a decline in the shop's status. Ladies like to aspire to their fashions, and to their modiste. It might suffice to be in Soho Square to start out, before moving up—which means moving west. To move eastward . . ." She gave a helpless shrug. "It would undo everything we've been working to achieve."

"It really makes that great a difference where we're located?"

"Sadly, it does."

"You would understand ladies' behavior better than I," he said after a moment. "His Lordship was disappointed."

Felicity tried not to think that the earl might decide their bargain was too much trouble, and not come back. Perhaps she should brace herself for more demands from the solicitor. "As was I."

CHAPTER FIVE

Evan drove home, brooding over the morning's outing. *It is not acceptable,* echoed her voice in his memory. *And why not?* he wanted to argue. Who was she, in decrepit Vine Street, to look down on a perfectly sound shop in Soho Square?

He crossed Regent Street, where traffic slowed to a crawl. He grimaced and waved one hand to clear away a cloud of dust billowing from a block where a new foundation was being dug. Construction had started near Carlton House and was slowly worming northward as Mr. Nash demolished, straightened, and rebuilt the street. And— as Miss Dawkins had said—it was filthy.

Perhaps she had a point. Evan couldn't see his mother venturing through this mess in search of a new dressmaker, not when it was far easier and more comfortable to go to Bond Street. And if his mother, who was a very reasonable woman, wouldn't go, it was a certainty that other, flightier, ladies wouldn't go, either.

On the other hand, Bond Street rents were quite high. As part of the diligence on Vine Street, Grantham had drawn up a list of the rents that properties across London fetched, to see what would be reasonable in the new Vine Street. Bond Street properties had been near the top of the list, which hadn't surprised Evan. He paid the bills his mother and sister accrued while shopping there. If Miss Dawkins wanted to be in Bond Street, she'd need to pay considerably more than thirty pounds per annum.

He turned into the mews and handed off the carriage to a groom. Perhaps he ought to have asked more specific questions about what she wanted before he agreed to this bargain. He thought about that as he went into the house and strode up the stairs to his study. What would he have done differently?

Not much, he concluded. The only real possibility, which he could still elect, was to let Grantham to handle the business. He had already spent far too much time thinking about Felicity Dawkins, often for reasons he didn't want to examine closely, and if he told Grantham to deal directly with her, it would free Evan from any obligation to see her again.

And yet, inexplicably, he didn't do that.

Instead he sent off a note to Mr. Abbott, the estate agent he'd had to leave standing on the step in Soho Square, detailing the sort of property Miss Dawkins wanted. Anticipating the man's first objection, he added that rents up to one hundred pounds per annum were acceptable this time. That could be negotiated with the landlord, once a place was found.

To his relief, the agent was very prompt. The next morning he arrived with a list of properties near Bond Street that might be suitable. Evan told him to arrange viewings, then sent a note to Follette's dress shop informing Miss Dawkins. The best and fastest way to get that woman out of his thoughts was to get her out of Vine Street. Once she was gone, his unwarranted fascination with her would fade. She would be occupied running her shop and he would be occupied with his building project. There would be no more distraction in his life, the way it ought to be.

Felicity received the earl's note as she went down to the salon. The seamstresses often arrived at nine and began work, but she didn't open the salon to clients until later. London ladies didn't shop early. The presence of a liveried footman peering through the window gave her a start, and she rushed across the room to open the door.

"With Lord Carmarthen's compliments," said the fellow as he held out a note.

"Thank you." She fingered the thick paper. Bracing herself, she broke the seal. But instead of the curt dismissal she feared, he wrote that he had located more properties and asked if she would be willing to view them, beginning this afternoon. This time he listed the streets, which were all west of Regent Street, and some were very near Bond Street.

She felt at once heartened and chastened, and resolved to be more diplomatic next time. She must stop thinking of the earl as an opponent and consider him a partner instead. When they viewed these properties, she must be clear and objective about them, and communicate clearly to the earl what was right and what was wrong. *A little explanation goes a long way,* she reminded herself, thinking of how she would approach a client.

"Will there be an answer?" the footman asked. "His Lordship asked me to inquire, and carry back any reply you wished to send."

"Oh! Of course. Tell him that will be perfectly agreeable, please."

The servant bowed and left, and Felicity went back into the shop.

She headed upstairs to the workroom, where her employees were busily sewing the gowns that should—*would*—set Follette's on the path to success and security. Felicity had asked everyone to be here today because it was time to tell them about Lord Carmarthen's plans. His note only made her more certain of what she would say. At her entrance they all looked up.

"Good morning," she said. "I want only a few minutes of your time. I have news."

She caught the worried looks exchanged between Alice and Sally, the two apprentice seamstresses. "Is it very bad news?" Sally asked hesitantly. She had been here for four years, since she was a child of twelve. She'd seen Felicity dismiss Mrs. Cartwright, which had not been a completely cordial parting.

"On the contrary," she said firmly, "I think it's very good news. But first . . . You must all have noticed the changes in Vine Street. Mr. White's tailor shop closing up, for instance."

"And the coffee shop at the end of the street," murmured Selina Fontaine. She had been at Follette's the longest and must be very aware of the recent decline.

Felicity nodded. "All the shops are closing up, I'm afraid." Anxiety seemed to ripple through the room. "The reason for this is a large improvement planned for Vine Street. Someone has bought every other building, and plans to build new sewers and install pipes for gas. To do all this, however, all the buildings must be torn down and rebuilt."

Delyth Owen gasped. Selina's face went perfectly still. Only Alice seemed undaunted. "But ma'am, that'll be a terrible mess. Look at Regent Street!"

"Precisely," Felicity agreed. "The gentleman expects Vine Street to be as fine as Regent Street, and to that end he wishes to buy this building as well." She paused, suddenly uncertain about what she was about to promise her employees, these talented, hardworking women who depended on her. Delyth had left a career designing costumes for the theater to come work for her; Selina had stayed with her through the hardest of times. Alice and Sally were learning a trade, but their wages helped support their families. Not only Felicity's family depended on Madame Follette's, and that meant they were all depending on Felicity's wisdom in making the right decisions.

But . . . She believed Lord Carmarthen to be a gentleman who would keep his word.

"The gentleman who has bought everything has made my mother a handsome offer for this building," she went on, tamping down her doubts. Her first duty was to be honest, but also optimistic. If Delyth and Selina left her before the coronation commissions were completed, Felicity didn't know what she'd do. They had already attracted several excellent clients. Delyth had secured a large commission from the Merrithew family, whose matriarch had been one of the leaders of London fashion in years past, and Selina was working on a number of gowns for the sister-in-law of the Duke of Barrowmore. Those were the sort of clients Follette's desperately needed. "We will only accept it when we have secured a comparable, if not superior, location for the shop. No one's employment is in danger, and neither is any commission your clients have made. We shall be able to complete every gown ordered for the coronation in time. But at some point, Follette's will be relocating from Vine Street."

"Where to?" asked Sally timidly.

"I don't know yet," Felicity confessed. "I hope not far from here. I'm going out later today to view more properties with Lord Carmarthen, who is improving the street. He's agreed to help us locate appropriate premises."

Delyth and Selina exchanged a glance. "You're quite certain everything will work out well?" asked Delyth.

"Yes," she replied immediately. One way or another, she would make it so. "I wanted you to know that we shall not close. No one will lose her place because of this, and indeed, I hope it will lead to even more commissions from society ladies, which will benefit us all. If you have any questions and concerns, please speak to me. I value each and every one of you, and your talents." She looked around, but no one spoke. She mustered a smile. "Then I suppose we should all get back to work."

CHAPTER SIX

Evan turned into Vine Street resolved to remain focused on business today. Yesterday he'd treated it too lightly, so confident had he been that the shop in Soho Square would solve the problem. He hadn't understood Miss Dawkins's position, and he'd made a bad choice. She must have feared as much; during the drive to Soho Square, he'd tried to tease her, and her replies had been a bit tart.

So today he would take careful heed of what she said. They had a bargain, after all, and Evan was keen to fulfill his side of it. He stopped the carriage and went inside the shop.

This time she was waiting for him, stunning in a raspberry walking dress. She said a quiet word to the young lady behind the counter as she tied on her bonnet, and then she turned to him. "I am ready, my lord."

Evan noticed the girl at the counter watching him very closely. He gave Miss Dawkins his arm and led her out to the curricle. "Am I hated by the whole shop now?" he asked, guessing what motivated the young lady's stare.

A faint blush colored her cheeks. "Of course not. Why would you think such a thing?"

"Your assistant is glaring at me." He tipped his hat to the girl, who was watching them through the window. She quickly turned her back, and Evan started the horses.

"I spoke to everyone this morning to let them know what is happening in Vine Street. I'm sure some had begun to wonder; I rarely leave the shop during the day, yet have done so several times this week because of . . ." She paused, clearly searching for the right words to describe it. "You."

He gave a short bark of laughter. "No wonder she stared! You make me sound ominous."

"Oh no!" she exclaimed, laying her hand on his arm. "I didn't mean that."

Her hand seemed to sear his wrist. Evan called himself three kinds of fool for being so aware of this woman. "Excellent," he said lightly. "It would be very distressing to be thought a monster."

She released his arm. "I wouldn't call you monstrous, sir, but disruptive. You cannot deny you've turned things upside down in Vine Street."

He thought about telling her how some of the other tenants and owners had jumped at his offers to buy. They recognized that Vine Street had two futures: It could remain as it was, growing shabbier and more neglected until it became a forgotten little alley overshadowed by Regent Street; or it could be transformed into an extension of Regent Street, just as modern, but shielded from the traffic of the thoroughfare. Sooner or later they must leave Vine Street, and Evan offered them good value to leave sooner.

Again he reminded himself that Felicity Dawkins had a different view, and that arguing his side of the story would only cause more discord. "Only with good intentions," he settled for saying.

"Yes," she said quietly after a moment. "I believe that."

Evan glanced at her from the corner of his eye, uncertain that he'd heard correctly. Her cheeks were still flushed—beautifully, he couldn't keep from noticing—but she was studying him thoughtfully.

"I do," she repeated with some force, as if he'd questioned her. "But I hope you can understand that I—and my mother—are reluctant to move for equally good reasons."

"Convenience," he said. "Security."

"I have four employees. Four women whose livelihoods depend on Follette's, and I am responsible for them as well as for my own family. Your offer to purchase our shop is generous," she allowed, "but my greater concern is to keep the business on sound footing, which requires clients. In Soho Square we would be even farther from Mayfair, making it less convenient for ladies to visit us. Yes, we can sew the gowns anywhere; but to have commissions for those gowns, we must have clients, and my seamstresses must be able to come to the shop in safety. We often work late hours, my lord, and I cannot ask them to walk all the way across London in the dark."

"I see," he said, mildly ashamed that he'd not thought of young seamstresses walking home at night. "I should have inquired more closely into your requirements for a shop, and for that I apologize."

She smiled, the same warm, dimpled smile that had snared his attention the first day he met her. "I accept." Her smile grew, and she gave a rueful little laugh. "When I told my brother about your first visit, he asked what an earl could want with a dress shop. He was right, of course; what could you know about being a modiste? I should have explained my position better at the start."

"I haven't the first idea about being a modiste," Evan admitted. "But I did research property values very thoroughly, and what improvements would yield the most benefit for the longest time."

"That is good sense," she replied. "And good dressmaking sense as well. I don't make gowns that cater solely to the fashion of the moment. A gown can be fashionable while still being timeless, so a woman might wear it for a few years at least, with alterations and different accessories."

"Perhaps we're not so different," he said, pulling up in front of the first shop to let. "We want to make things that will last."

Her lips parted in surprise as he jumped down and held out a hand to help her. "Perhaps not," she said, sounding pleasantly surprised.

Evan grinned. "Let's hope this shop is suitable, then, so we can both carry on."

Felicity Dawkins laughed, and then she took his arm, and Evan felt the strangest sense of something falling into place inside him. What was wrong with him? He was attracted to her—understandably, on purely physical grounds—but even when he tried to suppress it in the interest of furthering his architectural ambitions, talking business with her made him want her more. What lady in London would talk about creating things—even more, openly speak of being in business? Not one he could think of.

She tipped back her head to survey the building, and belatedly Evan did, too. He was pleased to see that Abbott had done better this time, finding a shop that looked every bit as clean and sound as the one in Soho Square, but located just steps from Bond Street.

The door opened and a man stepped out. "Lord Carmarthen?"

"Yes. And Miss Dawkins."

The fellow was already looking at her with far too much interest. "A pleasure, ma'am. Joseph Ferrars, at your service. Won't you come inside?"

"Thank you, Mr. Ferrars." She gave him a bright smile as they went into the shop. As she passed the man, his gaze raked over her in obvious appraisal. Evan tightened his jaw, and made certain to stand between him and Miss Dawkins.

"The salon is large," she said, oblivious to the way Ferrars was staring at her.

"A full fifteen feet from wall to wall," said Ferrars. "May I draw your attention to the windows? Newly glazed, and ideal for display. I believe you are searching for premises suitable for a milliner?"

"A modiste." She leaned forward to inspect the window, and Ferrars stole a glance at her bottom.

"It's a bit dark," said Evan. "North-facing shops always are."

"It has gas lighting." Unperturbed, Ferrars demonstrated the valve on the sconces.

Miss Dawkins walked around the room, studying the shelves behind the counter and the office at the rear. "There are no rooms that could be used for fittings."

Ferrars jumped forward. "Upstairs. Let me show you." He led the way up the stairs.

"Are you the landlord?" she asked him as they walked through three rooms on the first floor. Evan alternated between watching her face for any indication of approval, and keeping an eye on Ferrars.

"As it turns out, I am." Ferrars was watching her, and now he smiled, a rather predatory expression to Evan's mind. "May I ask if you're the owner of the business in question?"

"My mother founded it and now I am in charge." She ran her fingers along a window pane in the large front room. "This is small for a workroom, but it might suffice. The fitting rooms are quite generous."

"Yes, indeed they are." Ferrars glanced at Evan, who was standing with his arms folded. "Are you a partner in the business, my lord?"

"Oh no," exclaimed Miss Dawkins before he could speak. "His Lordship is merely helping me find a new situation. He has nothing to do with the shop. He is . . ." She hesitated, darting a quick glance at Evan. "A friend," she finished.

Evan's private delight at that appellation was instantly squashed by the satisfied look on Ferrars's face.

"And I believe you're interested in taking the lodgings upstairs as well?" the landlord asked as they went back into the corridor. Evan knew this shop was suitable, if small, but somehow he wanted to find fault with it. He didn't like the way Ferrars looked at her, and he didn't like the idea of Ferrars stopping in all the time. The man had keys to the place and he could let himself in at will. Evan told himself he was concerned for the welfare of all the women working at Madame Follette's, but the truth was he didn't want Ferrars prowling about Felicity Dawkins. He could only imagine how hard it would be for a woman, living alone, to fend off advances from her landlord . . .

"Yes, if they are available."

"They are," said Ferrars, "but they're not large. If you are searching for lodgings for a family . . ."

"No," she told him. "Only myself."

"Very good," murmured Ferrars with satisfaction. "Let me show you." He took out a ring of keys and unlocked a door at the rear of the corridor, opposite the stairs to the salon below. "A private staircase, as you see, ma'am." He swept it open and bowed. Miss Dawkins gave Evan a pleased look and started up the stairs. Ferrars turned to watch her go, a focused, hungry expression on his face, and Evan's sour mood condensed into one thought: The problem with the shop was Ferrars. He hoped some other shortcoming would put Miss Dawkins off the place entirely, because he found himself thinking that he'd have to set Ferrars straight, and perhaps post one of his footmen as a guard, if she relocated her shop here.

He brushed past Ferrars to follow Miss Dawkins up the stairs, putting out his arm to block the man when he started to come, too. "Allow us a few minutes to discuss things," he said, in a tone that brooked no argument. With only the tiniest flash of annoyance, Ferrars nodded. Evan pulled the door closed behind him, and jogged up the stairs.

Felicity Dawkins stood in the middle of a modest sitting room. She had taken off her bonnet, and the afternoon sun illuminated her hair into a glowing halo of gold. She turned to face him. "It's a wonderful location."

That was not what he wanted to hear. "Really?" he said vaguely, strolling around the room and taking a look out the windows.

"Oh yes." She came up beside him. "I think it may be suitable."

"You said the workroom was too small. That seems a great failing."

"It's smaller than I would like," she admitted. "But to be this near to Bond Street, I can make allowances."

Evan squinted at something in the street below. "What do you think of Ferrars?"

She paused. "What do you mean?"

He could see their reflection in the glass, his figure dark and hers bright. Her chin didn't come to his shoulder, and she was slimmer to boot. Ferrars was almost Evan's height, and probably outweighed him by a stone. Perhaps her brother would be around enough to keep the lecherous landlord at bay. Perhaps she was accustomed to warding men off and would have no trouble with Ferrars. Perhaps it wasn't his place to say anything at all—and yet . . .

"He seems excessively interested in you," he said abruptly. "I suppose you didn't notice him staring at your—" He coughed. "Staring at you rather boldly."

"No," she said, startled. "Was he really?"

Evan gave a curt nod. "He has keys to every door in the place. I gather your brother has his own lodgings elsewhere, and doesn't come to the shop every day."

"No," she said again. "Henry only comes a few days a week, unless I ask him . . . Are you certain Mr. Ferrars's interest was salacious?"

His jaw tightened, picturing again the expression on Ferrars's face as he watched the sway of her skirts. "If a man looked at my sister that way, I would beat him to a bloody mess."

She said nothing. Evan waited for her to express shock, outrage, disapproval . . . anything.

"My lord," she finally said, "are you actually trying to persuade me this shop is unacceptable?"

"I think I am."

"Because of Mr. Ferrars." She sounded disbelieving.

"Because you are a woman, living alone, with other young women coming into the shop. Perhaps your brother can keep him in line, but it's a risk I would not personally take, if I were in your shoes."

Her reflection turned toward his. Evan darted a glance directly at her. She was gazing up at him with worry. "Do you really think he's that bad?"

A caustic smile touched his mouth. Ferrars hadn't even been discreet about ogling her. "Would you welcome his attentions?"

"No!" she exclaimed with some horror. "Not at all." She cleared her throat. "Well. I don't think this shop will suit me after all."

The tension in his muscles eased as quickly as a bubble popping. Feeling immeasurably lighter and happier, Evan grinned. "Shall we visit the other property?"

The smile that lit her face was real. "Yes."

They went down to the salon, where Ferrars was waiting. "Thank you, sir," said Miss Dawkins politely. "Very handsome, but smaller than I require."

Ferrars's disappointment was obvious. "You'll have trouble finding a larger place this near Bond Street on these terms, ma'am."

"I shall risk it," she told him.

His mouth tightened. "As you wish. Good day to you." He followed them back to the salon, and closed the door with a bang behind them.

"He didn't take that well, did he?" muttered Miss Dawkins.

Evan glanced over his shoulder. Ferrars was watching through the window, and Evan made sure to give him an icy glare. "Never a good sign." Dismissing the landlord, he turned to the woman beside him, who was regarding him with far more warmth than she ever had before. "Shall we walk to the next possibility? It's nearby, and such a fine day."

Her eyes rounded in pleased surprise. "Yes." Evan motioned to a boy lingering hopefully nearby, handing him a coin to watch his carriage and horses, then offered Miss Dawkins his arm and led her toward Bond Street.

"Was he really staring at me?" she asked as they walked.

"Are you calling me a liar?" His eyebrows twitched upward.

She laughed. "Not at all! I only meant that I never caught him."

He glanced at her. "Do you often catch men staring at you?"

"Oh goodness, that sounds so vain." She had a way of wrinkling her nose in wry amusement that Evan found mesmerizing. "It does happen. Many so-called gentlemen have little respect for a woman in trade. More than one has assumed that since I make my own living, I would happily welcome any indecent overtures and propositions."

"Idiots," said Evan in a clipped voice. "I hope your brother sets them straight."

"Sometimes. Henry looks imposing, but he has the kindest heart, and no stomach for beating up a client's husband merely for having wandering eyes."

He scowled. "Your clients' husbands do this?"

"On a few occasions," she admitted quietly, before continuing in a more confident tone. "But my mother experienced it first, and she taught me to defend myself. Never cross a woman armed with pins and scissors."

Evan didn't think pins or scissors would stop a truly determined man, especially not if that man got her alone in a shop he owned. "You shouldn't have to defend yourself against your landlord. Nor anyone, for that matter. If any client's husbands make a nuisance of themselves, tell me."

This time the look she gave him was openly shocked. "That isn't necessary, my lord."

"Carmarthen," he said. "If your brother is hesitant to thrash someone who's harassing you because it might impact your clientele, I'll do it."

"Why?" She seemed to regret the question the moment she asked it; a beautiful blush stained her face, and she put one hand over her mouth. "I mean—"

"You called me a friend, back there," he said when she stopped. "Did you mean it, or was it just for Mr. Ferrars's benefit?"

"Apparently it didn't deter him from staring," she murmured. She wouldn't look at him. "I shouldn't have presumed to call our acquaintance such . . ."

"No." Without thinking he laid his free hand on hers. "It was a pleasant surprise. Can we be friends?"

She raised her head, giving him a wary look. "You want to buy my shop."

"And raze it to the ground," he agreed. "But not without fairly compensating you and seeing you settled into another, equally respectable, shop."

A glimmer of a smile teased her lips. "And you don't mind that I insisted you help with the latter?"

Evan grinned. "It's what I would have done, in your place, so I can hardly hold that against you."

Her eyes widened, her lips parted, and Felicity Dawkins burst into laughter. "Not really!"

"Something like it," he replied, inordinately pleased that he'd made her laugh. "Never waste a strong bargaining position."

"Well!" Still smiling, she shook her head. "I confess, I never thought you'd see it that way."

"I have always respected confidence and honesty. You've dealt fairly with me, and I've tried to do the same with you."

Her smile grew warmer. "I do appreciate that. So often—" She stopped and bit her lip. "Not every man would."

"Am I convicted of being just like every other man?" Evan made a face. "I doubt I have much in common with Mr. Ferrars, for one."

"No," she said at once, still smiling. "I didn't mean to imply that." She glanced up at him. "This has been a very illuminating conversation, sir."

"Carmarthen," he said again, not even sure why he wanted her to call him that. Every time she said "my lord" it felt like a sharp prod to his conscience, reminding him that they were from different worlds. Evan much preferred to dwell on the more pleasant title of "friend," which could possibly lead to something more intimate.

They turned the corner into Bond Street, and Miss Dawkins took a deep breath of pure pleasure. Evan stole a glance at her, and nearly tripped over his own feet. Her face glowed with eager excitement, nothing reserved or hesitant about it.

"I adore Bond Street," she said rapturously.

"Why so?"

She smiled, showing the dimple in her cheek. "Everything that is lovely and elegant and well-made can be found here." She nodded at the shop beside them. "The finest glover in London. And there, two excellent milliners. Jewelers, hatters, boot makers, china and lace and books and drapers!"

Evan looked around and saw shops, filled with ladies and gentlemen and servants carting boxes and packages in their wakes. The sight of so much commerce was gratifying, but he also noted the older buildings and how much they could use some improvement. "And that's why you want to be here?"

"Yes. To be in Bond Street signifies that your work is some of the finest in London." She stopped in front of a large window. "Merely strolling down the street is a joy. See how handsome the displays are!"

"Bolts of cloth."

She gasped at his dry statement. "Oh, but look how beautifully they're presented! You can see the glorious colors of this damask, and the print on that cotton. The velvet is arranged to catch the light and show off the rich sheen of the nap."

"Indeed." Evan gave it a closer examination. "Who would have noticed?"

Miss Dawkins laughed. "Only every woman in London. Several times clients have come to me with a length of silk, proclaiming it the most beautiful thing they've ever seen and wanting it made up into something."

"Do you?"

"Whenever possible. It's an extra challenge, of course, but I never like to disappoint a client."

"I feel ever so grateful for my own tailor now," Evan said. "He only asks if I've gained or lost any weight, then sends the finished garments."

Her eyes opened wide. "With no choice of fabric or cut?"

"No. What difference does it make?" Evan lifted one shoulder. "I expect my valet pays more attention to my clothing than I do."

"That, I believe," she murmured, studying his coat and waistcoat with a critical eye.

An unwonted thrill went through him. "What fault do you find?" he managed to ask, his mouth going dry as her gaze moved over him. He imagined peeling off each layer of fabric as she watched, perhaps even helped. The idea of her hands sliding over his skin seized his mind like a fever.

She raised her eyes to his. "Color," she said, her voice husky. "You lack color. But your eyes—" She stopped, her breath catching for a moment. "Your eyes are an unusual color, my lord."

Evan barely heard the last two words. She was attracted to him. The flush on her cheeks gave her away; her eyes were wide and dark and her breathing had sped up. Triumph surged through his veins, as potent as the finest whisky. "Thank you," he murmured.

Miss Dawkins—Felicity—wet her lips, and something inside Evan seemed to growl with hunger. If they hadn't been standing, stock-still, in the middle of the busiest street in London, he would have kissed her, and damn the consequences. "Let's go in."

Evan blinked. "In?"

"Inside the . . ." She motioned toward the door, a blush coloring her face. "Inside the draper's shop."

"Yes. Yes, of course." He would have gone anywhere she invited him right then. Evan swept open the door, and led her inside.

CHAPTER SEVEN

Felicity took a deep breath as they stepped into Percival & Condell's draper's shop, grateful for the moment to regain her poise. She must have lost her mind, telling the Earl of Carmarthen that his wardrobe lacked anything. Everything he wore was of fine fabric, well cut and expertly made. His outfit today had cost a very handsome sum, even though it was all in dark, somber shades.

And while she thought nothing of teasing her brother over an unfortunate choice of waistcoat, it was a very different thing to stare boldly and wantonly at the earl's figure. She could find no fault there, from his broad shoulders to his trim waist and strong legs. Her mother would smack her if she'd seen how Felicity had studied Carmarthen's trousers—which fit very, very well indeed.

But when she looked at his face, trying to save herself, she only felt more keenly aware of how handsome he was, from the loose locks of dark hair that regularly tempted her to comb her fingers through, to the brilliant blue of his eyes. Felicity had blue eyes herself; she had never thought blue a particularly arresting eye color. But the earl's were different, almost aqua-colored, like the sea on a fine day. And when he asked if they could be friends, and offered to beat up any man who bothered her, Felicity feared she would forget herself entirely and succumb to the spell of his voice and the temptation lurking in his gaze . . .

She took another deep breath. Theirs was a business relationship—a friendly one, but one that would end as soon as their bargain was fulfilled. She needed to remember that while His

Lordship escorted her around town, offering his arm and laughing when she was impertinent.

"May I help you?" A clerk approached, his head angled in question.

"We require some color," said the earl. "Or rather, I do."

Felicity flushed crimson. "Fine wool," she said quickly. "Shades of blue and green. Also damask and satins, nothing elaborate or fussy, but elegant."

"Yes, madam." The clerk headed behind his counter and began studying the bolts of fabric on the shelves that lined the walls.

"Elegant," murmured the earl as they followed. "Thank you for adding that. For a moment I had the most dreadful vision of a waistcoat embroidered with chickens or cabbage roses."

She smiled. "I would never suggest that. Everything in fashion must be chosen with the wearer's image in mind: Is he stern? Regal? Fun-loving and a bit rebellious?" The clerk laid three bolts of wool on the counter. "Not this," Felicity told him, dismissing one immediately. "What about that cerulean wool?" The clerk took it from the shelf and added it to her pile. She stripped off one glove and ran her hand over it. "No, the weave is too coarse. Do you have anything else similarly shaded, but finer?"

For the next several minutes she kept the clerk busy, running around the shop finding different fabrics as the bolts piled up in front of her. Carmarthen leaned against the counter and watched in amused silence, his arms folded. Felicity didn't doubt that it was his presence that kept the clerk's attention focused solely on them, even to the point of brushing off other customers begging his assistance. But she'd forgotten how much *fun* it was to shop. At the silk warehouses she had to keep several competing interests in mind: not just the color and the quality of the fabric, but the cost and what she could do with the cloth, and for which client. Today she could think only of the man beside her, and what would suit him.

"What image do you wish to reinforce for me?" asked the earl, when the counter was piled with bolts. "Rebellious, or regal?"

She laughed. "Neither." She had removed both her gloves by now, the better to assess the feel of the cloth. "Something vibrant and bold, befitting a man who would buy an entire street in order to tear it down." She held up a length of royal blue wool in front of his waistcoat. It went well with his charcoal trousers and gray coat. She put it down and studied the selection. "Something elegant and modern, as you wish to rebuild Vine Street in that style." She held up a sage green cloth, woven with a thin gray stripe. She tilted her head, considering it. "I like this one."

"You're very fond of color." His eyes dipped to take in her pelisse, which was as brightly pink as ripe raspberries.

Felicity smiled. "I am. But only those that suit me. When I was a child, my mother made my clothes from scraps." She made a face. "So much white muslin! It was all beautiful, but I got such a scolding when I got dirty."

"Were you raised in the Vine Street shop?" he asked, surprised.

"Yes." She held up a forest green satin with a pattern of leaves in gold thread. "Striking, don't you think?"

"Bold and vibrant," he said, echoing her earlier words. "What else suits me?"

Felicity reached for one of the damasks. It was woven in shades of blue, from deep indigo to hints of pale azure. "Rich," she said quietly, holding it up against his chest. "Suitable for a lord."

"I see. But does it match my eyes?"

She made the mistake of looking up. There was nothing regal about the way he was looking at her. Desire, pure and simple, burned in his gaze, and it ignited a reciprocal spark inside her own breast.

No, not ignited. That fuse had been lit some time ago. Felicity had been attracted to men before and been able to squash the spark. But every time she thought she'd got over her attraction to *this* man, it flared back into life the next time she saw him, brighter and hotter. If she didn't keep her distance from it—from him—she'd find herself scorched before long.

She cleared her throat and busied herself with rolling the damask back onto the bolt. "No, not a match. A complement."

"Excellent," murmured the earl. "Send the lot to Cavendish Square, number eighteen," he told the clerk, handing the man one of his cards.

Felicity's eyes widened. "All of it?" she said stupidly.

The earl picked up his hat and offered her his arm again. "You spoke so beautifully of each one, I couldn't choose."

He'd just bought twenty pounds' worth of fabric without batting an eye. The silk damask alone must have cost ten pounds. Forcibly reminded again that they were from different worlds, she took his arm in silence and let him lead her out into the sunshine.

"Here we are." He stopped at the next block of shops and flourished one arm. The same fellow who had been in Soho Square waited in the doorway, although he stepped back without a word as the earl held up one hand.

It was obvious that this shop was superior to the last. It was better maintained, for one, and occupied a corner, with Bond Street traffic on one side and a more sheltered street adjoining it. Unusually, it had large windows facing onto both streets, which meant more light in most of the rooms.

"So many windows," said Felicity in surprise.

"Shall we go inside?" He led her to the steps, introducing the fellow waiting with the keys as Mr. Abbott, letting agent.

The salon was smaller than Ferrars's, but Felicity couldn't take her eyes off the windows. There was even a bow window at the corner, where one could pose a full-sized mannequin in a gown. Already she could envision the displays she would set up to entice passersby to come inside. "A bit small, but very bright," she said, wandering over to inspect the counter. "What sort of shop was it?"

"A millinery shop, ma'am," said Mr. Abbott. "It should require very little work to make it suitable for a modiste."

"So it seems." She turned down the narrow corridor, lined with shelves and drawers, perfect for storing supplies. "There is only one small room. Are there more upstairs suitable for fittings?"

"Indeed." Abbott hurried forward to show them the way upstairs. The workroom was adequate, with plenty of cupboards and two stoves for heat, and three smaller rooms that would serve as offices or fitting rooms. When Mr. Abbot asked if she would like to see the lodgings above, Felicity nodded eagerly. Even though she told herself not to be too easily satisfied, she couldn't see anything wrong with this shop.

The rooms upstairs were small, but included two bedrooms as well as a sitting room. She walked through them, inspecting every inch. When she came back into the sitting room overlooking Bond Street, the earl was alone; Mr. Abbott must have gone back downstairs.

"What do you think?" he asked. He looked very much at home, resting one elbow on the mantel as if posed for a formal portrait—except for the fond smile on his face.

She turned in a slow circle. "I think it might be perfect."

He raised one brow. "Perfect?"

She lifted her hands and let them fall. "It's right on Bond Street. It's smaller than my current premises, but not much. The workroom is ideal, there are three rooms that could be used for fittings instead of two, as I have now, and the lodging is adequate." She smiled in amazement. "I retract everything unkind I ever said about your desire to tear down Vine Street. You are a godsend! Can this really be only thirty pounds a year? I never would have discovered it on my own."

Something flickered over his face. "With the increased prestige and ability to display directly on Bond Street, your revenue will surely increase."

Felicity's beaming smile dimmed. "I hope so, of course," she said slowly. "It's more than thirty pounds, isn't it?"

He flicked one hand. "Not much."

The warmth and goodwill she had been feeling drained away. She just looked at him, speechless with dismay.

He crossed the room to the window. "You'll have a fine view from here. And is this another closet?" He opened a door, revealing a small storage room.

"Carmarthen."

Warily he turned.

"How much is the rent?"

For a moment she didn't think he would tell her. Then he raised one hand as if quell any protest. "The owner is asking ninety pounds, but everything is negotiable—"

"Ninety pounds!" Felicity was appalled. No wonder the shop was so perfect; it was far too expensive for her. "Have you any idea how much a seamstress earns in a year? Twenty pounds—twenty-five, if she's talented and hardworking. Apprentices might not make thirteen. Ninety pounds! I didn't want to pay more than thirty!"

"I know," he said in the same soothing voice. "But hear me out: Let me speak to the owner on your behalf. I'll deal with him entirely. This shop earns him nothing by standing empty and he may consider a lower figure."

Felicity felt crushed by disappointment—not only that she wouldn't be able to take this lovely, ideal shop, but because Carmarthen had lied to her. He brought her to this Bond Street shop that was everything she wanted, knowing it cost three times what she could afford. "And when he says no, a shop this lovely is worth ninety pounds?"

He let out his breath, as if holding back his temper. "You don't know that he will."

She did, though. Felicity hadn't the earl's status or wealth to intimidate everyone she dealt with. The shop owner would laugh in her face if she offered a third of his asking rent. "He would have to be a very big fool," she said quietly. "Even bigger than I was, to think this might be affordable." She looked sadly around the cozy, light-filled rooms. "I need to get back to my shop, sir."

The earl didn't move. "Thirty pounds won't get you anywhere near Bond Street. I had to broaden the search."

She headed for the door, and the stairs, and the street. He followed her, not saying anything until they reached the pavement outside. "I appreciate your efforts, my lord," she said there, addressing the middle of his chest rather than meeting his sea-blue eyes. "I wish I could take this shop, but I cannot. I tried to be clear about what I could afford, so as not to waste my time or yours."

He ran one hand through his hair, tousling the dark waves even more. "You're despairing of it too easily."

Suddenly she wanted to be away from him, from his air of wealth and confidence and most of all from the feeling that she had frustrated him yet again. The easy banter and potent attraction that had sizzled between them only half an hour ago seemed a distant memory. Perhaps he hadn't meant to set her up for disappointment, but he'd known all along this shop cost too much and still he'd let her explore and exclaim over each feature and envision herself working and living there. How could he do that to her?

She had to clench her jaw to hide her feelings. She had no reason to feel betrayed or bereft; the Earl of Carmarthen was no more in her reach than this Bond Street shop. "Good day, my lord."

"Where are you going?" he exclaimed as she turned to start for home.

"It's only a short walk to Vine Street from here." A short walk, across an ever-growing gulf between his world and hers.

"Let me drive you," he said.

Felicity shook her head, unable to keep from looking at his offered arm with regret. Part of her wanted desperately to take it and listen to his promises. Another part of her, though, whispered it would only pave the way to greater heartbreak later. "I think I'll walk."

He stared. His arm fell to his side. "As you wish." Stiffly he bowed. "Good day. I apologize for wasting your time today."

It wasn't a waste, she wanted to cry. *It was wonderful—until the end.* She swallowed the words. "Good day."

She walked home feeling as if a dark cloud hovered over her. The elegance of Bond Street gave way to the bustle of Piccadilly, and she crossed the gleaming new Regent Street, at which point she could almost see the cloud close in around her and envelope everything. Two weeks ago she had thought Vine Street a little tired, decidedly old, but also quaint. Now she saw it as it was: paint peeling from doors, clogged drains letting water pool in the street, windows ominously dark and empty compared to the shops in the streets she'd just left. She went into Madame Follette's and was struck by how dim it was after the shop in Bond Street. What a delight it would have been to receive clients in that bright, airy salon . . .

Alice popped out of the corridor leading to the fitting rooms. "Oh, you're back, miss! It's been quiet since you left. Only Lady Giles Woodville came for a fitting."

Lady Giles Woodville was Selina's client, and the sister-in-law of the Duke of Barrowmore—who was Selina's lover. Felicity had seen the way Barrowmore looked at Selina, and thought it was only a matter of time before he married her. Then Selina would leave the shop and there was no certainty Lady Giles would continue patronizing Follette's. Perhaps Selina would patronize her, when she was a duchess . . . assuming Felicity still had any seamstresses to sew the gowns, to say nothing of a shop for them to work in. Delyth had steady work with the Merrithew family, so steady they had requested she move into their Portman Square home for the Season. If she were left with only Alice and Sally to help her . . .

Felicity took a deep breath and looked around her salon. It wasn't big or bright, but she still designed the best gowns in London. Somehow or other, with Lord Carmarthen's help or in spite of him, with or without her seamstresses, she would make it through this, delivering every coronation gown on time and saving Follette's.

She had to. No one else would do it for her.

Evan watched her go and said a dozen curses inside his head. He'd got so caught up in watching her face light up that he hadn't prepared better for the question of the rent, and now it felt like he'd lost all the ground gained earlier in the day. The discovery that she was attracted to him—perhaps as attracted as he was to her—had gone to his head, like a bottle of wine drunk too quickly.

But he'd had to do it. Her requirements were unrealistic.

"Will that be all for today, my lord?" said a voice behind him.

He swung around to see Mr. Abbott standing on the steps. "Yes. I'll inform you if I require anything else."

"Of course." The older man inclined his head slightly in the direction Miss Dawkins had gone. "I thought the lady found these premises highly satisfactory."

Evan's jaw tightened. "She did. It was the rent she found wanting."

"Ah." Mr. Abbott locked the door and put on his hat. "I am familiar with the gentleman who owns this property. I daresay he would be willing to negotiate if you, my lord, would provide a guarantee."

"What sort of guarantee?" Evan frowned.

"The owner is a man retired from the cloth trade himself; I believe this was his tailoring shop for many years, and he still has a fondness for shops dedicated to fashion." Mr. Abbott cast a polite glance after Miss Dawkins. Her raspberry dress stood out in the crowd. "He would likely favor a talented young modiste over other tenants."

"Then why would he want a guarantee?" asked Evan in irritation. Perhaps this fellow was the same as Ferrars, with less than noble intentions toward pretty young modistes.

"He is aware of what a tenuous existence fashion offers. A shop may soar to the heights of desirability one year, then fall from favor the next and leave the owner bankrupted. I have seen it many times," he added at Evan's frown. "The hatters, the glovers, the milliners, the tailors . . . Let one dandy or duchess set fashion on its ear, and people will abandon any tradesman who cannot adjust immediately. A modiste can be ruined by inventory." Mr. Abbott spread his hands. "I don't speak for the owner, of course, but if he were assured a shop would have capital to survive a few years at least . . ."

He could pay the excess rent. It could be called a loan, or an investment, or even extra compensation for her current shop. But he could mark it as an expense of the Vine Street project, where sixty pounds—even one hundred twenty, over two years—was hardly worth noting in the ledger. Evan's mood lifted as he thought about it.

But would Felicity accept? He tried not to think of the most obvious implication, that he would have an enduring excuse to call on her for months to come. He would have to phrase it carefully, just as he would have to apologize for not telling her the true rent before she saw the place in Bond Street.

If Evan had let himself think about it, he would have been unsettled by how important it was to him that Felicity be pleased. He wanted to see that astonished delight on her face again, and he wanted to be the cause of it. Instead he focused on the fact that this would move her out of Vine Street and allow his other plans to proceed. She'd liked it very much, and therefore she should accept any plan that ended with her taking up residence here, for only thirty pounds a year.

"Thank you, Mr. Abbott," he said. "Your advice has been most helpful. Would you be so kind as to let the owner know I expect to take this property, and he should not offer it to others?"

"Of course, my lord." With a pleased expression, Abbott bowed. "Good day."

CHAPTER EIGHT

In the uproar over the dressmaker's shop in Vine Street, Evan forgot that he had promised to escort his mother and sister to a theater benefit. When he hesitated, his sister leapt to prevent him from wriggling out of it.

"We never see you," she cried. "One might think old buildings are more important to you than we are."

He had to laugh at that. "More important? Never—but they don't require me to dance with them and their friends."

Emily made a face at him. "There won't be dancing tonight, so you've got to come."

Truthfully he didn't mind. Evan was pleased that they were in London again. With all his projects in town, he hadn't gone back to Wales much in the past year, but his mother and sister preferred to spend the winter there. He *had* been busy lately, and a night at the theater would take his mind off vexing golden-haired seamstresses.

"My goodness," said Emily in awe as they made their way through the crowded theater salon. "Mother, I see the most wonderful gown."

"Oh? On whom?" His mother began rummaging in her reticule for her spectacles. Evan wasn't sure why she didn't just wear them all the time—she was quite short-sighted—but she reacted with horror whenever he suggested it. Vanity, he supposed fondly. His mother was still a handsome woman.

"The lady in green, near the stairs. I don't know her." Emily stood on tiptoe, trying to see over the crowd. "We should walk past her so Mother can see the gown, Evan."

"As you wish." He offered an arm to each of them and they headed toward the staircase. Lady Carmarthen had her spectacles on, and remarked admiringly on more than one lady's gown as they made their way through the crowd.

"There, Mother," Emily whispered, squeezing his arm in excitement. "Do look—have you ever seen such a striking bodice?"

Lady Carmarthen turned her head, and Evan obligingly angled his body so she could face the owner of the incredible gown without obviously staring—and, to his astonishment, beheld Felicity Dawkins, standing with her brother at the foot of the staircase.

For a moment he did stare. She looked stunning tonight, and not just for the vibrant peacock green silk that clung to every curve of her body. Her dark blond hair was a pile of curls, artlessly arranged on top of her head, exposing her pale neck. Her splendid bosom was on display, with an edge of lace peeking out that sent his mind straight to the thought of undergarments. Her undergarments. Delicate and lacy, yielding to his hands as he kissed her . . .

"Marvelous," said his mother in delight. "We must ask her whom she patronizes. The color is perfect for her, and it takes a talented modiste indeed to cut a gown to flatter so well. There must be someone who can introduce us . . ."

Evan cleared his throat, then had to do it again. Felicity turned to look up at her brother, who was a big tall bloke, and the smile she gave him lit her face with impish good humor and delight. What wouldn't he give to see that smile directed at him, and to have her hand on his arm . . .

"I know who made her gown," he said gruffly. He steered his family away from her, not wanting his mother to notice his reaction to Miss Dawkins. "I'll try to bring her to our box at intermission, if you desire a word with her."

Emily gasped. "Do you know her, Evan? Oh, who is she?"

"Yes, who?" chimed in Lady Carmarthen.

"Let us hurry," he urged, quickening his steps until his sister stopped gaping at him. "We'll miss the opening act if we linger all night on the stairs."

By the time they reached their box, Evan felt a little calmer. It was unsettling that his heart still jumped every time he saw Felicity, and he would really like to stop thinking of her undergarments, let alone kissing her senseless while she wore little else. He was confident Emily wouldn't notice, but if he came face to face with Felicity, without time to prepare himself, his mother would recognize at once that there was something between them—

That thought stopped him short. There was *nothing* between them. They had made peace, but at best theirs was a friendship, not an affair. A little covert lust was nothing, after all; he couldn't act on it without jeopardizing the Vine Street plan, and he was adamant that nothing could do that.

"Who is she?" Emily demanded as soon as the door was closed behind them. "How do you know her, Evan?"

"Yes, dear, who is she?"

He decided it was best to answer directly. "Miss Felicity Dawkins of Madame Follette's dress shop. I met her because her shop is in Vine Street, my latest endeavor."

His mother's eyes rounded. "*She* is the seamstress? Good heavens."

This was the trouble with benefits, Evan thought; one never knew who might attend. "I've no idea if she created the gown herself, but her mother owns the shop and she manages it at present."

"Follette's," murmured Lady Carmarthen. "I didn't know they were still here."

"Do you know them, Mama?" asked Emily in surprise. "Why have we never gone there? I'm sure I'd recall a gown like that one. Oh Evan, can you persuade her to make one for me? I should adore a gown of that color!"

"Certainly not," said her mother tartly. "Not until you're older. And to answer your question, I thought they had gone out of business years ago. Once upon a time, a gown from Madame Follette was the pinnacle of fashion. She had a way with sarcenet and muslin . . . Unparalleled, I tell you. But judging from this . . . Miss Dawkins, did you call her? Miss Dawkins's gown suggests they've refined their look."

"You must bring her to be introduced, Evan!" declared Emily. "Please?"

Evan, who had been digesting his mother's astonishing revelations about the dressmaker's shop, started. "What? Why?"

"How wonderful it would be to discover Follette's before anyone else in town," Lady Carmarthen enthused. "Or rediscover, as the case may be, but they've been out of fashion so long it might as well be a

330

new shop. I must say, the gowns we ordered from Madame de Louvier are perfectly acceptable, but there is something missing . . ." She paused, her brow knit. "Imagination," she said, sounding a little surprised.

"I cannot wait to see if Miss Dawkins's gown is as beautiful from near as it is from afar," said Emily with longing. "Where is she sitting?"

Evan murmured something indistinct to hide the fact that his eyes had been searching the theater for her ever since they entered the box. She ought to be easy to spot—her brother was too big to miss—but he couldn't. Almost frantically his eyes moved over every box within sight. She had to be somewhere . . .

He leaned forward on pretext of adjusting his chair, scanning the theater all the while, and finally picked her from the crowd. There, in one of the lower boxes. Her gown glowed under the lamplight, and her face was bright with interest as she studied the rest of the crowd.

He let out a breath of relief even as he recognized the danger he was in. God help him. She was in trade. His mother wanted to *employ* her. But in trade or not, she was the most beautiful woman he'd ever seen. She made him laugh, she challenged him—and won—and she made him think, as the gas lamps were lowered and the performance began, that if he did nothing and she disappeared from his world, he might spend the rest of his life searching for another glimpse of her.

"Thank you for bringing me, Henry." Felicity gave her brother a smile as they made their way into the theater. She felt a twinge for coercing him into coming with her to this benefit, but only a very small one. Without his escort she would have had to refuse when Lady Marjoribanks offered the use of her box for the evening, and Felicity really wanted to go out.

For days now she'd done little but worry about Follette's future, including too many hours spent pining for the shop in Bond Street and wondering if maybe, somehow, she could afford the rent. Tonight she wanted to think about anything other than shop rents or which of her seamstresses might leave her first or—most importantly—what the Earl of Carmarthen might do next. She had neither seen nor heard from him since the disastrous day on Bond Street. As much as Felicity told herself she should expect nothing else from him, it was unsettling how much she wished he would stop by, just once more, so they could part on better terms.

"I'm sure it's good for you to get out of the shop," said Henry.

"And for you," she replied pertly. Henry must be as worried as she was about Follette's, though in his own way. Besides, Henry looked so handsome tonight, and the Kilchester family would be in attendance.

The Kilchester ladies had patronized Follette's for years due to some service Felicity's grandfather had done the previous Lord Kilchester. Lady Euphemia, the eldest daughter of the family and a true beauty, had commissioned several gowns for herself, and also one for her companion, a young woman named Katherine Grant.

Miss Grant was the sort of client Felicity adored: She had wonderful coloring and a lush figure, and cost was no object to her because Lord Kilchester was paying for the gown. She also had no sense of her physical attractions, judging from the drab and ugly dress she'd worn to her first fitting. Felicity had put her in crimson, cut to display her magnificent bosom, and Miss Grant had looked dazed when she stepped in front of the mirrors.

But when Felicity mentioned the handsome bill she expected to collect from Lord Kilchester for Miss Grant's gown, Henry's face had turned bright pink. Normally when she spoke of the Kilchesters, he merely nodded, as Lord Kilchester was one of the few aristocrats who paid his bills on time. She wasn't surprised to see her brother all but gape at Miss Grant when they met the Kilchester party in the theater's main salon. And it was so rare to see Henry look mesmerized by a woman, as he did now, that Felicity impulsively linked arms with Lady Euphemia and walked away from her brother, to let the full impact of Miss Grant's crimson gown soak into his obstinate male brain.

"Thank you," whispered Lady Euphemia as they walked. "Doesn't Katherine look lovely tonight?"

Felicity smiled. She'd known Lady Euphemia for years. "She does."

"And Hen—Mr. Dawkins looks very handsome in his evening clothes."

"He does," she agreed.

Lady Euphemia sighed happily. "Just as I intended!"

They settled into Lady Marjoribanks's box. Lady Euphemia tended to attract admirers, and she was soon occupied with them, chatting and laughing. Felicity busied herself with examining the crowd, scrutinizing every dress that caught her eye. It was such a shame when modistes took advantage of their patron's desire for the latest style, she thought, feeling a spike of pity for a petite woman in a nearby box. The poor lady was overwhelmed by the decoration on her gown, from the puffed sleeves and lace collar to the rows of ruffles that covered her skirt—all in a strong shade of pink that made her fair coloring fade almost to blandness. Felicity spent a moment picturing a pale blue gown with subtle embellishment, cut to emphasize the lady's graceful arms and neck. Oh, what she could do for that woman . . .

With a blink she moved on. To have a chance to clothe more ladies like that, she had to establish Follette's as the place for personal style instead of an ordinary shop that produced unimaginative copies of fashion plates. Her own gown tonight was part of that effort, cut from a sinfully luxurious bolt of peacock green silk after a customer canceled the gown it was bought for. It had been an extravagance, to be sure, and she'd hidden the bill from Henry to pay it out of her own funds, but already she had noted several women openly admiring it. All she needed was one person to ask where she'd got it.

The lights grew dim and the play began. Since it was impossible to see anyone's gown now, she let herself get lost in the farce, about two young ladies determined to win the hearts of two handsome brothers by any means possible. It was silly but witty, and ended happily, so there was a smile on her face as the lights came up at the interval.

Lady Euphemia went to rejoin her family, escorted by a Lord Waddell, who looked dazed to have her on his arm. Felicity was just beginning to wonder where her brother had gone to when a firm knock sounded on the door of the box.

"Good evening, Miss Dawkins." It was the Earl of Carmarthen. He stepped in, seeming to fill the tiny box. His piercing blue gaze locked on her.

Felicity's heart almost stopped; why was he here and why was he seeking her out? Heart pounding, face flushed, she curtsied. *What is wrong with you?* she chided herself silently. It was a benefit performance, open to all; she should have anticipated the chance of seeing him. As to his reason for seeking her out . . .

She summoned a smile. "What a pleasure to see you, my lord. Are you enjoying the play?"

"Yes. Mrs. Burton is superb."

"She is."

Silence descended. Felicity waited for the earl to explain why he had come, but he only looked at her. It wasn't a bold or rude gaze, but searching, as if he was trying to puzzle out something about her. It made her unaccountably anxious, and with a tiny jolt she realized she wanted him to see her favorably again—as a woman. A woman who spent far too much time thinking about him, and whose breathing became alarmingly erratic whenever he was near. Of course he was attractive—she had known that since the moment he walked into her salon—but even more, she liked him. He was clever and amusing and he listened to her. And in the draper's shop, when she'd held up a bit of blue damask and looked into his eyes . . .

Felicity knew what desire could do to a woman when it caught her in its coils, and as a result she'd spent most of her life avoiding it. Which was not to say she hadn't had flirtations, even an amour; a handsome soldier had won her heart years ago, but their romance only lasted as long as his regiment was in London. A lace merchant had once suggested she marry him, and one of the tailors who used to work for Mr. White, whose tailor shop had been across the street from Follette's, had tried to kiss her several times before Henry put his fist in the man's face. Her mother had taught her to keep men at bay, whether they were lustful husbands or brothers—or in one case, a father—of a client at Follette's.

She had a good idea what a man like Lord Carmarthen would offer her: an affair, perhaps even something formal with a house and a carriage. Follette's clients had included more than one kept woman, and Sophie-Louise had taught her daughter not to judge any woman's choice too harshly. After the last few years of hardship, wondering if she would lose her shop and home, Felicity understood quite well why a woman might take the security and riches offered to her. She had never thought it would suit her, though.

But if Lord Carmarthen asked her to be his mistress . . .

"I have a favor to ask," said the earl abruptly, putting an end to her dangerously tangled thoughts. "Might I present you to my mother and sister?"

Felicity's eyes grew wide with astonishment. "I would be honored, my lord."

He bowed his head and offered his arm, and slowly she put her hand on it. What could he mean by this? She didn't understand it, but as she walked out of the box on his arm, she felt an almost giddy swell of excitement.

"Thank you," he said as they made their way through the crowd. "They have been admiring your gown all evening, and are wild to examine it up close."

She forced a laugh. So that was why he'd come to her. The little bubble of unfounded hopes burst silently in her chest, which she instantly tried to discount. She should be pleased he was willing to present her to his family for any reason, let alone one that would benefit Follette's. "How flattering! It's one of my favorites."

His gaze dipped to her bosom. "And rightly so."

A shiver ran over her skin. Why did he look at her that way if he only wanted her to show his mother her gown? Lady Carmarthen could come to the shop any day and see it in daylight, without missing a moment of the play.

"I also wished to apologize," he said softly as they walked. "I should not have hidden the cost of the Bond Street shop from you."

"No," she murmured. "Thank you."

"I've not given up," he added. "But getting what you want may require some creativity."

She darted a glance at him. "Of what sort?"

"I'm still deciding that," he said vaguely.

When they reached the best circle of boxes, he opened a door and ushered her inside. Two ladies were waiting, and Felicity would have known them anywhere as his family. He had his mother's eyes, and his sister's bright smile was very like his.

"Mother," said the earl, "Emily, may I present Miss Felicity Dawkins. Miss Dawkins, my mother the Countess of Carmarthen and my sister Lady Emily Hewes."

"Thank you for interrupting your evening to come to us," said the countess warmly. "My daughter and I were struck, as if by lightning, by your gown. It is a marvel."

"Thank you, my lady." Felicity curtsied. "It's my own creation."

"So said Evan," cried his sister, giving the earl a fond look. "We begged him to secure an introduction."

Felicity looked at the earl, who was already watching her. Their gazes connected for a moment, his intent, hers uncertain. "That was very kind of him," she murmured.

"Kind to us!" Lady Carmarthen smiled. "I've been less enchanted by my dressmaker every season, and the thought of finding a talented new one fills me with delight."

Felicity tore her eyes away from the earl. What he thought, and what he wanted, would have to puzzle her another time. She fixed her attention on her potential new client. "Indeed. Whom do you patronize now, my lady?"

"Madame de Louvier." The countess brushed one hand down her dress. "She's very skilled at the latest fashions, but I vow, I've never owned a gown that suited me as well as yours suits you."

This, Felicity understood. She recognized the covetous look the other woman cast at her peacock gown. With a keen and unsparing eye, she catalogued the failings of the countess's own gown, and knew she had the perfect opportunity to win Lady Carmarthen's custom.

"Thank you, ma'am. None of my gowns come from fashion plates; every item we create at Madame Follette's is designed solely for the customer who orders it. There is no way a drawing in a magazine can take into account a particular woman's coloring, nor is it designed to flatter her finest features. Follette's believes a gown should do both." She smiled. "Naturally we include the latest fashionable features, but only in creating a gown uniquely suited to the lady who wears it."

"So I see." Lady Carmarthen studied Felicity's gown with admiration. Obligingly, she made a slow revolution on the spot.

"Lovely," sighed Lady Emily. "Mama, may we please visit Madame Follette's?"

"We shall indeed, very soon." Lady Carmarthen bowed her head. "Miss Dawkins, it has been a pleasure. Until we meet again."

"Thank you, my lady. Lady Emily." Felicity curtsied again, and the earl silently offered her his arm. In the corridor, she couldn't resist. "Thank you, sir," she whispered, unable to keep a beaming smile from her face. "It was an honor to meet your mother and sister." It would be an even bigger honor to see them wear her gowns in society.

"One that may soon be repeated," he said with a slight grin. "I daresay they'll visit Vine Street within days."

"How fortunate you've not started demolishing it yet."

He laughed reluctantly. "Am I never to be forgiven for that?"

"Forgiven! Are you admitting it might not be the very best thing that could ever happen to any street in London?" She felt light and happy, which must explain why she was teasing him again.

"I still believe, unequivocally, that it's the best thing to happen to Vine Street in years," he replied. "And I hope some day you will agree with me."

She looked at him from the corner of her eye. His profile was calm and assured, but, as if he could feel her gaze on him, he glanced her way. It was a cautious glance, questioning, curious . . . hopeful.

And suddenly her corset was too tight and her shoes were too big. She missed a step and stumbled against him, and in a flash his arm went around her waist. Felicity inhaled raggedly as he held her close for a moment, and when she raised her flushed face to thank him, every word fled. Carmarthen's expression was taut, his eyes burning bright with hunger.

Felicity knew she should not get involved with the earl, but that gaze incinerated every sane, sensible thought in her mind, leaving nothing but her own desire for him. "Carmarthen," she breathed, unsure if it was a warning or a plea.

He lowered his head until his lips almost brushed her ear. "My name is Evan."

The warmth of his face, so near her skin, nearly made Felicity's heart burst out of her chest. To use his given name was unmistakably intimate. She willfully closed her mind to the more contradictory signs and questions.

They reached Lady Marjoribanks's box and found it empty. Where was Henry? "My brother seems to have abandoned me," she said with a nervous smile.

"I would be delighted to see you home," said Carmarthen, watching her closely.

Felicity imagined her brother sharing a tender interlude with Miss Grant, and gave a nod. "That would be very kind of you, sir."

They went into the box and the earl closed the door. At the rear it was quiet and dim, although the brightly lit stage lay directly before them and the loud hum of conversation during the interval filled the theater. Without a word the earl reached out and untied the rope holding back the drape that could be drawn to provide some privacy. With a soft shush it fell closed, cutting off the light and sound even more.

He turned to her, his eyes glowing. "Do you want me to leave?"

Her heart was beating so hard, her hands were shaking from it. "What will happen if you stay?" she whispered.

Slowly his mouth curved. "Always direct. I admire that about you." He raised one hand and touched her cheek. Felicity's eyes closed and she swallowed hard. His touch felt so good on her skin. "I want to kiss you," he said, his voice a dark murmur.

With effort she pried her eyes open. "At times . . . At times I suspect you don't like me much . . ."

He gave a short, quiet laugh. "On the contrary, Miss Dawkins . . . *Felicity*. I like you far too much for my own peace of mind."

A shiver went through her at the sound of her name in his voice. She let her head tip slightly, nestling against his palm. "And after the kiss?"

His thumb stroked her cheekbone. "What do you mean?"

"Is that all you want?" Her throat was tight, making her voice husky. "A kiss tonight, then tomorrow we return to sparring over the fate of Follette's?"

He moved a step closer. Felicity realized she had unconsciously pressed up against the wall behind her, in the deepest shadow behind the drape. When the earl brushed his fingers over the bend of her waist, she arched her back, all but inviting him to slide his arm around her—which he did without a moment's hesitation.

"My dear," he murmured, drawing her to him. "Don't you realize you've won every match? I've no wish to keep sparring with you about anything. After this kiss . . ." His lips brushed hers, so lightly she gasped. "You tell me what you want to happen."

"And . . . You'll do it?" She looked at him in disbelief.

The earl—Evan—smiled. "Yes," he said simply, and then he kissed her.

His mouth was soft, tempting, seductive. Felicity's lips parted on their own and he tasted her, his tongue making love to hers. Every little worry in her mind about getting involved with him abruptly winked out, like candles doused by a bucket of water. He cupped her cheek in his hand and tilted her head so he could deepen the kiss. Her toes curled inside her slippers. Oh, how he could kiss. She sagged against the wall and clutched at his jacket so she could devote all her energy and attention to kissing him back.

The applause of the crowd made her jump; the second act was beginning. "No one can see us," the earl murmured, his breath hot on her skin as he kissed her throat.

She glanced at the drape. It only partially obscured them, but the lights were dimming, and it grew a little darker in their secluded corner. "What do you plan to do, that no one ought to see?" she whispered.

"This." He pressed his lips to the swell of her bosom above her gown. Quick and nimble, his fingers undid the fastenings holding the bodice closed in back, and then he eased it forward. "Just a taste," he breathed. "My God—you're so beautiful . . ."

Feverishly she stripped off her gloves so she could plow her bare fingers through his hair. Her lungs seized as his tongue traced circles on her skin, closer and closer to the edge of her corset. Shivers racked her body and her nipples grew hard, aching for him to unlace her and put his mouth *everywhere*. "Carmarthen," she said faintly. "Evan . . ."

He curled one hand around the nape of her neck and pulled her near, until her forehead rested against his. "Say my name again," he whispered, his lips almost touching hers.

"Evan," she said on a sigh.

He kiss her, hard and brief. "What now, Felicity?"

She made a soft noise of indecision. She knew what he was asking. Her heart hammered, both at the white-hot pleasure of his hands and mouth on her skin and in nerves at the prospect of taking him home.

"Do you want me to go?" His fingers were massaging little arcs along the back of her neck. "If you do, I swear on my life I'll go and leave you in peace."

"No!" She put her fingers on his lips. "Not that."

His eyes met hers. "I promised I'd see you home."

Desire made her quiver. "Have you changed your mind?"

"Not at all." His gaze dropped for a moment, to her exposed bosom. "I can do one of three things. The first is return to my mother and sister and allow you to watch the remainder of the performance, before summoning a hackney coach to deliver you home in dignified safety."

She wouldn't be able to pay attention to a word of the play now, not with the memory of his touch still scalding her skin. She gave a tiny shake of her head.

A grin, more feral than amused, flashed across his face. "The second choice is that I escort you home now, as I promised, and then return to my mother and sister."

That one was also not appealing. A few frantic kisses in the carriage wouldn't satisfy her now. "And third?" she asked, her voice husky and hesitant.

He inhaled slowly. "Third . . . I will go make arrangements now for a suitable escort home for my mother and sister, and then I shall take you back to Vine Street and make love to you for the rest of the night."

"Yes," she whispered, almost before he finished speaking. "The third."

With a muffled growl, he kissed her once more, so deeply and so well she wobbled on her feet when he released her. With a devilish smile playing over his lips, he turned her to face the wall and gently tugged her gown back into place. "I'll only be gone a few minutes," he breathed, kissing the nape of her neck as he did up the hooks and ties again. "Wait for me here."

Felicity barely managed to nod before he left, opening and closing the door with a soft click behind him. She rested her cheek against the gaudy wallpaper, dazed and half disbelieving what had just happened. The Earl of Carmarthen—Evan—wanted her. He was going to take her home and make love to her. The mere thought made her heart pound; giddy anticipation coiled in her belly, and she felt the most insane urge to burst out laughing in sheer joy.

She pushed away from the wall and smoothed her hair, albeit with trembling hands. Thank goodness Henry wasn't here. She was so flustered over the prospect of having Evan in her bed, she couldn't even wonder where her brother had gone or what he was doing. Hopefully it was something so diverting he wouldn't pester her tomorrow about what had happened with the earl.

And if Henry was off making love to Miss Grant, there wasn't a word Felicity would say to tease him about it.

CHAPTER NINE

By the time Evan returned, she had composed herself enough to leave the theater with dignity. Neither said a word as they went down the stairs, now almost deserted during the performance, pausing at the cloakroom to retrieve her cloak, and then proceeding out to the street, where the Carmarthen carriage awaited. He must have sent for it when he left Lady Marjoribanks's box. Silently he handed her inside, then climbed in and sat beside her.

"What did you tell your mother?" she asked softly, as the carriage rocked forward. It occurred to Felicity that if Lady Carmarthen knew she was the earl's lover, it might end any chance of the countess patronizing Follette's. She still wanted him too badly to change her course, but her practical side regretted that consequence.

It was too dark to see his face clearly. "I told her something unforeseen had arisen and I needed to address it at once."

Unforeseen. She smiled wryly at that. "I see."

"Do you?" His teeth flashed white in the dim carriage as he grinned. "I also made a silent promise that I would remove your gown very carefully, to avoid tearing it. My mother can forgive a fit of passion, but not the ruin of a splendid gown."

"I like your mother very much," she said with a short, surprised laugh.

He laughed, too, then sobered. "Felicity. You said something earlier about after the kiss—that tomorrow we would return to sparring over the fate of Madame Follette's. I don't want that to happen."

Felicity went very still. "Nor do I."

He turned on the seat to face her, and reached for her hand. "I can't stop the plans to tear down and rebuild Vine Street; there are other investors, and the Crown has approved the plan. But I made you a promise, and I will keep it."

"Creatively," she said after a moment, remembering his earlier words.

One corner of his mouth curled upward. "Yes."

She hesitated, but when he looked at her like this, he undercut all her righteous indignation. "Very well. I shall be patient and trust you."

"Thank God," he murmured, reaching for her. "I do mean to satisfy you . . ."

She wound her arms around his neck as he shifted his weight, dragging her on top of him until they sprawled across the carriage seat. "You can start tonight."

"I intend to," he said, and then his mouth was on hers, seductive and lazy, as if he meant to take all night to savor her. Felicity shivered as the thought sent molten heat coursing through her.

It was only a short drive from the theater to Vine Street. Still, Felicity felt as if a year instead of a few hours had passed since she left with Henry. Evan spoke to his coachman as she fumbled in her cloak pocket for her latchkey, and then he stepped up behind her, raising one of the carriage lanterns so she could see. Gratefully she unlocked the door and let them in. With a clatter of hooves and wheels, the carriage drove off as the earl closed the door behind them.

"Your brother lives elsewhere, I believe?" he said.

"Yes." Felicity watched, off balance and somewhat dazed, as he slid the bolt of the lock home.

A small smile played around his lips. "Show me your shop."

Her eyes rounded. "Now?"

"Why not?" He prowled toward her. "I'm curious."

"Well." Flustered, she waved one arm. "This is the salon." He chuckled. "There is the office," she went on, pointing it out, "and here are fitting rooms and our fabric closet." He followed her as she walked down the narrow corridor past those rooms. "Upstairs is the workroom," she said, going up the stairs. Did he really care to see all this? Henry's incredulous query—*what would an earl want with a dress shop?*—echoed in her mind. "And my lodgings are above."

"Show me," he said softly, remaining on the landing when she started to continue up the stairs to her personal quarters.

"Why?" she blurted out.

"Because it's where you spend your days. I want to understand what's important to you."

Felicity hesitated. In the lantern light, his face was focused on her, his eyes darker than usual. She took one step down, then another. "Very well."

The workroom occupied almost the entire floor. She led the way past the cupboards full of sewing supplies and the long worktable, to the wide windows overlooking the street. "Here is where most of the work is done." She gestured at the chairs set near the window. "Alice and Sally, my apprentices, do much of the basic sewing, although Mrs. Fontaine, Miss Owen, and I do a great deal as well."

"Do you still sew?"

"Of course," she said with surprise. "The only way to craft a beautiful gown is piece by piece. If one doesn't know precisely how to cut and drape and stitch the cloth, it will never resemble the sketch. I presume you must know something about how a house is built, in order to plan ones with sufficient space for all your modern plumbing and such."

His grin was white in the darkness. "Of course. But I don't do the plumbing."

She laughed. "A gown is far simpler than a house, I suppose."

It wasn't too dark for her to see the way his gaze slid over her. "Simpler, perhaps, but no less demanding."

Her skin prickled when he looked at her that way.

"They don't sew at the table?" He held up the lantern, illuminating the long, narrow worktable.

"No, that is for cutting. A good table is essential for cutting properly."

He skimmed one hand across it. "And what is this?" He swung the lamp toward an alcove opposite the fireplace. The room glowed as the light was reflected in the triptych of tall mirrors that stood there.

"It's a sort of fitting area." She crossed the room. "For an intricate gown, a client would stand upon this stool in her undress." She stepped up on it in illustration. "We make an initial pattern for the gown out of muslin by draping and pinning it to her figure, marking on the fabric where trim and embellishments should be. With the mirrors, a seamstress can see every side of the gown at once, as can the client. This way there are no misunderstandings about where the trims will be or how low the bodice is."

"Ah." He set the lantern on the small table nearby, meant to hold pins and other supplies. His arms came around her and tugged loose the bow holding her cloak closed. The cloak slid from her shoulders, and he tossed it behind him onto the worktable. "So if you were my client, you would come in and remove your gown."

Felicity's heart seemed to pause, then slam into her breastbone as she felt his hands at the back of her gown, untying and unhooking again. Unlike in the theater, where there had been a fevered haste to his actions, this time he was unhurried and deliberate. *I want to make love to you for the rest of the night.* "Yes."

His gleaming gaze connected with hers in the mirror. "Show me."

Trying to hide the faint tremor of her fingers, Felicity eased the delicate sleeves down her arms, the silk whispering over her skin and leaving a trail of gooseflesh in its wake. The earl—Evan—inhaled sharply as she eased it over her hips, letting it fall down over her petticoats. She almost lost her balance on the step stool as she stepped out of it, but his hands were at her waist, steadying her.

"For an evening gown," she said, "we would work over a lady's undress."

"Hm." His hands spanned her waist, then drifted up the front of her ribs. Standing on the stool, Felicity was the same height as he was. "This tormented me tonight." He ran one finger across the twist of fine net trim edging the bodice of her petticoat. "It winked at me like a beacon until I could scarcely look away."

She was having trouble breathing. "That was not my intent . . ."

"No?" His smile was wicked, his eyes heavy-lidded but intense. He bent his head and nipped the sensitive skin at the curve of her neck, and Felicity gave a gasping moan of pleasure. "That's what it made me feel," Evan whispered, his lips brushing the spot. "This is what it made me want."

Her breath shuddered as she watched in the mirror, his hands dark against her white undergarments as he unfastened the petticoat and peeled it from her shoulders, sliding it down over her hips, so she stood in her chemise and corset. From all sides she could see them, him dark and dangerous in his evening clothes, her pale and exposed in her white undergarments.

"Should I apologize?" Her voice was throaty and inviting, even to her own ears.

Evan smiled, the slow, roguish grin that never failed to make her heart skip a beat. "Never." His hand flattened over her stomach as he plucked the string of her corset. "I reveled in every moment of it. It was quite the most . . . uplifting evening I've ever had at the theater." The corset came loose, he pressed against her, and Felicity felt the hard, heavy length of him at her back. Uplifted, indeed.

He threw the corset on the floor and then his hands covered her breasts. Her back arched and she gasped, her hands reaching backward for him, trying to anchor herself against the storm brewing inside her body. His mouth was on her neck again, kissing, sucking gently, teeth grazing her skin just hard enough to make her flinch. "Evan," she gasped.

"Dear God, I love the way you say my name." He yanked at the string of her chemise, then pulled it down to bare her breasts. Felicity let her head fall back as his hands cupped her. His touch was firm, not rough, squeezing and then feathering fingertips. He played with her nipples until she squirmed, drawing a low laugh from him. His mouth opened in hot, wet kisses on her shoulders and neck, until she managed to turn her head. When his lips took hers, a charge went through her; her toes curled and her fingers flexed, digging into the fabric of his coat to hold him to her.

"Felicity." His voice rasped in her ear. "Tell me you've done this before . . ."

Head swimming, she nodded once. She could barely hear his exhalation of relief and then cool air swirled around her knees. She pried open her eyes a little and watched in the mirror as he slowly drew up the hem of her chemise. Her belly clenched in excitement, knowing what was coming, and her knees felt weak. When the chemise grazed her waist, Evan's breath hissed in her ear. "So beautiful." He kissed her again, his palm flat on her thigh, sliding up, up, up—

Felicity arched as his hand settled between her legs, warm and big. "So soft," whispered Evan, his voice guttural. His fingers stirred, and she whimpered. It had been a long time since any man had touched her there, but she was more than ready. He stroked, his fingers easing deeper between her thighs, and she almost fell off the stool at the first touch there, on the nexus of nerves. "So wet," said Evan, a taut undercurrent of need in his voice.

"Yes," she almost sobbed. "I want more—I want you—*Evan . . .*"

With a sudden movement he spun her around in his arms, his mouth claiming hers ruthlessly. Felicity surged against him, winding her arms around his neck. His hands went to her bottom, and when he lifted her, she curled her legs around his waist. Still kissing her, he turned and took a few steps before setting her down—on the worktable, she realized.

"Take this off." He flicked the drooping chemise. As she struggled out of it, he stripped off his coat and waistcoat. Felicity threw her garment aside, unabashedly baring herself to his gaze. Even though the lantern behind him was the sole source of light in the room, his eyes seemed to blaze with a light of their own.

"God almighty," he whispered.

"Take off your shirt," she said unsteadily. In white shirtsleeves, his shoulders looked incredibly broad and strong.

His wicked grin flashed again as he jerked at his cravat, almost ripping off the cloth before pulling the shirt over his head. In the low light, he was still magnificent, lean and strong. "As you command, love." He stepped forward, between her knees, clasping his hands around her hips and pulling her forward until they were pressed together from thigh to chest. For a moment they clung to each other.

Dimly Felicity wondered if he felt the same unnerving sense of oneness that she did. Even the feverish haze of desire seemed to recede for a moment as she wallowed in the strength of his arms around her, the steady thump of his heart beneath her cheek, and the feel of his breath on her shoulder. And in that moment, Felicity thought she'd never wanted anything so much, in all her life, as she wanted this to last forever.

He put one finger under her chin and tipped up her face. For a moment he just looked at her, something like wonder softening his face. Felicity stared back, helpless to look away. Why couldn't he have been a lace merchant or an attorney, she thought with some despair, someone—*anyone*—who might have contemplated forever with her?

To quell those thoughts she reached for him. She was not a fool; she knew what she was getting into.

When she put her hands behind his head and pulled him back to kiss her, his hands began to wander freely over her body. Shivers ran through her as his palms glided over her shoulders, her back, her hips. When his hands covered her breasts, she jolted upright, and he pressed her backward to lie atop her cloak.

"This table," he rasped, "is the perfect height."

It was higher than a regular table, to make it easier for the seamstresses while cutting. A wild, reckless smile crossed her face. "For what, my lord?"

He touched his finger to her lips. "Evan. Say it."

"Evan," she whispered.

His hand closed on her breast, compressing the flesh and rolling her nipple between his thumb and forefinger. Felicity arched off the table. "Again."

"Evan," she gasped. He bent over her and put his mouth where his fingers had been, suckling hard on her erect nipple. She flung her arms out, shuddering even as she pressed into his mouth.

"Again," he commanded, his fingers trailing down her stomach.

"Evan," she whimpered, her thighs tensing as he urged her legs farther apart. She gave a strangled moan as his palm moved to cover her center, now pulsing with want.

"When we are alone together, like this"—his fingers dipped into the soft, wet folds between her legs—"you are my lord and master, Felicity. You've enslaved me—you command me—"

She forced open her eyes. He loomed over her, dark and gorgeous and bare, his strong hands stroking her body into delirium, his blazing eyes fixed on her. "Make love to me, Evan," she said on a sigh. "Please."

His mouth curved before he bent his head again, to her other breast. Felicity barely had time to marvel at his words before he swept her away on a tide of sensation, with his mouth and with his hands.

Just when she felt herself approaching the brink, he pushed himself up. Leaving her gasping and tense on the table, he stepped back. "Just a moment," he said, his voice tight.

"Hurry," she moaned. Her heart was racing so hard, her pulse seemed to reverberate through her whole body.

Evan smiled, that dangerous feral smile, and turned around to fetch the lantern. He set it down beside her and pushed the shutter open all the way. "You'll drive me mad," he said as he unfastened his trousers. His eyes seemed to feast on her bare skin.

She rolled her head coyly. Her hair had come undone, and was spread across the table and her shoulders. "It would only be fair."

"Oh?" He stepped out of his shoes and trousers and kicked them aside. "How long have you wanted me?"

Her face heated. "The day you drove us to Soho Square . . ."

"My darling," he said, running his hands back up her legs, "I wanted you since the moment I laid eyes on you." Palm on her belly, his thumb dipped lower, pushing inside her for a moment, and then she felt his erection there, thick and hard. She was so wet, so ready, he slid home easily, but the fullness made her catch her breath. When he was deep inside her, Evan paused. "Try to wait for me, darling."

Her whole body was throbbing with incipient release. "I—I can't—"

"Try." He grasped her by the hips and pulled her toward the edge of the table until she had to hook her legs around his waist again for balance. And then he began to move, hard and steady but not nearly fast enough, flexing his spine with each thrust so that he seemed to touch something inside her that fractured Felicity's mind into pieces. She gripped his wrists, struggling to breathe, trying to hold back the approaching flood. "Evan," she begged, tears leaking down her temples. "I can't wait—"

"Yes," he rasped, and she let go. Pleasure roared through her as his thrusts grew harder, faster. The first wave had barely started to subside when he touched her. Felicity screamed at the intensity of the feeling, and Evan gave a harsh bark of laughter. "Again," he ordered, stroking her in time with the plunging of his hips against hers. Incredibly the pleasure peaked anew, until she was almost crying from it, and then Evan thrust deep and threw back his head and gave a shout of elation.

It seemed an hour before she could hear anything but her own ragged breath. When she managed to focus her gaze, she saw only Evan, leaning over her. His hands still gripped her hips, and he was still inside her. A sheen of perspiration slicked his skin, and he wore a heavy-lidded expression that put her in mind of early mornings.

He raised his head. Gently, almost reverently, he lifted her face to his. This kiss was different: soft, yearning, the sort of kiss a man in love might give. Felicity returned it with fervor, wondering if he would feel the same thing.

"Was that satisfactory?" he murmured, his lips brushing hers.

"Very." She ran her fingers through his hair.

"And it was only my first try." He pressed another tender kiss on her mouth. "Take me to bed, love."

Felicity's heart quivered at the last word. If only she *were* his love. She sensed she could find herself head over heels for him, with very little provocation.

But for tonight, this was enough; it would have to be. She pulled her crumpled cloak around her, took him by the hand, and led him upstairs to her bed.

CHAPTER TEN

The next several days were the grandest in human history, to Evan's mind.

Part of it was the anticipation of beginning the Vine Street project. He always felt a surge of energy and excitement when his plans, so long in the making, started to coalesce into stone and iron and plaster. He spent his days in the architect's office now, poring over last-minute alterations and adjustments.

It was true that Madame Follette's still sat in the middle of the street, occupied and open for business, while the last of the other tenants drove away in laden wagons, but Evan had a plan for that as well. He spoke to Mr. Jackson, who owned the Bond Street shop Felicity wanted. Jackson understood his request, but was dithering. What if Evan lost interest in the shop after a few months and declined to pay his guarantee, the man wanted to know. Evan was somewhat handicapped by not using Grantham for the negotiations, but thought he was getting on well enough without his customary solicitor. Sooner or later he and Jackson would find a way to agree, and then Felicity would have the shop her heart desired, he would have free rein in Vine Street . . . and he would have her.

Every evening, after Madame Follette's closed, he went to her. When he discovered that she had been accustomed to getting something to eat from the chophouse nearby, he began bringing dinner. They ate in her cozy sitting room, where she showed him sketches she had made for clients—who now included his mother and sister—and he recounted how he'd become enchanted with building. They talked of their childhoods, hers in a busy London

351

shop and his in rural Wales, and discovered they almost shared a birthday, being born just three days apart in October.

By tacit agreement neither brought up the relocation. Evan had promised he would find suitable premises for her; she had said she trusted him. They talked of everything else, and then they went to bed together, where no words were necessary to build a deeper bond between them than any Evan had ever experienced.

His visits grew longer and longer, until one morning he woke with Felicity in his arms and the sun in his face. And when she opened her eyes and gave him a sleepy smile, her golden hair wild around her bare shoulders, Evan had the thought that *she* was the missing piece in his life. Ever since he'd walked into Follette's salon and laid eyes on her, he kept feeling the same sense of contentment, as if life was now complete, and finally he admitted it was because of her.

And rushing her out of Vine Street would ruin it.

Accordingly, when he returned home around dawn one morning, after a night spent making her cry out his name in rapture, to find one of Grantham's clerks drowsing on his doorstep, his first reaction was to scowl. He knew what the man had come about, and he didn't want to face it. His signature was needed to begin the demolition, and Evan had purposely not given it yet. He sent the man off with a curt promise to visit Grantham's office in a few hours, but despite intense efforts while he washed, shaved, and changed, Evan had thought of no ideal solution to his problem when he was shown into the solicitor's office.

Grantham was as blunt as usual. "How do you progress with the immovable modiste?"

Evan turned his back to hide his expression. Just the thought of Felicity made him want to smile, even when Grantham called her that. "Reasonably well," he said, not directly answering the question.

"Thirty pounds per annum in the heart of Mayfair? It sounds nigh impossible to me."

"I gave her my word." He just needed Mr. Jackson to see reason. It was beginning to bother him that the man was delaying so long, and not for the first time Evan wished he could set Grantham on it.

Unfortunately he knew what Grantham would say: *Don't do it.* He would guess at once why Evan was so keen to guarantee Felicity's lease, and he would baldly ask if any woman was worth sixty pounds a year. Since Evan's answer to that query was a strong *yes,* even inching toward *worth any amount,* he had avoided the whole topic with his friend.

"You know as well as I do that your word was not a binding contract," Grantham reminded him. "Unlike these." He tapped a stack of papers, signed and stamped by the Commissioner of Woods and Fields, which had approved the Vine Street endeavor. "It's time to get on with it, Carmarthen."

"I know," Evan snapped. It was not simply his decision, now that significant money was at stake, including Treasury funds. Investors and tradesmen were waiting on him to give the order to proceed, and they didn't give a damn about Felicity's consent.

But he couldn't force her out before he presented her with an alternative. She was fiercely devoted to her shop, and she ran it well; it wasn't her fault that fashionable London kept moving westward, or that the development of Regent Street had cleaved her from that part of town. Madame Follette's meant as much to her as Carmarthen Castle meant to him.

There seemed no way he could press forward on schedule with Vine Street, and still please Felicity; delaying the demolition would ruin his reputation, while breaking his word to Felicity . . .

Might ruin the rest of his life.

"Well. You should thank me, then," said Thomas Grantham with a cocky smile. "I have solved the problem."

Evan frowned. "What? You found premises?"

"No, I have found the means to extricate you from that devil's bargain you seem determined to keep." Grantham leaned forward and held out a sheaf of paper. "You told me to send someone to query the residents of Vine Street. Watson turned up a stray bit of gossip, which he followed on a whim, and it led him to this."

He flipped the pages. It was an affidavit, signed by a Mrs. Mary Cartwright. "What is this?"

"Mary Cartwright was a seamstress for many years at Madame Follette's. She was turned off last year when the daughter took over. It seems she's grown bitter over that, and was all too eager to tell Mr. Watson every rumor and complaint she ever had with Mrs. Dawkins."

"What has this got to do with our *problem?*" asked Evan testily. It was wrong to call Felicity a problem, even though she was at the center of the chaos in his life.

"Read it." Grantham took off his spectacles and began polishing them with a handkerchief. "I'll wait."

With an odd sense of foreboding, Evan sat down and read. Much of it was minor complaints, such as the time Sophie-Louise altered a gown Mrs. Cartwright had made without telling her first, or how Mrs. Cartwright's pay was withheld once over a ruined bolt of lace, but on the third page, Evan saw what had pleased his solicitor so much.

Sophie-Louise Follette had fled Paris at the height of the Terror with the family who employed her as a ladies' maid, the comte and comtesse de Challe. They were stopped at the port, where the comte and his wife were detained while Sophie-Louise was allowed to get on the ship bound for England. Apparently thinking the revolutionaries guarding the port wanted to steal their money, the comtesse de Challe gave Sophie-Louise a notable—and very valuable—set of diamonds for safekeeping and urged her to continue on to London and wait for them there. Sophie-Louise took the diamonds, made it to England, and then sold the gems as if they were her own. With the money she bought Number Twelve Vine Street and became a modiste.

Mrs. Cartwright alleged that Sophie-Louise had confessed it all to her years ago, when they were working very late one night. The Frenchwoman had sworn her to secrecy at the time. Mrs. Cartwright had kept the secret because her employment depended on it, but now that Sophie-Louise and Felicity had served her so ill, she felt no obligation to remain quiet any longer.

Evan sat like a statue. The shop was purchased with stolen jewels. Grantham knew they could use this to coerce Sophie-Louise to sell the shop, and at a far lower price than Evan had expected to pay. And if the comte de Challe, or his descendants, could be located, they could send Sophie-Louise to prison.

Felicity would be devastated. She would lose everything she loved—and she would blame him.

"Do you believe this?" Evan asked, his thoughts racing.

Grantham shrugged. "It's got a tinge of revenge, but I made a few enquiries. Mrs. Dawkins—who married Josiah Dawkins in 1795, according to the parish of St. Martin's—purchased that building in

September of 1794. She paid in full, and I can find no record of a mortgage. Indeed, Mrs. Cartwight said Mrs. Dawkins was quite proud of the fact that she owned the building outright." He slid the spectacles back on his face. "Another interesting fact is that her daughter is likely not Josiah's child. There's a record of her age that suggests she was born before her mother's marriage."

It struck him like a slap to the face. Felicity was illegitimate. Her shop was built with stolen funds. Her mother was a thief and a liar.

And God help him, he wanted her anyway. He wanted her for the way her eyes lit up, for the teasing smile she gave him, for the way she blushed when he murmured seduction in her ear. He wanted to have her in his arms, in his bed, in his heart.

He folded the affidavit and slid it into his coat pocket. "Find them," he said quietly.

"Find whom?" Grantham's brows went up. "Carmarthen, this will ensure the Dawkinses cooperate, quickly and easily. Even if there's no legal recourse, one whiff of illegitimacy or thievery—from an aristocratic employer, no less—would ruin their name and trade."

"The diamonds." Evan got to his feet. "Find the de Challe diamonds, and buy them."

His solicitor stared at him as if he'd lost his mind. "Do what?"

"Buy the bloody diamonds! All of them!" He ran his hands over his head. He had no idea what he'd do with them, but it would gain him time to think of something.

"Carmarthen." Thomas Grantham rose from his chair and leaned over his desk. He lowered his voice. "What are you contemplating?"

"I don't know," he admitted, "but get those diamonds. If you can discover all this, I presume that shan't be a problem."

Grantham looked at him askance. "We don't need them to pressure Mrs. Dawkins."

"But I want them," he said through his teeth. He didn't have to explain himself to Grantham—not that he *could* explain, even to himself. "Will you find them or not?"

"Yes," said the other man after a moment. "If you wish."

Evan gave a curt nod and yanked on his coat. "Let me know when you have them. Until then, not a word of this to anyone. And learn what happened to the comte de Challe." He strode from the office, his brain roiled with uncertainty.

355

CHAPTER ELEVEN

Humming quietly, Felicity went down the stairs to open the salon. She ought to be tired, since Evan had spent the night again and only left two hours before Alice and Sally arrived for the day, but these days she hardly seemed to need sleep. She blushed a little at the thought of how Evan kept her awake. If she let her mind dwell on it too long, she'd end up staring into space, smiling like a fool in love.

Love. Even the word brought a bittersweet smile to her face. She had known that man was dangerous the first day she saw him, but she hadn't expected to fall so hard for him. He was an aristocrat while she was in trade, yet he treated her as his equal in intelligence and judgment. He listened to her, even when she spoke about the challenges of pleasing Lady Marjoribanks, who unfailingly requested gowns made in the least flattering colors—sometimes several within one gown. He amused her with stories of the things he'd found inside old buildings, from animal skeletons and diaries to the time his workmen tore down a wall and discovered some malicious maid, in the distant past, had emptied chamber pots into a hole in the wall. He brought dinner every night, which—after a long day that hardly allowed time to think, let alone eat—won her heart more than jewels ever could have.

To herself, Felicity admitted she was in love with him. To him . . . She didn't dare say the word. She was under no illusions that he would fall in love with her, but if she professed her love aloud, it would prompt him to point out that he never promised her love. If she kept it to herself, Felicity reasoned, she could pretend it was still possible that he might one day return the feeling.

She went through the shop and unbolted the door, opening it to let in some fresh air while she swept the steps. Vine Street was quiet these days; every other tenant had left. Felicity kept her eyes on her own steps as she whisked the broom from side to side, not wanting to think about the impending mess. Evan had given his word that he would help her relocate, and she had promised to trust him. He hadn't shown her a new shop in some time, though, and if she started thinking about it, she would wonder if he'd come to regret his promise, and if he'd end up forcing her out after all in spite of the wicked pleasures they shared in her bed every night. Therefore, Felicity tried not to think about it much. She didn't want anything to ruin the glow of happiness inside her, not yet.

A carriage turned into the deserted street as she finished sweeping. For a moment her heart skipped; could it be Evan? It was still early for clients. But it was a hackney coach, and when it stopped in front of Follette's and the door opened, a familiar figure stepped down.

Felicity's eyes rounded. "Mama!" She dropped her broom and hurried to help her mother. "What are you doing here?"

Sophie-Louise drew herself up and pinned a stern look on her. "I have come to save my shop, that's what I am doing. What do you mean by this suggestion we sell?" She pulled a letter from her reticule and flourished it in front of Felicity.

She winced. After Evan had given his word to help them relocate, she'd written to tell her mother. That had been part of *her* promise to Sophie-Louise, that she would write every fortnight about how the shop was going on. Her mother had demanded it as part of her agreement to take a holiday. "Yes, Mama. It's time to sell, but—"

Sophie-Louise flipped her hand in disgust. "Never!" She marched into the shop, leaving Felicity to show the driver where to deposit her mother's large valise. Felicity eyed that with alarm. It looked like her mother meant to stay. Not only would that put the shop into an uproar, it would end Evan's visits.

Her mother had gone straight up to the workroom, where everyone greeted her with cries of surprise. Sophie-Louise was in her element, hugging Alice and Sally, sharing a quiet exchange with Selina, whose face was flushed with delight. She wanted to see everyone's work, offering comments and compliments, until she paused in front of a gown on the wooden figure. "For which client is this?" she asked in surprise.

Felicity cleared her throat. "The Countess of Carmarthen, Mama." Evan's mother and sister had indeed come to Follette's, and ordered a good number of gowns. Unsurprisingly, the countess wanted something bold and modern, and Felicity had taken great pains to use the fashionable touches that would most flatter Lady Carmarthen. As a result it looked nothing like the gowns produced under Sophie-Louise.

Sophie-Louise's gaze narrowed, but she only said, "I see."

The day passed in a blur. Sophie-Louise resumed control of the shop as if she'd never been gone, leaving Felicity feeling oddly disgraced. She busied herself with her own work, focusing on Lady Carmarthen's gown and trying hard not to think of the lady's son. She managed to send a note to Evan around midday, informing him her mother had returned and he shouldn't call on her that night.

Her throat felt tight as she sealed it, unable to keep back the thought that it was likely the beginning of the end, if not the outright end, of their affair. She could hardly go to him, and he couldn't come to her while her mother was living with her again.

And for several days he didn't come. At first Felicity was relieved, but soon it turned to black despair. She missed him. She missed his wry smile, the timbre of his voice, the touch of his hands. She missed being able to do as she wished, without her mother's sharp eye observing everything. Every night her mother interrogated her about some facet of the business until Felicity could have screamed.

Henry came only briefly, long enough to tell his mother he was in love and planned to marry Katherine Grant. Sophie-Louise flew into ecstasy, demanding to meet the young lady and insisting on making her bride clothes, and then she utterly pardoned Henry for sending her away from the shop. Once again Henry could do no wrong, and Felicity had to defend every decision.

But the subject she most dreaded did not come up. Sophie-Louise railed against the development of Vine Street, but she didn't specifically ask about the man in charge of it. Felicity hoped that was out of ignorance, but finally her mother brought it up.

"Tell me about Carmarthen," she said one night as they sewed under the lamplight. It had been gray and grim all day, making Vine Street seem even more desolate than usual, and now the storm had arrived, thunder growling overhead and rain beating down. Felicity spared a worried thought for the leaky roof, and said a quick prayer Evan would yet locate some other suitable premises. She was sure her mother would agree to move in an instant if something like that Bond Street shop could be found.

She dragged her mind back to her mother's question. "He's bought everything else in the street. He wants to buy Follette's as well, so he can rebuild everything like it is in Regent Street."

"No, Felicity, tell me about *him*." Sophie-Louise turned a sharp gaze on her. "I hear he has been often to the shop, even in the evening."

The needle slipped right through the fabric, past her thimble, into the pad of her finger. Felicity winced. "He's an earl. His mother and sister ordered several gowns."

"He drove you out several times. Alice tells me he's very handsome."

Felicity pulled too hard on her thread, and it broke. "What are you asking, Mama?"

Her mother lifted one shoulder. "Is it Follette's he wants?"

She looked up and met her mother's eyes defiantly. "Yes."

Sophie-Louise didn't look convinced. "How will he react when he does not get Follette's?"

Felicity hesitated, then put down her sewing. "Mama, we have to sell." Sophie-Louise gathered breath to reply, and Felicity held up one hand. "He's right about Vine Street. It's falling apart, no longer fashionable or genteel. Our roof leaks. Every other building has been sold, and will be torn down any day now. Soon our clients won't be able to drive to our door, and the shop will be filled with dust."

Her mother's eyes snapped. "How can you defend this? This shop, it is my life!"

"Relocating is the only way to save it!" Felicity pleaded. "He's made a generous offer—"

"But what has he offered you?" Sophie-Louise demanded. "I will not sell to a man who trifles with my daughter, not even if he offers me ten thousand pounds." Shocked, Felicity fell back in her chair. Her mother's mouth firmed. "I have been waiting all week to hear about him. Can I not see the shadow that crosses your face every time he is mentioned? Henri tells me a little, Alice and Sally a little more, and Selina tells me the most: that you looked like a woman in love. But he has not come to call, nor have you spoken of him. If he has broken your heart, I will never forgive him, nor will I do anything to help him."

"Mama . . ." Her voice trailed off, stunned.

Sophie-Louise raised her brows. "Why do you think I came back to London? It's very pleasant in Brighton. Sea-bathing is a delight."

A full minute of silence reigned. Finally Felicity wet her lips. "He promised me nothing," she said softly. "I fell in love with him knowing it would never lead to anything. You mustn't blame him."

Her mother made a scoffing noise.

Felicity sighed. "Either way, it doesn't matter. I've not heard from him in days. Whatever was between us . . . is over."

Evan walked the streets of London for what seemed like hours before he finally turned into Vine Street.

The threatening sky had given way to a full-blown storm, and he was thoroughly soaked. Despite being only ten o'clock, it felt like the middle of the night, so dark had the day been. And that suited his mood.

He stood on the pavement across from Follette's, eyes fixed on the lights in the topmost windows. He knew the rooms well, after the many nights he'd spent there, talking and laughing and making love with Felicity. Just being here again after so many days away made his heart ache. God, he missed her.

Her note, warning him that her mother had returned and he shouldn't visit, had been both a relief and a cruelty. Cruel, because he thought he'd never needed her more. Relief, because it excused him from seeing her with such turmoil in his heart and mind.

Could he let her go? Could he keep her?

Grantham thought he was deranged. His mother was shocked. Evan had felt he had to tell them what he planned to do, but neither had helped put his mind at ease. So here he was, in the pouring rain, as wretched as any schoolboy.

Shadows at the window moved. Suddenly the curtain was drawn aside, and there she was, wrestling with the window, trying to pry it open a few inches. Evan's heart gave a great leap at the sight of her, and before he knew it his feet had begun moving, taking him across the street. Hesitant no longer, he raised his hand and pounded on the door to make her hear him over the storm.

Several minutes later a light glowed in the salon. Holding the lamp aloft, Felicity came forward and peered out into the darkness. Her face blanked in astonishment when she saw him, and she hurried forward to slide back the bolt and open the door.

"I know it's late," he said before she could speak. "I had to see you. May I come in?"

Regret flashed over her face. "Evan—"

"Please, darling," he said. "Hear me out."

At the endearment, something lit in her eyes, and a tiny smile curved her lips. With a nod, she stepped back and let him in, closing the door against the rain behind him.

"Who is there? Is it Henri?" Another woman came into the salon, lamp in hand.

Evan knew at once it was Felicity's mother. Sophie-Louise was the same height as her daughter, a little plumper and a lot grayer. The same blue eyes snapped in her face as she swept an imperious glance over him. "What is the meaning of this, sir?"

"Mama, this is Lord Carmarthen," said Felicity. "My mother, Mrs. Dawkins, sir."

"A great pleasure to make your acquaintance, Mrs. Dawkins." He bowed very formally, ignoring the rain that dripped off his shoulders.

"My lord." Mrs. Dawkins dipped a shallow curtsy. "The shop is closed."

"I know. I apologize for disturbing you, but . . ." His gaze slid back to Felicity, who wore an expression of composed anxiety. "I had to speak to Miss Dawkins and could not wait even until tomorrow."

"Ah. What have you come to say?"

"Mama," said Felicity under her breath.

Evan turned back to the older woman. "Mrs. Dawkins, I would like to purchase this building. My solicitor, Mr. Grantham, has written to you several times about it."

She sniffed. "I recall his letters."

"In your absence, I approached your daughter, Miss Dawkins." Again he looked at her. What would she say to this? "She repeated, very firmly, your opposition to selling, but at last we struck a bargain:

361

She would encourage you to sell to me if, and when, a suitable location was found elsewhere for Madame Follette's."

Mrs. Dawkins looked at her daughter with furious dismay. Felicity flushed, but gave a small nod.

Evan plowed onward. "We located a fine shop in Bond Street, but the rent asked was too high. Believing that Miss Dawkins found it perfectly suited to her needs, I negotiated with the landlord. I have come tonight to offer you the premises at Bond Street and Clifford Street for the rent of thirty pounds per annum."

Felicity gasped. "How on earth—?"

He'd bought the whole damn building from Mr. Jackson, just concluded that afternoon. He'd explain that later. "In addition, I am increasing my offer for this building by two hundred pounds," Evan said, holding up one hand to stay her. "Can we agree, Mrs. Dawkins?"

The older woman's face grew stern. "Am I to agree to this now? I have not seen this shop, and even then, we could not possibly remove from these quarters before Michaelmas."

"Mrs. Dawkins, workmen will begin demolishing Vine Street within the week. All the papers are signed and filed. It is imperative that you relocate at the soonest possible opportunity."

Her eyes flashed. She set down her lamp on the counter and crossed her arms. "My answer is the same I gave to your presumptuous lawyer: no."

"Mama, the shop he mentions is perfect," said Felicity urgently. "A vast step up for Follette's."

Her mother shot her a sharp look, but Evan thought there was a crack in her adamant refusal. He plunged his hand into one pocket as he crossed the room toward her. "Perhaps this will alter your decision." He pulled out a diamond bracelet and laid it on the counter, where it glittered in the lamplight.

Felicity, who had followed him, choked. "Goodness!"

Evan kept his eyes on Mrs. Dawkins. She frowned at the bracelet. He pulled out a necklace and put it next to the bracelet. Mrs. Dawkins's eyes flared in recognition, but she said nothing. He added a pair of earrings and a brooch before she spoke. "The diadem," was all she said, in a flat voice.

"Broken up," he told her. That was the only piece Grantham had failed to buy, because it had been split up several years ago.

Felicity held her lamp higher over the jewels, her face pale. "What is this?"

"It is a threat." Mrs. Dawkins looked at Evan grimly. "Sell, or you will expose me."

"No." He gazed back evenly, but reached for Felicity's hand. "It's not a threat." He glanced at Felicity, and smiled to banish her anxious expression. "I hope it will be a wedding gift."

Her lips parted, and her beautiful eyes grew bright. Evan folded her hand between his. "I've been lost without you these last few days. I love you, darling. Marry me, I beg you."

She looked stunned, raising a trembling hand to touch his cheek. "You love me?"

"Madly," he confessed. "Didn't you guess?"

An incredulous smile spread across her face. "I was so afraid to hope you might . . ."

His grip tightened on her hands. "Then . . . ?"

"Yes," she said, beginning to laugh. "Yes!"

"And?" he prompted, now grinning like a fool himself.

Her smile grew warm, and she put her arms around his neck, in spite of his dripping wet coat. "I love you, Evan."

He had time to brush his lips across hers before Sophie-Louise Dawkins cleared her throat. Felicity's mother was still pale, her eyes fixed on the diamond parure on the counter. "Where did you get these?"

"Here and there," said Evan vaguely. "All entirely legal, of course. The comte de Challe never made it out of France. It's been more than twenty years since his jewels went missing, which means no one can be prosecuted." He pictured Felicity sprawled in his bed, wearing the diamonds and nothing else. "And now they're mine, to give as I wish."

Felicity, looking between them, shook her head in confusion. "What are you talking about?"

Her mother reached out and gingerly touched the pendant stone in the necklace, a stunning diamond the size of an acorn. "These were the property of the comtesse de Challe," she said in a low voice. "My mistress in France. When the Terror came, she wished to flee. The comte delayed, to gather funds and valuables, and by the time we set off for England, the revolutionaries were at our heels. We were detained in Calais. My master thought they would be robbed of everything, so he gave me the jewels and some money and instructed me to continue to England and wait for them there." She raised haunted eyes to them. "I waited for months, monsieur. Months with no word, no aid. The money was gone and I—" Her gaze veered to Felicity, then away. "I had to support myself."

Evan guessed what she left unsaid: She'd been expecting a child, without a husband. His arms tightened around Felicity. Those diamonds had given her a safe home, a happy childhood, and then a livelihood. Thank heavens Sophie-Louise had sold them. "I don't blame you," he said quietly.

"You bought this shop with money from these," whispered Felicity numbly. "Oh, Mama . . ."

Mrs. Dawkins drew a deep breath. "Monsieur le comte, I accept your offer. If you are to be my son-in-law, I will not fear you sending me to prison. You may buy this shop, because . . ." She smiled, a bit uncertainly, at Felicity. "I trust my daughter's judgment. If she says the other premises are perfect, that is all I need to know. She has taken excellent care of Follette's in my absence."

"Thank you, Mama," said Felicity softly.

Her mother raised an eyebrow, glancing from the diamonds to Evan and back to her daughter. "I believe I should be thanking you," she said gently, and turned toward the stairs. "I am going now. You may kiss him to your heart's content." She left, taking one lamp with her.

Evan reached for the necklace. "How soon do you want to be married?"

Felicity pressed one hand to her forehead, looking overwhelmed. "I have commissions to finish—your mother—"

"She can wait. I cannot." He fastened the necklace around her neck and admired it, lying just above the swells of her bosom. "Next week?"

She gasped. "I haven't a gown!"

"Wear the blue one that you wore to Grantham's office. I nearly lost my wits when you walked in." He eyed the diamonds again. "And wear these."

She touched them. "How did you know about these? And why did you buy them?"

"I bought them so no one could ever harass your mother about them," he said, ignoring the first question. He'd explain about that later. "So we're agreed: The wedding will be next week."

Felicity began to laugh. "Must you win every negotiation between us?" He put his hands on her hips and boosted her to sit on the counter, putting his face level with her bosom. At the first touch of his lips on her skin, her laughter faded. "Yes," she breathed, "next week would suit me perfectly."

Evan grinned, and blew out the lamp. "Excellent. Now kiss me, to your heart's content."

In the darkness she smiled, pulling him close. "That will take the rest of my life."

If you enjoyed *Dressed to Kiss*, please consider posting a review of it online. Honest reviews help other readers decide if they might like it.

Thank you!

ABOUT THE AUTHOR

Caroline Linden was born a reader, not a writer. She earned a math degree from Harvard University and wrote computer software before turning to writing fiction. Since then the Boston Red Sox have won the World Series three times, which can hardly be a coincidence. Her books have won the NEC Reader's Choice Award, the Daphne du Maurier Award, and RWA's RITA Award, and been translated into almost twenty languages.

Visit www.CarolineLinden.com to sign up for her newsletter. You can also follow her on twitter or like her on Facebook.

~ALSO BY CAROLINE LINDEN~

2nd

CPSIA information can be obtained
at www.ICGtesting.com
Printed in the USA
LVHW082133210522
719421LV00017B/200

9 781534 699472